HIDDEN IN BLOOD & SHADOWS

HIDDEN IN BLOOD & SHADOWS

Songs of Shadow & Sorrow Book 1

K.D. EDLEY

K. D. Edley

For R.
Always

I

~ COLE ~

VALENCIA, 23RD APRIL 1672

Cole ran.

He skidded around a corner, hand scrabbling across the rough cobblestone as he struggled to keep his balance without slowing. He ran. No idea where to, which direction, just away. He wasn't fast enough.

Hands grabbed him, and a knife slid between his ribs. He felt it scrape against bone.

Dropping to his knees, Cole rolled. Letting instinct drive his hands, he lashed out and up. The man above him grunted in pain. Not enough though. Not enough to slow him. He kicked Cole, hard. Managing to get his feet back under him, Cole struggled up. He blocked a blow, and another, but the next was too quick. Everything was starting to spin. That damn knife had done too much damage. He could feel it. Life slipping from his body as blood oozed and bubbled.

Gods, he was going to die.

He staggered back, managing to dodge a punch by dumb luck rather than skill. All the trouble he had gotten into in his too short life, and this thug was going to take him down? Cole laughed at the stupidity of it.

There was a brief flicker in the air behind the man's left shoulder. Cole barely had time to register it before a blade burst through his attacker's chest. They both stared at the sword tip dumbly a moment, before the man went slack. He hit the ground, dead, a moment before Cole collapsed himself.

He landed hard on his knees. Lifting his head, Cole stared hazily up at near identical expressions of concern across the faces of the two men who had come for him, though this time, they'd arrived too late. He tried to muster up a see, told you I'd be fine, cocky grin. But his lips wouldn't cooperate. Neither would the rest of his body as he slumped, distantly aware of his face colliding with the cobbles.

Everything was dark, cold.

He heard voices. Were they arguing? No, they were pleading. Why? He was just a worthless street rat whose own mother had abandoned him. One who never should have survived this long. But apparently, he didn't know how to die. And these two weren't going to let him go that easily either.

He felt something warm and wet on his lips. Then, it felt like he inhaled a storm, and lighting surged through his veins.

***

2

~ Harper ~

Rivulets of blood tracked their way down the brick wall of the alley.

Harper ran her index finger through the nearest streak of red. A shiver danced across her shoulder blades. She reached out again, dragging her finger through the blood to break the line of the complex sigil it formed. The prickle of dread under her skin lessened with the symbol broken. Harper pulled her hand back, the sigil looming over her, a silent spectre unwilling to give up its secrets. Rolling the blood between her fingers, something about it made her itch, like the blood was seeping into her skin and crawling its way up her arm. It was fresh but not that fresh. Definitely not human.

Cold drizzle drifted in the police lights, almost sleet, but not quite. It'd be better if it would just snow. Harper rubbed her hands together. Another half hour and her fingers would be numb. She kept her back to the two cops behind her, both sodden and unimpressed.

One of them stomped his feet, trying to get feeling back in them. 'God damned freak.'

Harper rolled her shoulders as she stood, as if that'd slough off the slick echo of unease that scuttled about under her skin. Three hours sleep was not enough to deal with another bloody murder and narrow-minded cops, not before her first cup of coffee.

The cop stomped his feet again. 'I should have been in bed half an hour ago.'

His partner huffed. 'Yeah, and your old girl could have kicked you back out by now.'

'Can't say I'd blame her. I think my toes have turned to icicles.'

Harper fumbled with her phone. She agreed with the cops on one thing, why the hell did some bastard have to pick such a cold night to kill someone. She glared at the two officers, daring them to rush her. They held their tongue for now, but it wouldn't last. In her experience, cops were all useless at this sort of crime scene, too busy either looking down their noses, or checking over their shoulders for the bogeyman to do their job. She took photos of the sigils and the victim's body, cataloguing as much as she could before they lost patience with her.

Her position as Liaison between the Erinyes Council and human law enforcement barely granted her access to crime scenes, it certainly didn't buy cooperation. What was that human saying, the best Erinyes was a dead one?

She closed her eyes and took a deep, slow breath. The

victim deserved more of her attention than ignorant cops. A young male Erinyes in his late twenties, though it was hard to tell as they stopped aging in their thirties. He had no identification, just another John Doe who'd be lucky if the cops behind her logged a cursory report on his murder.

His death had been violent. Bruising on the face and torso, one eye swollen shut, ribs likely fractured. Three broken fingers on the right hand. Throat slashed. Humans...they made it all too easy to hate them sometimes. Though she shouldn't be so quick to jump to conclusions. An open mind is an investigator's greatest asset. She heard an echo of her father's voice, soft and patient in a way she'd never been. He'd said that so often. History however, told her most Erinyes who died a violent death, met it at the hands of a human.

The dissolving sigils hung heavy over her. This was the third crime scene in the last two years covered in these bloody Aionic symbols. Most murders she investigated were hate crimes, a violent meeting of opportunity and intolerance, wrong place wrong time. There was purpose here though, however disturbed. Nothing seemed typical. She rubbed her fingers together absently. She'd started dreaming about these damn sigils. Two years looking for answers and nothing.

Harper sighed. There were always exceptions, humans and Erinyes didn't all hate each other. Her father had been dead for sixteen years, but the memory of him she carried with her had a point. Toss out her preconceptions, focus on cataloguing the details. He had been a damn good investigator after all, and the reason she did the work she did.

The officers were becoming more vocal in their impatience

to clear the scene and clock off for the night. 'Waste of time, who's going to miss another feathered freak.'

She didn't bother looking up. 'Did you skip anatomy at school? Erinyes don't have feathers, moron.'

Sometimes it seemed the only qualifying characteristic to be a human cop, was to be an intolerable dick. There were a few exceptions. One walked towards her, carrying two giant cups of coffee.

'If one of those is for me, you'll be my favourite cop in the city.'

Detective Jacobs held out one coffee. 'You hate every other cop in the city, so that isn't saying much.'

Harper grinned at Jacobs, before taking the coffee she offered. 'Top of the shit heap's the best position to be in.'

Jacobs rolled her eyes. 'Charming. Can't imagine why no one wants to work with you.'

Harper took a gulp of the too hot coffee before Jacobs changed her mind and took it back. Jacobs was an excellent detective, one of Chicago PDs finest. She was also the only detective who willingly worked with Harper given her heritage. Personality had little to do with humans' unwillingness to work with her. It was hard to beat centuries of prejudice and hatred. Humanity and Erinyes may have been living in a fragile peace for two hundred years, but neither side were bastions of tolerance and equality.

She wouldn't have a job if they were.

The detective looked over the scene. 'When the call came in, I thought it sounded like one of yours.'

Harper took another sip of the coffee, burnt, like all good cop coffee. 'Victim's not human.'

Technically, she had the authority to investigate any Erinyes death in the human city. Officially, her title and authority meant exactly squat.

Jacobs waved her coffee at the sigils. 'And those?'

Harper took another photo. It could be the mad ramblings of a run of the mill psycho. She'd investigated enough of these crimes to trust her gut when it said it wasn't though.

'Not sure. They're similar to the Aionic script.' The sigils were the language of the long dead Aion who created her kind over two thousand years ago. But these didn't make any sense. It was like a child scrawling random letters on a page hoping to stumble across an actual word. 'They don't make any sense. Maybe the killer's a Descendant wannabe?'

Jacobs frowned at the sigils. 'Really?'

Harper shrugged. 'I'll look into it. Let you know if I find anything.'

It was a guess, and probably not a good one. The Descendants were a human cult who worshiped the Aion. They were idiot fanatics who didn't even bother to learn the language of those they worshiped, which could explain why the sigils made no sense. Her instincts said that wasn't it though. These weren't random sigils, they served a purpose, she just hadn't been able to decipher it yet. Now, another body had turned up. Harper looked away from the bloody sigils. Apparently, the killer intended to give her plenty of opportunities to figure it out.

The Detective didn't know about the other murders Harper was investigating. The good thing about being a liaison rather than a cop was Harper picked her cases. She didn't report to any human law enforcement, so kept her dealings with them to a minimum. It wasn't the most useful approach, but whenever she tried speaking to most cops or detectives other than Jacobs, she ended up wanting to put her fist through something. Probably best for all involved if she continued working alone.

The Erinyes had their own form of law enforcement, the Watchers. But even they didn't care what happened out here in the human city. Snobs and arseholes no matter where you go. She'd accepted that a long time ago. It was easier to keep to the fringes of both societies, investigating cases that caught her attention and no one else cared about. She glanced at the beaten face of the young dead Erinyes. Did anyone care about him?

He was just a kid really. By Erinyes standards. Dark blonde hair turned red with blood. She guessed this guy actually was in his late twenties. Erinyes abilities manifest at the same time they stop aging. Being young would have made him easier to target.

The head was almost detached from the body, with the jagged edges of the sliced throat like some sort of macabre smile. Just like the other two murders. She still didn't know what sort of weapon the killer used. Harper ignored the wounds, focusing on other details. Hands calloused like he worked for a living. With no identification on the body, finding out who he was would be her priority. Harper had no jurisdiction over the physical evidence, relying on the diligence of human medical examiners for any prints, DNA or the like. She wouldn't hold her breath for them to complete much of a report though. They rarely did for her kind. Just one of the things that made her job so hard.

The edge of a tattoo poked out from beneath the sleeve of the man's coat.

'Jacobs.'

The detective came over and knelt next to Harper. 'What have you got?'

Harper indicated his wrist. 'Right if I...'

Jacobs nodded, watching as Harper pulled the sleeve up. An intricate tattoo snaked its way around the man's forearm. The Erinyes families often used tattoos to identify themselves. If this was a family tattoo, it was one she was unfamiliar with. She took a photo. Even if it wasn't a family design, it would still help identify him. She had everything she needed for now. Backing up the photos to her secured cloud storage, she turned and walked away.

'Let me know if you find something,' Jacobs called after her.

Harper didn't bother answering. Her heritage may not be the only reason other cops didn't want to work with her, but frankly, if life had taught her anything it was that polite and decent got you nowhere.

She tossed the half empty coffee in the bin rather than finishing it. Cop coffee was fine in a pinch, but she needed a decent cup to get through a day of chasing leads to identify the victim and trying to uncover the meaning of those sigils.

A small crowd had assembled to gawk at the poor sap who'd had a worse day than them. Her steps faltered as a prickle of sensation ran across her skin, like the caress of a cold wind. Harper looked around. She could always tell when other Erinyes were nearby, her one true ability. She spotted him straight away. Tall, dark hair, hands in the pockets of his coat. He looked straight at her, startled almost. He held her gaze a second, before the air seemed to ripple around him and he disappeared. She had always envied one thing about her Erinyes brethren. The ability of near instant travel they called flight, though it was more like teleporting. Wherever he had gone, she had no way of following. She couldn't feel him or any other Erinyes now.

Curious. Did he know the victim?

She stared at the empty space where he had been standing but it wasn't going to give her any answers. Pulling her jacket tight, she trudged through the dim light of early dawn. Her wet boots making it even colder if that were possible.

***

3

~ GAGE ~

Gage shoved his hands in the pockets of his coat, hunching his shoulders against the cold. The humans flowed around him, like he was a crack in the pavement to be stepped around and forgotten. A kid bumped into him. Gage pushed a tendril of suggestion towards him without thinking. The boy looked around, brow furrowing when he saw nothing, before turning his attention back to the murder scene. Gage didn't want to be noticed, so he wasn't. It was easy, with the crowd's interest fixed on the grisly scene. The freezing cold was little deterrent to the almost euphoric fascination rolling off the humans as they watched with keen interest. He swallowed against the buzz of macabre curiosity.

Why did rolling heads always draw a crowd?

Gage shifted amongst the group. He couldn't see the body, but the sigils scrawled across the wall were all too clear. He stared at the red trailing down the brick as drizzle fell. He couldn't look away. It felt like the ground reached up and grabbed hold of him, like it wanted to pull him down beneath the sidewalk and entomb him in the cold earth.

It had been five years, but it felt like a breath ago. Like one tortured, endless breath, since he had first seen those symbols.

Damn it, get a grip. This was a chance to finally get some answers. He looked away from the sigils and noticed one of the cops looking at him. Her brown hair was pulled into a messy bun like she had grudgingly dragged herself out of bed when the call came in, but her gaze was sharp, missing nothing. Not a cop, he realised, another Erinyes, one who stared right at him when every other person's eye skimmed past.

What the hell was an Erinyes doing investigating with the cops?

Gage shifted his shoulders, taking flight. He pulled himself into the void, letting it fold around him for the briefest moment, before stepping back out again. He didn't go far, landing out of sight in a small alcove down the street. He shifted weight from one foot to the other as he waited, not that it helped much, it was still freezing. He watched as the body was taken away, a shapeless lump hauled up and tossed into the ambulance like some sort of by-catch. The officers wiping their hands as they slammed the doors shut and drove off, hoping for a more valued catch next time. With the corpse gone the onlookers started to disperse, the rain washing away blood and their attention alike.

Breaking away from the other bystanders, a man walked down the street to join Gage. His dark blond hair slicked back, wet from the rain, yet he still managed to look graceful if a little menacing around the edges. He also looked entirely too comfortable for someone wearing only a dark green t-shirt and jeans in this sort of weather, especially for someone born human. That was Cole all over, unexpected and contradictory.

Cole stared at him with too knowing green eyes. 'You okay?'

Gage nodded, though they both knew he wasn't. He looked down the street, avoiding Cole's concern. The body had been found outside a warehouse in the human city, but the wall of the Enclave was visible between the buildings. It was only a few hundred meters away. Had the victim been drawn out here? For the most part, Erinyes lived within the confines of the Enclave. Those walls were meant to keep them safe. Not that they always did.

Gage looked back to where the body had been. 'Did you find anything?'

Cole shrugged. 'Nothing useful.' He had mingled with the crowd of onlookers, trying find anything out about the dead man. 'No one had seen him in the area before.'

They walked down the street to the half-heartedly taped off crime scene. Nothing. Someone else was dead, and they still had nothing. Gage wanted to punch something. He pushed his hands deeper into his pockets instead.

Gage took a deep breath, trying to centre himself. Cole toed a pile of tape left on the pavement, quietly giving Gage a moment to regain his composure. The smudge of blood where the body had been lying caught Gage's attention. Aside from the sigils, there was little other blood. No sprays, smears, splatters.

'He was killed somewhere else?'

Cole nodded, seeming relieved Gage had pulled himself together enough to notice the details. 'He fought back. With his wounds, there should have been a lot more blood, signs of struggle.'

Gage took a deep breath. Cole had undoubtedly already noted and filed away every detail about the scene, in triplicate. The man could be frustratingly cavalier, but at the same time meticulous.

'Any idea who he is?' He didn't care who the boy had been, not really. Only that his death might provide some fresh lead.

'Not yet. I'll look into it.'

Gage nodded absently. Cole had an uncanny knack for finding out things. His eyes drifted back to the sigils, much as he wanted to look anywhere else. 'Okay, good.'

Red sigils dripping down the wall, just like before, long dark hair, a mocking grinning slash across her throat. He swallowed down the sick feeling in his gut and looked away, gaze falling on Cole instead. The thin t-shirt was starting to stick to him, soaked from the rain. The sight made Gage shiver, even if Cole didn't seem to care. It was fucking freezing.

'Let's get out of here.' Gage forced his feet to move. 'Wet and shivering is really not a good look on you.'

Cole followed him, laughing. 'Everything is a good look on me.'

Gage resisted the urge to take flight and leave Cole to the freezing rain. 'Where'd you park the damn car.'

***

4

~ HARPER ~

Harper tucked a stray stand of hair behind her ear as she claimed an out of the way table in the back of the Blue Dawn café. Out the window, clouds drifted above the Enclave. Dark bottoms hanging ominously, like any moment they would fall from the sky and smother the streets below. The Enclave wall loomed across the street, tall and solemn, marking the line between the human and Erinyes sectors of Chicago. It had once been the only thing standing between the Erinyes and death, a thin line of protection during the many conflicts and massacres they'd faced at the hands of the humans. She sometimes wondered if it wasn't a trap, to keep them in, contained.

She had lived her whole life in its shadow, unsure which side she belonged on.

Opening her phone as she waited, an unread email blinked at her. Her thumb hovered over the link, knowing what that message was about. She had reapplied yet again to undergo the Trials to become a Watcher. They had finally responded. She didn't belong to a family with enough influence to have their own Watcher, so the Council had to approve her admittance as an unaligned one. One who would represent others like herself, Erinyes from families decimated by the many conflicts with humans, or just not that big to start with. Watchers were respected, it was an honour to become one. An honour apparently the Council didn't think she deserved. Harper sighed. If she didn't open the email, she could avoid the outcome a little while longer.

The café was busy. With so many Erinyes in one place, a relentless buzz brushed against her senses. Her one ability really was a joke. Erinyes were empathic, sensing emotions. But not her. It wasn't something useful she felt, like knowing when someone was angry or being deceptive. She just felt this dragging, uncontrolled turmoil of sensations. Like a bone chilling winter draft or the unease of someone watching over her shoulder. Everyone felt slightly different, like recognising the voice of a friend in a crowded room. In crowds like this though, they all mixed in a muddy discord that made her grit her teeth. It was a debilitation more than anything else. An ability she couldn't even control, a fact the Council jumped on every time they blocked her application.

What did it matter that she had been training to be a Watcher since she was six years old, determined to follow in her father's footsteps no matter how small she had been. Arrogant bastards. They only saw an Erinyes who couldn't even fly.

She kept applying, though. More fool than any of them.

Harper closed her eyes and took a deep breath, held it a moment before huffing it out. Turning the phone off, she placed it face down on the table and wilfully ignored the sensations from the Erinyes around her until they faded into the background. Sometimes, it was easier to walk beyond the walls amongst the humans who hated her, then here amongst her own kind.

Harper opened her eyes, startled as Viridian dumped a plate of pastries and two coffees on the table. He kicked a chair out and sat down across from her, already chewing one of the pastries and staring at her appraisingly. Harper resisted the urge to roll her eyes. In a hundred years he might unsettle her, but right now he was just a kid seeking approval and hoping no one saw through the cool guy act. He was maybe forty, and just settling into his abilities. Erinyes were little different to humans during their childhood. It wasn't until their thirties or forties that their abilities started to develop. The ability to fly, their empathic skills. Though some manifested earlier. Harper remembered being that age, back when she thought she may still fully manifest. She'd given up that hope a long time ago.

'You know, I've seen homeless people who look like they have more fun than you,' Viridian said.

Viridian split his time between the clubs at night, where pretty much anything went, sex, drugs, no holds barred fights, training with the Watchers, or working at the Blue Dawn café during the day. She'd asked him once when he slept, he'd said Tuesdays. Harper wasn't that much older than him, but the frantic pace he took life made her feel ancient by comparison.

'Don't be a dick.' Harper picked up her phone again and opened the crime scene photos. 'I need some help on this one.'

He gave her a quick smirk before picking the phone up. His expression turned serious as he flicked through the photos. Harper spent as much time outside the Enclave as within it these days. Viridian was her source on things happening inside the walls. She watched him as he studied the crime scene photos. Viridian was smart and heard things. He was also unaffiliated with any Erinyes families, which made for less politics. She'd met him five years ago on a case that took her to an underground fight club Viridian had been passing his time in, hellbent on misspending his youth. Somehow, he convinced her to provide an introduction to the Watcher who trained her, while she gained another bad mark on her record for investigating within the Enclave where she had no jurisdiction. He had been training to become a Watcher since and enjoyed helping her on her cases, even though most Erinyes didn't give a damn what happened outside the Enclave. It'd be a few years yet before he'd be ready to take the trails himself, if he didn't turn up dead from some misadventure first.

Viridian absently chewed on the pastry. 'I heard about this earlier.'

'Do you recognize him?'

'No, sorry.'

'He had a tattoo.'

Viridian flicked through to the photo of the tattoo. His brow knitted as he looked at in, zooming in and out. 'It does looks familiar.'

'You've seen it before?'

'No, but something similar.'

Viridian pulled up the browser on her phone, typing something in. Finding what he was after he pushed the phone back across the table. 'You recognize this?'

Of course, she did. It was the family crest of the Aesir, one of the oldest Erinyes families. If you believed the rumours, they traced their lineage back to the Aionic wars when their kind was first created. They kept to themselves though, stayed out of the politics most of the other families engaged in as they jockeyed for power in the complex and unstable hierarchy that passed for Erinyes self-government. The Council consisted of family and unaligned Watchers elected from each Enclave. Elections could be cutthroat. Even if they kept out of the power plays amongst the families, no one was game to mess with the Aesir. Their family not only contained some of the oldest Erinyes alive but was rumoured to have some of the purest Aion lineage that still existed. If you believed the stories.

'It's not an exact match, but too close to be a coincidence,' Viridian said.

He was right. A family like the Aesir wouldn't allow just anyone to bear a mark with such obvious similarities to their crest.

'Do you know any Aesir?'

'Hell no, out of my league.' Viridian picked up another pastry. 'I know there are a few of the family in the city though. I can put some feelers out, maybe with some luck, get you an introduction.'

Viridian's eyes brightened at the idea of helping track down Erinyes powerful enough to make Harper and Viridian look as harmful as chubby toddlers by comparison. Yeah, the kid was definitely going to get himself killed one day.

'That's alright.' She tapped her fingers against her phone. 'I could make an official request to the Council, see if they'd tell me what family this is, if any?'

Viridian raised an eyebrow. 'They'll tell you nothing, you know that.'

She rocked her cup back and forth. It left a coffee ring on the table. 'Well, it's worth a try.'

The Council was as rigid and narrow minded as the cops who refused to work with her. She'd damn well work around them if she had to. It wouldn't be the first time. Viridian studied her, lips thinning like he knew exactly what she was thinking. She pushed the cup away, looking out the window rather than watch him debate the futility of reminding her about the thin line she walked with the Watchers after the last time she'd pushed outside of her authority.

Viridian sighed. 'I can find a way to get you an introduction. The Aesir are old and not the friendliest bunch. They're far from the worst of the families though.'

That was true. She still didn't like it. If one of them took offense at Viridian poking around their business, it could get messy. 'Forget about it. It's probably nothing anyway.'

Harper had never met one of the famed family. Her father told her stories about them as a child, the mighty Aesir were feared almost as much as they were revered. She doubted even half the stories were true. But, even if they were only half as powerful as rumoured, she wouldn't risk sending a kid like Viridian looking for them. He'd been in the city on his own since he was sixteen and made it this far, but she didn't want to draw him into a case like this. He was better off away from sigil drawing serial killers and family politics. She'd find the Aesir on her own.

Harper looked up as a man in a long coat walked out the door of the café. He was gone before she got a good look at him. Her brow creased, something about him familiar but she couldn't place it. She shrugged the thought off. There were a lot of people she vaguely knew in the Enclave, few she knew well. She tossed a twenty on the table for the pastries, got up and left.

'Always a pleasure,' Viridian called after her.

***

Harper pulled her coat tight against the cold as she made her way along the waterfront. The Enclave was always busy. Especially here along the lake with its trendy food and night-clubs. She hadn't eaten anything while talking to Viridian, so dropped by her favourite bakery. It was a tiny place, about a block from her apartment. There was a line-up at the serving window. The girl behind the counter smiled at each customer. She knew the regulars' names, knew how they took their coffee. When it was Harper's turn though, the girl stared at her blankly. Harper pointed at a cinnamon raisin bagel and asked for a flat white coffee. Her usual. Not that anyone ever remembered.

She debated what to do next as she waited for her order. The cases she investigated almost exclusively involved the deaths of Erinyes with no family to care what happened to them. If anyone had reported the victim from this morning missing, she'd know about it by now. Assuming he had no family, the best place to start would be the lodges. Lodges were scattered throughout the Enclave. They provided accommodation and help for Erinyes new to the city or those unaffiliated with an Erinyes family. Harper had been lucky her father had been a Watcher. They'd always had a home, even if they had no other family. The lodges were a good way of tracking down information.

Harper ate the bagel as she made her way south. The Enclave covered only a small part of the greater Chicago city. She could walk across it in about twenty minutes. The population had grown in the last hundred years, but they remained confined within the walls. She looked up at the high-rise apartments along the lake and couldn't help wondering how much more it could grow. It was home to around ten thousand, mostly Erinyes, though humans too who were friendly with her kind. It might lay within the confines of Chicago, but it had the feel of a small town, with the Erinyes always looking out for each other. They'd had to. The first Enclaves had been created almost two thousand years ago, but so many of them had fallen, besieged by humans. The Erinyes had given up on assimilation into the human world a long time ago. They developed their own way of doing things instead. There were fewer cars within the Enclave for one thing. What was the point when the Erinyes could fly. Well, most of them.

She finished the last of her coffee as she arrived at the first lodge. She tossed her cup in a bin and pushed open the door. The man behind the counter smiled at her. His name was Daniel, but everyone just called him Dee. He was human, but some days she picked up a slight sensation from him. Erinyes blood affected any human that consumed it, like a drug. It gave a temporary boost to stamina, agility, or healing. The effects varied but didn't last. Not unless the human received regular doses over several years. Harper had known Dee for a few years. She'd never asked, but assumed he got the blood legally, most likely through friendship with one of her kind, otherwise the Watchers would have dealt with him by now. He was usually willing to answer her questions, even though technically he didn't have to. Today there was barely a tingle against her senses. It must have been a while since he last consumed.

'Harper, I'd say it's a pleasure, but you're never here for anything pleasant.'

'Hey Dee.' Harper took out her phone. 'I'm investigating the death of a young Erinyes.' She pulled up a photo of the victim's face. 'I'm trying to find out who he was.'

Dee's smile faded. He studied the photo a moment. 'I'm sorry, I've never seen him before.'

Harper wasn't surprised. She spoke to Dee for a while longer, emailing him the photo and asking him to contact her if anyone else on the staff knew who the dead man was.

No one remembered seeing the victim at the next two lodges either. She was almost to the fourth when she felt it again, a cool touch like the first delicate frost that won't survive the sunrise. The same sensation she'd had from the Erinyes watching the crime scene this morning. Harper kept walking, senses on alert. This wasn't the busiest part of the enclave, but there were people around. She turned a corner, stopping abruptly. The footsteps behind her stopped too. She waited but couldn't hear anything. She could sense the person following her still nearby. There was a slight shift in the air.

'Why are you following me?' Harper said.

'Who says I'm following you?'

The words came from behind her. Harper quelled the instinct to jump. She turned around slowly. A man leant against the wall, looking as if he had been there all along. The alley she'd turned into was dark, the shadows almost concealing him. More than that, the shadows clung to him like a cloak of impossible fabric that drunk in the light before it could touch him. A trickle of cold crept over her, it was definitely the same man from the crime scene. Was he involved, a curious onlooker, a creepy blood sigil drawing psycho?

'You were at the crime scene,' she said.

'I know.'

'And you followed me down West Street for at least three blocks.'

The man tilted his head, studying her. 'Most people don't see me unless I want them too.'

He hadn't answered her implied question. 'Why are you following me?'

'Curiosity.'

'About what?'

He shrugged. 'You. The murder.'

He looked bored rather than curious. Following her wasn't something just a curious onlooker would do. 'Why are you interested in the murder?'

His lips twitched with a suppressed scowl. 'I didn't do it if that's what you're worried about.'

'Right.'

He didn't bother hiding the scowl this time. 'Of course, why should you believe me.'

Harper's fingers toyed with the handle of one of her knives, undecided whether to pull it. He had made no move yet. In fact, he all but lounged against the wall like this was his daily routine, and she was interrupting him. She generally trusted her instincts, but right now they weren't telling her much.

'Do you know what happened,' Harper said, hoping to keep him talking to get a read on him.

'To the dead guy? No idea. Hence the curiosity.'

Harper gritted her teeth in frustration at his flippant tone. 'Who are you?'

'You can call me Gage.'

Finally, a direct answer. 'Gage?' She asked, looking for a last name.

'Yes,' he answered, back to unhelpful.

Harper couldn't read this guy at all. There didn't seem to be any immediate danger, but she didn't exactly feel safe either. She discreetly kept a hold on her knife.

He watched her as she debated what to do next.

'You're looking for one of the Aesir?' He said, before she could decide.

She flexed her fingers. Had he been following her longer than she thought? 'How did you know that?'

He ignored her question. 'Why are you looking into them?'

She remembered the man she'd seen at the café. It must have been him, and he overheard her conversation with Viridian. Harper glanced toward the nearby street. People were walking past, but none of them looking in her direction. Harper looked back at Gage. Maybe she could get some useful information, assuming he wasn't the finger-painting murderer himself. 'The victim. He had a family tattoo.'

'You think he was a member of the Aesir?'

'No, but I'm hoping they might have some information.' She studied him closer, dark hair, tall. If he wasn't examining her like she was an irritating pebble in his shoe, she'd say he was attractive. You could never tell the age of an Erinyes by looking at them, but Harper got an idea by how they felt to her senses. He didn't feel old, but not young either. If she had to guess, she would say around a couple hundred years of age. 'Do you know any Aesir here in the city?'

'Everyone knows the Aesir,' he said, which didn't answer her question.

It wasn't a no though. 'Can you get me an introduction?'

'The Aesir don't work like most other families. They keep to themselves.'

'So how do I find one of them?'

'You don't.' He shifted, standing straighter. The shadows shifted with him as he backed away. 'They find you.'

He was gone before she could say anything else. 'Enigmatic bastard.'

***

5

~ COLE ~

PARIS, 16TH OCTOBER 1690

Cole slid a coin across the table. He didn't particularly like gambling, but he was good at it. He tapped his cards as he studied his opponent. Sebastien was a naive young Lord. A younger son of a younger son. An overlooked spare who seemed determined to throw away what little inheritance he had. Glancing down at his cards, Cole knew he had the man beat.

Cole leant back in his chair, letting a grin slide across his lips. 'So, you really know one of the Aesir?'

Sebastien puffed out his chest. 'I do, dear boy.' He matched Cole's bet. 'Filthy creatures, but even animals have a certain nobility.'

'A certain savagery too.'

The men around the table laughed.

Idiots, the lot of them. They had no idea. 'How exactly does a Parisian Lord know any Erinyes?'

The Paris Enclave no longer existed. It hadn't for a hundred years, and there were very few Erinyes in the city.

Sebastien waved a hand lazily. 'I met them through some investments I recently made.'

That was a lie.

Cole forced his shoulders to loosen, lifted his chin and grinned. He laid down his cards. Sebastien looked down at them, laughed, and tossed his own cards aside.

'You win again. Why do I play with you?'

Cole shrugged. 'Because I'm such good company.'

'Ha.'

'And I'm buying.'

The men all cheered as he stood and made his way to the bar. He tossed his winnings down and ordered everyone a round. Sebastien soon followed. He took a stool and Cole pushed an ale across in front of him, hoping it would help loosen his tongue.

Cole waited until the second drink was gone before asking. 'How do you really know the Aesir?'

Sebastien stared at him, wide eyed. He wet his lips. 'Truthfully, I don't. I've been looking for them.'

'Why?'

'I really shouldn't say.'

Cole leaned in. 'But you want to, don't you?'

Sebastien looked around, like he expected the devil to be hiding amongst the crowd. 'I recently made some new acquaintances who are capable of removing a few obstacles for me.'

'Obstacles?'

'My cousin.'

Cole nodded, like it was perfectly normal to want family dead just to inherit more wealth. 'And in return, they want you to find the Aesir for them. Why do they think you can?'

'My grandfather was obsessed with history. He collected all sorts of rare books, forgotten histories. Terribly dry stuff.'

'I've heard of your family's library. They say the King himself likes to peruse its collections.'

Sebastien seemed to nearly glow. 'He does indeed.'

'Well, fancy that. Here I am, drinking with someone who rubs shoulders with kings.'

Sebastien laughed. 'Your company is as fine as any at Versailles.'

'Oh, I doubt that.' Cole leaned closer to Sebastien. 'The Aesir have villas up and down the Mediterranean, why would anyone need some old books to find them?'

Sebastien shifted in his seat. 'I have no idea.'

Cole studied him a moment. He really didn't know, which was unfortunate. But maybe he could still be useful. 'These new friends of yours, do you trust them?'

Sebastien looked around again, dropping his voice. 'Hardly. Can anyone ever truly trust the English?'

Cole suppressed a smile. Apparently, his French accent was at least good enough to fool a drunk French lord. 'English?'

'Damn Londoners. But with what they are offering, I'm willing to overlook that flaw.'

It was more than a flaw. France and England were

currently at war. Sebastien was willing to commit treason to better his station.

Cole let the conversation drift to another subject, making sure Sebastien's ale stayed full. It didn't take long before the Lord staggered to his feet, weaving his way through the crowd and out into the back lane to relieve himself. Cole followed. Sebastien was too drunk to notice. He didn't notice the two men waiting in the shadows for him either.

Cole had spent years amongst the Erinyes and learned to sense them instantly. It was like a sixth sense all humans had, a base awareness of their empathic abilities that were always reaching out, though not everyone was good at recognizing it. Erinyes could reign in their abilities to some extent, though it was nearly impossible for them to hide altogether. But even the most ignorant human would feel it now.

Sebastien stiffened, like a deer sensing a predator. He turned to face Cole.

'You wanted to find the Aesir.' Cole shrugged, almost feeling sorry for him. 'They found you first.'

The next morning, as Cole looked out over the river Seine, the lord's body was already turning grey somewhere in its waters. Cole turned away and headed towards the docks. They were almost ready to set sail. Sebastien had talked. A lot. Not that he knew much. But enough to be sure someone was hunting the Aesir and where to find more answers.

London. Why did it have to be London.

Cole would do anything for the Aesir. Even return to the city of his birth, when he swore, he'd never go back there.

**

6

~ HARPER ~

The Tower of the Watchers was an imposing monolith of a building standing tall in the middle of the Enclave. A spartan stone edifice with a history of Erinyes blood and pride in the mortar that held it aloft, casting a vigilant shadow over the Enclave. Harper walked up the steps, ignoring the others coming and going from the building, as they ignored her. She remembered running up these stairs, laughing and swinging from her father's hand when she had been too little to understand the weight of duty demanded by every step.

In this building, few were friendly towards her, even less so since her father died. Carellen was an exception. Harper waited outside his office. He had no official title, but everyone referred to him as the Commander. The towering grey-haired Erinyes had been the Watcher for his family for the better part of two centuries. Harper suspected he took it on himself to be her superior. She doubted the Council even remembered their liaison with human law enforcement half the time. Carellen had always been kind to her though. A remnant of his long friendship with her father. Harper had known him for as long as she remembered. She wasn't sure she would class him as a friend, but probably as close to one as she had. Certainly, she respected him more than anyone else she knew.

She looked up as the office door opened. Unlike the still unread email from the Council, a request from Carellen to meet wasn't something she'd ignore.

Carellen waved her in. He didn't offer her a seat, their meetings rarely lasted long enough for that.

He didn't look up from the papers he was signing. 'Harper, keeping busy I presume?'

'Always, Commander.'

Harper was required to file reports on all her investigations with the Watchers, which she did with a bare minimum detail. She'd completed thorough reports in the beginning, before realizing no one cared, her reports undoubtedly filed somewhere and never read.

Carellen pushed aside the last of the papers, looking at Harper. 'Anything interesting this week?'

'Conviction for that murder on the river was upheld.'

Harper put a lot of work into that case, a young Erinyes couple beaten to death. Both too young to have abilities manifested to protect themselves.

Carellen nodded. He and Harper both knew one conviction wouldn't stop the violence against Erinyes. It still felt good though.

'Anything new?'

Harper debated what to report. As with the other cases, there wasn't much to go on. The two previous victims had been random nobodies, no families, young, no one to miss them. If the latest victim had family, they could provide some leads. Her position didn't allow her access to the Watcher records, but if she got access, maybe she could find a next of kin to talk to.

'A murder yesterday.' Carellen didn't react. There was a murdered Erinyes somewhere every week. 'He's unidentified, I'd like to find out who he was.'

Carellen nodded, fingers tapping on his desk, and his attention already wandering back to whatever filled his day.

'Human attacker?'

'Unclear.'

The Commander's attention flicked back to her briefly.

Harper hedged her bets. 'I'd like to run a search in the Watcher's database, see if I can identify the victim so we can notify the family.'

Carellen looked at her for a moment. Notification to the family was the only leverage she had. Even if the Council wouldn't investigate crimes outside the Enclave, they always respected the right of families to collect their dead. With no next of kin to collect the body, the medical examiner would cremate and dispose of the remains.

Carellen nodded. 'I'll grant you access for a search.'

'Thank you.' Harper turned to leave.

'You haven't been to a training session in a while, everything okay?'

Harper smiled. She had been sparring with Carellen since she was a kid. Making her fall flat on her face seemed to be one of the few things in life that gave him genuine enjoyment. He was a hard teacher, always had been, but she was a decent fighter because of him.

'I've been busy.'

Carellen looked at her for a moment. 'I suppose it's too much to hope you've found a personal life?'

Harper's jaw tightened. 'I'm fine.'

He sighed. 'Of course, you are.' Carellen leant back in his chair, rubbing a hand tiredly over his face. 'Sit a moment.'

Harper looked at the door, already knowing what he wanted to discuss. She sat down, sighing.

'Harper, they rejected your application again.'

Just reading the bloody email would have been easier than hearing it. She looked away, staring out the window at the grey afternoon. The sky was too heavy for daylight to break through. There was still no sign of snow. It'd probably rain again later.

'They will keep saying no, you know this.'

'I know.'

'Then why do you keep applying?'

She turned back to him, jaw set. 'Because, one day they might tell me why.' She had been asking that since her father died. Why? 'They won't let me take the trials until I somehow prove myself more than I am. Yet none of them will give me a chance to prove anything.'

'No. They won't.'

She shook her head, laughing. 'No, they won't.' She stared at Carellen. 'If my father was still here--'

'But he's not.'

Her father had been dead for sixteen years. She still didn't know how he had died. She looked at Carellen, wondering yet again, if he knew. Carellen had been the one to find her in the Watcher training rooms the day it happened. He'd led her out of the building in a numb haze while everyone stared. It felt like they had never stopped staring, a distant scrutiny that followed her, even through the indifference. Something had changed that day, but she didn't know what, or why. There had always been a lot of politics within the Watchers. Something she wasn't good at. Was it just prejudice against her lack of abilities that saw her receive rejection after rejection? She had requested the file on her father's death multiple times, but the Council refused. Just like they rejected her application to the Watcher Trials. They never gave a reason. Until they did, she'd keep applying.

'You can do good where you are.' Carellen looked away, jaw twitching like he wanted to say something before reconsidering. 'Make peace with that. Or they will dismiss you.'

Carellen was the only reason she had her job as Liaison. She'd always been grateful, thinking it enough. How much longer would it feel that way?

Carellen turned back to the paperwork neatly ordered on his desk, dismissing her. 'If that's all, I've got work to do.'

Harper made her way from Carellen's office to the archives, anger lengthening her stride. She had no office or desk, so used the visitor computers in the public archives whenever she gained permission to access the Watcher's databases. She logged on, hoping she didn't have to wait around for Carellen to provide authorization. The temporary passcode waiting in her inbox did little to sate her irritation.

The murders were connected, though she didn't know

what linked the victims. She'd been told, more than once, her inability to let things go was her biggest downfall. Maybe they had a point, but this killer wasn't done yet. It had been two years since she stood at the first crime scene. The deliberateness of it, the violence, the ritualistic nature of the sigils, stuck with her, and now it had happened twice more. She scanned the victim's profile into the system and ran it through facial recognition. It was a long shot, many Erinyes never dealt directly with the Council so wouldn't be in the database.

Tapping her fingers on the desk as she waited, Harper noticed a Watcher across the room. She was from one of the smaller families in the Enclave. Harper couldn't remember which one. The woman watched Harper for a few seconds before looking away, hunching her shoulders like the sight of Harper in this bastion of Watcher history was offensive. Harper tapped her fingers harder against the desk, the sound loud in the quiet of the archives. The woman scowled, bundled up the books she was reading and left. Harper smiled tightly at her as she passed, before turning back to the screen.

The authorisation Carellen had provided would only allow her this one-time limited access to the Watcher databases. Might as well make the most of it. She needed to find answers, no one else would. Dismissing a fleeting thought for the repercussions if they found her poking at things she had no authority to poke, Harper ran a search for other crimes with similarities to her three cases. The nature of the crime scenes was purposeful. She couldn't shake the idea that the killer wouldn't have spontaneously started killing and leaving such elaborately staged scenes with sigils that clearly meant something to him. She had already looked for other murders outside the Enclave with her limited resources and found none. The victims were all Erinyes, she had jumped to the assumption it was a human killer. But maybe it wasn't. Maybe that was just her own prejudices, and he had started killing here, inside the Enclave and that's why she hadn't heard about it.

Tap, tapping her fingers, she looked around as she waited for the search results to come back. The archives were quiet with no one nearby, they usually were, that's why she worked here whenever she came to the Watcher tower. A few minutes later she had the results. A few dozen matches for cases with sigils at the crime scene. She skimmed through them, eliminating any with superficial similarities. She looked around again, there wasn't time to be thorough. She was able to quickly narrow the search down to six results, she printed what details she could access. The reports were only cursory overviews of the cases, but they would have to do. She didn't have authorisation to access anything else. Four were in different cities, which she hadn't considered before. Her contacts with human authorities were tentative at best, she hadn't the forethought or means to undertake a wider search beyond the city before. Two cases were in Chicago though, one five years ago, and another a few months ago.

The older murder had been a young female victim, found dead in her own home, which was different to the three cases she had so far. She could only access a brief entry from a Watcher's daily report, anything else likely to send up a red flag. She skimmed over the file. It held little information. There was a reference to further details in an official report, but Harper wouldn't be able to access it. It wasn't much, but more than she'd had before.

Harper waited until the facial recognition search finished. She logged off when it came back with no matches and made her way out of the building. She paused on the steps, watching people come and go. It had been five years, but maybe a visit to the crime scene would help her get a feel for how similar the murder was to the cases she had been investigating. If it was related, maybe the fact the killer had attacked this victim at home could offer a different angle or lead to follow.

Investigating inside the Enclave now might be the last straw with the Watchers and Council. She glanced up at the Tower before striding down the stairs. Only if they found out.

***

7

~ GAGE ~

Gage ordered another drink, ignoring the phone buzzing in his pocket, undoubtedly Cole checking up on him. He just needed a minute to himself. The bartender eyed him. It was early, almost no one in the dingy bar except a few pickled regulars. Gage didn't care, he wasn't here for the company. He stared down at his glass, running his thumb over the smooth surface, back and forth.

Sometimes he just wanted to forget.

Other times, he tried to hold on to the fading edges of memories from a better time, but it was like trying to catch smoke in his hands.

Mostly, he was just angry. Kind of hard to be anything else, when all his memories of her were blotted over in the ugly black of dried blood.

Gage closed his eyes. That bar smell, the sweet malty stench of old beer and lost hopes, stuck in the back of his throat. It reminded him of the reek of rotting apples laying abandoned in an orchard, the men meant to pick them lying dead on battlefields on the other side of the world. The smell brought a memory back, vivid despite the years that had passed. Thousands of miles away, a world war had been killing millions, while Gage lay bleeding in a field of decaying fruit. He'd been stupid, careless, and let himself be ambushed. They drained his blood. He watched them gulp it down, high on the temporary boost it gave. Between the gnarled trunks of apple trees, he'd watched the men who'd left him for dead walk away laughing. He'd barely survived that day and had thought nothing could hurt more.

He'd been wrong.

He squeezed the glass tighter, not enough to crack, but enough to make his fingertips whiten. Taking a breath, he let it settle in his lungs until his grip loosened.

Gage opened his eyes, pulling his phone out. Two missed calls, and a text. He opened the text. Cole had found information on the woman from the crime scene. Gage had a way of going unnoticed. The Erinyes woman spotting him this morning had rattled him. Few saw through his illusions, Cole being an exception, always able to find him. Her name was Caitlan Harper, the Council's Liaison to human law enforcement in Chicago. That explained what she had been doing at the murder scene. She had several infractions for exceeding her authority and jurisdiction and looked to be doing it again. Harper had run a search for similar cases in the Watcher records. Cases from within the Enclave.

One of the cases she accessed was Ara's. Along with a search for the address of the building where she'd been killed.

Gage stared at the screen. Pixels of light so small a thing to hold something so heavy. The glass cracked beneath Gage's fingers. The chair spun idly as he disappeared.

***

8

~ HARPER ~

The building stood empty, abandoned not derelict. Harper picked the lock, resisting the urge to glance up, the windows like eyes heavy with silent disapproval at her lack of respect and good judgement. She slipped inside, gently closing the door behind her. Furniture and personal items filled the rooms, everything still in its place as though its owner would come back any moment. The layer of dust and cobwebs covering everything told the truth though. No one was coming back.

Harper worked her way upstairs. The body had been found in the bedroom on the second floor. The stairs groaned under Harper's weight as she moved, loud in the otherwise quiet building. After investigating in the human world for so long, it felt odd the house remained unoccupied. Erinyes didn't view death the same way as humans though. Human lives were fleeting compared to the Erinyes. Even with her weak abilities Harper would live far longer than any human, hundreds of years likely. At the scene of a murder like this, any Erinyes who entered the building would feel it, a slick slide of unease over their skin, the weighty residue of a violent death.

The better question was why no one had torn down the building. She'd investigate who owned it later, maybe it would lead to the victim's family who might know more about what happened.

Pushing the bedroom door open, the first thing to catch her attention was old blood etched onto the wall, sigils still visible. The room was bare, whatever furniture there had been long since removed, sullied by what it bore witness to. The crime scene photos had shown the body hung from a hook in the wall using bindings on the woman's wrists. Whether the killer hammered the hook in himself or used one already there had been impossible to tell from the photos.

A shiver ran down Harper's spine. The air in the room so thick with the memory of violence and terror it was greasy on her skin. This was the same killer. She was sure of it. Harper stared at the old blood for a moment, before looking around the rest of the room. There wasn't much to see. As Harper turned to leave, marks on the door frame caught her attention. There were more scuff marks in the hallway.

The woman had struggled. Desperately.

Harper followed the marks down the hall.

'What are you doing here?'

Harper jumped, turning to see the Erinyes who'd been following her. Gage. The casual ease from earlier gone. His eyes flashed with anger, more apparent for the calm of his words.

'What are you doing here?' He repeated.

Harper reached for her knife. If she'd been unable to read him last time, she was having no trouble now. Instinctively angling her body to ward off any attack as waves of barely suppressed violence rolled off the other Erinyes.

Gage's eyes flicked to the knife, the sight of it giving him pause. She doubted he felt threatened though. He took a step back, making Harper aware of how much he'd been looming over her, and she wondered if he hadn't realised until then either. She didn't relax her stance any.

Gage looked away from her for a few seconds, taking a deep breath. She got the impression he didn't like losing control as she watched him reign in his emotions.

'This is private property,' Gage said, looking back at her somewhat calmly. 'My private property.'

Did creepy killers purchase the properties of people they killed?

Harper flexed her fingers on the knife, trying to get her heartbeat under control. Think damn it.

She studied the man, trying to appear calm despite the thoughts scurrying through her mind like a skipping film reel. Had he followed her again? Was this his house or was this some weird possessive thing because he'd killed someone here. Serial killers kept trophies, could a whole house be a trophy?

Thoughts circled for a moment before she realized the atmosphere of imminent threat had dissipated.

She weighed her options. 'I was following a lead.'

'From the murder yesterday?'

Harper nodded.

'Hmm,' was his only reply, looking for all the world like he'd lost interest in her presence.

The bedroom door remained open, the fading sigils just visible from where they stood. Gage looked at them, shoulders stiff, hands clenching and unclenching.

'You think they're connected,' he said.

He looked almost...a house haunted with loss. Shit, he owned the house.

Harper sheathed her knife. The overwhelming sense of standing in a mausoleum pressed in on her. She'd wondered if the victim had any family left to question. Now, it seemed likely she stood face to face with one, and she didn't know what to ask. Not when they were so close to where the woman had been brutally murdered. A muscle in Gage's jaw twitched, his expression tight with emotion he seemed to be ruthlessly trying to extinguish.

Harper tried to give him a moment. But couldn't help asking. 'Who was she?'

'I'm sure you've got that in a file somewhere.'

Harper wanted to push for answers, but the raw threat from a few moments before lingered. There was little information in the file she had, and no mention of a name or any family.

She chewed on her lip, thinking. 'You think they're connected. That's why you were there yesterday.'

'I don't know,' he said quietly.

Gage looked away from the room, pushing past her and down the stairs.

He waited near the front door when Harper caught up. Gage didn't look at her, his attention on a grouping of photos on the mantle over the fireplace in the front room. She recognised the victim in a few of them, looking out with bright eyes. She turned to watch Gage. He swallowed, looking lost. Whatever he saw there, he seemed to come to some decision.

Gage dropped his head, shoulders slumping. 'Ara was home alone. The front door was smashed in, but I think she let the killer in...she knew him. There were two cups of tea half full in the kitchen.'

Gage didn't look up. No inflection in his voice, like he was reciting a report, but none of those details were in the one Harper had. She didn't interrupt, afraid he'd stop talking. It was the first real information he had offered.

'She fought...Ara was young, but she was strong. There were things missing, photos I think.' Gage looked away from the mantle and the images of the dead girl and her friends and family, running a hand through his hair. 'There wasn't much evidence, and no one saw or heard anything.'

Harper nodded, storing away what he'd said to think over later. 'The Watchers investigated?'

'They found nothing useful.' Gage opened the front door. He paused, his fingers gripping the handle like he was caught between lingering and running, a moment of fragility he quickly pushed aside. He looked up at her. 'Look around all you need,' he said before walking out.

Alone again, the house felt emptier, colder.

Harper walked over to the mantle, curious if the photos would answer the question Gage evaded about his relationship to the victim. Most of the photos showed groups of people laughing, some at the beach, others in what looked like a club. The only one with Gage in it showed a laughing Ara kissing Gage on the cheek while he scowled at the camera. The girl looked young, and so alive. It didn't provide any definitive answer though.

Not sure why, Harper took the photo out of the frame and slipped it into her jacket.

When she got back to her car, something had been tucked behind the wiper blade. Great, a parking ticket. Harper reached over and picked it up. It wasn't a ticket though. It was a business card, dark grey with an embossed sigil on one side. She didn't know what the sigil meant, but recognized the word written beneath it. Aeternus. It was an Erinyes run nightclub.

Handwritten on the reverse side of the card it said, 'ask for Hael'.

Harper looked around. There was no one else in sight. Did Gage leave it on his way out, or someone else? Harper pocketed the card. It didn't matter who left it.

Anyone even half informed about happenings in the Enclave knew of Aeternus. It was rumoured to be owned by the biggest information broker in the city.

***

Harper stood across the street from Aeternus, debating whether to go in when her phone rang.

Viridian didn't bother saying hello, he usually didn't. 'Put the word out you wanted to meet any Aesir willing to talk.'

Harper sighed. 'That wasn't necessary.'

'I know. I got nothing anyway. These guys don't like being found, maybe you should drop it.'

Viridian sounded concerned, though there was something else there as well.

'Maybe.' She had no intention of dropping anything.

'I mean, you don't want to mess with these guys. Just, think about it at least. It was a long shot they'd help anyway.'

It was a hunch as much as anything. The tattoo possibly had no relation to the Aesir crest it resembled. Her gut said otherwise though.

'I'll think about it.' Harper hung up, thoughts already elsewhere.

She toyed with the edges of the business card in her pocket. Those damn sigils, she couldn't get them out of her head. Some humans thought Erinyes powerful magical creatures capable of wiping out humanity with some arcane spell if they so desired. That was bullshit paranoia. If they could, why would Erinyes have suffered centuries of persecution and atrocities at the hands of humanity? Millennia ago, when the Aion who sired the first Erinyes walked the earth, maybe things had been different. Doubtful though. The Aion fell after all, one by one until there were none left. The last Aion died two thousand years ago. He met that death at the hand of a human.

The power from Aionic sigils was passive. An echo of the Aion's power that offered protection, refuge and concealment. Even then, only at the hand of someone who knew what they were doing. They provided a sentimental connection to their heritage more than anything else.

Why this killer used the sigils was a mystery. Hell, maybe she was wrong, and it was just some sort of calling card, nothing more.

Aeternus was positioned amongst several warehouses on the edge of the Enclave. Some of the surrounding buildings had been converted to loft apartments. The building was unassuming, with the name in surprisingly discreet lettering above the door. People, both Erinyes and human, talked about Aeternus being as much a meeting place as a bar. She'd never been here before, despite its reputation as an information hub.

Inside, the bar was what she had been expecting. Low lighting, clusters of people, little dark nooks and crannies for people to engage in whatever illicit activities they desired with privacy. She'd been expecting the overall effect to appear sleazy, a den of shady deals and sex, but it wasn't.

More...a sensual sort of classy.

The bar itself was all glossy glass and metal running the length of one wall. Harper waited until she got the attention of the woman tending behind it. She gave Harper an artfully indifferent glance.

Harper leaned on the bar. 'I'm looking for Hael.'

'Sweetie, ain't everyone.'

Harper pulled the business card out of her pocket, sliding it across the bar to the woman. 'I was told to ask for him?'

The bartender looked at the card, before studying Harper with more interest.

'Name's Harper. I'm here about...'

The woman reached across the bar, putting a hand in Harper's forearm. 'Not here. If you're business is with Hael, talk to him in private. Rooms have ears, honey.' She pushed the card back across the bar towards Harper. 'This way.'

Harper followed the woman. Out from behind the bar

she was shorter than Harper, and all sultry grace. Her dark red hair catching the light as it flowed around her shoulders. More than one head turned to follow their passage, unsurprisingly. The woman exuded effortless sex appeal, likely the sort that burnt more than a few who got too close. The lace and leather outfit that slunk around her curves made Harper appear conservative by comparison, with her sensible shoes and a utilitarian jacket. Harper glanced down the woman's figure. Nowhere to conceal knives in that body-hugging outfit. Unlike her own.

The woman led her to an elevator where she waved a card matching the one left on Harper's car over the scanner. There weren't any other buttons. The doors closed, and Harper stood in silence, sensing the other woman regarding her with a curiosity that bordered on predatory.

The elevator stopped at a more intimate room than the bar below. A small landing out from the elevator led to wide walkways off to the left and right. A sunken lounge area took up the centre of the room with comfortable leather seating bracketing the space, before stepping back up to a small bar on the other side. Off the walkways around the oval shaped room hallways led deeper into the building. The space was large, but there were only a handful of people in it.

'Few people gain entry to the private lounge.'

Harper looked at the woman who hadn't offered her name, but the tag she wore said Ash. She had dropped the easy sexuality and felt far more dangerous.

She flicked her eyes to the card Harper still held. 'The man who gave you that must have had his reasons. Anything you hear in this room--'

Harper bristled at the implied threat. 'What happens at Aeternus stays at Aeternus?'

'I don't care what happens downstairs, but here...you won't live to regret betraying the trust entrance to this room implies.'

The woman's inflection barely changed, but Harper knew she was deadly serious.

She gave Harper one last cold look, before turning back to the elevator. 'He's at the bar,' Ash said before the doors closed.

Harper looked across the room. The only person at the bar was behind it. She walked down the steps, taking in more details of the room. There had been security cameras in the elevator and multiple one's downstairs, but none in this room. Two men sprawled on the seating that curled around the wall of the sunken area. One with dark blonde hair and green eyes, the other darker toned with slate grey eyes. Across from them sat a couple too wrapped up in each other to notice anyone else. They were all Erinyes, except one. The blond man was human, eyes flitting up and down as he looked over Harper with a flirty smirk. His coat looked tailored and expensive, though he wore it with a casual indifference over a simple tee-shirt, and faded jeans.

Harper studied him as she walked across the room, wondering if he was fully human. The Erinyes families had always taken in select humans, offering their blood as a sign of trust. Sometimes they were offered the choice of consuming enough blood for its effects to become permanent. Those that did, were called Eshari. The effect often doubled their lifespan. Their abilities were never particularly powerful, it was a roll of the dice, with one or two minor skills developing. Maybe they'd be stronger, or heal faster, but it was only an echo of Erinyes abilities. The choice to become Eshari was offered to few humans, as once fully blooded, they became as much part of the family as those born into it.

The Aion created Erinyes by forcing humans to drink their blood. The Erinyes were adamant humans become Eshari by choice for that very reason.

The Eshari weren't powerful enough to register as anything more than a slight tingle of sensation to Harper. They were a diluted shadow of those first blooded humans who became the Erinyes. She felt nothing from the blond man, he probably was human, and not why she was here. She ignored the others and walked straight to the bar. The man behind it had his back turned, busy pouring a drink.

'A drink, Miss Harper?'

Harper eyed the man, though the relaxed slant of his broad shoulders gave her little to work with. He wore a dark grey Henley and jeans with the nonchalant ease of someone who knew they looked good in them.

She swallowed down a rush of nerves. 'Scotch.'

Hael looked over his shoulder, one side of his mouth curling up in a smile. 'Woman after my own heart.'

He poured a second glass, before turning and handing one to her. He leaned back against the bench, an impressive array of expensive liquor either side of him. Harper spotted bottles of scotch and vodka she could never afford, before turning her attention to Hael. His expression a complicated mix of curiosity, calm, and flirtation, carefully crafted to tell her precisely nothing. She took a sip of the scotch. It was smooth and smoky, with a hint of something more just below the surface, much like the man who had given it to her she suspected.

Harper pulled out the card again. 'Someone told me I should talk to you.' She tossed it on the bar, so the hand-written note was face up.

Hael's lips twitched in a flash of amusement. 'Gage, has such a way with words, doesn't he?'

She'd been pretty sure Gage had left it for her, too big a coincidence to have been anyone else, but it was nice to have it confirmed. 'He seems to have a personal interest in my investigation.'

Hael's expression turned serious. He studied her with eyes full of shrewd intelligence. Harper's senses roared, her skin prickling with heat like she stood too close to a raging fire. Old, ancient, like parchment turned to dust. This man was the oldest Erinyes she had ever sensed. As quick as it came, the sensation disappeared, replaced by a heat more akin to the sensual caress of fingers up and down her spine. Any sense of his age and power gone so entirely she wasn't sure she hadn't imagined it.

Hael's smile turned wicked. 'If that kid's got any sense, he'd be taking a real close interest.'

Harper didn't know whether to roll her eyes or laugh at the innuendo. She hated sleazy guys, but this one....she doubted he had the least bit of interest in getting in her pants.

'I'm investigating the murder yesterday. Outside the en-clave?'

Hael nodded. 'I'm aware'

'Cops have got no idea, and care about as much as you'd expect. I'm trying to identify the victim.'

Harper pulled her phone out and brought the pictures of the victim up. She handed it to Hael, letting him flip through them.

'Sorry. I don't know him.' Hael kept flicking, pausing when he got to the tattoo. He zoomed in on the photo, quiet for a moment, before handing her phone back. 'This is why you were looking to meet an Aesir?'

'The similarity to the Aesir crest, thought it was worth following up.'

Hael swallowed down the last of his scotch. 'I can get you a name in a few hours.' He turned back towards Harper. 'The tattoo...It's an offshoot of the Aesir family.' He shrugged, like that was common knowledge. It really wasn't. 'I assume that's not all you had?'

Harper took another sip, debating what to tell him. If he could get her the victim's name, that alone was more than she'd been able to do on her own so far. The rumours about the owner of Aeternus being an information broker played in her mind.

'You own the bar downstairs?'

'I own the building. And the bar. I have a rather nice chalet in the Italian alps. Did you want to discuss real estate, or did you want to discuss the files you have on the other murders?'

Harper watched Hael smile benignly at her, trying to find her footing. She was used to dealing with humans in her investigations. In this room, she was a mackerel swimming with sharks.

'How do you...never mind.'

Hael had been expecting her. Presumably Gage told him

about her visit to the old crime scene at Ara's house. Still, she had barely spoken to Gage in their brief encounters. Shrugging it off, Harper pulled out the files she'd printed.

He looked through them in silence for a couple of minutes. Harper watched as he read. Cultivating a relationship with someone as well informed as Hael could only be beneficial. She knew little about him. There had always been rumours, the hot-headed bar owner, unpredictable and fickle who drank too much and took nothing seriously, but who no one seemed willing to cross. She didn't care for rumours and would see for herself how volatile or useful he might be.

Harper had always been slow to form opinions on those she met. Her father had always smiled in fond amusement at her natural lack of trust, wondering where she got it from. He'd always had such good instincts about people, it's what made him a good investigator, and well-respected Watcher. Harper loved him for never trying to change her or force her to make friends as a child. He'd always smiled and said when she deemed someone worthy, she'd stand by them no matter what, so it was a good thing she took her time getting the measure of people.

Hael tossed one of the files back to Harper. 'This one doesn't fit.'

Harper looked at the file. The sigils had been less extensive than in the other cases. The kill clean, less...frenetic maybe. 'What makes you so sure?'

Hael shrugged almost lazily. 'She had a habit of betting on her own matches in underground fights, then lost unexpectedly.' He pushed the files aside.

Hael fixed himself another scotch, as he did Harper caught

sight of a shimmer on the wall behind the bar. Protection sigils flared, lining the walls of the whole room, before they faded back out of sight.

'You have barrier wards?'

'Wouldn't be much of a private lounge if just anyone could fly in.'

Sigils may not hold the power humans believed, but one of their more useful functions was to ward a room or building. The right sigils formed a barrier no Erinyes could cross. Or in the hands of someone skilled, let only selected Erinyes pass. They had no effect on humans though, which Harper assumed was why there were more traditional security measures to access the elevator, like the passkey embedded in the card Gage left her.

She watched as he finished pouring another scotch for himself, starting to think the rumours about him drinking too much might have some truth to them.

Hael studied her as he swirled the amber liquid in his glass. 'What's your official duty in this case, you're not a Watcher?'

Harper still wasn't sure what she was doing here, but this question she was used to at least. 'I'm the Council's liaison with human law enforcement. Officially, I aid Police in investigations that have Erinyes involvement.'

'And unofficially?'

'Unofficially...I have no jurisdiction outside, or inside the Enclave. I'm a living breathing PR stunt to show how progressive relations between us and humans have become, when they're no better at all.'

The words tasted bitter in her mouth, but they were the

truth. She glared at Hael. She'd never admitted that out loud before.

'Sorry.' He shrugged, not looking the least bit apologetic.

Erinyes mind tricks. A shiver ran down her spine at the memory of power and age she had gotten from him earlier.

The corner of Hael's mouth ticked up in a smile that made her want to punch him in the face. 'I see the truth of things.'

All Erinyes had some abilities. Flight the obvious one, but most were empathic, sensing emotion from others. They healed quicker than humans, were faster. Some conjured simple illusions to misdirect, confuse. A rare few even saw the echo of memories, though Harper wasn't sure how true that was. She was just as unsure about the myths of half-bloods who could make a person believe they were on fire or dying of thirst, freeze with a touch the way the Aion had been able to. If any of that were ever true, Harper had never seen it.

Some were strong enough to sway thoughts. It was near impossible to get someone to do something they didn't want to, but easier to influence them towards simple choices they were already considering. Like a truth they had been avoiding admitting. A far cry from the mind control humans feared, but still disconcerting.

Hael had so slickly suggested she voice a truth she'd been struggling with for a while now, that she hadn't even noticed it until the words were out. She hated him for it.

She thumped her glass down on the bar. 'My authority might be limited. I'm not a Watcher, and I'm not a cop. But I do what I can.'

Hael seemed satisfied with her answer. 'I'll contact you

when I find a name for your dead man.' He grabbed a note pad and pen, pushing them across the bar. 'Your number?'

'With your resources, I'm sure you'll find a way to contact me?'

He shrugged. 'I could. But this is much simpler, don't you think?'

Harper glared at him, but he was right of course. She scribbled down her number, not trusting he would do as he said. She walked back to the elevator, anger fizzing under her skin, and refusing to look at anyone in the room. It was hard to avoid a truth once it had been spoken aloud.

***

9

~ GAGE ~

Gage watched Harper as she stepped into the elevator. She seemed determined to keep poking where someone more sensible wouldn't. A sure-fire way to find trouble, but also potentially useful. Let her rattle a few cages, see what falls out.

'You done lurking back there?' Hael asked as he poured another drink for himself and filled a second glass with Russian Vodka. He slid the vodka across the bar as Gage walked out of the back room.

Gage ignored the offered drink, glaring at Hael who smirked back at him. 'I had to use the service entrance.'

'Security measures, you know how it is,' Hael said.

'Ash had to let me up.'

Hael shrugged, feigning an innocence Gage knew him incapable of. 'A strange woman turned up with your access card, I had to adjust the ward's until I was sure you weren't compromised.'

Gage picked up the vodka and swallowed it in one gulp. 'You're such an asshole.'

Hael grinned, with far too many teeth. 'And yet, you keep coming back.'

'It's a good thing you know how to mix a decent drink, or you'd get awful lonely.'

Hael laughed quietly to himself as he started mixing two more drinks. He studied Gage as he did, dropping much of the act he usually put on. 'You sure about her?'

'No.' Gage absently drew circles in the moisture ring left by Harper's drink on the bar, half forming sigils before scrubbing them out. 'I don't know.'

He wasn't sure why he'd told Harper anything. Or maybe he did. Ara deserved better. He couldn't turn down help, just because it meant someone else going through the details of her life, pulling them apart, scrutinising, until she was nothing more than cold facts.

Hael sipped at his drink, looking towards the elevator where Harper had exited. 'She's hard to read in a lot of ways. But there's an...honesty to her.'

Gage nodded. He trusted Hael's impressions of people, especially their own kind. Gage understood humans, could read them better, pass himself off as one if called for. Hael understood everyone, human, Erinyes, it made little difference to him. He saw the truth of them.

'Let her investigate. She'll either find something or she won't. Either way, she could be useful.' Hael looked back at Gage. 'You okay?'

Gage hadn't been back to Ara's house since she died. A phantom cold crept down his spine, squeezed at his ribs. It trickled down his arms and pooled in his fingers. His ever-present icy anger wanting to be let loose. He wouldn't allow it out though, clenching his fingers to contain it. The habit a coping mechanism that barely suppressed the urge to lash out.

Gage watched the clear liquid slosh back and forth in his glass, before taking a mouthful. 'Okay enough.'

Hael's watchful gaze felt a little like the summer thaw as he shuffled around Gage's emotions, like he was deliberately letting Gage know he was reading him. Not that it would be very hard at the moment. Gage had no doubt his feelings were flooding out for any Erinyes to sense, especially someone as attuned to them as Hael. Gage took a deep breath, forcing his control back in place. Hael didn't say anymore on the matter, which Gage was grateful for.

Across the room, Gage felt Cole move, tracking the void where his presence should be. Gage read emotion off humans as easy as breathing, every human except Cole, who was remarkably adept at concealing himself. Of course, Cole wasn't entirely human anymore. Few outside this room knew of Cole's unique condition, and with his skill at appearing to be nothing more than a simple human, he was very good at keeping it that way. He'd had centuries to perfect the act after all.

'The dead kid's name was Arty.' Cole sat next to Gage. 'Harper was on the right track with the tattoo.'

Gage remembered the blond hair stained dark with blood. 'So, he was Aesir?'

'Cousin of some sort. One of Bodhi's.'

Gage nodded. Bodhi headed an offshoot from the Aesir.

Not big into politics, more due to being a small family rather than by choice, like the Aesir.

Cole looked at Hael. 'That makes five.'

Five dead Aesir in the last five years. The Aesir were a big family, scattered across the world, but five murders, that wasn't a coincidence. Gage gulped down his drink and waved the empty glass at Hael. Cole grabbed it out his hand before Hael could refill it. Gage glared at him.

Cole gazed back at him unflinchingly 'Arty had a brother.' He set the glass down out of Gage's reach. 'He's here in the city.'

Cole and Hael shared a look. Hael probably reading whatever emotion Cole was pushing at him, like having a conversation without words. Gage narrowed his eyes, trying to decide is he should be annoyed at whatever was being communicated, but his empathic skills weren't as good as Hael's. He got nothing beyond a vague feeling of concern.

Gage pushed down a spike of frustration. 'I'll talk to the brother. See what he knows.'

Hael looked back at Gage. 'I know this started with Ara, but...'

Gage met Hael's steady gaze. 'I know.'

Gage had spent years chasing dead leads searching for Ara's killer. He'd raged and rampaged, but still found almost nothing to fill the ache she left inside his chest.

Hael reached across the bar and put his hand on Gage's shoulder. 'Be careful, there's something more to this. These aren't just random murders.'

Gage nodded, not sure what to say.

'I'll give you a few hours before I call the lovely Watcher Liaison and give her the information.'

'Thanks.'

Hael cuffed him on the back of the head. 'Now, stop drinking all my good booze. Get the hell out of here.'

Gage smiled as he stepped back. He gave Cole a brief nod, before disappearing.

***

Gage once spent a summer working his way through a trafficking operation in eastern Europe that had better house-keeping than the dive bar Arty's brother Yuri was drowning his grief in. Yuri was blonde too, with the same jawline as his dead brother, but not much else. He was bulkier, older, and very drunk. Clearly, he'd been here most of the night. He didn't give Gage a chance to talk.

'I know who you are, and I don't give a shit,' he slurred, looking up at Gage with an expression full of anger and resentment Gage wasn't expecting, but understood. 'You turn up now. What's the point? My baby brother is dead. Slaughtered. You and yours don't care.'

Gage took the barstool next to Yuri, resisting the urge to wipe his hands on his jeans. 'I can't help your brother, but I can find who did this to him.'

Yuri looked at him, scoffing in disbelief. 'What, you're going to swoop in with some Watcher justice and make everything better.'

'I'm not here as a Watcher, Yuri. I want to find who did this to your brother.'

Cole caught Gage by surprise as he slouched on the bar on the other side of Yuri.

'I don't think the whole truth and justice approach is going to work with this one,' Cole said, looking Yuri up and down. Finding something lacking, he turned to check out the bartender next, a bouncy blonde girl who looked far too put together to be in a place like this.

'Oh, glory be, they sent the pet human.' Yuri swallowed down his drink, some of it dripping off his chin.

Gage hadn't realised Cole followed him. 'What are you doing here?'

Cole shrugged. 'I was bored.'

Yuri laughed bitterly. 'Screw you.' He haphazardly waved his empty glass at the bartender.

Cole smiled dangerously. 'Only if you ask nicely.'

'Cole,' Gage warned, not sure how Yuri would take Cole's flippant irreverence.

Cole slapped a hand on Yuri's shoulder. 'It's all good. I offer to remove the head from whoever killed Yuri here's brother, and he'll probably buy me a drink.'

Yuri looked at Cole like he was trying to figure out if he was insane. Gage could have saved him the bother. Cole was definitely insane. Hell, he'd been raised by the most dangerous person Gage had ever known, the odds were never in favour of Cole being well adjusted.

Yuri lifted his hand, drunkenly stabbing a finger at Cole's chest. 'You cut that bastards head off, I'll buy you a whole fucking bottle.'

Cole grinned at Gage, all insincere and daring him to say something. Gage resisted the urge to roll his eyes, or maybe laugh. Cole had a strange way of getting to people that was always surprising. They trusted him in ways that made no sense. Frankly, Gage would never understand how Cole didn't get punched in the face more often.

Cole caught the bar tender's attention with a smile that was all easy charm. 'Three of the best scotch you've got.' He looked back at Yuri. 'Actually, just bring the bottle.'

Cole poured the drinks once the bottle was delivered. 'For Arty.' He raised his own glass and took a mouthful.

Yuri drank, looking resigned to the company he clearly didn't want.

'Arty was into cars, wasn't he?' Cole asked.

Gage had no idea when Cole had the time to gather information on Arty. Maybe he got it from Hael. who collected random bits of information that might be useful one day. Wherever he got it from, the detail was enough to draw Yuri's attention away from his drink.

'Yeah, he was.' He looked at Cole more appraisingly. 'He worked in a garage outside the Enclave.'

'Erinyes don't appreciate a good car. You lazy bastards fly everywhere.' Cole poured another round of drinks. 'Me, I love a good fast car and road enough to open her up on.'

The corner of Gage's lips tilted upwards. Cole loved his fucking cars, but drove like he lived his life, recklessly. He once wrapped a car around a tree while Gage was in the passenger seat. It was a damn good thing he healed quickly.

Cole looked across at Gage and shrugged. 'Not that I'm any good at driving them, I just like going fast.'

Yuri picked up his glass and gulped the scotch down like it was water. 'That's what Art always liked. The speed. He was into street racing. He pretty much liked anything he could bet on.' He held out the empty glass for Cole to pour another drink. 'He was a good kid, but not always the smartest.'

Gage swallowed down his scotch, barely able to feel the burn of it. All he could think of was Ara's bright smile. She had a laugh like the first rays of morning sun, fresh, full of possibilities and so much life. For a long time, he hadn't been able to remember her smile. All he saw when he closed his eyes was the blood in her hair, torn fingernails where she'd fought so hard to hang onto life, and the jagged line of her slit throat that made a mockery of every smile she had ever given him.

His fingers tightened on his glass. Gods, he wanted to punch something. Let the rage loose, it'd be so fucking easy. He set the glass down on the bar, slow and deliberately, willing his fingers to loosen. Cole watched him, shrewd and observant, the man always had a way of seeing things, even when you didn't want him to.

'Do you know where Arty was the night he was killed?' Gage asked.

Yuri looked down at his glass, eyes shining. 'Art liked to bet on the cage fights at Fifth and Coleman.'

'Tyriel's gig?' Cole asked.

Yuri nodded. 'How bout you take the pretty Watcher here, maybe someone will stab him in his useless heart.'

'Ah, what heart.' Cole smirked. 'Gage gave his away a long time ago. He's all clockwork and wiring in there now.'

Gage glared at Cole. 'Look who's talking, arsehole.'

'Nah, I never had one to start with. It's like the Sahara in here baby.' Cole tapped at his chest. 'Nothing but dust.'

Gage shook his head, fond despite himself. 'You're an idiot.'

'Piss off already.' Yuri grabbed the half empty bottle from Cole and poured himself another drink.

Gage stood, putting a hand on Yuri's shoulder. 'I am sorry about your brother,' he said softly, before grabbing Cole and pulling him away from the bar, leaving Yuri to his grieving.

Cole turned the collar of his coat up against the cold as they walked outside. His joking demeanour sliding away like it was nothing more than a mote of fluff whisked away by the winter wind, letting a little of the real Cole shine through. He looked across at Gage, watching him as they walked, like he was deciding whether to say something. He looked away, to Gage's relief. Even now, he never wanted to talk about it.

'One of those cases your Liaison friend dug up was on a fighter at Tyriel's,' Cole said after a moment.

'Yeah, so Hael said. He didn't think it fit the pattern.'

'Maybe not. Hael doesn't believe in coincidences either though.'

That was true. For the first time in a long while, he had direction. He'd barely been able to feign sorrow at Arty's death, too numb to truly care beyond knowing with a fresh murder there would be new leads to find the bastard who killed Ara.

Cole looked across at him. 'Tyriel starts his fights around midnight. They should be nearly over.'

'Can you get us in?' Gage asked, unsurprised when Cole nodded in answer. Of course, he could. Cole could talk his way in anywhere. He was also a downright catalyst for strife who couldn't help getting involved in things, even when he shouldn't. 'Want to go cause some trouble?'

Cole's smile filled with the lack of self-preservation he approached life with. 'Always.'

***

Gage pushed through the crowd. It was late, but the fight club was still in full swing. He didn't bother with subtlety, shouldering past human and Erinyes alike, too impatient to let the ebb and flow carry him. In the centre of the room stood the fight cage. A raised platform boxed in with steel mesh. The cage rattled as a fighter was thrown against the mesh, the sound swallowed by a roar of approval. Gage curled his fingers. The muscle in his jaw tightening as the sour slide of violent delight rolled off those around him, skulking over his body like the creeping touch of unwanted hands. Scenting blood the crowd shifted with a primal, vicious energy. They were a mass of roiling movement, churning, like the frenzied feeding as a bait ball reaches the ocean's surface.

The thunderous cheering as another brutal punch connected drowned out Gage's growl of frustration. He'd thought the fights would be over by now. They'd never find answers in this crowd. He couldn't even hear himself think.

Technically, these fights were illegal, but no one put much effort into shutting them down. There was too much money involved. Collecting bets on no rules fights that didn't end until one fighter was out cold, or dead was big business.

Gage turned to Cole, who made his way more easily through the crowd, shifting and swaying in time with its frantic movements. Cole was better at getting people to talk about things they didn't want to and doing it in a way, so they didn't even realise. Gage suspected it had something to do with a subtle use of suggestive ability, like how Hael encouraged people to tell the truth. Cole insisted he was just that charming. Hell, maybe he was right.

Gage had to lean in and shout in Cole's ear. 'Where the hell do we even start?'

Cole tilted his head. 'There.'

Gage followed Cole's line of sight. A man in a suit sat in the VIP area. Security and a few wealthy looking people surrounded him. The man wasn't talking to anyone or watching the fight. Instead, he sat with his elbows on his knees knocking back drinks like they were in danger of evaporating if he didn't empty them as soon as possible. He was an odd island amongst a vast sea of people, forgotten and overlooked. He wasn't insignificant though.

Gage knew who that was. Tyriel, the owner of the club.

'You sure that's a good idea?'

Cole didn't answer. His gaze drifting back to the fight, eyes tracking every movement.

'Cole.'

Cole gave a slight jolt as one fighter went down onto his knees. Covered in blood, the fighter's arm looked broken, but he wasn't tapping out. He couldn't, the fight wouldn't end until one of them couldn't get up again. He was only a kid but appeared resigned as he stared up at his opponent. He had nothing left to block a sickening round house kick. Even over the noise of the crowd, Gage heard the kid's jaw shatter. The boy hit the floor, out cold. At least it was over now.

With the fight over, the crowd pulsated around them, making Gage aware of just how still Cole had become. He stood motionless, like deceptively calm waters with a torrent of barely contained rage flowing beneath the surface. Two men entered the cage to drag the unconscious fighter out, and Cole's expression shuttered into a blank state, as if someone flipped a switch and erased everything.

Shit, he knew better than to bring Cole somewhere like this. They should have left as soon as he realised the fights were still underway. He'd been so caught up with finding a lead on Ara's killer that he hadn't thought. He reached out to grab Cole's arm, but he shook Gage off, moving through the crowd with an ease Gage struggled to match.

'Cole.'

It was no use. Gage moved faster, pushing and shoving people out of his way. Cole slipped through the crowd, well ahead of him though. Cole grabbed one of the security team at the door of the cage, shoving him to the ground. He punched another in the jaw, before shoving past him and stepping into the cage. Cole slammed the door behind himself.

Shit.

Cole looked out at Tyriel. The club owner set down his drink with a curious half smile. Cole's expression filled with icy defiance. It was the sort of look that made lesser men run. Tyriel watched a moment, seeming oddly fascinated before nodding to his security team who backed away, leaving Cole to face the next fighter.

These sorts of places didn't take well to anyone withdrawing once they stepped into the cage. There was nothing Gage could do. Cole was on his own.

***

10

~ COLE ~

LONDON, 27TH OCTOBER 1690

Cole hated London.

It had been a lifetime since he'd last been in the city, yet the moment he arrived the years melted away. He remembered the smell, the way the air felt, its streets and people. He had been born here, and his feet wanted to take him straight along the Thames before cutting through the streets to Cheapside. It was all so familiar. It wasn't the same though, and neither was he. When he'd last been in London, he had been a half-starved fourteen-year-old and the city had been on fire. The glow of the Great Fire consuming the city had shrouded everything in orange as he drifted down the Thames with the crazed Erinyes who tore apart the slave pits of the old city, and killed the Masters who'd made Cole's life hell.

That was twenty-four years ago. So much had changed.

The buildings replacing those that burnt could be seen from the walls of the Erinyes Enclave. Construction works were still under way. The stonework of St Paul's the most notable. Cole watched as lanterns around the building site flickered out. It was almost midnight and Hael's meeting with the Councillor still hadn't finished. Cole blew out a breath of air that hung in the cool night air. He could get to the church and back in an hour. Hael wouldn't even notice he'd gone.

The London Enclave was old, its streets narrow and dark. Cole made his way to the gates leading out to the human city and slipped through unnoticed. The last time he walked these streets, everything had been on fire, people running and screaming. It was quiet tonight. No one bothered him as he walked a winding route towards St Paul's Cathedral. Everything was laid out much the same, though not as crowded as it'd been, the streets wider after the fire for one thing. He passed through the Cheapside markets. He'd run through the old market as an orphan, picking pockets, stealing food from inattentive vendors when he got so hungry, he could barely stand.

Those times had been almost happy.

Cole paused a few streets away from the markets where the buildings were all new, mostly brick now compared to the wooden ones he remembered. He'd been begging for food, maybe ten years old, when everything had changed.

He still remembered the man's face, black eyes, a strong straight nose.

The man had grabbed Cole off this street and pulled him into an alley that no longer existed. Cole had screamed until his lungs hurt, but no one listened. The man knocked him out to shut him up, and he woke sometime later, already in chains. It wasn't uncommon. No one cared.

Cole had been sold to the slavers for three pounds. A horse would have been worth more.

It could have been worse. A lot of kids stolen off the streets ended up dead in a ditch. Cole had kicked and bitten anyone who tried to touch him after, which only made the slavers laugh. They called him a hellion and threw him in the pit for his first fight against a boy three years older. In the slave fighting pits, if you wanted to live, you didn't lose.

Cole hadn't lost.

He shoved his hands in his pockets, looking up at the new buildings standing in the ashes of the old. Nice respectable businesses. He wondered if the men who owned them ever came to watch him fight.

Cold air settled on his shoulders as he stood staring at the building, unable to make his feet move. His fingers ached, and he realised they were clenched in fists. He forcefully loosened them, remembering the ache in the back of his throat from the smoke as the slave pits burned. The fire reflected in Hael's eyes as he held out his hand, covered in blood. Cole had hesitated, but only for a moment. He spent four years in those slave pits. The night Hael freed him, Cole killed the Master who ran the slave pit and the guard who took the most joy in tormenting the slaves along with a few others whose faces he couldn't even remember. Hael killed just about everyone else.

He never asked Hael why he'd done it. He just ran into the night with the strange Erinyes and never looked back.

He thought he'd put the trauma of what happened in those fight pits behind him. Apparently, it wasn't that easy.

Cole turned and walked down the street, making his way to the Cathedral. It reminded him of the cathedrals in Rome, though this great dome was currently little more than a skeleton. Over the last twenty years he'd seen architectural marvels across Europe. Their history fascinated him. It was hard not to be when either Hael, Wrathe or both would have some story about whatever building or ruin they visited. The first time they explored the Coliseum Cole had realised just how old Hael and Wrathe were. Hael quietly told him stories about the gladiators with such forgotten minor details it was as if Cole heard echoes of them, dying while crowds cheered. There was something in the way Hael reached out his hand to the rough surface of the underground cells, fingers shaking, breath catching in his throat in harsh sounds, like the surrounding space was suddenly too small. It took Wrathe several minutes whispering words too softly for Cole to hear, to bring him out of it. That day Cole knew he would never ask Hael why he had destroyed the London slavers. Some things were better left to silence.

Cole snuck into the cathedral work site. Not that there was anyone around to stop him. He swung his way up the scaffolding, making his way along one of the completed sections of roof. Unlike some churches, this one didn't have any angel statues that he could see. Angel statues amused him. Everyone knew they were modelled after the Aion who long ago died out. A race of beautiful, winged people who brought their endless war to this world. They had been powerful, dangerous and deadly. The angel statues created in their image always had feathers. All the great sculptors, and an orphan boy from London knew more than they did. The Aion didn't have feathers any more than the Erinyes did. Maybe feathers were just easier to sculpt than flowing waves of light. Though that didn't explain why they usually looked so peaceful.

Cole scrambled down onto a ledge on the south side of the building, running his fingers over the raised outline of a stone phoenix. Below it was an old piece of gravestone with the word resurgem carved into it. Cole smiled. Rising from the ashes as something new was an idea he appreciated.

A muffled cry drifted up from the street below. Cole shifted his hold, turning to see where it had come from. There. Three men were pushing a smaller figure into an alley, pulling whatever she was carrying away from her. She cried out again, but softly, like she knew no one would help her. She kicked and struggled, but it wouldn't make any difference.

Without thinking, Cole leant out, and let go.

He dropped thirty feet onto the paved street. The landing was awkward, twisting his left knee. It felt like something snapped, shooting pain up his thigh and making his stomach roil. He'd been an Eshari blooded to the Aesir family for a while but was still figuring out his limitations. Apparently, a thirty-foot fall was overly ambitious.

He braced himself against the wall a moment, before pushing off towards the attackers. He could walk, but it hurt like hell. Genius move.

The three men were human. The young woman was not. As he got closer, she spotted Cole, eyes widening in fear. Cole saw fleeting hope fading in her expression. She was young, not even twenty. As helpless as a human at that age. The men still hadn't noticed him. Cole held a finger up to his lips and the women stopped struggling. One man laughed. Cole attacked him first.

He aimed a vicious kick at the man's knee, his own injured one screaming at the move. Cole gritted his teeth, slamming a fist into the man's face as he fell. One of the other attackers reacted quickly, getting in a hit to Cole's jaw, and another to his ribs before he could block them. Cole grabbed him by the collar, swinging him to the ground.

Cole looked over his shoulder at the woman. 'Get to the Enclave.'

She didn't hesitate, running out of the alley as the men got back to their feet and faced Cole. He'd back himself over three street thugs any day. Of course, that'd be if his knee wasn't buckling, no longer able to take his weight. Cole laughed. He couldn't help it. The men looked confused for a moment, before advancing. The rest of the world seemed to drop away as Cole's focus narrowed. Learning to be a person, to live the life Hael had given him had been complicated, but this he understood, this was simple.

Losing wasn't an option.

***

II

~ GAGE ~

Gage cursed as he was jostled by the crowd. People were scrambling to place bets before the fight started. He doubted they'd be backing Cole. As far as anyone else knew, Cole was just a human, and any human stepping into these sorts of fights should lose.

But Cole wouldn't lose, that was the problem.

Cole had been an orphan in London, taken by slavers and beaten and worse in places like this for years before Hael had found him. Gage had heard the story of how Hael saved a skinny half-starved fourteen-year-old human who'd have been lucky to see fifteen, and those traumas paled in comparison to what came later. Gage ran his hands through his hair. He'd fucked up and had to fix this. He pulled out his phone, calling Hael, panic straining his words as he explained what was happening.

Cole circled his opponent. The fighter was Erinyes, tall

but young. Cole waited for him to make the first move. When he did, Cole dodged, bobbing to the left and twisting, far quicker than the other fighter expected. He used his momentum to strike at the other man's ribs. Cole didn't let him recover, following up with a flurry of hits. The fight ended in less than a minute. Cole stood unnaturally still over the unconscious man. He wasn't even breathing hard and looked unaware of the crowd roaring around him. Cole exited the cage, waiting for his next fight with a thousand-yard stare Gage doubted saw anything in this room.

Indentured fighting was a weak spot for Cole, and Gage knew that. He should never have brought Cole here. Everything about this place was filled with triggers, and one had clearly been tripped.

Hael wasted no time, taking flight before Gage could end the call. He didn't even bother with the door, somehow landing in the middle of the crowded club next to Gage.

Gage pointed to where Cole stood. 'He'll keep winning.'

Hael nodded. 'I know. That's why I brought Deacon.'

Looking around, Gage spotted Deacon circling the fight cage. Deacon was Gage's nephew, though he was almost two hundred years older than Gage. Hael had raised Deacon, who looked up to Cole as a big brother, and was one of the few people able to talk sense into him.

'If that doesn't work?' Gage asked.

'I go in there and pull him out myself.'

Gage looked up at Hael. Tonight had gone to shit way faster than usual. 'I'm sorry, I should've known something like this would happen.'

Hael wouldn't look at Gage. 'Yes, you should have.'

They watched as Deacon got close enough to get Cole's attention without being noticed by Tyriel's security. Deacon spoke to Cole, who didn't seem to know he was there at first. After a few minutes Cole turned his head toward Deacon, he said nothing, but Deacon kept talking, leaning in closer. Gage didn't know what he could say that would make any difference. Cole was far from any logic right now. Cole's name was called for the next fight. Deacon grabbed Cole's arm, but Cole shrugged out of his hold, making his way back into the cage.

His opponent this time was older, stronger and more experienced. A human should stand no chance against him, and the crowd knew it, calling for blood. Cole didn't move as the fight was introduced, eyes tracking his foe, the rest of him eerily still. The other fighter made the first move, he was fast, but Cole seemed to just flow around him like water, weaving to avoid the series of blows aimed at him. Cole barely acknowledged a savage punch that connected, catching him in the jaw. He twisted with it, using the power of the hit to rotate his body. He lifted his elbow and struck his opponent in the temple. It barely dazed him, but it was enough of an opening for Cole to take advantage of. He went on the offensive, striking out while the other fighter was off balance. Cole's counter strike was a blur, brutal in its precision as his fist snapped his opponents head back. He was out cold before hitting the ground. The crowd buzzed with a mix of surprise and disappointment the fight was over so quick. Cole walked out of the cage, acknowledging no one.

'Shit,' Gage said, turning to Hael before realising the other man had gone.

Gage turned around looking for him. The defeated fighter

was being dragged out, still unconscious. Gage spotted Hael next to the cage, talking to Tyriel. Hael leaned in after Tyriel shook his head, saying something into the club owner's ear. Tyriel looked at Hael a moment, before shrugging and stepping into the cage.

'Ladies and gentlemen.' Tyriel waited until he had the crowd's attention before continuing. 'We have a change in the draw tonight. An old friend, well I guess we're not that close.' Tyriel smiled with no warmth. 'An old acquaintance, has decided he needs to blow off some steam.'

'Fuck,' Gage muttered to himself as he started pushing his way through the crowd.

'We will only have one more match tonight. Something different. I have a challenger who has thrown the gauntlet down to all remaining fighters to step into the cage. One against...' Tyriel made a show of counting the fighters outside the cage. 'One against, let's say, ten.'

Hael stepped out into the cage. A murmur ran through the crowd as bets were laid.

Gage reached the side of the cage. 'Are you insane,' he called out to Hael.

Hael looked down at him and shrugged. Of course, he bloody was.

'Stop Cole from doing anything stupid,' Hael said quietly.

Right, because enough stupid was already happening. With everyone's attention on the cage, Gage made his way to where Deacon held Cole back.

'What the hell were you thinking,' Gage said.

Cole stared straight through Gage. 'He was just a damn kid, he shouldn't have had to fight,' Cole said quietly, eyes still not focusing on Gage, like all he saw were a hundred other fight rings, and dead fighters who owed money to the wrong people.

'What the hell were you going to do about it?' The words came out harsher than Gage wanted to be.

Cole didn't answer. The muscles in his jaw almost quivering, like his lips were the only thing holding back a brewing storm of fury.

'You go into that cage and keep winning, people will ask questions,' Gage said gentler.

Questions even Gage didn't know the answers to. Cole was always careful, tucking away his secrets so well, no one even knew to look for them. Usually.

The fight went out of Cole as he looked across at Hael standing in the cage, like he'd just noticed what Hael was doing. Hael stood with his back to them, but he looked like he was waiting for someone to serve him a drink, rather than about to face off against ten cage fighters.

'And when he wins?' Cole asked quietly.

A muscle twitched in Gage's jaw as he looked across to Deacon, who gave a small shake of his head. Gage felt hollowed out, knowing what Deacon meant. 'He won't win. He's smarter than that.'

Deacon put a hand on Cole's shoulder as he started to shake, turning pale as reason worked its way back into his head.

'Shit, I'm sorry. I'm sorry,' Cole said over and over to no one in particular, eyes not leaving Hael, the man he had called father for centuries.

Everyone knew Hael as the fiery owner of Aeternus, broker

of information, who served a mean drink and threw an even meaner punch. He'd probably thrown a few of those in the crowd here tonight out of Aeternus over the years. Hael loved breaking up fights almost as much as he liked starting them. At least that's the image Hael had carefully curated since they settled in Chicago a few decades ago.

People tended to underestimate a reckless hedonistic hot-head. Hael was a known quantity people dismissed because they thought they knew him. Very few did.

In a pulse of movement and sound, the crowd made a flurry of bets, before cheering wildly as the fight began. Hael moved with the same fluid agility as Cole. It was graceful, but brutal. He attacked a big bulky Erinyes who looked like he was closely related to a brick wall. With a burst of movement and quick efficient hits, Hael dropped him to the floor cold. The man had barely slumped in a heap before Hael shifted to the next challenger, getting in a few quick hits before he took a hit to the jaw himself. Another fighter took advantage of the distraction and rushed Hael with a series of punches and a well-timed kick that knocked Hael to the ground. Hael spat blood and looked up grinning at the man who'd hit him. The easy charm and friendliness gone, his smile now all feral and taunting. Hael moved, fiercely launching himself from the cage floor. He grabbed one man by the throat and flung him at a female fighter, sending them both sprawling on the floor. Hael twisted in the air, kicking out at a third fighter, knocking him out with a perfectly timed move. The fight turned scrappy as Hael took several hits, but gave plenty of his own, managing to stay on his feet. The crowd rumbled with morbid delight. Whether they were cheering for Hael to beat the odds, or for him to be killed was hard to tell.

Gage couldn't take his eyes of the fight. The crowd surged around Gage, like he was the calm eye of a storm amongst the frenetic crowd.

Hael had taken out half of his opponents. He could probably have taken out the rest just as easily, if that had been the point. Blood streamed down the side of Hael's face, turning his smile red. He looked manic. He wasn't even bothering to block the hits he took now, almost like he relished in them, like he wasn't even feeling them, as he struck his opponents again and again. Another fighter fell, but it left Hael's back turned to two of the remaining fighters. They grabbed hold of him, while another rained a vicious series of blows to Hael's torso before he could shrug off the men holding him. Hael laughed, the sound chilling.

'What the hell is he doing,' someone asked loudly, though Gage barely heard them. It was Harper, shouting to try and get his attention over the noise of the crowd. 'Is he trying to get himself killed?'

Gage jerked, looking down at her. He had no idea when she had arrived. He stared at her a moment, confused why she was here, before remembering Hael had promised to send her the name of the dead man. She'd probably spoken to Yuri as well. He didn't bother answering her, just turned back to the fight, swallowing tightly as his fingers curled into fists.

Deacon shifted on his other side. 'You know we can't do anything,'

Gage tried to force his fingers to loosen, with only mild success. 'I know.'

Harper watched the fight, looking caught somewhere between fascinated and appalled. 'What was he thinking, throwing out a challenge like that?'

Cole flinched at her words.

One of the fighters grabbed hold of Hael's right arm, yanking it backwards at an impossible looking angle, before Hael managed to break away, stumbling out of reach.

Gage shifted closer to Cole, trying to reach out to him without drawing any more attention. 'They aren't good enough to kill him,' he said quietly.

Cole's lips thinned in a bloodless line. 'I know.'

Harper looked at them a little stunned. 'There are ten of them.'

Gage tucked away any flare of emotion as she glanced up at him. 'Three now,' Gage said with a shrug as Hael knocked out the fighter who'd grabbed his arm.

There might only be three left, but Hael was injured. His right shoulder was dropping, and he kept it angled away from the attacks. Hael looked over at their group and winked, before he seemed to misstep. It was a minor mistake, but Gage knew it was deliberate. It left a small opening in Hael's defences for one of the remaining fighters to take advantage. With one last vicious blow, the fight looked to be over. Hael dropped to his knees. He was still conscious, though unable to get back up. Tyriel didn't step in to stop the fight. The three remaining fighters paused, momentarily uncertain. Hael's shoulder and arm hung uselessly, flopping about, clearly dislocated. He was having trouble breathing, probably from broken ribs. But he was awake, and Tyriel's fights had one rule. They didn't end until the loser was unconscious.

One of the fighters moved forward. He reached down, picking Hael up by his dislocated shoulder. Hael let out a cut off scream that dissolved into something resembling laughter, though it was too wet with the blood Hael coughed up to be sure.

'Screw this,' Cole said, trying to step forward but Gage grabbed hold of him.

'He told me to not let you do anything stupid,' Gage said.

Cole spun around to look at him. 'How can you watch this?'

'You think I...' The rest of Gage's words seemed to drown as he had to swallow thickly. He tightened his grip on Cole's arm. 'He's my brother, I hate this as much as you do,' he continued, the words barely audible.

Cole looked stricken as he turned back to the fight. There was no need to interfere anyway. The man who had hold of Hael viciously punch him in the head several times in quick succession. This time when he slumped to the floor of the cage, Hael was out cold.

It was over.

***

12

~ HARPER ~

Harper hated crowds. At least half the patrons at the fight club were human, but there was still a throng of Erinyes around her, battering away at her senses. Her head pounded, and it felt like insects were scuttling about under her skin. Harper clenched her fists as the crowd jostled her. She'd been here once before. This was the club where she met Viridian five years ago. She hadn't liked it then, and she didn't like it now.

Hael had sent the name of the victim in her case an hour ago, as he'd promised. She'd found the brother, Yuri, at a bar drinking his way to oblivion. He'd mumbled something about already sending the other useless pricks to Tyriel's. She had arrived just in time to watch the human from Hael's club win his second fight and then to watch Hael himself step into the ring.

What the hell had Hael been thinking? The rumours about him being reckless seemed well founded.

Tyriel walked into the cage and stood over Hael where he lay prone on the ring floor. He wasn't moving, out cold. Tyriel looked down at him for a moment that seemed to drag before lifting his hand and calling the fight over.

Harper turned to Gage. 'What the hell was that about?'

He ignored her question completely, turning to the man whose arm he had hold of. 'Cole...' He didn't get any response. He turned to the other man with them, shoving Cole towards him. 'Deacon, get him out of here.'

Cole protested, but Deacon had him now. Cole looked pale, holding himself stiff. The man was trying to keep himself from shaking, she realised.

Gage stepped closer, looking Cole steadily in the eye. 'I messed up, not you,' Gage said low and earnest, holding Cole's gaze until the other man nodded slightly. 'I'll take care of Hael. We'll meet you back at Aeternus.'

Cole looked like he wanted to argue, before his expression slid into blankness as he watched Tyriel's men drag Hael out of the cage. Harper felt a rush of cold, recognizing that look. It was the same emotional shut down she'd witnessed many times as a child watching her own father's eyes shutter like that, like someone turned off the light behind them when memories and past traumas got too much. There was a history here she didn't understand. Any impulse Cole had to resist was gone and he let Deacon pull him through the crowd towards the nearest exit. Gage glanced at Harper once before moving towards where Hael, still unconscious, was being dumped on the floor of the VIP area.

Harper was debating whether to follow him, when she felt someone grab her arm. Viridian, of course he was here.

His eyes were bright and wide, caught up in the excitement. 'That was Hael, from Aeternus. You're here about the case, aren't you?'

'I thought I told you to stop coming to places like this.' She had repeatedly. He never listened.

He just shrugged and grinned.

Harper looked around. Gage was still moving through the crowd. She had overheard Gage's conversation with Cole as she arrived. Hael was Gage's brother, and for whatever reason, he had lost that fight on purpose. It couldn't have been easy to stand there and watch and she doubted Gage was acting rationally at the moment. If he did anything to provoke someone like Tyriel, she should stay the hell out of it. But she was curious and still had no answers for her case.

Viridian nudged her. 'Does this mean you found the Aesir? Can I help?'

Ah crap. She wasn't about to let Viridian follow her while she did something stupid. 'No, Vir. I gotta go. We can talk later.'

She pulled away before he could argue, following Gage. By the time she caught up to him, Tyriel's security was already confronting him as he tried to enter the VIP area. Gage grabbed one of them by the throat, pushing him against the wall.

'Get out of my way.' Gage's expression and voice were perfectly calm.

Another guard pulled a knife and pressed it to Gage's ribs. 'Private access only.'

Gage didn't appear concerned. 'I wouldn't try that.'

Starting a fight with security at one of the most notorious fight clubs in the city was a dumb idea. But it seemed to be the night for dumb ideas. It might also be the best way to understand Gage's interest in her murder case. Harper moved, grabbing the guard with the knife. She used a quick sharp hit to force him to drop the weapon and twisted his arm into a hold he wouldn't break easily. Gage didn't even glance at her or show any hint of surprise.

'I am an officially registered family Watcher, and you are impeding family business,' Gage said, almost politely. He let go of the guard's throat, not even bothering to wait for a reaction before walking through the barricade.

Harper dropped her hold on the guard. She held her hands out to the side, waiting to see if they would attack, or try to stop her. When they didn't, she followed Gage through into the VIP area, trying to contain her surprise. Gage was a family Watcher? Or had he just been bluffing? There wasn't any time to try and figure it out. They walked into a room bristling with Tyriel's security, with the club owner sitting calmly, Hael lying on the floor at his feet. Gage stood braced ready for a fight as he stared at Tyriel, eyes not dropping to his brother. The guards who'd tried to stop them walked in behind Harper.

'He says he's a Watcher,' one said, still rubbing at his throat where Gage had held him.

'That so.' Tyriel looked Gage up and down. 'And what would a Watcher be doing at one of my fights?'

Gage tensed, fingers twitching. He appeared to be debating

his options, leaning heavily towards bodily harm she'd guess. Harper decided to give him a less violent option.

'My name is Caitlan Harper. I am a Watcher liaison. We came here tonight following a lead on the death of Arthur Vanir. I was hoping to question him,' Harper said, nodding her head towards where Hael lay motionless.

'Well, that's unfortunate,' Tyriel said. 'This man cost me a great deal of money tonight.'

Gage snorted. 'I doubt that.'

Harper was relieved and surprised Gage looked willing to follow her lead.

'Maybe not,' Tyriel conceded, looking far too pleased with himself. 'I have to say, having the infamous Hael in my cage was an unexpected event.'

'You have no hold over him.' Gage looked down at his brother for the first time. 'He owes you nothing.'

'Yes, curious isn't it. Hael turning up at my club the same night as a human makes it past two rounds in the cage.'

Gage looked back up at Tyriel. 'Is it? I wouldn't know.'

Harper didn't miss the way Gage's hands tightened into fists at the mention of Cole. Nor how Tyriel's sharp eyes noted the reaction.

'Yes, and with such interesting terms. Why exactly would someone like Hael lay down a challenge against ten fighters?' Tyriel asked.

Gage laughed. 'You obviously don't know Hael.'

'But you do.'

Gage shrugged. 'You think anyone really knows someone like Hael? He's hot headed, impulsive. You think taking on ten fighters is out of character for him? He's more than a little insane.' Gage shifted his weight, his attention drawn back to Hael who groaned as he started to stir back towards consciousness. 'I'm pretty sure the idiot actually enjoys throwing himself head-first into danger.'

Tyriel laughed. 'That's probably true.'

'We will be taking him with us,' Harper said.

Tyriel turned his gaze on her for the first time, sharp eyes taking her in. 'I heard about young Arty's demise. Pity. He was a regular.' Tyriel waved his hand dismissively at Hael. 'He's all yours.'

Harper waited as Gage moved forward to lift Hael and half drag him towards the door. 'There was another case, a few months back,' Harper asked, ignoring the look Gage gave her as he paused, shifting his grip on Hael who was only partly awake and leaning heavily on Gage. 'A young woman I believe was one of your fighters.'

Tyriel nodded, eyeing her thoughtfully. 'Yes. There was.'

Harper knew how places like this worked, she would have to be careful with what she asked next. 'Anything I should look into with it?'

Tyriel watched her for a moment, his expression carefully neutral. 'She was a good fighter,' he said, words deliberate.

Harper nodded, hoping she understood what he wasn't saying. The fighter's death had nothing to do with betting on fixed fights

'Thank you,' she said, turning to go.

'She and Arty had a mutual friend,' Tyriel said before she could leave. 'A young dark-haired kid. I don't know him, but I've seen him a few times. Pretty sure he was here the night Arty was killed.'

Harper looked back at Tyriel. She hadn't expected him to answer her question, let alone offer something voluntarily. Gage caught her attention, shaking his head. Whatever Tyriel's motivations, they should go before he changed his mind about letting them leave unharmed. She nodded and followed Gage out of the club. Once they were out in the cool air of the alley, Gage propped Hael up against a wall as he regained full consciousness. He looked at Gage, eyes still a little glassy.

'Well, that was fun,' Hael said, coughing painfully.

'I'm sorry...'

Hael lifted a hand and patted at Gage's shoulder, like he was the one in need of comfort right now.

Harper cleared her throat loudly. 'What the hell is going on?'

Gage looked at her like he had forgotten she was there.

Hael rolled his head so he could see her. 'Ah, the lovely Miss Harper,' he said, somehow managing a halfway charming smile. 'So nice to see you again.'

Harper looked between the two men. Either they were insane, or something more was going on here. 'What were you thinking in there?'

Hael's laugh turned to coughing. He wasn't in good shape. 'Just blowing off some steam.'

Gage shrugged, like his brother trying to get himself killed was something that happened regularly. Maybe it was.

She looked at Hael. 'Really? I'd heard people say you were reckless, but that was bordering on stupid.'

Gage moved away from his brother. 'Thanks for your help, but I've got it from here. You should probably leave.'

Harper gritted her teeth, bristling at the dismissive tone in his voice she had heard so many times in her life. Cole and Hael stepping into that ring had been about something bigger which they didn't want her to know about. Fine. She didn't want their help any more than they wanted hers.

'Right, sorry.' She lifted her hands, retreating into sarcasm. 'What was I thinking, intruding on quality family time. Is this a thing? You come and enjoy the fights together.' Gage stepped closer to her, the shadows in the alley shifted around him, making him seem even taller. She refused to back away. 'Do you get off watching? The bloodier the better I suppose. Maybe you want to go back, toss him in for another few rounds.' She regretted the words as soon as they left her mouth but couldn't pull them back.

Hael peeled himself off the wall, like it hadn't been the only thing holding him up and stepped between her and Gage. 'I really do suggest you leave. Now.'

She looked up at Hael, his stony expression making her take a step back. His words settled on her shoulders, heavy and cold, pressing down on her with an impossible weight. This whole evening had been confusing. She was on the outside looking in, but it was like the glass surrounding these two men was opaque, and she only caught glimpses of shadows moving. Harper nodded. Before she could say anything else stupid, she turned and walked away.

***

13

~ GAGE ~

Gage took a deep breath, annoyed he let Harper's words get under his skin, it wasn't like she knew the impact they would have. A few decades ago, Hael would have killed someone for implying he enjoyed coming to fighting rings like this. Gage was just glad Cole had left before she said them, or he wasn't sure what would have happened.

He reached out to steady Hael, who started to sway a little. 'We should go.'

Hael pushed him away and he took a few steps, before disappearing. Gage followed him. It wasn't until after they landed back on the private floor of Aeternus that Hael allowed himself to slump against the wall, and Gage to keep him from sliding down it.

'Stubborn arsehole,' Gage said.

Hael smiled, looking tired. He was pale, but had stopped coughing up blood, which was a good sign. Cole and Deacon were waiting for them as Gage steered Hael towards the lounge. Hael groaned as he sunk down into the seat, leaning back and closing his eyes. Gage studied him, the cuts on his face had already stopped bleeding, but he was obviously still in a lot of pain. Hael might heal faster than others, but his injuries were serious, broken ribs and concussion, internal bleeding probably. He'd fully heal in a day, but that didn't mean he wouldn't feel pain now.

'Everything okay?' Deacon asked

Hael waved his good arm vaguely in the direction of the bar. 'Drink.' He opened his eyes when no one moved. 'I'm okay,' he said quietly, looking over at Deacon and Cole.

Gage wanted to protest as Hael sat up but couldn't find the words.

'Drink first. Then someone can put this back in,' Hael said, trying to shift his still dislocated shoulder.

Gage flinched as he stared uselessly at his brother's immobile arm. He really was a thoughtless arsehole tonight. He should have put the shoulder back in place before his brother flew with it.

Deacon came over to stand next to him. 'You get the drink. I've got this,'

Gage nodded and moved to the bar, grabbing a glass and a bottle of scotch. He closed his eyes when he heard an unnerving popping sound behind him and Hael stifling a growl. Hael was pale when Gage turned around but seemed to hold himself easier. Gage held out the glass. Hael waved it away, grabbing the bottle instead.

Hael tipped his head back and swallowed a few good mouthfuls before setting the bottle down on the coffee table.

'I think we should lodge an official request to give Harper access to all the Watcher investigations on the murders. There are five dead Aesir now, maybe some new eyes will turn something up.' He looked up at Gage. 'Request she be given all the cases. Including Ara's.'

Gage stared at him. Hael rarely opted to use official channels for anything that affected their family. He took a shaky breath. It meant only one thing. Hael didn't trust him to finish this.

'I messed up tonight. It won't happen again,' Gage said quietly.

'I know. That's not the point.'

'Hael, I can do this. You let me replace Deacon as Watcher. Let me finish this.'

'I'm not asking you to stop. Just...if you put an official request through as a Family Watcher, the Council won't be able to block it.' Hael shifted, looking at Gage steadily. 'Harper doesn't have access to everything. I think she can help. She seems to have the same instinct for finding answers that her father did. She won't stop looking. Give her the access she needs to find those answers for us.'

Gage swallowed the words of protest that wanted to trip off his tongue. What could he say anyway? He'd screwed up. The anger that boiled and bubbled inside since Ara's death evaporated as Hael stared at him, unyielding, before deliberately letting his eyes shift to Cole, who hadn't said a word since they got home.

Hael shifted trying to get Cole's attention, but Cole wouldn't meet his eye. 'Kid, this isn't your fault. I'd have killed half the people in that room if it wouldn't have drawn too much attention.'

Gage didn't doubt it. He understood all too well the hatred Hael held for cage fighting. Most fighters tonight might have been there by choice, others not so much as they were forced to fight to pay off debts. It made little difference. Fight rings like Tyriel's were only one step removed from the slave fighting pits that existed in Veracruz in the mid 1800's. The pits that almost took Cole from them. Any last vestige of anger drained out of Gage leaving him hollow and empty.

When Cole didn't answer or even react, Hael stood up gingerly and walked to him, pulling the man into an embrace with his one good arm.

Cole didn't move, didn't even seem aware Hael held him. 'He looked just like one of the kids they tore apart in Veracruz.'

The air in Gage's lungs seemed to freeze as Cole stared out over Hael's shoulder, distant, like he was looking back through a hundred and fifty odd years to some long dead kid who died in the fighting pits of Veracruz. The same hell where Cole had been held captive for twenty years before Hael and Wrathe could rescue him. Years spent fighting every day for his life as the fight masters came up with new and more depraved ways to torment their slave fighters. Years that somehow felt all the worse because Cole had already escaped the same sort of slave pits as a kid.

Gage couldn't watch. He'd known the scars the older man carried. How could he be so stupid? So caught up in his own fucking grief he had forgotten Cole's. An acidic well of self-loathing filled his gut. It had been years since Cole's last episode, but that was no excuse. He remembered long nights filled with screams, others where the only way Hael could get Cole to come back to himself had been to let him fight. Hael was always there to take the hits. Their sparring, if you could call it that, lasting hours, sometimes until they both could barely stand. On those nights, when Cole finally looked at Hael, and saw the man who raised him instead of the nightmares that clung to him like water, Cole would walk out, and they wouldn't see him for days.

It was one thing to be the cause of his brother taking a beating to protect the secrets they all carried. But to scrape and scratch at the scar tissue around the traumas Cole carried...that was unforgivable.

Gage ran his hands through his hair. Gods, what had he been thinking, taking Cole to a fight club when he knew the effect it might have. It didn't matter he had thought the fights would be done for the night. He'd stayed, hadn't even thought to leave until it was too late. Cole had done everything he could over the last five years to help Gage find Ara's murderer, and this was how he repaid him, by being an obsessed, self-centred bastard. He couldn't breathe, a heavy weight in his lungs. He needed to get out of here.

Deacon reached out and grabbed his arm as he walked out, his gaze steady on Gage. 'It's not on you either.'

Gage pulled away. 'Yeah, it is.'

He took the bottle of scotch on his way out and walked down the hallway. He sucked in a thready breath. It felt like there were giant hands around his ribs, squeezing and squeezing. He'd messed up. He'd messed up so much since Ara had been killed. And to what end? Her killer was still out there.

In his blind grief it had taken too long to realise they'd been targeting the Aesir the whole time. And tonight...What if they had lost Cole or Hael tonight because of his stupidity?

He stopped, leaning against the wall as he tried to breath. Closing his eyes, he tried desperately to call up some happy memory of Ara. She had always been happy. It should be easy. She had laughed like there was never a dark day in her life. But there had been many. He was drawn back to that day in the apple orchard. Ara had been four years old, at home with her mother when the men had ambushed Gage. Even when he thought he was going to die, he'd held onto that thought, that at least his beautiful little girl was safe. But she hadn't been. He hadn't been able to protect her in the end. His ribs ached, like the wounds from that day echoed in his bones, the same way pain blotted out every happy memory of his daughter.

He felt scattered in too many pieces to put back together. Hael was right. He had to send an official request through to give Harper access to the files on the murders, before he screwed anything else up. Before he lost anyone else.

He opened the scotch and took a few long mouthfuls before taking flight, disappearing before anyone could come looking for him.

***

14

~ COLE ~

LONDON, 27TH OCTOBER 1690

Cole was barely conscious when he heard Hael call out his name. He shifted and his knee flared white hot with pain. A nice contrast to the aching ribs, humming pain in his head, and general dull throbbing from half a dozen other injuries. Cole groaned as he pushed himself upright enough to slump against the wall. At least the sound drew Hael's attention, because he probably wouldn't make it out of the alley without passing out.

Hael rushed to him. Cole clenched his jaw when he put too much weight on his injured knee to keep balance. Hael grabbed hold of him, supporting Cole when he swayed. He stared dazed at one of the men he'd fought lying on the ground. He wasn't moving. Cole thought he might be dead. It'd been a while since he killed anyone. He felt sick in the stomach and was pretty sure it had nothing to do with his broken ribs.

Hael gently reached up, turning Cole's head so he could get a better look at him. 'Hey, are you okay?'

Cole managed a nod. He hated seeing Hael worried. Right now, he looked torn somewhere between mother hen and avenging angel. Cole swayed again, and Hael tipped away from retribution towards concerned medic, which was probably for the best.

Hael took more of Cole's weight, pulling him close to his chest. 'Hold on.'

Cole wasn't sure he could do anything else, but clenched his fingers in Hael's coat anyway, tighter than necessary for Hael to fly them away, but he wasn't too proud to admit he'd thought he might not see the Erinyes again somewhere during the fight. He wasn't even entirely sure how he'd managed to take down one of the men, and it was sheer dumb luck that the others had ran off instead of killing Cole.

Cole felt the shift as Hael stepped into the void. He closed his eyes, letting his head fall on Hael's shoulder as they landed in his room within the Enclave. Hael maneuvered him so he could sit on the edge of the bed.

Hael looked him over. 'What's most serious?'

Cole groaned as Hael accidentally bumped his knee. He was used to triaging his own injuries. 'Knee, broken ribs.'

Everything else was mostly bruising, maybe a bit of concussion. He'd been lucky, the worst of his injuries he'd done to himself.

Hael nodded. He quickly stripped off Cole's shirt and pants. Cole managed not to scream when he pulled his boot off and decided to call that a win. He stared at the ceiling while Hael examined his knee. Cole didn't need to look to know it was swollen. There was something torn in there for sure. Hael looked grim as he finished his examination, strapping Cole's ribs in silence.

Cole sighed, ignoring the twinge it caused. Hael had determined he wasn't about to die and was quickly working himself up into righteous indignation at Cole's stupidity.

Not that Cole blamed him. He had been stupid.

Hael sat back on his heels once he'd finished, looking at him. Cole pretended not to notice he was waiting for an explanation.

Hael sighed. He never was one much for patience. 'The girl was very grateful.'

Cole smiled a little. That was something. 'She okay?'

'A little shook up.' Hael paused. 'What were you doing outside the Enclave?'

'I was bored.'

Hael stared at him. 'So, you decided to get beat up by a few street thugs?'

'That wasn't the plan.'

Hael raised an eyebrow. 'Are we pretending there was a plan involved? How exactly did three humans get the jump on you?'

Cole shrugged, plucking at a loose thread in the blanket on his bed. 'I may have busted my knee jumping off the roof of the Cathedral.'

Hael stood up, throwing his hands in the air. 'Are you kidding me? Why the hell would you jump off the roof?'

'I heard her scream.'

'So?'

Cole stared at Hael, faltering with disbelief. 'So...what was I meant to do, watch?'

Hael started pacing, getting more agitated. 'What business was it of yours?'

'Right.' Cole resisted the urge to fold his arms. 'Because you'd have just stood by and let them do what they were going to do.'

'That's not the point.'

Cole couldn't help but huff out a bitter laugh at the irony. 'Pretty sure it is.'

'Being blooded to the Erinyes doesn't make you invincible. Have some common sense.'

Sometimes Hael made him feel like the angry teenager he'd once been with impulse control issues who tended to solve problems with violence. He didn't let the fact that was still true more often than he'd like keep his anger from building, not when Hael was just as bad. 'And where exactly am I meant to learn that from, you?'

Hael stopped mid stride, turning to face Cole. 'What's that meant to mean?'

'That you're the patron fucking saint of acting impulsively.'

Hael looked like he might relent but was too stubborn to let go of his point. 'Damn it, Cole, your life is worth too much to throw away on some random stranger.'

'Because you knew me so well the night you freed me?'

Hael held his arms out to the side. 'I didn't die saving you.'

He could have. 'No. You burnt down half the city.'

Hael looked away, swallowing thickly. Cole closed his eyes, instantly regretting the words. Hael hadn't intended for the fire to consume the city. He hadn't even realised it'd started until it was too late. They were never sure how many people died in the flames, but their deaths weighed on Hael nonetheless. Frankly, Cole was surprised they'd come back to London even this soon. Cole wasn't the only one with terrible memories of the city. Hael still drowned himself in guilt anytime they talked about the city, as much as he tried to hide it.

'I'm sorry.'

Hael forced a smile. 'It's fine.' He ran a hand over his face, looking tired. 'Cole, you know I never regretted saving you.'

'I know.' Hael didn't need to say it. Cole felt it coming off the man in waves, a sense of certainty as unshakable as bedrock. It was kind of humbling. It also highlighted his point. 'I don't regret helping the girl tonight either.'

Over Hael's shoulder, a dark figure appeared in the doorway. Cole slumped back against the wall, half propped up on pillows, ready for a lecture from the other man who had raised him. Only this lecture didn't involve words and was a lot harder to ignore. A mass of emotions rolled over Cole, concern, rebuke, worry. A big, tangled mess all at once that was overwhelming yet oddly comforting. Cole looked down, flattening a crease in the blankets with his fingers. He hated making either of them worry.

Satisfied he had gotten his point across, Wrathe leant against the doorframe, almost hidden in the shadows. 'He's too much like you sometimes.'

Hael didn't react. Cole wasn't surprised, the two of them always knew where the other was. 'I know. More's the pity.'

Wrathe lifted his chin, the movement causing long, dark hair to fall away, revealing icy blue eyes. 'Would you prefer if he took after me?'

Cole couldn't help smiling. He was pretty sure he was turning into an amalgam of both of them, and the thought terrified him some days.

Hael sighed. 'Relations with the humans are strained. They're paranoid about this war of theirs, even if you aren't an Erinyes, they're suspicious of anyone who could be a French spy. Try not to make yourself a target.'

Cole said nothing, not wanting to make a promise he might not be able to keep. He excelled at finding trouble, even if he wasn't looking for it.

Hael reached over and pulled a bottle of Scotch from the bedside table. He poured a glass, then took out a knife and sliced the tip of a finger. He held it over the glass squeezing several drops of blood into the liquor before handing it to Cole.

'You know that doesn't do much for me anymore.'

It didn't. But Hael still insisted on giving it to him every time he got injured doing something stupid.

The first time he drank Hael's blood had been like swallowing a lightning storm. The effects had never truly faded. After the second it had become permanent. He knew it shouldn't have happened that quickly and that he had stronger abilities than other Eshari. Like the strange way people talked to him now when he wanted them too. The effects of a human drinking Erinyes blood varied, but it should have taken several years of regular doses for it to become permanent. But Hael's blood was purer than most.

Being blooded to an Erinyes family was an honour. One he wasn't sure he was worthy of.

Hael waved the glass at him. 'Just drink it.'

Cole rolled his eyes but did as he was told. There was no storm now, just a pleasant static sensation and a metallic taste spoiling the liquor. He frowned down at the empty glass. 'This is my good scotch.'

Hael kept hold of the bottle as he stood up, taking a mouthful from it. 'Not sure idiots should get the good scotch.'

Wrathe stepped into the room and took the bottle from Hael. 'Then you definitely shouldn't have it.'

Hael looked like he wanted to argue before shrugging and grinning like the lunatic he was. They made an odd pair. Wrathe the dangerous dark shadow to Hael's nova bright volatility.

Cole tried not to laugh, clutching at his ribs. 'If you're finished telling me how stupid I am. Get the hell out of my room.'

Wrathe set the bottle back down on Cole's bedside table before crouching down next to him. He reached out, hand hovering over Cole's knee. Cole drew in a breath at the cold emanating from Wrathe's fingers.

'Have you learnt whatever point Hael was trying to make?' Wrathe asked.

Cole smirked. 'Don't jump off buildings before attacking street thugs?'

Wrathe didn't smile. He rarely did, but his eyes brightened with humour. 'Good boy.'

Hael threw his hands up in the air. 'Gods. He breaks his neck next time, I'm blaming you.' He grumbled about the vexations of family as he walked out of the room.

Wrathe looked at Cole, expression intent. 'You know he only gets angry because he cares so much.'

Cole felt the warm glow of Hael and his affectionate concern receding as he moved further away. 'I know.'

The ability to feel the shape of emotions from Erinyes was one of the more useful abilities he had received from Hael's blood. It'd been the one thing that helped him understand the complicated natures of the two men who had given him the only home he'd ever known, both of whom were very good at concealing the truth of themselves.

Wrathe nodded, moving his hand and wrapping lean, strong fingers around Cole's knee. Cole gritted his teeth at the pain from the soft pressure. It was only a moment before cool relief started to spread. Wrathe couldn't heal with a touch, no Erinyes or even the Aion had been able to do that. But he did the next best thing. How many times over the years had Wrathe used his abilities to soothe bruises or sprains Cole ended up with? Cold radiated from Wrathe's fingers, easing pain, and after a while, it would help with the swelling.

Wrathe didn't move, eyes closed as he concentrated. 'You learn to live with the pain.'

He didn't mean the physical pain. Gods, the smell of the Thames had brought it all back so vividly. Cole looked down at his hands, almost expecting them to be covered in blood. He had been so young the first time he took someone's life. Kill or be killed had been the only options in the fighting pits. He'd tried so hard to forget. But there was no forgetting.

He looked up at Wrathe. 'Have you?'

The corner of Wrathe's mouth twitched. 'I wouldn't still be alive if I hadn't.'

For a moment, Cole could sense the immense pain and guilt Wrathe carried. The sort that would drag you down into the depths if you allowed it. He let Cole see it, the whole ugly mass of it. Cole wasn't the only one who struggled with the things he'd done.

Closing his eyes, Cole breathed a little easier as tendrils of power penetrated his muscles, almost like they were hunting the pain. It amazed Cole that someone with so much fury you could almost see it rippling away under the surface of his skin, was capable of such inherent gentleness. Wrathe interacted with so few people, keeping himself hidden away. Cole had no idea how old he was, but it was older than anyone else he'd ever met. In all Wrathe's long years, how many had seen this side of him? A side in many ways truer than his seething rage capable of burning cities to the ground. And it had.

As Cole drifted off to sleep, he couldn't help wondering, who was keeping who from tumbling over the ledge into darkness?

***

15

~ HARPER ~

Harper was barely out of bed when a message from Carellen came through, asking her to meet with him. The Commander was waiting for her when she arrived. He didn't look particularly happy, although sometimes it was hard to tell. It's not like Carellen ever smiled.

'Close the door.'

Harper closed the door to his office and sat. She clasped her hands in her lap to keep from fidgeting. Carellen said nothing. He watched her from the other side of the desk. Twisting her fingers together, Harper tightening her jaw as she stared back at him. She'd known the man since she was a small child, and he sometimes still made her feel like one. He had watched her fall flat on her face the first time she attempted to copy her father in a complicated spin kick far beyond her abilities as a six-year-old. He'd been there every time she had been rejected for the Watcher trials, and when she spread her father's ashes over Lake Michigan on a bleak Autumn evening sixteen years ago.

'I take it you've been busy?' Carellen asked finally.

'Just following some leads,' Harper hedged, waiting to see where this conversation was going. Carellen almost never called her to his office.

'Always looking for answers, aren't you,' Carellen said, looking out the window at the impressive view of the Enclave. He laid his hand on a stack of files in front of him, fingers tapping. He sighed and pushed them across the desk towards her. 'There has been a formal request for you to investigate some ongoing cases within the Enclaves and outside your current jurisdiction.'

Harper tried to keep her face passive as she nodded. She wasn't sure what she had been expecting. Someone to have reported her for breaking into an old crime scene maybe. For the Council to be rid of her once and for all. Anything but this. In all her years working as a Liaison for the Watchers, no one had ever requested she investigate a case. She hadn't even known it was possible. It couldn't be a coincidence that she met a family Watcher yesterday, and now this. But why? She leaned forward and picked up the pile of files. She flicked through them. Five case files.

'I hope you know what you're doing,' Carellen said.

Harper looked up at him. 'Why?'

'Five murders, all from or related to one of the oldest Erinyes families.'

Harper looked closer at the files. The cases were all for murdered members of the Aesir family. Shit. She reread the names, the case file for Ara's murder was included. As was

Arty's. She'd only retrieved a redacted file on Ara's murder yesterday, with no name recorded. It wasn't uncommon for larger families to maintain strict privacy, and the Aesir were famous for it.

'The Watcher who made the request?' Harper asked.

'Is not someone I nor the council could refuse.'

Harper chewed on her lip, wanting to ask, but knowing it would break protocol. Information on Watchers, particularly Family Watchers, was held in strict confidence. Gage must have made the request, though Carellen would never confirm it. But why? She'd left both Hael and Gage angry last night with her thoughtless words. She didn't know either well enough to understand their actions, let alone motives. The cases assigned to her were all for the Aesir family, and the request had been processed without question. The only way that made any sense was if Gage was the Watcher for the Aesir family. It was the only reason that the Council would have been unable to refuse.

She stared down at the files. What had he told her the first time they met...you didn't find the Aesir, they found you. Apparently, the words hadn't been the enigmatic dismissal she'd thought at the time.

'What do you know about the Aesir?' Carellen asked.

Harper shrugged. 'They're a large family, spread across Europe and the Americas. Keep to themselves, don't get involved in Council politics.'

'They don't anymore. They were founding members of the first Council two thousand years ago.'

Harper looked up from the files. Few families traced their lineage back that far. 'So, when you said one of the oldest...'

'They go back further than that, if you believe the rumours.'

'And do you believe them?'

'Usually I wouldn't.'

Harper raised an eyebrow. Carellen wasn't one to dally in idle gossip.

'I met Ishta once,' he said. 'Far as anyone can tell she is the head of the family. I'm pretty sure she was there when they crowned Charlemagne.'

'She'd be over 1200 years old.'

Carellen shrugged. 'I wasn't going to argue with her.'

Harper huffed. She wouldn't have either. Only a handful of Erinyes were that old, and they weren't people you wanted to contradict.

'Ishta married into the Aesir. I can't be certain, but I don't think she's the oldest of the family. They keep to themselves and like to feed the rumours that persist about them. It's a good way to keep people from knowing the truth...or believing it.'

Harper studied Carellen, curious. 'Believing it?'

She never put much stock in the stories people told about the Aesir. Not even when it had been her father telling them.

'If the rumours are true, about how old some of them are, how pure their bloodline is, I'd sure as hell want to keep anyone from believing it.' Carellen looked away from her, gaze settling on the view outside his window again. It was still grey outside, but the clouds weren't as heavy today, shy streaks of blue peeking through here and there. 'How many people, human and Erinyes alike, would fear a family that is rumoured to have Aion half-bloods amongst them?'

Harper studied Carellen's profile, shocked not so much by

his words, but that he seemed to find some credibility in the rumours. She looked down, straightening the files in front of her. She'd never thought about it that way. People would fear a half-blooded Aion, and people generally wanted to destroy what they feared. Wrapping the truth up as myth would have its benefits. They were a large family, wealthy, with a lot of influence, but betting on their mystery to keep them safe was a gutsy move.

'Do you know why they're not part of the Council anymore?' she asked.

'Not for sure. They suffered more losses than most during the last war. They could have just wanted to be left alone.'

Harper nodded. The last war between the Erinyes and humans had been 200 years ago. Her own father had fought in it. He'd suffered from nightmares when she had been a child. She remembered him screaming in his sleep. She'd made the mistake of running in to wake him once. He'd thrown her across the room. She had barely been six years old. After that, she always waited outside his door until he woke himself. Then she would creep in and curl up by his side until his shuddering breaths eased. The war had been brutal and bloody. It left its mark on countless Erinyes, even long after the signing of the peace treaty.

'Harper...be careful.'

'I will.'

Carellen sighed again. 'Not everyone will be happy about this. A family Watcher requesting your services is unusual to say the least. Family politics, whether or not they are on the Council, it always gets messy. It won't end well for any outsider who gets involved.'

'I know. I have no interest in the Aesir family. I just want to close my case.'

'That's what I'm afraid of.' Carellen watched her sadly for a moment. 'If I ask you to let this go, you won't, will you?'

Harper chewed on her lip. She didn't enjoy disappointing Carellen, but this might be her only chance to work an actual Watcher case. 'No.'

Carellen nodded. 'If you're doing this, make the most of it.'

She looked up in surprise. 'What do you mean?'

'If a family Watcher, especially an Aesir one, owes you a favour. You could use it to ask them to sponsor you.'

She leaned forward as the air in her lungs seemed to vibrate. A sponsorship? The Council would never block a family sponsored candidate from the Watcher Trials.

'Harper, the Aesir wouldn't have asked for this lightly. You succeed...I know the Aesir's reputation. They will repay you.'

'Would they sponsor me though?'

'It would cost them nothing. It'd give you the chance the Council has been denying you. The rest would still be up to you. You fail, they've repaid their debt. You succeed, they've still paid their debt and have a friendly relationship with a new unaligned Watcher.'

He was right. Sponsorship was an unusual honour, one that only granted a place in the Trials, with no guaranteed outcome. They were usually reserved for younger members of a family who already had an established family Watcher who wasn't ready to stand down. It gave them a chance to gain experience, with no need to displace their existing Watcher. Sometimes it might be a family member who wanted to join another family or start a new branch. Occasionally it was a way to repay a debt to someone who had done a great service for a family. She tried to dampen the hope scampering about inside her. She'd need to successfully assist the Aesir family first. But if she could…It would be the chance she had been waiting for. That was all she needed, all she'd been asking for. A chance to prove herself.

'But Harper, if you take this.' He pointed at the files in front of her. 'You may end up making more enemies than friends.'

Harper nodded. 'I know.' The fizz of excitement trickled out with a breath. A bubble of hope stayed behind though, lodged somewhere underneath a rib. 'I have to try.'

With the Aesir cases officially assigned to her, Harper could access the full resources the Watchers had on their murders. She took a corner desk in the archive and methodically read through each of the cases. There were crime scene photos, forensics, witness statements. Harper made notes, took copies of what she needed, but she could already see why the murders remained unsolved. There was no real evidence, the only witness statements were from those who found the bodies, the crime scenes clean of all prints and DNA, no surveillance footage of any kind. The only thing linking the victims were the sigils left by the killer and the fact the victims were Aesir.

The five Aesir cases were spread across Europe and America. Harper made notes on a rough timeline. Ara's case was the first, killed five years ago. Then a 12-month gap before the next Aesir murder, a man in Prague, then St Petersburg, New Orleans, and back to Chicago with Arty's death. Scattered between the deaths of the Aesir were the two cases Harper had investigated, and the five other cases she had found in her illegal search a few days ago.

Harper sat back in her chair, tapping her pen on the desk. A serial killer traveling around the world? It didn't make sense. Why sometimes members of the Aesir and other times not? Why did the killer keep coming back to Chicago? She had a lot of questions and very few answers.

Harper pushed aside a paper, looking at her notes. There was another connection between two of the victims. Two of them had been at Tyriel's fight club. The club owner had said Arty and the dead fighter had a common acquaintance. Tyriel ran an illegal fight club, if he knew more, he wasn't likely to talk to her, even if she wasn't truly a Watcher. She was surprised he had offered any information at all. Maybe Arty's brother knew more, and would be more willing to talk. If he wasn't too hung over. Harper collected all the copies of the files and bundled them into her bag. For the first time in years, she felt her father with her as she walked through the Watcher Tower. She had a lead to follow on an actual Watcher case, maybe she could make him proud yet.

***

Yuri had an apartment in the Enclave, but he didn't answer when Harper knocked. He was probably still passed out drunk. He'd been nearly incoherent when she spoke to him last night. She took a step back, looking up at the building, wondering if she should commit a second break in within as many days.

'He's not here.'

Harper spun around. Tyriel was standing on the steps behind her.

He smiled at her. 'Just in case you were thinking of breaking in to check.'

'And how do you know he's not home?'

Tyriel laughed. 'Because I beat you to the petty act of villainy. I already popped in and checked.'

The ability to fly certainly made break and entering easier she supposed, but she couldn't help raising an eyebrow at his ease in admitting it to her. 'Are you telling me I should be arresting you?'

'You could try, I suppose.' It was a gentle dig at her lack of authority to do so, but his tone implied no real barb behind the words. He bowed at her. 'I don't believe I introduced myself properly last night. My name is Tyriel.'

'I know.'

His expression closed off a little. 'I suppose you do.'

She narrowed her eyes, studying him. He didn't seem to like the reputation he had. 'What are you doing here?' She asked.

'Same thing as you I suspect. Hoping Yuri can answer some questions.'

Her brow crinkled, a little thrown. 'Why.'

'Because despite what you might think, I care what happens to my fighters.'

He had read her reaction precisely. She'd assumed he wouldn't care about those who fought in his club beyond callously profiting of them. The fighter who had been killed, Helena, she'd been dead for months. No one else seemed to have given her a second thought.

Tyriel looked up at the apartment Yuri had shared with his brother. 'Helena was young, liked to drink and dance. She would often join the crowd when she wasn't fighting herself.'

'You said she knew Arty?'

Tyriel smiled sadly. 'I think she was a little sweet on him.' He looked back down at Harper. 'When Helena died, I tried to find out what had happened. But I didn't find anything.'

'There's a lot of that going around.'

He smiled ruefully. 'Seems so.'

'I don't suppose you know anything more about the friend you thought Arty and Helena had in common?'

Tyriel shook his head. 'No, sorry.' He looked back at the door to Yuri's place. 'Helena always said the brothers were close. Yuri likely knows their name.'

Harper nodded. If she could find him, that was.

Tyriel looked up, watching a sleek, black modern muscle car drive down the street towards them. 'I think that's my cue to leave.' He smiled politely. 'If I can be of any help, you know where to find me.'

He sauntered away down the street before she could say anything else.

The car pulled up next to Harper. Cole got out. He hesitated a fraction when he saw Tyriel walking away. Expression darkening, he slammed closed the driver's door, and leaned against the car. Cole watched the club owner, distracted for a moment, before he turned back to Harper and his demeanour brightened.

Cole smirked, green eyes intent. 'Hael said you'd be here.'

'Of course, he did.' He seemed the type who liked knowing what people were going to do before they did.

Cole folded his arms, lean body relaxing and lips tilting in a lazy smile as he openly appraised her. The graceful menace from the cage fight was nowhere to be seen. It was like he was a different person, all languid ease with nothing to hint at his fighting ability. There was no sign of the post traumatic episode last night either, despite seeing Tyriel here. Instead, he looked like someone who'd never known a moment of darkness in his life. All sun touched, with honey blond tipped hair swept back and warmth dancing in his charming smirk.

Harper's phone buzzed in her pocket. Cole's smile slipped just a bit, not quite reaching his eyes. 'You'll want to answer that.'

Harper pulled her phone out of her pocket. It was Detective Jacobs. 'Yes?'

'Morning to you too,' Jacobs said without any of the amusement she usually expressed to Harper abruptness.

Work related then. 'Do you have another case for me?'

'An Erinyes was found dead in an alley a few blocks outside the Enclave,' the Detective said.

Harper had a sinking feeling. 'Murdered?' She didn't need to ask. Jacobs wouldn't have called if it wasn't.

'Definitely. Thing is,' Jacobs continued. 'The victim...he's the brother of the dead guy from your current case.'

Harper looked up at Cole who was still watching her. 'Yuri Vanir.'

'That's him.'

'Send me the address.' Harper stabbed her finger at the disconnect button. So much for getting any answers from Yuri. 'You knew,' she said to Cole.

He shrugged. 'Hael likes to know things.'

Harper shoved her phone back in her pocket. 'Right.'

Cole tipped his head towards the car. 'Get in. He's waiting for us.'

She paused with a brief flicker of doubt about getting in a car with a man she didn't know, to meet with Hael, who she didn't know any better. Well, she never claimed to make the smartest choices, a fact that Carellen lamented frequently. She got in the car.

They made their way towards the edge of the Enclave. She'd assumed Hael would be at his club. 'Where are we going?'

'Hael wants to know what happened to Yuri. Thought you could help get us access to the scene.'

She laughed under her breath. 'Doubt it. Doesn't work like that.'

'So how does it work?'

'You think the human cops appreciate having to let an Erinyes investigate cases they'd rather ignore?'

He smiled. 'Probably not.'

Out the window, the Enclave wall appeared as they drove through one of three great stone gates allowing entry into the human city. Only a solitary Watcher slouched against the wall of the guardhouse. He was scrolling through something on his phone and didn't look up as they drove through. He'd probably pissed someone off to be posted here as the gates went mostly unguarded these days. Some days she wasn't sure she belonged in the Enclave, but leaving it for the human world was like stepping into a shadow that got deeper and darker the further from the Enclave she went. She might be ignored by her own kind, but out here, she was hated along with every other Erinyes.

She unfurled her fingers, laying them flat on her thighs. 'Most of the time I'm lucky if the cops haven't cleared the scene before I get there. They don't answer questions or bother gathering evidence before it's lost. They just want to dump the body off at the morgue as soon as they can so it's off their hands.' She looked at him. 'They won't let me bring anyone else into a crime scene.'

Cole glanced at her before looking back to the street. 'Okay,' he said casually.

'The request to have the Watcher cases assigned to me...'

'Was Gage. Unless you've met some other tall, dark and handsome Watcher recently, who'd want to help you.'

Harper let out a huff of air. 'Hardly.'

'Yeah, most Watchers are blowhard dicks who'd step on you, rather than walk around you.'

She chewed her lip, wanting to know for certain Gage was the Aesir Family Watcher, and why they had assigned the cases to her, but not wanting to ask. On the off chance she was talking with a member of the Aesir family, she didn't want to piss them off, the chance of securing a sponsorship heavy in her thoughts.

Cole hadn't taken his eyes off the road but grinned at her. 'Are you wondering why we asked for your help, or if we're who you think we are?'

Harper just about jumped out of her skin as a soft laugh sounded from the rear seat. She spun around to see Hael, calmly staring back at her like he had been there all along, which he hadn't.

Hael's mouth twitched into a lopsided smile. 'Both, obviously.'

Harper faced the front, heart racing.

Cole took yet another turn. 'Yeah, he does that. I'd get used to it if you plan on sticking around.'

Harper glared across at Cole. His lips pressed together, trying not to laugh at her shock. She took a deep breath, impressed at Hael's obvious flight skills. The Erinyes called it flight, but from what she understood about the ability most Erinyes possessed, it was more like folding space. She didn't understand it. They didn't need to see where they were going, passed through walls, travelled across the city near instantly. A rare few could travel across oceans. The further they went, the more energy and control it took.

There was a nursery rhyme about a young Erinyes who tried to travel through the world. She couldn't quite remember it, something about trying to hold together two part of space that were too far apart. His grip slipped. Space streamed through his fingers. Like pulling a piece of string taut, it rippled and reverberated, flinging him far, far away from everything he had known.

Having enough control and precision to land in a moving vehicle was remarkable.

She looked at Hael in the rear-view mirror. He wore a short-sleeved shirt, she saw a slight discolouration extending down his right arm from the dislocation, but otherwise he looked fine, not at all like he'd been in a vicious fight last night. It wasn't until he leaned forward that he winced, holding himself stiffly.

'Broken ribs?' She asked.

Hael shrugged gingerly. 'One or two.'

'You're lucky you're not dead.'

Hael looked amused. 'Why Miss Harper, were you concerned?' Harper rolled her eyes at him, and he laughed, low and soft. 'Don't worry, it'd take a lot more to put me down.'

She wanted to know what possessed him to pit himself against ten cage fighters. She didn't think he'd answer if she asked. He held a hand to his ribs discreetly. She wasn't sure how he was even upright with the beating he'd taken. He tilted his head as he caught her watching him, she felt a little like a mouse in the gaze of a hawk. No doubt he had collected an entire dossier about her since they met and was just using the opportunity to see where the pieces of her history he'd uncovered fit.

Harper maintained eye contact. 'Cole says you want my help to access the scene. That's not going to happen.'

Hael shrugged. 'I assumed as much. Guess I hoped you'd be inclined to share what you find with us.'

'Is that why Gage had the Watcher cases assigned to me, so I'd share what I found on the cases outside the Enclave?'

'Maybe he can find something you missed.'

Harper looked away, caught between a knee jerk retort at the implied insult, and fear Hael had a point. She'd found nothing in two years, after all. 'So, I guess he gave me his cases so I can find what he missed.' When she glanced back, Hael looked out the window and she realised the truth. 'It wasn't his idea, was it.'

'Not at first,' Hael said quietly. 'You understand, with five dead Aesir it's not something the family will let go.'

No, probably not. All the Erinyes families took personal attacks to heart. 'Am I going to be stuck in the middle of a vendetta if I investigate?'

Hael looked at her, weighing up her worth. 'No, I'll ensure your safety...as much as I can. If this is someone with a grudge against the Aesir, you might not want to get involved. You seem the sort who can't let something go once you start looking for answers. If you wanted to get out now, it'd be the smarter move.'

Harper wasn't good at doing the smart thing. 'I'll be fine.'

Hael nodded. 'Well, don't say I didn't warn you.'

As much as she found someone protecting her smothering, she believed Hael meant it. How long since anyone other than Carellen had been concerned for her? This man, who'd thrown himself into a cage fight with no apparent concern for his own wellbeing, why did he care about hers? She didn't get it.

'What happened last night?' she asked.

He glanced at Cole, before looking back out the window, his head resting against the glass. His reflection flickered with emotion. Harper looked across at Cole. The muscles in his jaw tensed, but otherwise he didn't react. It was Hael who answered, just when she thought neither would.

Hael's head still rested against the glass, watching the street pass by. 'Gage hasn't been able to let go of Ara's death. He lost himself for a long time. I thought he was getting better, but he made a mistake last night because he wasn't thinking.' Hael looked back at her. 'Guess I'm just hoping a fresh perspective might help him.'

Harper held his gaze for a moment, trying to figure out what to think. Hael's expression was open and honest. He looked like someone worried about their brother, and not sure how to help him. The moment passed, and his expression closed over again.

'Anyway. This has gone beyond Ara now. I need to know if the Aesir are being targeted,' he said.

Harper looked back out the windscreen. She would need more than one honest moment to trust Hael. But his motives in asking her to investigate the Aesir cases didn't feel like anything she needed to worry about, not yet anyway. If Hael and Gage were brothers, it meant he was an Aesir too. From what little she knew of his reputation, that made him more dangerous. Surely it would be common knowledge if the biggest information broker in the city was part of one of the largest and oldest Erinyes families. Of course, it was also possible it was more useful as a collector of information if no one knew he was a member of one of the largest and oldest families.

There was one thing she needed to know though. 'What was Gage's relationship to Ara Aesir?'

Hael smiled, leaning back in the seat. 'Gage thought you suspected him of somehow being involved when you met him at the house.'

Harper shrugged. 'He was following me. It was suspicious.'

'Of course, it was. He's hardly full of sunshine and rainbows either, is he?'

Understatement. 'No. He's not.'

Hael looked away, his expression a mixture of fond and sad. 'He wasn't always that way.'

Cole looked up at the rear-view mirror at Hael for a moment. 'Well, he was never exactly Mr Sunshine, but he smiled more.'

Hael laughed a little, more sad than happy. 'Yeah.' He

stayed quiet a moment, before looking back to Harper. 'Ara, was his daughter.'

Harper wasn't sure what she had been expecting. Friend, sister, girlfriend maybe. She remembered Gage's hollow expression as he looked at the photos in Ara's house. Daughter made a lot more sense.

Cole watched the traffic lights out the windscreen, waiting for them to turn green. 'Ara was a sweet girl. She laughed a lot, loved to tease her father for being so serious. He loved her like she was more important than breathing.'

Hael was quiet, his expression dark. 'Gage hasn't always had the easiest life, but she made him want to live it again. And after...'

He trailed off mid-sentence, like he hadn't meant to say that aloud, before disappearing as quickly as he'd appeared. A puff of displaced air ruffled her hair as she stared at the seat where he had been like it could provide insight into the man, but it had nothing to offer. The lights turned green, and Cole drove off. Neither of them spoke until they pulled up near the alley where Yuri's body had been found.

Cole shoved his hands in his pockets as they walked. A couple of cops milled around. She needed to be quick if she wanted to see anything before they took the body away. The obligatory onlookers stood around. No one seemed bothered about keeping them away. Cole stopped when they were close enough to see the body. The cops ignored him, just another human gawking at a dead Erinyes. When she glanced up at Cole his expression said otherwise, not that the cops noticed. A fine lacework of anger and sadness fell across his features like a veil, delicate and complex, before he stiffened and irritably pushed it aside. She paused by his side, as she waved her identification at the cops trying to get their attention,

'Did you know him?' she asked.

'Not really.' Cole stared at the scene, but it was like he was a thousand miles away. 'I bought him a bottle of scotch yesterday. He was a mess after his brother's murder.'

Harper nodded. She had forgotten Gage talked to Yuri to get the same lead to Tyriel's fight club.

The cops finally noticed her and let her through the tape. She didn't bother talking to any of them. Yuri's body slumped against the wall, like a forgotten coat someone had dumped on the floor. He'd been beaten, one of his arms broken, a few of his fingers too. His throat cut, dried blood flaking on his shirt. She'd only spoken to him briefly last night. Cole was right, he had been a mess, desperately trying to drown his grief. He would have been an easy target. Apart from the slit throat, there were no other similarities to the sigil murders. She took a few photos before the cops waved her away when the coroner's van arrived.

Harper found Cole on the edge of the gathered onlookers. She handed him her phone with the pictures. 'There were drag marks. He was dumped here.'

Cole flicked through the pictures before looking around. They had parked on a busy street at one end of the alley. The body had been dumped last night sometime. Even at night that street would have been well lit.

Cole handed the phone back to her. 'They would have accessed the alley from the other end.'

Harper nodded. 'Come on.'

They walked down the alley, it led to a smaller service lane running along the back of several buildings. There were no cameras or lights. They turned the corner, and Hael was waiting for them. His expression was shuttered. Whatever raw honesty and openness she had seen in the car was gone.

'There were no sigils,' Cole said.

Hael nodded. 'But killed a day after his brother.'

'Yeah, I know, that can't be a coincidence.'

Something further down the service lane caught Harper's attention. She walked away from the two men. There was a smear of blood on the pavement. Not much, but maybe the sort of smear you'd get if you pulled a body out of a vehicle. They were only a hundred metres from where Yuri's body had been found, yet she couldn't hear any noise from the cops or the onlookers. You could park here at night and dump a body with no one hearing or seeing you. So why had they dragged the body towards the busier end of the alley? It was always going to be found quickly. The killer could have dumped the body in one of the dumpsters and not have it found for days. It was like they wanted it to be found. She looked up at Hael and Cole as they walked towards her.

The sound of a boot scraping on metal grating echoed dully in the alleyway. Harper barely registered the sound before Cole reacted. He moved fast, grabbing her by the shoulders. A gunshot sounded, muffled by a silencer. Cole twisted, pulling her out of the way. She felt his body jerk as the bullet hit. Warmth spread near her hip. Blood, but it wasn't hers.

Hael picked up a piece of loose pipe, she watched in a daze as he swung, letting it fly towards a fire escape from one of the buildings. It sounded loud as it banged against the metal railings, everything just that little bit too sharp as adrenaline surged. The pipe dinged the railing with the force of Hael's throw. She realised the shooter must have been there, as Hael shifted to stand between them and the direction he had thrown the pipe.

She moved, cursing her delay. Blood soaked her shirt. It stuck to her skin. She rolled Cole over. The shot had hit him low in the abdomen, a little to the left. She pressed her hands down on the wound, fingers slick with his blood, but he waved her away, struggling to his feet.

Hael glanced at him. 'Cole?'

'M'fine.'

'He's shot,' Harper said.

Hael looked down at the blood.

'I'm fine.' Cole repeated.

Harper looked up at the sound of running feet, two men were coming towards them.

Cole stood a little straighter, moving toward the attackers. 'Get her out of here.'

He looked over his shoulder at Hael once, before moving faster. Hael grabbed her hand, pulling her towards another fire escape on the opposite side of the alley from the shooter.

'Wait.' She looked back at Cole incredulously.

He was already fighting. His movements sure, and fast. Cole wasn't quite as graceful as he had been last night in the cage, but he quickly subdued one attacker. She thought Hael intended to drag her up the fire escape, but he grabbed hold, pulling her close to his chest. Harper drew a breath to protest, when everything lurched. It felt like the air was sucked from her lungs, her heart froze for an agonising second, before everything shifted again, and they stood in the street near where Cole had parked the car. They'd landed in a little alcove outside an empty building, out of sight of the people walking past.

'What...' Her lungs expanded too quickly, sucking the rest of her words away.

Hael steadied her for a moment, before disappearing again. She could only presume back to help Cole. What the...She leant against the wall, breathing in deeply through her nose. A flock of spots swept across her vision. She had just flown. It'd felt like Hael gathered reality in his hands and bent it to his will. He'd flown out of the alley and a few hundred metres down the street carrying her with him. She hadn't known that was possible. She was pretty sure it shouldn't be.

Shaking her head, Harper pushed the shock aside, gritting her teeth with a spike of anger. She pushed away from the wall, intent on going back to help. She was far from helpless in a fight. A hand grabbed her from behind. She spun, instinct already moving her body to throw the person to the ground. A sickly-sweet scent overwhelmed her. Everything shimmered as the ground seemed to disappear from beneath her feet. Her knees buckled, the sensation oddly far away. The building over her swayed, blurring in and out a little. Her head rolled to the side and coarse pavement pressed into her cheek. She saw boots, black leather with thick tread. A blurry shape knelt to look at her. Hands grabbed her, shifting her so she lay slumped in the alcove instead of on the pavement.

'I have a message I'd like you to deliver.'

Harper tried to pull her senses together, but everything moved like it was sinking into deep waters. The man reached over and tapped her cheek, oddly gently.

'Maybe I should have written it down,' he said, chuckling.

She tried to make her muscles cooperate and look up at his face but couldn't. She could just see his boots, and the light catching on the wet pavement. She didn't remember it raining. Everything she saw past his boots was a little bit too shiny. Shimmering, and dancing about so much it was hard to focus on anything.

'Tell your new friends, I know what they have hidden. Can you do that for me?' He reached down, brushing the hair back from her cheek. 'You really shouldn't have gotten involved, Harper.'

The man stood. She watched the boots walk away, everything going oddly bright around the edges. Her eyelids were lead weights, too heavy for her to keep open. Everything faded away.

***

16

~ GAGE ~

Gage landed next to Cole's car. Good, they were still here. He'd followed as soon as the trace on the Watcher database alerted him to someone poking around Harper's records. He hunched his shoulders, using his abilities to pass unnoticed by the humans. He hoped he was just being paranoid, until he spotted Harper laying in an alcove. He rushed to her. She moaned, pushing at him feebly. She was covered in blood. He grabbed hold of her, checking for wounds, but she didn't seem to have any. She jerked, coming back to consciousness. Her eyes widened, pupils dilating as she pushed him away, looking like she had no idea where she was.

'Harper?'

She looked up at him, eyes focusing. 'Gage? What happened?'

'I was hoping you could tell me that.'

She grabbed hold of him, using him to pull herself to her

feet. She swayed but seemed steady enough. 'Yuri...they used the body to draw our attention.'

'What are you talking about?'

'They wanted me here...' she shook her head, like the movement could clear it. 'No, not me. They knew the Aesir would come.' Her eyes widened and she looked down the street. 'Cole...'

Gage hurriedly pulled his coat off and wrapped it around Harper, hoping no one was paying attention. 'What happened?'

She grabbed his hand pulling him along. 'Cole was shot.'

Shit.

Harper directed him to an alleyway where the police were clearing the murder scene. As they moved past, Gage pulled Harper closer, hoping like hell no one noticed the blood on her. She led him further down the alley and into a service lane. Gage spotted Hael, he was holding Cole upright, one arm around his waist to keep him on his feet. Gage didn't bother running, he flew, appearing at Hael's side and grabbing Cole to help support him.

'Cole, hey look at me.'

Cole scowled. 'Don't worry. This is nothing. It kind of tickles.'

Gage peered at Cole, his expression was a little tight with pain, but his eyes were clear and alert. 'Guess I should leave your ass to drive yourself home then.'

Cole laughed. 'Why is it you only find a sense of humour when I get hurt?'

Hael shifted his hold, taking more of Cole's weight. He looked over Gage's shoulder at Harper. 'You okay, Harper?'

Gage turned back to see her leaned against the brick wall. He let Hael steady Cole and returned to her. She was pale, but still tried to fend him off as he peeled her off the wall. 'Concussion?'

She shook her head. 'Drugged.'

Hael looked up. 'What. When?'

She waved a hand towards the street. 'After you left. Some guy. From behind.'

Whatever she had been drugged with was clearly still affecting her. Her mouth thinned at whatever expression Hael was wearing. Without looking Gage knew what it would be. Guilt. The same guilt that crawled around inside Gage's ribcage. Cole had been shot, Harper drugged, and he hadn't been here to help.

'I'm okay, just groggy.' She waved at Cole. 'He's not.'

'I'm fine,' Cole said to no one in particular.

Hael rolled his eye as he fished the car keys out of Cole's pocket and tossed them to Gage. 'Sure you are kid.' He pulled Cole close to him and they disappeared.

Harper stared at the empty spot where they had been. 'Where did they go?' She asked, the words slurred.

'Back to the car. Hael can't take anyone far.'

She nodded as he helped her back the way they'd come. Maybe in her drugged state that made sense. Erinyes couldn't take passengers with them when they flew, at least none except Hael as far as he knew. Hael talked about the dark, empty space in-between that all Erinyes skimmed through when they flew like it was home. His brother felt the void differently and was somehow able to manipulate it easier.

Once they got to the car, he helped Harper into the

passenger seat. She pushed at him unsteadily, mumbling something about not needing help, but her words were too quiet and sleepy. Hael was already in the back seat with a hand pressed to Cole's abdomen, hopefully stemming the blood loss.

Hael looked up at Gage. 'I think it's through and through. He'll be fine.'

'Told you so,' Cole said, with far too much smugness for someone with a hole through their guts.

Gage ignored him and started the car.

***

Gage parked in Aeternus' underground garage, and they took the elevator up. Blood had soaked through the thin material of Cole's shirt, and down the side of his jeans. Hael bypassed the club and headed straight upstairs to the apartments. Gage directed Harper to follow. Even dazed, her dark eyes were curious, looking around rooms only those closest to Hael ever saw. This had been home for decades. There were six apartments on the upper levels of Aeternus, along with several common rooms, and a kitchen they shared. It was to the kitchen Hael took Cole now.

Gage guided Harper to sit at the table. She sank into a chair, watching as Hael helped Cole lie on one of the benches.

Her brow knitted in concern. 'I assume you have your own doctor?'

Gage nodded his head towards where Deacon hurried up the stairs.

'Oh,' Harper said.

Gage grabbed a glass, filling it with water. He handed it to Harper and knelt in front of her. Putting a hand to her cheek, he tilted her head to look at her properly. Her pupils were still dilated. If anything, she seemed a little high. She looked at him, dazed, but his touch seemed to ground her. She felt warm beneath his fingers.

Harper drew in a slow breath, before shrugging him off. 'I'm okay, just a little shook up.' She looked around. 'Everything's too shiny maybe, but I feel okay.'

Gage studied her a moment longer, but she seemed okay, much steadier and more focused at least. 'Okay.'

He moved over to where Deacon was cutting away Cole's shirt. The wound was neat, the bullet had been small calibre. Gage let out a shaky breath at seeing Cole bleeding again so soon after what happened last night. Gods, this could've been much worse.

Deacon rolled Cole, his fingers deftly finding the exit wound, shaking his head to himself. 'How many times have you been shot now? The human gods damn target.'

Cole grinned at him, wincing as Deacon probed his wound. 'Yeah, I tend to attract everything. Men, women, bullets and knives.'

'You're an idiot, just so you know.'

Cole smiled at Deacon, small but sincere. 'Sorry.'

Deacon looked at Cole briefly, before he set to work, putting a few stitches in the wounds. Gage glanced across at Harper, hoping she was too out of it to realise how quickly the bleeding eased. Another perk of the abilities Cole shouldn't have.

Hael squeezed Cole's shoulder, before quietly moving to

sit across the table from Harper. A little too quiet. Taking the lion's share of guilt was something he and his brother had in common.

Hael looked across at Harper. 'I'm sorry.'

She smiled at him. 'Not your fault.'

Hael looked down. 'You're okay though?'

Harper waited until Hael looked up again before nodding at him. 'I'm fine, really.'

She was covered in Cole's blood. Gage walked down the hallway to Ash's rooms. Deacon's sister tended towards well fitted clothes designed to show off her body, but there was probably something for Harper to change into. He found a t-shirt. It was old and worn thin but looked like it'd fit Harper.

He handed the shirt to Harper when he got back, pointing to a room off the kitchen. 'You can get changed in there if you want.'

Harper looked at the shirt he handed her, and then down at her own, pulling at the material that was tacky like she had forgotten about the blood. 'Oh, thank you.'

Gage sat down next to his brother when she left. 'What happened?'

'They were waiting for us. Three-man team.'

Gage nodded. 'The trace I had on Harper's records and the case files picked up an unauthorised search. Someone tried to find where the request for her services came from.'

Hael looked at him, thoughtful. 'I think the shooter was aiming at her, if Cole hadn't gotten himself in the way.'

'Then why drug her, and leave her on the street?'

'Maybe you interrupted?'

Gage shook his head. There had been no one in sight when he arrived.

'Pretty sure I wasn't the target.' Harper said, walking back out to sit with them. 'They wanted me to pass on a message,'

Hael narrowed his eyes at her. 'What message.'

Harper looked over at Cole, her brow furrowed. Deacon had finished and sat with Cole's feet across his lap. Both men were watching Harper.

'Everything is a little fuzzy, but there was a man. Black boots.' She paused, eyes going distant as she tried to remember. She looked back at Gage. 'He knew my name.'

'Are you sure?'

'Yes.' She nodded. 'He said I shouldn't have gotten involved.' She looked up at Gage. 'But if I wasn't the target, how did they know any of you would be there?'

'Someone ran a search on your records in the Watcher database this morning. Looking for who requested you investigate the Aesir cases.'

'How do you know?' Harper asked.

Gage looked across at Cole. Harper followed his gaze.

Cole shrugged. 'I may have hacked the Watcher's database, years ago.'

Harper laughed. She looked back to Hael. 'Of course. You have a reputation as someone who knows a lot of things. Guess you have to get your information from somewhere.'

Hael smiled at her, the devil hiding in the depths of it, all mischievous charm. 'Oh, I get my information from a whole lot of somewheres.'

Harper smiled at Hael's innuendo. His brother liked to play the flirt when it suited him, but that's all it ever was, playing. He used his charm as a tool, while keeping everyone at arm's length.

Hael melded his smile into something gentler, and more sincere. 'What was the message?'

Harper looked between Hael and Gage. 'He said, tell your new friends, I know what they have hidden.'

Gage didn't miss the way his brother stiffened. 'Was he a little more specific? I mean, Hael has information on everyone on the Council and half the Watcher's in this city, just for starters,' Gage said, allowing his brother's reaction to slide away like it hadn't happened at all.

Harper shook her head. 'That was all he said.'

Gage tapped his fingers on the table. Much like Hael, he didn't believe in coincidences, and an attack hours after they put through an official request for Harper's services wasn't something he could write off as mere happenstance. 'I'm sorry you got caught up in this.'

Harper shrugged. 'It's not the first time I've gotten a bit banged up on an investigation.'

Gage smiled. He didn't doubt it. She was stubborn and a bit on the abrasive side at times. She probably had a talent for pissing people off. He rather admired it.

'You should stay here...' Gage reached across, putting a hand on Harper's forearm as she started to protest. 'Just for a while, at least until the effects from the drug are gone.'

Harper stared at him a moment, chin held high and clearly wanting to argue, before looking away and nodding reluctantly. The drug must be affecting her more than she wanted to let on for her to agree.

'Good.' Gage looked down realising his hand was still on

her arm. He pulled back. 'I'll get a room ready for you. You can stay the night.'

He stood and walked out before she could disagree.

***

17

~ HARPER ~

Harper had no idea what she'd been drugged with, but it wasn't pleasant. She felt on edge, like she'd been dumped in a pit of spiders, their legs digging into her skin like a thousand tiny, creepy fingers. Shapes and shadows shifted on the periphery of her vision. Whenever she turned towards them, they moved, keeping just out of clear view. She didn't say anything about it. It was disturbing, but she'd rather deal with it on her own then let people she barely knew see how unsettled it left her. It was obviously a psychotropic effect of the drug. She'd gone through enough of a rebellious stage when younger to realise that.

She looked around the kitchen. It was modern, stone and glass, but welcoming and well lived in. Cole lay on a pillow covered bench positioned to take in the view through a floor to ceiling glass wall. The view out to the east sparkled with the lights of the Enclave at the moment, but it was the sort of spot that would be lovely in the mornings. They'd shown a lot of trust bringing her into their home, which left an uneasy pit in her stomach. She needed their trust if she wanted to wrangle a sponsorship out of this. But looking down at Cole, his eyes closed as he recovered, that trust felt unearned.

Deacon sat on the other end of the bench, watching her with a mild disinterested hostility, if that was possible, like she was a threat he hadn't yet fully assessed. She didn't blame him, the two men seemed close, and she was the reason Cole had a bullet hole in him, not that she asked for his help.

'This isn't the first time you've had to patch him up?' She asked him.

Deacon looked down at Cole, whose feet were propped across his legs, the bench not quite long enough for him to stretch out. 'No, he has a habit of ending up on the wrong end of pointy things.'

Cole didn't open his eyes, but he lips twitched in a slight smile.

She shifted in her seat. Oddly both annoyed, and grateful to Cole. 'He pulled me out of the way.'

'Yeah. He does that.'

Deacon looked away as someone walked into the kitchen. It was the woman who'd led Harper to Hael's private lounge. Harper thought for a moment, Ash, that was her name.

Ash barely glanced at Harper, before ignoring her and walking over to Deacon. She leaned down and kissed him on the forehead. 'How is he?'

'He, is just fine,' Cole said, not bothering to open his eyes.

Ash reached over and poked Cole in the leg. 'Wasn't asking you.'

'Deac, tell your sister to bugger off. It's not nice to poke sick people.'

'You're not sick. Just a little holey.'

Cole threw one of the pillows at Ash.

Deacon smiled. 'He'll be fine.'

Ash tilted her head, looking down at Cole intently for a moment, as if to make sure he really was okay, before tossing her hair and walking over to the kitchen. She opened the fridge, pulled out a bunch of grapes, and jumped up to sit on the kitchen bench. She popped a grape in her mouth as she looked at Harper with a deliberate air of disinterest.

'Deacon said you got drugged. What with?'

'I don't know,' Harper answered.

Ash waved her hand, encouraging her to elaborate.

'He held a cloth over my mouth. It smelt sweet, sickly sweet. Burnt like hell.'

Ash ate another grape, considering a moment. 'Made everything glowy?'

Harper nodded.

'Hmm, if you're seeing things, that should go away in a couple of hours.'

Cole rolled his head to the side, opening one eye to look at Harper. She shrugged. 'Figured it would.'

'It's an herbal mix,' Ash said, still chewing on grapes completely unconcerned. 'It will knock you on your ass, feel a bit trippy for a while, visions, unwanted treks down memory lane that sort of thing. But it's harmless.'

Cole lifted his head, concerned. 'You sure you're okay.'

Harper smiled at him, nodding.

He looked at her a moment longer before letting his head

drop back down. 'Gage is right, you should stay. We've got plenty of room.'

Harper swallowed, trying not to show any pain. It felt as though she'd breathed in fire, embers that sparked and flared all the way down her throat. 'That's really not necessary.'

Ash jumped off the cupboard, tossing the grape stems in the bin. 'Effects can last up to a day, so they're probably right.' She smiled at her brother, winked at Cole and walked out.

Deacon half smiled. 'My sister, the soul of caring.'

Shifting Cole's legs so he could stand, Deacon got up and put on the kettle. Harper barely noticed him moving about the kitchen. The shadows flickering at the edge of her vision intensified. She turned towards them, seeing flashes of light like she'd looked too close to the sun. It reminded her of the days her father took her to the park. They'd lie on their backs on the grass, looking up at the sky so blue and deep sometimes, it was like it would swallow her if she stared at it long enough. She'd held her father's hand tight, as if it was the only thing keeping her tethered to the ground. His eyes had been as blue as the deepest winter sky.

'...Harper. Hey.'

Harper flinched, realising Cole had been trying to get her attention. 'I'm okay.'

'No, you're not.'

She looked out the window at the grey light. It'd probably rain again later. She'd loved the rain as a kid, laughing with her father as the thunder made them jump when it sounded too close. She turned back to see Cole was sitting up, watching her. A blanket was draped over shoulders, torso still bare after Deacon cut his shirt away. Even injured, he looked to be all lean strength.

She smiled at him. 'I'll be okay. Just got lost in a memory.'

He nodded his head towards the table. 'Deacon made you tea.'

Harper dug her fingers into her thighs, trying to ground herself. Deacon must have made the tea and left, as had Hael at some point. She been too distracted to notice.

She felt oddly vulnerable and didn't like it very much. Growing up, she learned to be independent. Her father doted on her, but he worked hard, bringing his cases home and spending long nights pouring over them. She barely remembered her mother but never needed a family beyond her dad. After he was gone, she made sure to need no one else. Harper stared at the cup of tea Deacon had left on the table in front of her. She wanted to go home to her apartment, to the comfort of her own bed and an empty room with no one watching her. Out the window the grey clouds drifted low over the city, the gloomy light seeping into her bones and making her feel heavy. She missed her father. She missed seeing the light under his office door, the way he laughed and looked at her.

Harper studied Cole as she sipped the tea. 'You're Eshari.'

Cole looked down at himself. 'Huh, you know, I think you're right.'

Harper couldn't help but smile. 'I mean, I don't think I've ever met another human who'd been accepted into a family. Not properly, anyway.'

Cole shrugged. 'It's not that uncommon.'

It wasn't. But Harper didn't have much to do with Erinyes families. She spent years training to be a Watcher, before they rejected her application. Since then, her work took her out of the Enclave into the human city. In all the time she had been a Liaison, she'd seen the worst of humans. The way they treated Erinyes, the violence and prejudice. She investigated cases where humans killed Erinyes for no other reason than they could. Guess she'd never taken time to consider not all humans were like that. Not all of them hated her kind blindly.

There had to be a story behind how Cole ended up part of the Aesir. 'If I ask how that came about, you wouldn't tell me I guess.'

'Hael saved me.'

Harper looked across at Cole. She hadn't expected him to answer.

Cole watched her, green eyes sharp. 'It was a long time ago. I was an orphan on the streets of London, with the bad luck to be taken by one of the slaver's fighting pits. I was ten.'

He didn't look away. She wanted to flinch at the words but didn't, not when his expression dared her to pity or judge him. It was too easy to imagine what a young boy endured in a place like that.

'He got you out?'

Cole nodded. 'He did.'

Erinyes being sold into slavery was once as common as human slavery. Underground rings that forced Erinyes to fight persisted after the slave trade officially ended. 'Was it run by Erinyes or humans?'

'Does it matter?' The muscles in Cole's jaw tightened, but his expression remained resolute. 'Very few people know that story.'

That wasn't surprising. Cole gave little of himself away. 'Then why tell me?'

'Gage told me what you said last night, outside Tyriel's. I want you to understand why you should never say something like that around Hael again. I was fourteen when Hael found me, half starved, feral. I'd killed more people than I care to count because I refused to let my end come in a place like that.' He looked away, swallowing. 'Hael tore apart most of the fight masters. I killed the rest. He took me with him, gave me a home, a family. It wasn't the only slave fight ring he raised to the ground. He despises anyone who enslaves another person and isn't afraid to act.' He looked back at her, expression all the steelier for its vulnerability. 'A sentiment I'm sure you can understand I share. Tyriel is lucky he didn't end up dead last night.'

Harper couldn't look away from Cole. The spectre of past pain in his eyes, but so much more strength. There was an indestructible iron core to him, beneath layers of anger fuelled molten lava. She could see the feral child who killed to survive a hell that would destroy most. But also, a man who would kill to protect the family he'd found, because despite everything, Harper was certain he was still capable of a depth of love few were.

'Hael is the only father I have ever known. I've read your file. I know you understand that kind of love.'

Harper nodded. 'If I'd known, I never would have said what I did.'

He smiled at her. It was a small and gentle thing she felt oddly privileged to see.

'I know.' Cole pulled the blanket tighter around himself as he stood, grimacing a little. 'You really should get some sleep.'

He was right, she was exhausted. She couldn't help smiling back at him. 'I will. Thank you.'

Gage came back shortly after Cole left. He led her through the hallway to an apartment. It was small, but cosy, with a kitchenette and one bedroom.

'If you need anything, I'm next door, or Cole is across the hall.'

Harper shut the door and stood in the middle of the room. The effects of the drug were fading, but it still clogged up her brain, making it hard to focus and leaving her feeling hollow. How exactly had she ended up here? The last two days had been crazy. Cole saved her life tonight. Gage and Hael trusted her enough to bring her here. Her instinct was to leave, but she didn't.

From what she'd seen of them, they were an honourable family who were close and protective of each other. Helping to stop whoever was targeting them to gain a sponsorship left her feeling like a grubby fraud. She closed her eyes and just breathed for a moment. Being a Watcher was all she'd wanted since she was a kid. There was no one watching her back. She was on her own. What did it matter if she got something out of helping the Aesir?

Being tangled up with whatever family secrets were involved was the last thing she wanted. She opened her eyes, looking at the closed door. This was about getting a sponsorship. She didn't understand why they asked for her help, or why Cole felt the need to tell her about his past and didn't need to. She kicked off her boots, wishing it was as easy to toss her doubts aside. Turning out the lights, she got into the bed with its crisp clean sheets. She needed sleep but spent half the night tossing and turning, drifting in and out dreams as the drug continued to dredge up a myriad of memories.

She was a little girl, arms trembling as she tried to hold the same pose as her father, before spinning, her foot arcing high, high, too high, as she stumbled, falling in a heap. Her father laughed, low and soft. He picked her up, tossing her over his shoulder and spinning around so fast the room blurred.

'One day, little bird, one day you'll be big and strong. No one will be able to stop you.'

Laughing, she held out her arms. Flying.

She was older, angry, frustrated. Bruised as she trained harder and harder. She'd never fly. He still smiled the same way and said it didn't matter, she'd be a better Watcher then him one day.

Carellen walked across the training floor. It was raining outside, his coat wet and his usually stoic expression gone pale. A wave of whispers passed around the room before everyone suddenly went quiet, and nothing was the same again. Her father was gone. Everyone stared, but no one spoke to her. She was left with only her grief and a silence that made her want to scream.

***

18

~ Gage ~

Gage found Hael after everyone had gone to bed. He was drinking alone out on one of the balconies overlooking the Enclave. His expression troubled, no doubt over the message given to Harper.

Gage studied him, wondering if he knew more than he was letting on. He usually did. 'If you know what this is about, tell me.'

Hael shrugged. 'I don't know.'

'Okay...then do you have any guesses?'

'Brother, that message could have been about any one of a hundred secrets I have uncovered over hundreds of years.'

Gage looked down, resting his hands on the balcony railing. Technically a truth, but also evasive. And not even in clever way. Hael knew more than he was saying, and whatever it was, it had unsettled him. 'They attacked after we put the request in for Harper, that message was for us.'

Hael took a deep breath, letting it out slowly. 'It's safe to say someone is definitely targeting our family.'

A hollow, angry thing squirmed in Gage's gut. He'd spent five years searching for the person who killed Ara. Somehow, he missed the fact that the same person was targeting the rest of his family. How long ago had Hael figured that out?

'Someone who didn't react well to Harper getting involved.' Hael continued. 'Maybe they think she is a threat?' He looked out at the night sky. 'Maybe she knows something we don't. I don't know, I need more information.'

Gage looked down at his hands. 'The man who attacked her, knew her name. He had access to the Watcher database.'

Hael swallowed down the last of his drink, he stared down at the empty glass. 'I've worked with less I suppose. If it's someone that knows her, I'll see what I can find out.'

Hael rarely let anyone see his true emotions, or the damage that centuries of protecting their family wrought. But it was all on display right now, a myriad of ghosts dancing in the shadows of his brother's eyes. It hurt to see so much sorrow and anguish in someone who gave everything to make sure his family was safe and happy.

Gage had been seven years old the first time he met Hael. It was at a family gathering in Georgetown. There must have been a hundred people at the garden party, a mass of swirling skirts, and large hats that fascinated Gage. He remembered how beautiful his mother looked in her fancy clothes. A far cry from the laughing woman who chased him barefoot around their own small garden. Gage's mother was human. His father, Kazimir, had been married when they met, and the affair resulted in a messy parting of ways with his wife, Ishta.

In the end, his relationship with Gage's mother didn't survive either. But his father insisted they were part of the Aesir family, and always invited them along to any gatherings.

Gage remembered he had been eating an apple, chewing slowly and enjoying the sweet squelch of juice across his tongue, when he noticed a man he'd never seen before walking up to where he and his mother had found a quite spot to keep out of everyone's way. Unlike so many of the others, this man smiled warmly at Gage's mother, reaching out to take her hand and kiss it with a flourish as he looked down at Gage and winked.

The man knelt and looked Gage in the eye. 'Do you know who I am?' He asked.

Gage shook his head, staring at this curious man with grey green eyes and hair that took on a bronze glow in the sun.

'My name is Hael. I'm your brother.'

Gage stared at the man a moment before looking up wide eyed at his mother. She smiled at him, reaching out to nudge him a little. Gage knew he had brothers and sisters. They never talked to him though. Gage glanced across the garden to the mother of those siblings.

Hael followed his gaze. 'Ishta is not my mother.'

'She's not?'

Hael looked back at Gage. 'No. My mother had red hair, redder than mine.'

Gage stared up at the man's blond hair that glowed like fire in the sun.

'She was beautiful. Just like yours.' Hael glanced up at Gage's mother, who blushed.

Gage giggled. No one ever made his mother blush. 'Is your mother here?'

Hael smiled, though it was somehow sad. 'No, she died. Many, many years ago now.'

'I'm sorry.'

'Thank you. Maybe one day, I'll tell you about her.'

Hael stood with them for a while, talking quietly to Gage's mother about boring grown up things, occasionally asking Gage a question, or telling him about impossible things he saw in his travels. Gage listened intently, chest filled with warmth every time his new brother made his mother laugh. It was the first time Gage had seen her enjoy one of these family gatherings. It hadn't lasted long enough. Ishta walked across to them. Shoulders stiff, and eyes cold as she demanded to know what Hael was doing in the Americas. It would be decades before Gage realised the grudge Ishta held against Hael was far older and deeper than the one she ever held against him.

Hael had wanted Gage and his mother to return to Europe with him, arguing bitterly about it with their father. Hael eventually left alone, and it was twenty years before Gage saw him again, although his brother wrote regularly. Gage still didn't understand why his father stopped Hael and had hated Kazimir over it for a long time, knowing how unhappy his mother had been living in the same city as Ishta. His mother died when he was twenty-seven. Hael arrived a week later to take Gage to Europe.

Gage may never have built a relationship with the rest of the family if it weren't for Hael. His brother could be kind, thoughtful, but also deadly and ruthless. He would lie, threaten, kill if he had to.

Gage's hands stilled on the railing as he stared at the view, not really seeing it. 'He didn't say he knew something you'd found, or a secret.' Gage looked across at his brother, watching for his reaction. 'He said something we had hidden.'

Hael stiffened, ever so slightly, just a minor tension in his shoulders. Most people wouldn't have noticed, but Gage knew his brother well. It was the same reaction he'd seen when Harper said the words earlier, before Hael schooled his expression into something more passive.

Gage let go of the railing, turning to Hael and catching his gaze before he could look away. 'Maybe you don't know specifically what they meant, but you had a gut reaction when Harper said those words.'

Hael looked down, taking a long, steady breath. 'If the wording was deliberate, then yes, that would shorten the list of possibilities.'

'How short?' Hael didn't answer. He flinched when Gage reached out to his shoulder. 'Hael, please.'

'I know a lot of things. I carry a lot of secrets, my own and others.' Hael paused. He still wouldn't meet Gage's gaze. 'There are things I'd die to protect. Some I would kill for.' He looked up at Gage, his expression haunted. 'And there is what I'd kill hundreds to make sure stayed hidden, forgotten. What I spent centuries erasing every trace of.'

The Aesir worked hard to obscure their heritage in rumour, none harder than Hael. There were stories told about their family, about how they were around centuries before the Council was even formed, and even more dangerous, about the purity of their bloodline. They'd made sure no one really believed those stories.

Millenia ago, the godlike Aion poured though the gateway that connected this world to their own, bringing an endless war with them. So much had been forgotten about that time, but at some stage, one side looked for an advantage and forced humans to drink their Godblood, changing them for ever. Giving them abilities so they could fight and die in a war that wasn't theirs. Those abilities were passed onto their children, and their children's children, down through the generations.

The Erinyes didn't get sick, or old, but died by the thousands in wars with humans over the centuries. Not a single one had died of old age. They weren't invulnerable. The Aion hadn't been either. Do the right sort of damage, and they died easy enough. Sever the brain stem, destroy the heart or enough organs, massive blood loss. Anything that killed them quicker than their enhanced healing could counter. The humans had always vastly outnumbered the Erinyes, and they were inventive, finding new and better ways to kill. Most Erinyes alive today were born in the last 500 years, with almost none older than 1500 years.

The Council held extensive records on any known Erinyes with Aion blood. Those not only descended from the first humans turned by ingesting pure Aion blood, but born from the union of those first Erinyes and an Aion mother or father. Half-breed Godchildren stronger than any Erinyes. They called them the Furiae. The Council's official database held no record of any Erinyes with more than a quarter Aion heredity still alive.

Of course, those records had very little detail on the Aesir family.

Hael had ensured no records were left on Kazimir, their father, that showed the truth. Kazimir was half Aion, a first generation Furiae, and over two thousand years old. As far as Gage knew, no record had ever existed on who the mother of Kazimir's oldest child was, and he could count on one hand the number of people alive who would know.

Most people dismissed stories of the Furiae. They long ago assimilated into the rest of Erinyes society. After a few generations their Aion blood diluted, and their descendants weren't any different to the Erinyes anyway.

Gage gently gripped Hael's shoulder. 'The biggest thing I can think of that our family has hidden is what our father is, and who your mother was.' Gage searched his brother's face, though he wasn't sure for what. Was it possible Hael had known something that could've helped in Ara's case all this time? 'But you don't mean that, do you? Tell me.'

Hael shook his head. 'I can't.' Ripples of heat collided with Gage. Little subtle shifts of warm wind that couldn't make their mind up which way to blow. Hael shifted his weight, fingers flexing restlessly. 'I've never told anyone, not even Kazimir.'

Gage couldn't hide his surprise. Hael and their father had always been close. Far closer than Gage had ever been to Kazimir. He had no idea what Hael would feel important enough to keep hidden from him. Unless...Gage closed his eyes. Of course.

There were only two things in this world Hael put above

the safety of the rest of his family. Cole, and the man who helped Hael raise him.

Gage took a deep breath, opening his eyes. 'Just tell me one thing...does this have anything to do with how Cole got his abilities?'

Gage could almost see Hael mentally packing away his emotion into whatever boxes he stored them in, but the process wasn't as neat as usual, as if some of the boxes wouldn't close quite right.

Hael nodded, swallowing like someone had shoved jagged glass down his throat. 'Indirectly. If anyone knew that, it'd could lead to other questions that shouldn't be asked.'

Gage didn't really know the true extent of Cole's abilities. It was something they never talked about.

Cole sometimes knew things he shouldn't. It was more than people telling Cole things, deep dark secrets things, they just gave up willingly. It was like he reached into their heads and plucked secrets out. He had felt Cole's anger frost the air, and the man was truly deadly in a fight. Cole never should have survived in the fighting pits of Veracruz, let alone for twenty years. Gage had never asked how. Just like he never questioned Cole's age, only helped him hide it.

No one, except Hael, knew how Cole got his abilities.

In many ways, Gage still felt like an outcast amongst much of his family. Hael was the only sibling he was close to, despite their massive age difference. After Ara died, Hael, Cole and the twins...they were the only thing that stopped him letting go. He had leaned on them, and they'd always been there. He trusted his brother, always did. If Hael thought no one, not even him should know, he would back that play.

Gage nodded, tightening his hold on Hael. 'Okay. Okay.'

Hael let out a breath lowering his head. When he looked back up, the mask was fully back in place. This was the brother who walked in dark places to keep their family safe, and never asked for anything in return. His voice was steady, full of steel and the cold certainly of mountains crumbling beneath glaciers. 'You better pray to whatever gods will listen, that no one's found what I've kept hidden for two thousand years.'

Two thousand years? Cole wasn't quite four hundred years old.

Gage might not know what the secret was, but he was certain he now knew whose secret it had to be. And Hael would absolutely kill to protect them.

***

19

~ COLE ~

LONDON, 28TH OCTOBER 1690

The room was dark when Cole woke. It took a moment for his eyes to adjust and see more than just the silhouette of Wrathe sitting in a chair by the foot of the bed. Wrathe dozed, his head tilted forward. Cole shifted hesitantly. His ribs uncomfortable, and knee a dull throb, but not as bad as he'd expected. The swelling had receded more than it should have. Wrathe must have continued to use his powers to ease the pain as Cole slept. He looked up at the ceiling. An injury like this a few years ago would have taken months to heal, and even then, probably wouldn't have healed right. With Hael's blood, it might take a week. He'd be useless for a few days though, the more he used it the longer the healing would take, even for an Eshari.

Cole looked across at Wrathe. An undercurrent of fondness and worry wafted from the man. Wrathe was easier to read when he relaxed, which wasn't often. Wrathe rarely let his guard down. It was easier to read emotions from those Cole knew well. He tended to only get spikes of more intense feelings from anyone else. It was probably the weakest of the gifts he'd received, though perhaps the most useful. He had always been good at reading people, finding their weakness, exploiting it. That was how he survived four years as a slave fighter when he had been smaller than most of his opponents. His new abilities made him even better at it.

Wrathe stirred, waking from his doze. Cole felt the shift in awareness, a bright spark of relief when he saw Cole awake and well, which quickly dulled into something blander and nondescript. That was the emotion Cole generally got from him. It had taken him a long time to realise it was an emotional state Wrathe carefully cultivated. Wrathe didn't like letting anyone know when he cared about something. A result of having so much taken from him.

'Do you feel better?' Wrathe asked quietly.

Cole stretched, muscles stiff. He knew if he tried to do anything beyond sit up, there'd be a lot more pain. 'Better than I should.'

Wrathe looked down. 'Good.' He held something, absently running his thumb across its surface over and over again. Wrathe shifted, and Cole saw it was a little stone horse.

Cole found that horse in a ruin somewhere in the Ottoman Empire when he was younger, maybe a year after Hael freed him. It was probably ancient Hittite. Cole had been excited when he found it. A tiny piece of history that fit in his pocket. He'd quickly hid it, unwilling to trust things wouldn't be taken from him. Hael and Wrathe had given him everything he owned. The horse had been Cole's alone. He found it, it was his, and just his. He'd carried it on him for almost five years as they travelled across Europe until they were attacked in Constantinople. Cole never knew why they were attacked, some old grudge or another. All he knew was that men ambushed them, and Wrathe saved him. Hael had been busy fighting off five attackers, another half a dozen or more cornered Cole and Wrathe. It happened so quickly. Cole watched as a sword suddenly protruded from Wrathe's back. Blood dripped off the end of it, falling on Cole where he'd crouched on the ground. Wrathe had put his body between Cole and the blade.

The wound had been serious, the sword shredding one of his lungs and nicking his heart, along with several other critical injuries he took as they fought their way through the men. Hael eventually carried Wrathe unconscious from the street that was stained with his blood. It took him a week to heal. Wrathe should have died. Cole sat by his side, refusing Hael's efforts to get him to sleep. It was his fault Wrathe had been so badly injured. If he hadn't needed to protect Cole, those men never would have stood a chance. On the third day of fevered coma, Cole slipped the little horse into Wrathe's hand, begging him not to die, and gave the one thing he considered his own as some sort of offering. Cole never thought to ask for it back after Wrathe recovered. That was almost twenty years ago. He hadn't realised Wrathe kept it all this time.

Wrathe moved, hiding the little horse away. 'Hael said to let you know, the man in the alley was still alive.'

Cole let out a shaky breath of relief and rubbed his ribs, not sure what to say upon finding out he hadn't killed someone. He just nodded and said nothing.

Wrathe sat in silence for a long while, before looking back down at his hand where the stone horse was hidden. 'I'll always choose to save you,' he said softly. 'No matter the cost.'

The words were quiet but hung heavy and solemn in the dark. It felt like Cole was back in that room, an unworthy boy, begging the best person he knew not to sacrifice everything for him. The feeling of it was visceral, almost tangible, like someone had lit a candle in his mind, making the shadow of the memory dance in the room around him. Then, it was gone, falling away to nothing.

Wrathe forced a small smile, the expression sad more than anything. 'If you're up to it, you have two young visitors hiding outside,' he said, changing the subject before Cole could say anything. 'I think Hael sent them as a peace offering.'

Cole swallowed thickly. 'Okay.'

Wrathe stood, putting the chair back against the wall.

'Wrathe...thank you.'

Wrathe paused but didn't look at him, just nodded once. He opened the door and stepped out. 'If you two are done hiding, you can go in.'

Two heads peeked around the door frame, matching grey eyes wide and a little scared watched him.

Cole put on a brighter smile. 'Come here.'

The two children bounded into the room. The twins were a handful. Cole didn't remember having as much energy when he was their age. Of course, he'd been begging on the streets, while Hael made sure Deacon and Ash wanted for nothing. They paused at the edge of his bed, wide eyes taking in his injuries.

He reached out a hand, Ash took it hesitantly. 'I'm okay. I promise.'

She smiled at him, though it trembled a little at the edges. 'Deac was worried about you.'

Deacon pouted, crossing his arms. 'Was not.'

'You cried until Dad said we could come see Cole for ourselves.'

'You cried too.'

Cole couldn't help smiling at them. They were adorable, as much as he'd deny the sentiment out loud. He teased them a lot instead. Of course, they were being raised by Hael, so took any resistance to their charm as a challenge. Cole had avoided them when they were babies. He convinced himself when Hael took in the orphan children of his brother five years ago, there would be no place left for him. Hael very loudly and extensively pointed out what an idiot he was for the thought, while Wrathe watched with one of his rare smiles.

Ash scowled at her brother, squeezing Cole's hand in both of hers. 'Bad men beat up our brother. I'm allowed to cry.'

Cole swallowed thickly. Ash was only six but looked so determined and protective. That was the first time either of them called him brother. She looked up at him, little face daring him to contradict her.

He reached out and ruffled her hair, making her scowl. 'It's okay to cry when people you care about are hurt.'

Ash smiled, turning to stick her tongue out at Deacon. 'See, I told you so.'

Deacon looked like he wanted to start crying again. Cole held out his other hand to the boy, pulling him up onto the bed when he took it. Deacon snuggled into his side and Cole gritted his teeth, ignoring the flare of pain from his broken ribs. He pulled Deacon closer, making room for Ash as she scrambled up onto the bed as well.

'We wanted to come in earlier, but...'

Cole smiled. The two cheeky kids were in awe of Wrathe. It frustrated Hael no end that they were polite, perfectly behaved children full of shy smiles whenever Wrathe was in sight.

Cole shifted his knee so it lay more comfortably. 'That's okay.' He toyed with the edge of the blanket for a moment. 'You really think of me as your brother?'

Deacon looked up at him, his little face serious. 'Aren't you?'

Cole looked down at the twins. They were no blood relation at all, but he was finally realising that didn't matter. When Hael and Wrathe took him in, Cole had been too old to call either father, unlike the twins who hadn't even been walking yet. Hael and Wrathe raised him from an orphan slave boy to whoever he was now. He may never call them father, but they were the only ones he'd ever known.

Cole closed his eyes, holding the twins closer. 'Yeah, I guess I am.'

***

20

~ HARPER ~

Harper woke, feeling like she hadn't slept at all. It was overcast and barely light. Good, she wanted to leave before any of the others woke. She ran her hands through her hair, before shoving on her boots, fumbling with the laces. The drug had worn off, but she still felt uneasy, half remembered dreams lingering just out of reach. Shoving the feeling aside, she quietly made her way out of the room. She paused in the kitchen, looking out the glass wall. The light coming through was so frail it was doubtful she'd feel any warmth, even if she stayed long enough to sit. She'd probably never see how nice it was on a sunny morning. Her own apartment faced north. Sunshine never managed to find a way inside. Harper straightened her shoulders when she noticed Gage watching her.

She waved her phone at him. 'I got a message from the Commander. I have to report in.'

'Carellen?'

'You know him?' she asked.

'Not personally.'

Harper gripped her phone tighter, resisting the urge to fold her arms. So much for slipping out unnoticed. Waking up in someone else's home had been disorientating enough without having to talk to anyone.

Gage studied her, his eyes a little narrowed. 'I didn't think you reported to anyone?'

Harper shrugged. 'Carellen insists on paperwork always being in order.' That wasn't a lie, he did.

'Okay.' He looked away from her. 'I guess we got you caught in the middle of this.'

It wasn't exactly an apology. She studied him. From what Hael and Cole said yesterday, this case had obsessed Gage for five years, for obvious reasons. His state of mind troubled them, even she could see that. She wondered if Gage did.

He was right though. They put her in the middle of something when they assigned the Watcher files to her. She got herself into enough trouble, without other people doing it for her. She'd accepted the cases though, too desperate for any opportunity to prove her worthiness to be a Watcher. Did they realise that when they asked for her help? Did they know she would never refuse no matter the danger?

She wasn't the only one who had been put in danger. Was Yuri killed because they had talked to him? She had been too muddled from the drug to think about it last night. 'I wanted to ask Yuri about someone his brother knew. He was killed before I could talk to him again.'

Gage looked back at her. 'The friend Tyriel said he had in common with one of the other victims?'

She nodded. 'Maybe Yuri knew something.' She chewed on her lip, thinking. There had been people around when they spoke to Tyriel at the club. Someone could have overheard them. She had thought it odd the body had been found so quickly. Did the killer use it as bait? To see who would come to investigate? If so, she doubted it was to draw out her, she was easy enough to find. But the Aesir? She looked up at Gage. 'Hael thought someone was targeting your family. I'm going to assume he was right.'

Gage sighed, rubbing a hand across his face. 'It seems so.'

He looked tired. She had heard voices across the hall sometime around two in the morning as she tossed and turned. Gage and his family were an unknown. Without a doubt, there was plenty they weren't telling her. But Cole had offered a tiny part of himself last night, a little glimpse behind the curtain of a broken human this powerful family accepted as their own. Looking up at Gage, she saw a grieving father looking for anything to ease the pain. She didn't want to care, to get to know them as people. Part of her wanted to run out the door, as far from any messy emotions as possible in case any of them accidentally got on her. Part of her wanted to know more. One of those urges seemed dangerous, fortunately it was the easier one to ignore.

Harper's shoulders stiffened. 'Next time you and your brother want to drop someone in the middle of your family drama and get them shot. Don't call me.'

Gage looked up at her. 'Harper...'

She didn't want an apology. They had to have known how

easy she would be to entice. Dangle the possibility of a favour, a tantalising glimpse of sponsorship and watch her jump. 'If you're about to say sorry, I don't want to hear it.' Harper flexed her fingers, easily sinking into the comforting embrace of anger.

Gage's lips tightened. 'I was going to say, you seem perfectly capable of getting yourself into trouble without our help. Giving you the Watcher files was a mistake.'

That probably wasn't what he'd been about to say. She had a habit of pushing people to heated words. Even when that wasn't her intention. Right now though, she wanted to make Gage angry. To push him away.

'A mistake? No. You need my help.' She shrugged, knowing just which button to push. 'Or at least, your brother thinks you do. If he trusted your ability, he never would have asked for me.'

Gage's expression darkened. It was like watching a late evening storm cloud roll in. 'Hael is overprotective. What he does or doesn't think about my abilities is none of your damn business. You should go. I'm sure Carellen is waiting with bated breath for your important report.'

Gage turned and walked away. Harper took a deep breath as she watched his rigid silhouette disappear down the hallway. Once he was out of sight, she walked downstairs, the need to run growing with every step. This was why she always worked alone. It was so much easier without other people's problems getting in her way. She'd lied about Carellen calling, but she could use one of his training sessions right now. Hitting something would ease the tension clawing at her shoulders.

Ash was waiting by the front door to Aeternus. She unlocked it, holding the door open for Harper. Even in a t-shirt worn a little too thin and leggings, hair pulled up in a simple ponytail like she'd just gotten out of bed, Ash was still beautifully intimidating.

'Deacon's worried you'll get somebody we care about hurt.' Ash's mouth thinned. 'Well, more hurt than Cole being shot.' She jutted her chin out, expression full of flint. 'I think he's right. You should drop this case and let us deal with it.'

Harper stared at her. It didn't surprise her Deacon was worried. She got the impression he was naturally suspicious of anyone unfamiliar. That didn't bother her, she kind of respected it. Ash however, made Harper want to punch her in the face. Maybe it was because Ash seemed the sort of person used to getting exactly what she wanted.

Harper smiled with fake brightness that practically screamed screw you. 'Have a nice day.'

She pushed her way past Ash and didn't look back as she walked down the street, feeling claustrophobic, like she couldn't put enough distance between herself the family she needed to trust her. If only she could get what she wanted, without having to care.

***

The Watcher training rooms were quiet when Harper arrived. It was a massive space. Light streamed in the windows high above, the exposed framework of timber beams casting a crisscross of muted shadows. Only two other people were training. She liked it when it was quiet like this, more comfortable going for harder holds and hits. That's what she needed this morning, to get lost in the back and forth of their training sessions. The familiarity of standing opposite Carellen and knowing at some point he would put her on her arse. After the last few interesting days, she needed something predictable. Twenty minutes into their sparring and the tension in her muscles dissipated. Her anger slipped away too. She felt foolish for reacting to Gage the way she did earlier.

He seemed so close to Hael, Cole and the others. Family, she never really understood how it worked. You're born and they're just there? Her father had always been ready with a comforting hug when she needed it and a fond smile for her antics. She never had to find family. Her father was just there. Until he wasn't.

If she was honest with herself, she missed having somewhere to belong. And maybe, her definition of what family meant was so narrow, because if she expanded it, she might have to let someone else in one day.

She was distracted, and Carellen clipped her in the side of the head. Just enough to get her attention.

'Is it true another Aesir was killed last night?' He asked.

Trying to pay more attention, Harper ducked a kick. 'Kind of.'

'He was kind of killed?'

Harper laughed. 'His name was Yuri Vanir. They're some sort of offshoot of the Aesir family.'

'Vanir. I've heard of them. Thought they mostly lived in Europe?'

'I don't know. I met Yuri a couple of days ago. His brother was the last victim in my case.'

Carellen dropped his hands, studying her as he bounced on his feet. 'You think he was killed because you talked to him.'

Harper wiped the sweat from her brow. 'Maybe. There was something I wanted to ask him but didn't get the chance. Gage and Cole questioned him as well. It'd be more likely Yuri was killed for talking to them, than to me.'

Carellen nodded. 'Maybe. You need to be careful though.'

She took the chance to suck in a few deep breaths. Caring about her didn't make Carellen any more inclined to go easy on her when they sparred.

She bounced on her toes. 'Do you know Hael, the owner of Aeternus?'

Carellen let out a huff of air. 'I'd be a poor Watcher if I didn't know who Hael was.'

Carellen gestured for her to take her guard again. Harper moved around him, feigning a hit, the Commander blocked her strike easily. She barely dodged his counterattack. She was still distracted, and it cost her when Carellen swept her feet out from under her. Harper fell hard on her back. She lay looking up at the ceiling of the training rooms, massive timber beams that had witnessed Carellen pull that move on her an embarrassing number of times over the years.

Harper may have the skills to take down half the Watchers who trained in this building, but she rarely bested Carellen. He seldom took on students anymore. She got a petty kick out of the fact he'd been her instructor since she was a child, when so many others wanted to train with him. He was always willing to spar whenever she needed to bleed off the anger that had been with her since her father's death.

She let out a big breath, pushing the sentimental thoughts

out with it. 'Gage, the Watcher who had the cases assigned to me. He's Hael's brother.' She looked up when Carellen said nothing.

His brow furrowed. 'Are you sure?'

She nodded as he reached down to help her to her feet.

Carellen didn't let go of her hand when she got to her feet. Reaching his other hand out to cup hers within both of his instead. 'Harper...I suggest you don't mention that fact to anyone else.'

Harper looked up at Carellen. He was truly worried about her. Usually, he expressed exasperation at her rash actions, but this was more. 'Gage is the Aesir Watcher, isn't he?'

'You know I can't answer that.'

She didn't need him to.

'Hael is a dangerous man, with dangerous enemies. I always suspected, but...' Carellen trailed off, letting go of her hand. 'I don't really know who Hael is. I'm not sure anyone does. He arrived in Chicago with that human of his about forty or fifty years ago and set up Aeternus. He ran a similar club in London for decades, possibly Spain before that. Those Aesir siblings, Deacon and Ash have always been close to him, and Gage more recently. But there's no record of him being an Aesir. Which probably doesn't mean much.'

'What do you mean?' she asked.

'The Council keeps records on everyone. Always has. They obsessed over keeping the Erinyes bloodline pure for a while. A lot of people didn't agree with it. When the Aesir left the Council after the peace treaty was signed two hundred years ago, no one questioned it. They weren't the only ones who did.

But that was also the time the Council started centralising records.'

Harper nodded. 'You think they were trying to hide something?'

'I don't know. They're a powerful family with a lot of influence. They didn't just step down from the Council, they withdrew all their Watchers, dropped off the radar for a while.'

Harper adjusted the strapping on her hands. 'No one thought that was strange?'

'Sure. But everyone also knew they lost a lot during the last war.'

The Erinyes were no different to humans when it came to grief, they all handled it differently. She thought of Gage and his drive to find his daughter's killer. He hadn't even packed up her house yet, after five years. She cleared all her father's things out of the apartment the week after he died.

Carellen stretched, sensing she'd had enough for the morning. But he kept talking. 'They retook a more public presence again about fifty years ago. The Aesir own a lot of businesses now. They're smart, adapted to the modern world better than most. There is an Aesir in Mexico City rumoured to have been one of the driving forces behind the start of the Internet. Zaffre I think his name is.'

Harper laughed. 'Seriously. The Internet?'

Carellen smiled. 'My point is, they could have wiped records of Hael.'

It was certainly possible. Cole hacked into the Watcher database after all. She wouldn't put it past them.

'No one wants to mess with the Aesir, and for good reason. They protect their own, ruthlessly.'

'Don't all the families?' she asked.

'True. But...do you remember the myth about the heart of the storm your father used to tell you?'

Of course, she did. Her father loved telling her stories almost more than she loved listening to them. The heart of the storm was one he told her when she was little. He would make her promise not to tell it to another living soul. She'd solemnly nod and cross her heart. Harper remembered shivers creeping down her spine as she lay awake at night, wondering if the man who fell in love with the wrath that burns at the heart of the storm was still out there. The man who showed the storm kindness when everyone else feared it. Her father always ended the story by telling her, some say, the man who embraced the storm saved us from its fury, others that his madness only made it more unpredictable, but do you know what I think? I think the truth is far more complicated than that. He never told her what that truth was, even when she begged him to tell her the story every night for months.

'I remember,' she said.

Carellen nodded. 'I've only met Hael a couple of times. But each time, I thought of that story.'

She remembered the way Hael laughed while he fought in the cage and understood what Carellen meant. There was an uncontrolled wildness to Hael, beneath the surface and behind his charm, that felt unknowable and dangerous. Did that make Hael the man or the storm? Neither was a particularly comforting thought. In the story, together the man and storm raised entire cities. It was an odd sort of tale to tell children.

Carellen laughed, shaking his head. Harper couldn't help

staring at him. She wasn't sure when she last saw her mentor laugh.

'You know, Hael would be a smug enough bastard to not even change his name.'

'What do you mean?' she asked.

Carellen picked up a towel from their bags. He leaned in closer as a group of people came into the training rooms. 'About 400 years ago, there was an Aesir named Hael. He had been their Family Watcher for a long time. Centuries, I think. He disappeared after the death of one of his brothers. Everyone assumed he died.'

Carellen had always taken an interest in Watcher history. He would tell her about some of the best Watchers he'd known or read about while they trained. 'You think that actually was Hael.'

'Maybe. He could easily pass it off as a family name. Wouldn't be that hard if you were clever. If it was...what sense did you get from him?'

Harper remembered that one small flash she'd had when she first met Hael. She'd almost forgotten about it. 'Old. Very old.'

Carellen's lips tightened. 'I hope he's not the same person.'

They picked up their bags, moving out of the training room. Carellen walked close so he could keep his voice soft.

'It was before my time, but they tried to put that Hael on trial for destroying half of Constantinople in the 500's. There was a revolt, the human's turned on the Erinyes sheltering in the city. They slaughtered hundreds of Erinyes during the night. There are records of several Aesir being amongst the dead. By morning, half the city had burned to the ground and part of it was nothing more than a crater. The Council never proved anything, and no one wanted to punish someone for avenging the deaths of so many Erinyes, so it was forgotten.'

She stared at Carellen. 'If he's the same person, he'd be well over 1500 years old. Is that even possible?'

'Maybe. No one talks about it, but I know there are two Erinyes here in America who are about that old. There are probably some older than that still alive somewhere.'

She couldn't shake the idea the Aesir family knew something about the murders. Hael tried to hide his reaction when she delivered the message from the man who attacked her yesterday. He reacted in a way that Gage hadn't. The message had almost certainly been intended for Hael in particular. The man was a broker of information, she could only imagine the secrets he'd gathered.

Carellen put a hand on her arm. 'I'd tell you to stay out of anything to do with the Aesir, but I'd be wasting my breath.'

He would be. Surprisingly, it wasn't only her driving need to find answers compelling her to keep investigating. It wasn't even the possibility of a sponsorship. Someone was targeting the Aesir, and even if she didn't understand why, the idea of anyone harming them didn't sit well. She remembered the way Cole nodded to Hael in that alley yesterday, the simple gesture enough to make Hael leave Cole alone and injured so he could fly her to safety.

Harper looked down at her hand, rubbing her fingers together. Since she'd seen the sigils at the first murder scene, Harper had known something was different about this case. But it continued to elude her. The feeling when she touched the blood sigils had settled in her bones, a heavy weight of dread she'd carried with her. She'd felt nothing from Erinyes sigils before beyond a slight tingle of awareness. Harper curled her fingers tight, nails digging into her palms. They were just creepy bloody sigils. She sounded like a paranoid human.

Harper hadn't intended to tell Carellen about the attack yesterday. He'd only tell her not to get involved in Family business. Something she knew well enough on her own. As much as she wanted to blame Gage, she'd already involved herself by investigating the murders. She could have chosen not to go with Hael and Cole yesterday. Handing the cases back would be the smart move. She didn't want to do that though.

'Someone tried to kill me yesterday. Or at least I think they did.'

Carellen's fingers tightened. He started to say something, before looking away and taking a deep breath. 'I'm guessing you had no intention of letting me know.'

Harper shrugged. 'I'm okay. But someone doesn't want me involved in the cases Gage gave to me.'

'Which I assume only makes you more interested in them.'

'Pretty much.'

When Carellen suggested the prospect of a Family sponsorship, the possibility helping the Aesir meant she would care what happened to them hadn't even occurred to her. She'd been an idiot. No family would just hand out a sponsorship to a stranger. A sponsorship would only ever happen if she let herself care enough to stick her neck out for them. Even if it meant getting her head chopped off. She would just have to hope, they cared enough in return to pull her back in time to dodge any swinging axes.

She looked up at Carellen. 'If you hear about anyone overly interested in the Aesir, will you let me know.'

'Of course.' Carellen looked thoughtful for a moment. 'I have a source who likes to track the more disreputable message boards. I'll see if he's come across anything.'

'Thanks.'

Carellen looked at her a moment, expression solemn. 'Just, try not to get yourself killed. Sponsorship is no use if you're dead.'

Harper smiled. 'I'll try.'

Yuri's body had been left where it would be found, a trap for whoever came to investigate. Someone had shot at her, but she was pretty sure she hadn't been the intended target.

***

Viridian was waiting for her when she finished showering. He leaned against the wall in the corridor outside the change rooms, looking bored. She'd forgotten he trained with Carellen on Wednesdays.

Harper walked past him, and Viridian peeled himself off the wall, following her. 'I heard you found the Aesir you were looking for.'

'In a way.'

'That's all I get?'

Harper shrugged. 'I met their family Watcher.'

'And?'

'He's a bit of an arsehole.'

Viridian laughed. 'Can't say I'm surprised.'

'Why's that?'

He didn't answer, shoving his hands in his pockets and hunching his shoulders. She knew what he meant anyway. Viridian had a strong aversion for the power and privilege of the Erinyes families, having grown up with nothing himself.

'You heard he had cases assigned to me?' She asked.

Viridian nodded. He watched her, chewing on his lip. 'You really think taking them was a good idea?'

'Probably not.'

He smiled at her. 'But you need answers.'

Hael said a similar thing to her yesterday. Her obsessive need to find the truth had gotten her into trouble more than once. She'd pestered and bribed numerous Watchers, aides, and clerks at the Council to find information about her father's death. Whatever bridges she had left with the Watchers, she'd burned almost every one of them over the years since his death, chasing answers she never found.

Harper shrugged. 'Some would say persistence is a good thing.'

'Persistence maybe. Obsession not so much.'

She glared at him, and Viridian held his hands up in surrender, laughing. 'Did I say obsession, I meant passion. You have an unyielding passion for answers most rational people would give up on finding.'

Harper shook her head at him, unable to stop a smile slipping out.

Viridian didn't seem to care she rebuffed his continual attempts to befriend her. Or maybe he just liked a challenge. Either way, it wasn't a smart move. He was training to become a Watcher. Any affiliation with her would only harm his chances given the state of her relationship with the Council and the Watchers.

Harper had trained since she was six years old to join the Watchers and follow in her father's footsteps. After his death, any chance of that happening had been taken away, and she'd never known why. The only thing she knew for sure was her father had been killed while investigating a case and that another Watcher had been killed as well. The other man had been a well-respected Watcher for hundreds of years. She assumed the Watchers blamed her father for his death, and that's why they didn't want her in their order. Whatever had happened, she lost the Watchers as much as her father with his death.

Viridian would do well to distance himself from her if he wanted to be accepted.

They turned a corner, almost running into a tall, uniformed brick wall of a woman. Irene stood in the middle of the corridor, looking about as amused as a pet rock lost in a field of other ordinary rocks. That was pretty much her default expression.

Harper said nothing, just crossed her arms and waited for the Watcher to chastise her about whatever issues were bothering her this week. Irene had been one of the more vocal in her disapproval of Harper over the years, especially after Harper became a representative for the Watchers with human law enforcement. Never mind the position was essentially meaningless.

Irene stood straight, shoulders pulled back imperiously. 'Are you sleeping with the Aesir?'

Harper dropped her arms to her side. What the hell? 'Excuse me?'

After all the years Irene spent making life difficult for Harper, she could guess exactly where this was going.

Irene sneered at her. 'Are you sleeping with him? Is that why he ignored protocol and assigned Watcher cases to you, when you had no right to them?'

Yep, there it was. Harper gritted her teeth together, before she could respond with anything unwise. The urge to punch Irene in the face harder to suppress. She curled her fingers tight, breathing through her nose.

'Whether I'm sleeping with him or not, I am sure the Aesir family Watcher is perfectly capable of interpreting protocols.'

Irene snorted. 'Whatever hold you have over him, however you convinced him to give you access to the cases, I will find out.'

'I'm sure you will. Or you'll jump straight over the facts to assumptions and accusations.'

Harper tried to push her way past Irene, but the taller woman moved to block her. Viridian looked between them like he wanted to intervene but wasn't sure if he should. If he was smart, he wouldn't.

Irene smiled down at Harper, about as friendly as a cobra swaying before its prey. 'It's only a matter of time before you screw up so big the Council can't look the other way, and even you won't be able to talk your way out of it.'

Harper stared at the woman, trying to figure out when she'd ever talked her way out of anything with the Watchers or the Council. They sure as hell never looked the other way when it came to her infractions against protocol. They'd suspended and barred her from the Watcher Tower six times in the last decade. The most recent less than a year ago when they refused her entry to the building for three months after she lost her temper with a human suspect in a murder case. She broke his nose and fractured three ribs. Considering the Council rarely cared what happened outside the Enclave, and even less about the human involved, she'd thought the suspension overly harsh.

As if the thought summoned one, Councillor Adelina walked around the corner. She stopped when she spotted them. 'Ah, Irene dear. I believe Councillor Varan is waiting for you.'

Irene smiled politely. 'I was just on my way.'

Harper watched Irene walk away. She curled and uncurled her fingers, breathing deeply through her nose until the muscles in her hands stopped shaking with the need to hit something. As much as she wanted to lash out, it wouldn't help. Irene had been a thorn in her side since the day her father died. That wasn't likely to change any time soon.

Most of the Watchers hated her. Sometimes, she wondered why she kept trying so hard to become one of them.

Viridian nodded his head deferentially at Adelina. 'And Carellen is waiting for me. See you soon Harper.' He smiled at her and made his exit, leaving her with the Councillor.

Adelina smiled kindly at her. 'I hear you have been assigned some cases?'

Harper stood a little straighter, ready to defend her right to investigate the cases if needed. 'I have.'

'Such strange murders. What do you make of them?'

The question threw her, she hadn't expected a Councillor

to be interested in her opinion. 'I'm afraid I have no leads at the moment.'

Adelina smiled benignly. 'I'm sure you have some thoughts?'

Harper shrugged, she didn't really. That was the problem. She thought back to the conversation with Jacobs at the scene of Arty's death. 'The Descendants are a possible avenue of investigation.'

'Really. Why is that?'

'The sigils at the scenes. They make no sense, like the killer doesn't really understand them.'

'An interesting thought. But the Descendants are misguided fools looking for something rebellious to distract themselves with. Hardly killers surely?'

Harper shrugged, distracted. 'It was just a thought.'

The Councillor looked vaguely disappointed. 'Well, I'm sure you'll find some leads soon.'

'The sigils clearly mean something to the killer. Perhaps if I could enter the archives?'

'I'm afraid not. The Aesir Watcher may have requested you be given access to the cases involving his family, but that is the extent if it.' Adelina studied her a moment. 'It sounds like you have very little to go on. Are you sure the Aesir did you a favour by asking you be given the cases? I'd hate to think he was toying with you.'

Harper clenched her jaw at the condescending tone. 'He seems perfectly capable of confronting me directly if that's his intent.'

'Hmm. Well, you probably know him better. I've never actually met him.' She looked at Harper, expression soft and sympathetic. 'I know how hard the other Watchers have made things for you after your father's death. Ridiculous of course, as if you have anything to do with what happened.'

'I don't even know what happened.'

'Terrible business.'

'What- '

'I'm sorry Harper,' Adelina cut her off. 'I really must be going.' She smiled. 'It was nice meeting you.'

Harper dipped her head politely as the Councillor walked away, even though she wanted to run after her and demand to know what happened to her father. It would do no good. After all her years prying for information to no avail, Harper had concluded that most Watchers knew little about what happened that night, and those few who did had vowed to never speak of it. That the Councillor even mentioned her father was unusual.

Harper tilted her head back, looking up at the ceiling as she let out a deep breath. She wasn't going to get any answer about her father, so forced her focus back to the case. Had Yuri known something that could have helped? He was killed only hours after they spoke to him. Using his body to draw them into an ambush had to have been a hurried plan. Maybe there was a chance whoever killed him had made a mistake in their rush?

Harper pulled out her phone and tapped out a quick message. She wasn't going to find anyone who would help in the Enclave. Maybe it was time to use her contacts outside it.

***

21

~ GAGE ~

Gage was pacing. He tried to stop, but it was like his feet itched every time he stilled. Cole was watching him.

'What?'

Cole shrugged, directing an insolent smile in Gage's direction. 'Nothing.'

Smug bastard. He wasn't sure what Cole was being smug about, but it was irritating anyway. He came to a stop where Cole leaned against a brick wall. They stood across the road from a fruit shop of all places. Hael called after Harper left with a lead on the men who attacked them yesterday. Gage and Cole had been following the man they thought led the team, Henry, for about an hour, apparently while he did his grocery shopping. They hoped he'd lead them to the rest of his crew, but all he'd done so far was go into a bakery, and now the fruit shop.

Gage resisted the urge to sigh, before deciding he didn't

care, and letting out a rush of breath. Cole was always better at this. Gage hated the waiting. Cole was one of those annoying people who seemed happy standing in the same spot all day. Which the more you knew of Cole seemed contradictory to the rest of his nature. The man was utterly explosive more often than probably healthy.

Although, in a way it made perfect sense. Cole enjoyed nothing more than being contrary.

Gage huffed again. 'Who goes shopping for fruit the morning after trying to kill someone?'

Cole rolled his head to look at Gage, raising one eyebrow.

'What? When did you last go to a bloody fruit shop?' Gage asked

The corner of Cole's mouth twitched in amusement. 'How exactly do you think the fruit in our kitchen keeps appearing?'

A suitable reply didn't present itself. Gage folded his arms, resisting the urge to pace again.

Cole wasn't in the mood for brooding silence it seemed. 'Did you see the lovely Harper off this morning?'

Gage didn't look at Cole, though he sensed the other man watching him. It seemed he was always bloody watching some days. 'I saw her briefly.'

'I assume you were elegantly charming and offered our apology for getting her caught in the middle of this.'

Gage didn't answer.

Cole laughed. 'Of course, you didn't, or you did in some truly obtuse way that pissed her off.'

'I get the impression it's not all that hard to piss her off.'

'Probably not.'

Gage looked across at Cole, who's expression was distant, but he was smiling just a little. 'You like her.'

Cole didn't answer, eyes shifting back to the fruit shop as the man they were following came out. He pushed himself off the wall. Gage followed. They kept far enough back not to be seen.

'You like her,' Gage repeated.

Cole glared at him. 'You sound like you're twelve years old. Is it really the time to discuss this?'

'What. You're the one who always says two people walking and talking is less suspicious than walking in silence.'

Cole sighed in an exaggerated sort of exasperation. 'That's because I'm usually with Deacon, or Hael, who are both far more interesting than you.'

'Nah, you love me.'

'Sure.' Cole said in a deliberately placating tone. 'Doesn't mean you're not about as interesting as a lump of wood.'

Gage huffed indignantly. 'Screw you.'

Cole laughed, a free and easy sound that made Gage smile. Cole had a knack for defusing his gloomier moods, usually by being an irritating bastard. Why the hell it worked he had no idea. Cole just seemed to know the exact buttons to push and when Gage needed him to push them.

Cole hadn't been born into the family like Gage, yet he seemed to fit so well. Though Cole didn't think he did. Maybe that's why they got on so well, neither of them believing they really belonged.

After Gage's mother died, Hael insisted Gage travel around Europe with him, meeting as much of the family as possible. Cole came with them, always ready with a bright smile, open arms or a smartarse comment for all the Aesir they met. Gage had always felt awkward in comparison. It had taken a while to notice that after the boisterous greetings and shameless flirting, Cole always retreated. It was only really with the children that Cole let himself be drawn back out. He loved telling them wild implausible stories to make them laugh. For someone who seemed to have no interest in starting a family of his own, Cole was damn good with kids. He had always been able to get Ara to settle when she was a baby, cradling her in his arms as she drooled peacefully in her sleep. Gage rubbed at his chest, shoving the painfully sweet memory aside.

Cole was one of the most damaged people Gage knew, but he possessed a depth of kindness that was almost frightening. Gage worried it would be his undoing one day. A worry he knew others shared.

The man they were following wandered through stalls in the open markets on West Avenue. He poked through wares and chatted to the vendors. He was obviously a local. Cole stopped now and then to look through stalls himself, making a decent showing of being just another market goer. They stopped at a fruit stall. Cole bartered with the stall owner for a while, all smiles and twinkling charm. He bought two apples, tossing one to Gage. Gage stared down at the apple, rubbing a finger against its red streaked skin, before taking a bite. Apples never tasted as sweet as they did when his was a child.

'You okay?'

Gage looked up. 'Just remembering my first trip around Europe.'

Cole smiled. 'If I remember right, you were an awkward bastard. I nearly had to kick you to get you to talk to anyone.'

Gage shrugged. He had just lost his mother.

Cole looked across at him. 'With good reason, I guess. I was always sorry I never met her, your mother.'

'She would have liked you. She had a soft spot for idiots.'

Cole laughed. 'Good thing, seeing as she raised one.'

Gage looked down at the apple. 'You didn't come with us the first time Hael took me to Russia, did you?'

'No. I stayed in Naples.'

Gage took another bite of the apple as they moved, keeping their target in sight. 'That's right, you and Wrathe stayed behind.'

Hael had argued with Wrathe the day before he suddenly decided to take Gage to Russia. Gage didn't know what it had been about, but he'd never forgotten how anger simmered between the two of them yet neither raised their voices. Gage and Hael travelled for months before his brother's temper had settled enough for them to return to Naples where Hael had been living at the time. Cole took a bite of his own apple, his expression a little guarded. They rarely spoke about Wrathe. For good reason. They had different perspectives on the man.

Wrathe had been as much responsible for raising Cole as Hael. They took in a traumatised, angry young teen, and gave him not only a home, but the means to figure out who he wanted to be. Gage wasn't sure how someone as damaged as Hael, and dangerous as Wrathe, managed it. There was no doubt Wrathe was the most dangerous person Gage ever met, and he'd met some disturbingly dangerous people in his time.

Cole was utterly loyal to them. His brother pulled Cole

from hell as a child, but it was more than that. They gave him a home and family when love had been a foreign concept to Cole. There were many, even members of their own family, who thought Hael himself incapable of truly loving someone. They were wrong. He was capable of a love that was absolute and had a way of inspiring the same in return. Gage had seen firsthand how Hael happily destroyed himself to save those he loved, none more so than Cole and Wrathe. Cole's history left him scarred, he rarely let people in. Yet he loved Hael and Wrathe in a genuinely unconditional way.

Gage didn't know Wrathe well. The man disappeared for long periods, and Gage hadn't seen him in at least fifty years. That was one reason he held a very different view of Wrathe than Cole. Gage never understood how Hael and Cole loved someone who left them so often.

Gage looked across at Cole. Did he know what secret Hael had hidden? If it was to protect Wrathe, how far would either of them go to keep it hidden?

Gage tried to keep his expression casual. 'Have you heard from Wrathe lately?'

Cole nodded. 'He calls now and then.'

'He knows how to use a phone?' That thought was almost disturbing. There was something kind of old world about Wrathe.

Cole smiled. 'Of course, he does. He texts a lot, with an absurd number of emoticons.'

Gage stared across at Cole. The last time Gage saw Wrathe, television had still been a novel invention in parts of America. The idea of him texting didn't want to compute.

Cole laughed at Gage's expression. He pulled his phone

out, tapping a few times before holding it up to show Gage. There in black and white was a conversation between Cole and Wrathe about the merits of cocktails with umbrellas in them being served in Siberia. The eloquence of the absurd text conversation wasn't surprising. Cole refused to use abbreviations, a sentiment it appeared Wrathe shared.

'Okay, I lied about the emoticons.'

But not the texting. Gage looked away as Cole shoved his phone back in his pocket. He always assumed when Wrathe disappeared, he dropped out of contact with everyone. 'Does he talk to Hael?'

'I don't want to argue about this again.'

'I know. Just...

'Wrathe doesn't leave because he doesn't care. The opposite, actually.'

Gage took a loud bite out of the crisp apple. Chewing aggressively and trying to swallow his perplexed judgement. 'That still makes no sense.'

'Do you know how long they've been friends?'

He didn't. Hael rarely spoke about his early life. If you've been alive for two thousand years, there's probably a lot you don't talk about. 'Not really.'

'Neither do I.'

Gage looked across at Cole surprised. Cole had known Hael twice as long as Gage had. He probably knew Hael and Wrathe better than anyone.

'He never told you how they met?'

'Oh, he did. He just left out most of the details. Wrathe was being held prisoner, tortured and experimented on. Hael set him free. Pretty sure a whole bunch of people died.'

That sounded like Hael. 'What's your point?'

'Hael can look out for himself. And there's probably dirt that isn't as old as their friendship. You think you get a say in how they treat each other?'

This was an old argument. One he wouldn't win. Hael and Wrathe's relationship was complicated, and almost impossible to categorise. Gage didn't understand the nature of it, and probably never would. It wasn't like Hael was an open book, even to those who knew him best. He was too good at using his charm, anger and recklessness to keep people at arm's length.

'Our family is really fucked up.'

'Obviously.' Cole studied him shrewdly. 'Why are you asking about Wrathe now?'

'Something Hael said yesterday, about the message given to Harper.'

Cole stopped, grabbing Gage's arm. 'What do you know?'

Gage debated what to tell Cole. 'I assumed the attack was about some bit of information Hael had on someone. But the wording...'

'It's about something Hael has kept hidden. It's not a secret we know about someone else. It's about one of our secrets. I know.'

Gage nodded, surprised, though not sure why. Cole had a habit of putting things together quicker than everyone else, a quality he shared with both his fathers.

'Yes, and I can think of only a few things dangerous enough for Hael to react the way he did yesterday.'

Cole nodded, green eyes dark and unreadable. He would give nothing away.

'Cole, I think you should go back to Europe, maybe spend some time with Bard and Creed.'

Bard and Creed were two of the oldest Aesir alive. They were close to Hael, and Cole spent decades with them in Naples after everything that happened in Veracruz.

Cole's expression hardened. 'I'm not going anywhere.'

'Cole...'

'No. You think this has something to do with me. With what I am?'

Gage nodded. 'Partly, at least.'

Cole looked across the marketplace to where the man they were following sat at one of the food stalls, drinking coffee and reading something on his phone. Gage had lost track of him, distracted by their conversation, obviously Cole hadn't.

'What did Hael say exactly?' Cole asked.

'That if anyone found out how you have your abilities, it would lead them to questions they shouldn't ask.'

Cole let go of Gage's arm. He laughed, the sound almost pained. 'I told them they should have just let me die.'

'What are you talking about?'

Cole ran a hand across his face. His eyes bright with some emotion Gage didn't understand. 'Nothing. Hael will be pissed you told me that. I wouldn't tell him if I were you.'

'Why?'

'That's not important.' Cole looked back at Gage. 'What matters is, Hael is right. If anyone figures out my secret, they'll discover an even bigger one.'

'You won't tell me what that is either, will you?'

'It's not mine to tell.'

Cole looked like he was suddenly a thousand miles away.

He had a way of drawing everything about himself inwards, like if he let no one see what he cared about they couldn't take it from him. Hael kept people at bay by putting up a smoke screen of false shallowness, all empty flirtation and impulsive hedonism. Cole masked himself in the same way with irreverence, like they were nothing more than reckless idiots who cared for nothing.

'Screw this,' Cole said, moving towards their target.

Gage barely caught up to him when they reached Henry. Cole pulled a gun and dug it into the man's ribs. He leaned in over him, so no one else could see the weapon.

Cole smiled, broad and chillingly friendly. 'Henry. Fancy meeting you here.'

Henry looked up at the two of them, body stiff. His hand moved to reach for his own weapon.

Cole twisted his gun, digging it painfully into the Henry's ribs, making him wince. 'I really wouldn't.'

Gage looked around, trying to place himself to block any curious onlookers from seeing too much, while also putting himself into position if he needed to stop Cole from doing anything stupid. He could be hard to predict at the best of times. This didn't feel like the best time. Gage regretted saying anything, though keeping Cole in the dark usually ended worse. He watched as Cole's fingers tightened on the gun. Though it wasn't the weapon he needed to worry about.

Cole lifted his other hand. He traced a finger down Henry's cheek. The man stiffened at the touch, eyes going wide. Henry drew in a shocked breath, like he'd just fallen in ice cold water. Goose bumps followed in the wake of Cole's touch. Henry held both his hands out, slowly setting them on the table palms down.

'That's better. Now, I assume you will do me the courtesy of not pretending you don't know who I am,' Cole said.

Henry looked up at Cole, he started to shiver. 'I tried to kill you yesterday.'

Cole leaned down, smiling. 'You didn't try very hard.'

Gage shifted his weight. Doing this in a public place was stupid, but if he stopped it now that would draw more attention. 'I suggest you answer my friend's questions. He tends to get twitchy when people make him wait for anything.'

The man glanced at Gage, but his eyes were drawn back to Cole when he moved his hand to the back of Henry's neck, fingers caressing the bare skin. Gage had only seen him do this once before, but he knew Cole was using his abilities to convince Henry's body it was getting colder.

Henry swallowed loudly. 'Sure. What do you want to know?'

Cole leaned in closer, speaking into Henry's ear. 'I want to know why you didn't try very hard to kill me yesterday? A smart man would've aimed for my head, not taken a shot at the girl first.'

'Those were our orders.'

Gage studied the man. 'Your orders were to shoot Harper?'

Henry shook his head. 'She wasn't meant to be there. We got a change in our orders when she turned up with you.'

'Changed how?'

'We were told to take a non-fatal shot at her first.'

Cole tightened his fingers. 'What were your original orders?'

Henry looked at Gage. 'You were meant to be there.'

Gage drew in a slow breath. It had been a while since anyone came after him directly. 'Me?'

Henry nodded. 'We were hired to take a shot at the Aesir family Watcher.'

Cole glanced up at Gage. 'Just a shot?'

'They didn't want him dead, just roughed up a little. The orders were to take out anyone else who turned up with him. But that changed when the girl turned up with you.'

Gage frowned at the man. 'So, the person who hired you was there?'

'I don't know. Must have been.'

'Who hired you?'

Henry cringed. 'I don't know man, I swear.'

Cole smiled coldly 'Come on now, Henry. You're the brains of your little operation. You were the gun. The two bozos with you were the muscle.'

Henry swallowed thickly. 'I don't know who he was. He never gave a name. I told him to fuck off when he first approached me.' He glanced sideways at Cole. 'But it was a lot of money.'

'I'm sure it was. Most people are smart enough to refuse taking a shot at an Aesir. But you really screwed up.' Cole shifted his grip on the man's neck, seeping a seductive suggestion into Henry's body, insidious cold creeping out from his fingers. 'Not only did you take money to shoot at my friend here. But do you know who the other man in the alley was?'

Henry shook his head.

'His name is Hael. I'm sure you're smart enough to know who that is.'

Henry stiffened, trying to look up at Cole without moving.

Cole smiled again. It was tinged with ice. 'Ah, not so stupid after all. Now see, thing is, Hael is oddly fond of my young friend here. I'm not sure why. Personally, I think he's a bit of an arsehole. But Hael isn't pleased you accepted a contract on Gage. And I'm not particularly happy you put a hole in me either. In fact, I'd take a great deal of pleasure in snapping your neck, right here, and I bet none of these people would even notice.'

Gage took a step forward, putting both hands on the table and leaning in. He hoped Henry took it as menacing, but he was trying to get Cole's attention.

'Hael is not usually a forgiving man.' Gage shrugged graciously. 'But I could put in a good word, if you're helpful.'

Cole glanced up, and Gage held his gaze for a moment, keeping his expression calm and steady. Cole's whole body looked tightly strung. He had been restless since the incident at Tyriel's, and whatever he'd figured out about the message delivered to Harper was pushing Cole towards an edge he was usually better at not jumping off. But now, Gage was worried about him doing something stupid. For all his unpredictable nature and general lack of self-preservation, Cole was surprisingly level-headed and too damn smart to go off the deep end without a plan for how to get back out, even if no one else could figure out what that plan was. Cole spent three hundred and sixty years learning the fine art of reckless genius from Hael. Hopefully, that genius was lurking in his actions at the moment.

'If you don't know the name of the man who hired you. What else can you tell us?'

Henry looked up at Gage, his expression a little desperate. These days, Hael rarely had to kill people. The fear he could, and would, enough to keep most people from acting against him. Though it was probably Cole instilling the fear Gage saw in Henry's eyes right now. It took a powerful ability for an Erinyes to affect someone like Cole was, to make them believe they were freezing to death, and Cole wasn't even Erinyes.

'He came up to us at Tyriel's. He was young. Dark hair. Kind of harmless looking. He had cash. That's all I know. I swear.'

Cole patted Henry on the back, pulling his hand away. 'Thank you, Henry. I'll make sure Hael knows you were real helpful, see if it improves his mood any.'

Gage straightened, and walked away, breathing easier when Cole followed him. He doubted Henry would still be in the city come morning.

He said nothing to Cole until they were a block away and out of the crowds, his thoughts racing. This was another connection to Tyriel's. No way he'd let Cole go back there. He grabbed hold of Cole, shoving him up against the wall where no one could see them.

He leaned in close to Cole. 'What the fuck was that?'

Cole lifted his chin defiantly. 'Didn't see the point in following him back to the others. If anyone knew something, it was him.'

Gage studied Cole, trying to understand what pushed him to not only use the powers he took great lengths to hide, but to do so in public. The reaction Cole had at Tyriel's had been the first time in years Gage saw him loose himself. Or maybe he'd been too caught up in his own problems, his grief and anger, for the last five years to notice Cole struggling with his control. Hell, Gage practically loaded Cole like a gun, aimed him and fired, so many times over the last couple of years in his search for answers. Cole was capable of great violence, and Gage took advantage of that with little regard for the effect it might have on Cole.

Gage cared for very few people, but Cole was one of them. It was time he remembered that.

He closed his eyes, taking a deep breath, before looking back at Cole. 'And pulling a gun on him in the middle of the markets seemed like a good idea?'

Cole shrugged, liked it was nothing. 'It worked.'

Gage stared at him, scrabbling to think of a better way to do this. Nothing came to him, and he didn't have time to do this gently. 'It's no wonder Hael keeps you around. You are just like Wrathe sometimes.'

Cole's shoulders stiffened as he glared at Gage. His lips tilted in a smile that turned to dust somewhere before it reached his eyes. 'I'll take that as a compliment.'

Gage laughed, a twisted ugly sound. 'You really fucking shouldn't.' He tightened his grip on Cole's shoulders, leaning in. He had to make sure Cole didn't follow him to Tyriel's. Bad-mouthing Wrathe was a sure-fire way to piss off Cole. 'He's a twisted emotionless bastard who doesn't care about anyone.'

Cole's expression darkened dangerously. Gage tried not to flinch. He'd seen that stony look so many times before, but never directed at him. Cole reached up and wrapped his fingers around Gage's forearm. His grip wasn't tight, it was almost gentle. Gage couldn't help the shocked inhale of air as trails of cold slithered out of Cole's fingers. There was an inexorable slide of sensation, like glacial ice grinding against stone as it pushed its own pathway through his skin, following the network of veins like they were valleys, the easiest and quickest path to his heart. He had never felt Cole's ability before. It was no wonder it freaked people into talking. He knew it wasn't real, but that didn't seem to matter. It felt as real as if he'd fallen through thin ice on a lake, and looked up, watching it freeze in over him, with no way back to the surface.

Cole leaned forward. 'Get your hands off me.'

Gage drew in a deep breath and held it, hoping the barb about Wrathe would hurt Cole just enough to make him leave and go home, out of harm's way. He stepped back, letting go of Cole.

Gage walked away.

Cole didn't follow him.

It felt like a slab of ice swished around in his gut. There'd probably been a better way to do that. But, asking Cole to stay away from Tyriel's hadn't been an option. Cole never did what was best for himself.

***

22

~ COLE ~

LONDON, 5TH NOVEMBER 1690

Cole really was as stupid as Hael insisted sometimes.

His knee twinged as he walked. It had been a week since he was injured, and the forced bed rest had been driving him mad. It was still too early to be putting his knee through this much strain, but Cole had insisted he was fit enough to help. He gritted his teeth against the ache, and quickened his pace, keeping the man he was following in sight.

Hael and Wrathe had been busy while Cole recuperated. They had found the Englishman Sebastien spoke of, the one seeking information on the Aesir. After some investigating, they had discovered he was involved in some sort of cult. Cole's initial reaction was to dismiss him as a religious lunatic.

Hael thought otherwise. He hadn't said why. They had managed to identify a few members of the cult, including the man Cole was following now. Even if Wrathe and Hael disagreed, they needed Cole's help tracking what the members were up to. Busted knee or not.

The man headed towards the markets. Cole hurried to close the distance between them as the street grew more crowded. He moved between market stalls, ignoring the noise and bustle as people bartered. The man slowed, looking around, trying to appear casual but he was checking if he was being followed, before entering a small alley off the market. Cole waited at the entrance. He couldn't hear the man's footsteps over the market noise and risked looking around the corner. The man had his back to Cole, crouching to push aside a sewer cover before lowering himself down, and pulling the cover back in place after he was through. Cole ran to the cover, kneeling even though his knee protested. He heard the scuff of boots on a ladder followed by a splash as the man jumped to the sewer floor.

'Not at all suspicious.' Cole muttered to himself.

He was only meant to follow the man, see where he went, who he interacted with. Hael insisted that under no circumstances was Cole to engage with him. They didn't want the cult knowing they were being watched, but mostly, he thought Hael was just worried about Cole's injury. People didn't just wander into the sewers for no reasons though. Following was a risk, but it was also the only way to see what the man was up to.

Pulling the cover back, careful not to drop it, Cole slipped through, leaving it ajar in case he needed to exit quickly. He moved as quietly as possible. The sound of footsteps ahead bounced around the tunnels, hard to pinpoint. Pausing at the first junction, he listened until he was sure the noise was coming from the left. Cole followed the sounds for a few hundred meters, making three more turns, before his foot caught on a loose brick. His knee buckled and he stumbled, managing not to fall, but his feet splashed loudly, the sound echoing and distorting in the tunnel. He stilled. Hoping against hope he hadn't been heard.

No such luck.

He looked around, thinking quick. He grabbed his wallet, took the money out, and tossed the wallet on the ground, then pulled off the silver ring he wore. He scruffed his hair, and hoped he looked dirty enough after being in the sewer to pass as a street rat. One who had just pickpocketed someone and made an escape through the sewers.

It wasn't a good plan, but all he had time for.

The man he was following backtracked, wary as he turned the corner and spotted Cole. He had a knife drawn but didn't immediately attack. Cole took a few steps back, trying to appear startled as the man looked Cole up and down, noting the abandoned wallet on the ground. Hopefully the hasty ruse would be enough to make him doubt Cole was following him.

Cole rushed forward, trying to push past the man who shoved him away. He let himself stumble, before throwing a punch without any finesse. The man wasn't any match for him, making it easy to fake the panicked attack. If he was acting the pickpocket, he might as well make it convincing. Cole spotted an amulet around the man's neck, grabbed and ripped it free, before pushing away, and scrambling down the sewer tunnel, trying to look like he knew where he was going. He ran through the sewers far enough to be sure he wasn't being followed, before finding an exit, coming out somewhere south of the markets.

Cole walked another few hundred meters, making a few turns and twists, before slumping against a wall in a quiet lane, breathing heavy. He was wet, cold, and his knee was sending spikes of pain up his leg. He rubbed his thigh. Not that it helped. Well, that had gone well. Frustrated, he thumped his head against the wall, before sighing and slowly making his way back to the Enclave.

Hael was waiting for him in the kitchen when he made it back. Taking in Cole's dishevelled appearance he raised an eyebrow. 'Are you okay?'

Cole waved Hael's concern away. 'I'm fine.'

Hael looked him up and down. 'I told you not to push yourself.'

'I'm didn't.' He lied. His knee was swollen. He'd probably set the healing back a few days.

Hael glared at him. He did that a lot. Cole sometimes wondered if his sole purpose on this earth was to vex Hael.

'I lost him in the sewers.' Cole said, annoyed with himself.

Hael looked like he wanted to argue more, before deciding against it. 'Sewers seem like an odd place to take a stroll.

'I thought so too.'

'We'll find him again tomorrow. Maybe enlist some locals.'

Cole shifted his leg, trying to ease the aching and decided to just ask what had Hael so concerned. 'Why do you think this cult is a threat?'

Hael stood with his back to him as he set the pot on the

stove to boil. His hands stilled and he sighed, turning around to look at Cole.

'A few centuries ago, there was another religious group. They liked to capture Erinyes, see what made us tick, how to better kill us. They called themselves the Order. Have you heard of them?'

Cole shook his head, careful to keep his expression blank. He had heard of them. Sometimes, Wrathe screamed in his sleep.

Dark things seemed to dance in Hael's eyes, demon shadows that dissolved and shifted shape. 'You haven't heard of them, because Wrathe and I wiped them out. A long time ago.'

Hael had been the Aesir's Watcher for centuries. He was very good at protecting his family.

Officially, Hael had stood down from the Watcher position to raise Deacon and Ash after their father, Hael's brother, had died. Cole doubted he would ever take up the title again though. He had become a little too well known and thought he could do more to protect his family from the shadows. Hael was still grieving his brother's death, still blaming himself for it. Cole had been wondering if that was making Hael over cautious about this cult. But it was hard to argue with someone who had been dealing with threats like this for literally centuries.

'Do you think this is related?'

Hael sighed, leaning against the kitchen bench. 'No. I don't know.'

'But you need to be sure.'

Hael nodded.

Cole could understand that. 'Next time, just tell me that.'

Hael rubbed his face, looking drawn and tired. 'I was trying to protect you.'

'I know.' Cole stood up, he put a hand on Hael's shoulder as he walked past. 'But I'm not a kid anymore. And if something happens to you, or your family, because you didn't trust me to help. I will not be happy.'

Hael looked at him, smiling sadly. 'It's your family too.'

Cole looked away.

Hael sighed. 'I hope you can believe that one day.'

Cole smiled tightly, not sure he would. 'I need a bath.' He walked out of the room. It wasn't just deflection. He really did need a bath. He stank of the sewers.

It wasn't until after he bathed that he remembered the small medallion he'd taken from the man. Cole searched his dirty clothes, finding it in a pocket. He ran his thumb over its surface. It was marked with seven stars, the Pleiades constellation, an unusual decoration. He looked through the rest of his pockets for the ring he'd taken off, but it wasn't there. With a sinking feeling he searched the clothes again, but it was gone. He must have dropped it. Cole sat on his bed. Hael had given him that ring. It had the Aesir crest on it.

Shit. If the man found that ring, he would know Cole wasn't just some pickpocket.

If this cult had been using the sewers to go somewhere unseen, they would have to find where. He shouldn't have lost the man, and they may have been one step closer to answers. Instead, he may have tipped the cult off and they'd be that much harder to find.

***

23

~ GAGE ~

Tyriel's club was closed when Gage arrived. He stormed his way past the lone security guard on the front door to find only a few cleaning staff inside. Gage stared at the fight cage for a moment. Oddly, it seemed more menacing standing empty amongst the trash left behind by the patrons. Gage's fingers tightened into fists, something inside his chest screaming for release.

He ignored the staff as he waited. It didn't take long for Tyriel to emerge from the back rooms, two security guards flanking him.

The man leered, crossing his arms as he stopped in front of Gage and looked him up and down.

'Watcher. What can I do for you this fine day? Did you leave another witness lying around my club?'

Gage forced his fingers to unclench, though every muscle

ached to slam his fist through this man's face. 'I just had a few questions.'

Tyriel laughed. 'Questions, questions. You Watchers always have questions. Though I'm pretty sure you're not here as a Watcher, are you?'

Gage didn't answer, and Tyriel let out another soft laugh.

'See, I've tangled with a few Watchers over the years. Family, unaligned, doesn't matter. They all have the same sanctimonious tone. They all drape themselves in honour, and swear to uphold the peace, when all they really want is power. Their own, their family's. But a little bird told me, you haven't been a Watcher long.' Tyriel smiled. 'In fact, they told me, you never even went through the training. You just showed up one day, the newly minted Aesir family Watcher. Now if I was a betting man, and I am. I'd put money on our mutual acquaintance, Hael, being the one to smooth the way for you with the Council. Am I right?'

Gage still didn't answer. Though it was harder this time. The man was disconcertingly well informed. Tyriel's security watched but kept back for now.

'That's okay.' Tyriel shrugged nonchalantly. 'You don't need to answer if you don't want. But if you don't, I'm probably not going to be in the mood to answer any of your questions.'

Gage took a steady breath, let it settle in his lungs awhile, before letting it out. 'No, I never took the Trials.'

Tyriel smiled. 'Of course, you didn't.' He turned and walked towards the back rooms. 'Come.'

Tyriel took Gage to a small private sitting room. He waved a hand at one of the leather couches, but Gage couldn't make himself sit, too agitated. It felt like his whole body was vibrating.

Tyriel poured himself a drink and sat. 'Suit yourself.'

Gage gritted his teeth. Ask the damn questions and get out of here. Preferably without hitting anyone. Much as he wanted to. 'I'm looking for someone.'

'Aren't we all?'

Gage glared at the man. 'Someone put a contract out on me. The contractor generously informed me they made the contract here.'

Tyriel studied Gage for a moment, fingers tapping on the arm of the couch. 'I assume you're smart enough to know I had nothing to do with it.'

Gage nodded.

'Do you know why?'

Gage looked around the room. He'd never met Tyriel before the other night, and only knew his reputation. But he was getting the impression there was more to him than people thought. 'Not really. I assume you wouldn't want to piss off my family.'

Tyriel tipped his head. 'Yes, partly. I've met the lovely Ishta. She's a fine woman. Not someone to cross if it can be helped. But most of your family in America lives on the west coast. We don't cross paths much.'

Gage shrugged. 'We have a reputation though.'

'Sure. People like to talk. There was some particularly juicy gossip about your mother when she was alive.'

Gage took a step forward, ignoring the security guards who moved towards him before Tyriel waved them away.

'I meant no offense. Just that you aren't favoured by the lovely Ishta.'

Gage stood still, swallowing the urge to do something stupid. 'No, I am not.'

Tyriel studied Gage a moment, before turning to the head of his security. 'Leave us.'

'Sir?'

'Now.'

The security guards filed out of the room, leaving them alone.

Tyriel waited until they were gone, leaning back in his chair. 'Your brother isn't well favoured by her either. Even less so, if I understand correctly.'

Gage's body stiffened, though he tried not to let his reaction show. 'I have several brothers.'

'Sure. But only one of them is in Chicago.'

Gage stilled. Few people knew Hael was one of the Aesir, even less who'd admit to knowing. 'What makes you say that?'

Tyriel leaned forward. 'I know Hael is your brother. I also know it's not Ishta I'd need to worry about if I was stupid enough to take out a contract on your life. Ishta is clever, but she has a foolishly persistent hatred for your brother, given he is the one to fear if you're smart.'

Gage swallowed, not sure what to do, other than hedge his bets and figure out exactly how much Tyriel knew. 'She's never forgiven him for her son's death.'

Tyriel nodded. 'I met Shade once.' He smiled at Gage's obvious surprise. 'He was a thousand-year-old Erinyes few dared cross. I never understood why Ishta blamed Hael for his death.'

Gage did. Ishta's strained relationship with Hael had nothing to do with Shade's death, while having everything to do with it. He had no idea how Tyriel had met Shade, who died well over three hundred years ago. Gage only knew the story because Cole had told him.

In many ways, Hael was an only child, born at the end of the Aionic wars when the world was neck deep in death and destruction. He lost his mother young, and his father moved on to make a new family, and then another, and another through the millennia. Kazimir's children were the Aesir. His sons and daughters and their descendants born over the last two thousand years. Hael loved those families, his half siblings, their children, and their children's children. He protected them all, but it left a lot of blood on his hands.

Ishta hated Hael, because he was necessary.

Kazimir might be the father of the Aesir, but it was Hael who kept them safe. He killed and bribed, blackmailed and maimed anyone who threatened them. Ishta had wanted to keep Shade as far away from Hael as possible. She wanted to keep him safe from the damaged monster Hael turned himself into protecting her and every other Aesir. Shade never listened to her. Ishta blamed Hael for her son's death, because Shade loved Hael and refused to let his brother take on the burden of protecting their family by himself.

It didn't help that Shade chose Hael over his own mother to be the guardian of his children Deacon and Ash.

Tyriel waved at the seat. 'Sit. Please.'

Gage sunk down onto the couch, not taking his eyes off Tyriel, who poured a second drink and handed it across to Gage.

'I have no direct quarrel with Hael, or you.'

Gage took a swallow of the scotch, nearly choking on it as it burned down his throat. He remembered the way Hael watched Cole fight a few nights ago, the restrained rage within him. 'Are you sure about that?'

Tyriel sat back, swirling the dark liquid in his glass a moment before taking a mouthful. 'I know his opinion of fight rings.'

'Really? If you do, you were surprisingly calm letting him fight here the other night.'

'Calculated risk.'

Gage snorted. 'A pretty big risk. You know how many places like this he's torn down?'

'I have some idea, yes.'

Gage wasn't sure what to make of this man who seemed so calm and sure of himself. Shouts came from outside in the fight club. Neither of them moved, despite the sounds of a scuffle. Gage curled his fingers tightly around the scotch glass, trying to keep his expression blank, when Cole walked into the room.

Tyriel sat back in his chair, smirking up at Cole. 'Well, if it isn't the human who fights like one of us.'

Shit.

The head of Tyriel's security burst in, grabbing hold of Cole, who didn't react, just stared at Tyriel.

Tyriel remained unflinching in the face of the stone-cold look being thrown at him. 'It's okay, Billy. Cole was just running a little late for our meeting.'

Tyriel had an impressive poker face. The guard let go of

Cole, looking contrite at mistakenly putting hands on an expected visitor who wasn't expected at all.

'Sorry sir. Will that be all?'

'Yes. Leave us. I've business to discuss with my friends.'

Cole continued to stare at Tyriel until the guard left. 'Gage, did you just finish reaming me out for doing something stupid and reckless, and then come straight here, alone I might add, to do something stupid and reckless yourself.'

'Possibly.'

Cole's eyes were wild around the edges, and his smile held too much of the dry desert about it to contain any true humour. 'I take it back. You are more interesting than a lump of wood.'

Some of the tightness in Gage's chest loosened. 'Glad you approve.'

Cole rarely held a grudge, even when Gage said stupid things he didn't mean. Hell, it had probably only taken him minutes to figure out Gage said what he did to keep Cole from following him here. He was too smart for his own good sometimes.

Tyriel chuckled. 'I didn't recognise you the other night when you stepped into my ring. But it's hard to not see the resemblance now. You're Hael's adopted human, aren't' you?'

Cole shrugged. Gage recognised the feigned casualness hiding the struggle to control himself, now that he was looking for it. It was an improvement over the impulsiveness from earlier. Maybe. Providing it didn't unravel.

Tyriel smiled, amused. 'You certainly have Hael's dramatic flair for recklessness.'

Cole studied Tyriel calculatingly. 'What do you know about Hael?'

Gage shifted in his seat. 'Quite a bit it seems.'

Cole finally looked at Gage, before taking the drink out of his hand and swallowing it. He sat next to Gage, bumping his elbow into Gage's thigh, the gesture his silent way of asking if everything was okay. Gage dipped his head in a small nod.

Tyriel studied Cole. 'You know, for a human, you fight particularly well.'

Cole plucked at a fray on the knee of his jeans. 'There's a secret to that.'

'What's that?'

'It's real easy to win fights you shouldn't, when you go into them expecting to die.'

Tyriel watched Cole for a long moment, before he looked back at Gage. 'I know why your brother hates fighting rings so much, because I know about Veracruz.'

Cole stiffened next to him, though his expression gave nothing away. Gage shifted his leg so it pressed into Cole's, hoping to offer an anchor so Cole remained calm.

'And what is it you think you know about Veracruz?'

Tyriel smiled, nothing amused in the expression now. It was cold and deadly. 'Quite a lot. I was there.'

Before Gage could even react, Cole jumped out of the chair. He grabbed Tyriel by the throat, slamming him back into the wall. Gage stood warily.

Cole leaned in close to Tyriel, every muscle in his body taut. 'What do you mean, you were there?'

Tyriel tried to swallow. He didn't make any move to

throw off Cole. If anything, he looked far too in control. 'Let go of me.'

'If you were at Veracruz, I won't be letting you go until your head is no longer connected to your body.'

'I was there.'

There was no way he could stop Cole, even if he wanted to. He stared at Tyriel in shock. Impossible, if Hael had any idea a fight master from Veracruz still lived, he'd have hunted him down, and would never let one draw breath in the same city as he and Cole lived. Especially not one still running fights.

Gage swallowed, his mouth gone bone dry. 'You were a fight master at Veracruz?'

Tyriel shook his head. 'No. I wasn't.'

Gage stared at Tyriel. If not a fight master, that could only mean one thing. 'Cole...let him go.'

Cole didn't react, fingers still locked around Tyriel's throat. Gage took a step closer. He reached out to Cole's shoulder. The muscles tensed and shifted beneath his hand. Whatever control Cole had was fraying, tattered edges drifting in the torrents of his stormy ire.

'Cole, if he wasn't a master, he was a fighter.'

Gage left the, just like you, unsaid. Even if Tyriel had been at Veracruz, didn't mean he would recognise Cole.

'Cole...'

Cole shifted his grip, fingers loosening a little, but not letting go. He stared at Tyriel, throat working for a moment before he could get any words out. 'If you were a fighter at Veracruz, how could you possibly run your own fighting ring? How could...'

Tyriel's eyes searched Cole's face, expression softening, like he recognised the rage there. 'It didn't start this way.'

'What do you mean?' Gage asked.

'Did you ever wonder why Hael never tried to shut me down. He could have.'

Cole let go of his hold on Tyriel. Gage pulled Cole towards himself until his back bumped into Gage's chest. Cole's body still rigid.

'I suggest you explain yourself,' Gage said quietly.

Tyriel held his hands out to the side, calm and compliant. 'When I came to Chicago, this ring was like every other fight ring. The fighters little more than slaves. I killed the master and split the money he had stashed away between the fighters, gave those who had nowhere else to go a place to stay. I wanted to shut it down, they asked me not to. They wanted to keep fighting and receive a cut of the take. You have to understand, most of them had no family, nothing except debts they couldn't pay.'

'That's what you tell yourself. You pay them, so it's okay?'

Tyriel dropped his hands. 'Hael told me, if I could live with what I was doing here, he wouldn't interfere.'

Cole shrugged off Gage's hand and stepped back towards Tyriel. His expression hard and unyielding. 'And can you?'

Tyriel hadn't reacted when Cole had his hands around his neck ready to kill him, but now, his calm confidence faltered. A flash of emotion slammed into Gage. He almost couldn't breathe, feeling like a man drowning, with no idea which way it was back to shore. As quick as it came, the emotion receded. Tyriel's expression closed off and he looked away without answering.

Cole stepped back. 'I'll be waiting outside.' He left without looking at Gage.

Gage said nothing. He waited for Tyriel to push himself off the wall and sit.

Tyriel stared down at his hands. 'What did you need to know?'

He sounded almost defeated. The sudden switch left Gage floundering, wondering who this man really was.

Gage pulled out his phone, bringing up a photo of Henry. 'This is who took the contract on me. He said the man who hired him approached him in your club. It would've been the night we were here.'

Tyriel looked at the photo and nodded. 'Henry. He's a regular. I don't remember him being here that night, but I don't spend long on the floor. I can ask around, see if anyone saw who he talked to.'

'I'd appreciate it.'

Gage stood to leave, and Tyriel looked up at him. 'Hael destroyed the fight pits at Veracruz because someone he cared about was a prisoner there, didn't he?'

Gage hesitated, before nodding.

'He saved my life that day.'

'He saved a lot of people that day.'

Tyriel ran a hand across his face. 'I hadn't been there long, compared to some of the fighters. A couple years, maybe.' He looked the kind of weary that had nothing to do with lack of sleep. Like he lay buried under a mound of stones, and the world kept adding more to the pile.

'From what I understand, a year in that place would've felt like a decade.'

Tyriel nodded, looking away. His expression drifting more and more distant. Many fighters hadn't lasted more than a few weeks in the pits of Veracruz.

Tyriel wasn't the man Gage thought he'd be. He'd expected the owner of the fight club to be a sadistic arsehole. He might be an arsehole, but there was nothing sadistic within Tyriel. Masochistic maybe. Gage couldn't help wondering if keeping the club fuelled a need for penance. Some people had been hurt so much they thought they deserved more of the same.

He should leave, but he wanted to know something. 'Why did you let Hael fight the other night, knowing he saved you all those years ago?'

'Would you believe me if I said it was actually a favour?'

Surprisingly, he did believe it. 'What do you mean?'

Tyriel looked at the door Cole left through. 'Your human friend never should've gotten into that cage. And he definitely shouldn't have won.'

'Cole wasn't himself the other night.'

'I assumed so. I recognised the look in his eyes.' Tyriel paused, almost like he forgot he had been talking before he continued. 'People asked questions about him winning two fights. If I'd let him walk away, they'd have asked more. Hael getting into the ring was a distraction. Most people forgot all about some human who fluked a couple of wins, after watching the owner of Aeternus get his arse kicked.'

Gage nodded. That's why Hael did it. He was surprised Tyriel had known.

Tyriel looked up at Gage, searching for something. 'You know, there was a human at Veracruz who won fights he never should have too.'

Gage held himself still as he watched Tyriel, trying to figure him out. 'Humans have slaughtered our kind for millennia. They win fights with us they shouldn't all the time.'

Tyriel looked away, his fingers absently drifting to trace the scars Gage only now noticed, winding their way down his forearms, faint white lines almost faded from sight. 'Aint that true. I never saw the human at Veracruz fight, more's the pity. They say he was rather spectacular.' He looked back up at Gage, a hint of a smile on his lips. 'Of course, I guess he's quite dead by now.'

Gage stared at Tyriel, caught between terror at how much this man had figured out about Cole, and curiosity at his apparent disinterest in acting on that information. 'I'm sure he is.'

Tyriel said nothing else as Gage walked out.

Cole was waiting for him outside the club. He pushed off the wall he leant against and stalked over to Gage. 'You know what no one ever remembers?' He glared a long moment, eyes hard. 'No one ever seems to remember, Hael wasn't alone the day he saved me from Veracruz.' He shifted his weight, agitation streaming off him in waves. 'That's fine, Wrathe prefers it that way.' Cole stepped back. 'But you...you know better.'

Gage looked down, swallowing, his throat tight. Cole was right. Wrathe had searched relentlessly for Cole over the twenty years he was missing, driven near mad with the need to find him when all evidence pointed to Cole being dead. Gage knew his own abandonment issue clouded his judgment when it come to the man. 'I know.'

Cole nodded, jaw tight 'Next time, why don't you try just telling me to stay in the car.'

'Would you have?'

Cole made an irritated scoffing noise before walking away.

'That'd be why I didn't ask,' Gage mumbled.

Not that his way turned out any better.

***

24

~ HARPER ~

Harper ignored the whispers as she walked through the police station. She rarely came into the building. It was like being a lone lion accidentally wandering into the middle of a pack of hyenas, hackles raised everywhere and only a matter of time until a disagreement broke out. It had been a few hours since she texted Jacobs to review the security footage of the alley where Yuri's body had been dumped. Harper hoped she had found something. Anything, at this point. Jacobs sat at her desk. A half-full cup of coffee that looked to be long cold perilously close to her elbow.

Harper pulled up a spare chair and sat. 'Did you find anything?'

'I'm good, thanks for asking. How are you?'

She reached across and moved the cup of coffee before Jacobs knocked it over. 'Hello, Jacobs.'

Jacobs smiled at her insincerely. 'See, wasn't so hard, was it?'

'If you say so.'

Jacobs was a hard to offend sarcastic jerk. That's probably why they worked together well.

'Have you reviewed the surveillance footage?'

Jacobs sat back in her chair and looked at Harper. 'I have.'

'And?'

'None of the cameras showed a view of the alley.' Jacobs tapped her fingers on the desk. 'Do you want a coffee? I want coffee. Come on.'

Harper followed her out of the station. They bypassed the diner across the road where most of the cops got their coffee. Instead, Jacobs led the way to a café two blocks away. Harper waited impatiently as Jacobs ordered them both coffee and they settled in a quiet lounge by the window.

Jacobs raised an eyebrow at the amount of sugar Harper stirred into her coffee. 'You know, even if I found anything on the surveillance tapes, I wouldn't be able to share it with you.'

Harper tapped the spoon against the side of her cup. 'I know.'

'Next time don't ask in the middle of the station. I get enough flack for helping you as much as I do.'

Harper took a mouthful of her coffee. It was pretty good. 'Sorry.'

'Yeah, I'm sure.' Jacobs wrapped her fingers around her own cup, seeking the warmth. 'What's so important about this case?'

Harper looked out the window. In the ten years she'd known Jacobs, she never shared much about her cases with the detective. She worked on her own, avoided the need for warrants and red tape where possible. She gathered whatever evidence she could and provided it to the human authorities and hoped they pursued a prosecution. Sometimes they did, sometimes they didn't. This case was different. The killer was likely one of their own, an Erinyes. That seemed almost certain after going through the Watcher cases. The chances of a human killing several Erinyes within the Enclave were low. If she found any evidence, this time she wouldn't turn it over to the cops. Gage and Hael were better positioned to stop the killing than any human cop. Still, she needed Jacobs' help. It couldn't hurt to fill her in on the case.

'I've been following a killer for two years.'

Jacobs put down her coffee. 'The sigils the other day?'

'That was the third case.'

'Third. Jesus, Harper. Why didn't you tell me?'

'What were you going to do?'

'If you've got a serial killer, maybe I could get resources to help you.'

'I doubt it. Who cares about a few dead Erinyes?'

Jacobs stared out the windows, expression tight. She couldn't argue against Harper's logic. Prejudices ran deep and the cops were underfunded, they wouldn't waste resources on Erinyes cases, even for a serial killer.

'Besides, I don't think the killer is human.'

Jacobs looked back at her. 'Why not?'

Harper tapped her fingers against her coffee cup. It'd break protocol to share Watcher information with a human outside the Enclave. She wasn't sure she cared.

'There are more than three cases. I just found out there have been another five murders inside the Enclave over the last five years.'

Jacobs looked at her, before sitting back in her chair. 'Shit.'

'Yeah.'

'Aren't the Watchers investigating if there were deaths inside the Enclave?'

'Most of the victims aren't from any of the families. I don't think they've paid much attention. The only family who has had members killed is looking into it, but they don't have much more to go on then I do.'

'I sometimes forget your lot are just as bad as humans sometimes.' Jacobs sat her coffee down, studying Harper. 'You think Yuri's is another victim?'

Harper nodded. 'I do. There weren't any sigils, but he died after a Watcher and I spoke to him about his brother's murder.'

'You don't think that was a coincidence?'

'No, I don't.'

'Okay.' Jacobs pulled a notebook out from her jacket. 'I did find something from the cameras.' Jacobs pulled a page out of the notebook and handed it to Harper. It was details of a car registration. 'There's no footage of Yuri, but that's the only vehicle to enter the alley within a few hours of the body being dumped. It might be nothing, or...'

Harper looked up at Jacobs. 'Or it might be the first break in two years.'

Jacobs shrugged. 'I put out a search for the van. Maybe we'll get lucky.'

Harper studied Jacobs. 'You have something else, don't you?'

Lips twitching, Jacobs took a sip of her coffee. 'Maybe.'

Sometimes Jacobs enjoyed playing mum, and Harper was

the two-year-old she was trying to convince to use her words. Harper slumped back in her chair, resisting the urge to look heavenward, like there was anything up there to help.

'Care to share?'

Jacobs smiled. 'I will if you will.'

Or they were both just two-year-olds and that's why they got on so well.

Harper sighed. 'Okay, one time offer, ask anything you want to know?'

Jacobs grinned, in that annoying I just won sort of way. 'Every time I ask about the Descendants, you fob me off with a mumbled variation of idiot wannabes.'

Harper tilted her head, that wasn't what she expected. Given free rein to ask anything, and Jacobs went with the Descendants?

'You want to know about the Descendants?'

Jacobs nodded.

Harper expected a probing question about Erinyes powers, or more worrying, something to do with feelings. 'Um, what about them?'

'Who are they, what do they want, why haven't the Council wiped them out?'

Harper thought for a moment. She'd never considered what the Descendants wanted. 'They're humans. Obsessed with Erinyes. Well, obsessed with the Aion might be more accurate. They're just some human cult, I don't really know a lot about them.'

Jacobs looked at her with a deadpan expression. 'Seriously, that's all you're giving me?'

Harper shrugged. 'I don't know anything else.'

'Right, so a human cult obsessed with the Aion, that has been around since the dark ages, and you're telling me the Erinyes Council finds them about as interesting as gnats in a swamp?'

'The dark ages?'

Jacobs laughed. 'You really are the worst Erinyes I've ever met. Yes, the dark ages. They've kept a low profile, but they've been around as long as your Council. Aren't you always telling me your mentor loves boring you with history lectures while he beats you senseless during training?'

'He usually talks about the Watchers. Don't think he cares much about human history.'

'They're one and the same, aren't they? You're all part human.'

She wasn't wrong. 'You say that to the wrong Erinyes, it won't end well.'

Jacobs laughed. 'Probably not.'

'Why do you want to know?'

Jacobs tapped her fingers. 'The van, it's owned by someone connected with the Descendants.'

Jacobs' phone vibrated on the table before Harper could respond. She picked it up, flicking through her messages.

'Shit.' Jacobs pulled out a ten-dollar bill and tucked it under her cup, waving at Harper's coffee. 'You'll have to leave that. You've got more bodies.'

***

The call came straight to Jacobs so there were only two uniform cops on the scene when they arrived. The stench of fresh blood still thick in the air, cloying. Harper imagined it sliding down her throat. The bodies were in a warehouse in the industrial area. Quiet, abandoned, you didn't want someone to see or hear you, this was the sort of place you came. The scene was a mess. Blood splattered everywhere, arcing up and across the walls, arterial bleeds. Some was nearly dried. Some was fresh and still dripping in slow congealed blobs.

Harper stood still, looking around. Whoever did this took their time.

The bodies were strung up, side by side on one wall, big heavy-duty metal pins driven though their shoulders and wrists, arms pinned outstretched. Sigils were scrawled across the wall above them. It was her serial killer, no doubt, but unlike the other scenes, this wasn't just a staged dumping ground, they'd been killed here. Slowly.

Jacobs let out a breath, the sound harsh in the silence. 'Shit.'

Harper took a slow shallow breath herself, trying to ignore the smell of blood screaming at the primitive part of her brain to run. She stepped closer, careful not to walk in any. It was a man and a woman, well dressed, or they had been, most of their clothes now ripped to shreds. Torn, bloody sigils covered their bodies, cut into the flesh. More of them this time, the sigils more distinct, like the killer was getting surer of them.

Jacobs stood next to her, looking up at the blood covered wall. 'You said these sigils had nothing to do with the Descendants last time?'

Harper looked around. She'd dismissed the possibility previously. 'I always thought the Descendants were simply children playing with things they don't comprehend. The sigils they use are gibberish. It's like they know the letters of the alphabet, but not how to put them into words. This makes little sense either, but it feels...' Harper let out a huff of air, not sure how to explain it. These sigils made her skin crawl in a way that was simultaneously thrilling and terrifying, like she wanted to reach out and touch them while also wanting to run the other way. 'This feels different.'

Jacobs shrugged. 'Maybe they're using another language.'

Harper looked away from the sigils, starting to catalogue the two bodies, how they were strung up, the wounds. 'The Aion only spoke one language.'

She paused. As soon as she said the word, they didn't feel right. The Aion only spoke one language, but that wasn't the only thing they or the Erinyes used sigils for. Erinyes used them for wards too, like the barrier wards at Hael's club. The Aion used wards even more extensively, though any knowledge of how was lost long ago.

Harper focused on the victims' faces. They were familiar. She took another step closer, looking between the two bodies. They were both dark haired, the remnants of their clothes refined, probably tailored. She didn't know them but was sure she'd seen them somewhere recently.

Jacobs noticed her shift in concentration. 'What is it?'

Harper didn't answer, letting her attention shift across the bodies. The woman was slender but fit. She'd probably been graceful, full of life. The man wore a nice suit, but it was rolled up at the cuff, the collar unbuttoned, so stylish, but with a casual flair. It clicked and she remembered where she'd seen them.

Harper turned to Jacobs. 'You're not going to like this, but I need you to let someone on the scene.'

Jacobs grabbed Harper's arm as she pulled out her phone. 'What? I can't just let anyone into an active crime scene.'

'He's a Watcher, if that helps.'

'Not really.'

'He can ID the bodies.'

Jacobs looked back at the bodies. 'You want me to let someone who knows them in here, to see this?'

Harper hesitated. She didn't have Gage's number, so called Aeternus instead. Ash answered. 'Ash, it's Harper.'

'What do you want?'

'Is Gage there?'

'Oh sweetie, if he didn't give you his number, he's probably not interested.'

Harper swallowed down her knee jerk reaction, this wasn't the time. 'Ash, this is serious, is he there or not?'

'Not.'

Harper let out a breath, debating her options. 'The first night I came to Aeternus, there was a young couple in the private lounge.'

Ash said nothing for a moment. 'Yes, there was.'

'Do you know them?'

'Harper, what's going on,' Ash said, dropping her usual disdaining tone.

'They were Aesir, weren't they?'

'They are my cousins, so I suggest you tell me why you want to know?'

'I'm sorry, but...I think they're dead.'

The line went quiet. 'Hold for a minute.'

The line clicked. Harper waited, aware of Jacobs watching her. The line picked up again. It was Hael.

'Where are you?'

Harper hesitated, watching Jacobs. 'I'm at the scene.'

'Harper? Tell me where you are. Now.'

Jacobs shook her head.

Harper chewed on her lip, thinking. She needed someone who understood the Erinyes. Who understood wards and what the killer might be doing with the sigils. She needed help to figure out what madness drove them if she wanted to stop the murders. Who better than Hael?

She hoped this wouldn't blow up in her face. '1789 Holloway. The industrial estate.'

Harper had barely hung up and shrugged unrepentantly at Jacobs, when she heard Hael's voice. The cops tried to stop him. Hael ignored them, walking into the room like some sort of sentient storm with one of the cops trailing behind trying to get his attention.

Jacobs sighed, waving at the cop that everything was okay.

Harper watched Hael, trying to predict what his reaction to the scene would be. This had probably been a terrible idea. Hael didn't appear to see the bodies at first, he looked up at the sigils, steps faltering. He seemed shocked, like the sigils were the last thing he expected, though he must have known to expect them. Harper doubted the blood bothered him, given his reputation.

Hael collected himself and moved towards the bodies. Harper watched the muscles in his jaw tighten, his eyes dark and unreadable. He was eerily calm otherwise. He reached out and Jacobs moved forward as if to stop him from contaminating the scene, before she thought better of it. Hael didn't touch the bodies though. His fingers hovered in the space between them, before he pulled back.

Hael looked down, taking a slow steady breath before looking up at Harper. 'Their names are Thorn and Valerie Aesir.'

Harper nodded. 'I'm sorry.'

Hael's gaze returned to the bodies. 'You'll make sure they're returned to us.'

'I will.'

Hael stepped back from the bodies but seemed unable to look away. A growing number of voices sounded outside as more cops arrived. A detective whose name Harper could never remember walked in.

'Detective Jacobs, do I want to know what you're doing at my crime scene?'

'Your crime scene?'

The detective's smile made Harper want to punch him in the face. It screamed arrogance.

'Yes. I guess the brass thought the case needed someone more capable, given it's the second ritualistic killing in a week.' He looked at Hael, all but sneering. 'The investigation has to be handled properly. We don't want any Erinyes magical nonsense getting out of hand after all.'

He clearly recognised Hael as Erinyes. A course on honing the human ability to sense Erinyes was mandatory at the police academy. Harper suspected the detective's prejudice drove him to perfect it.

Hael's attention shifted from the dead bodies of his family to the detective. His expression darkened dangerously.

Harper swore heat was coming off him. She discreetly reached out and grabbed his arm, as if that would stop him if he did something stupid.

The detective didn't seem to notice Hael's mood. 'I assume there is a reasonable explanation for what two civilians are doing at my scene?'

Harper pushed her fingers firmly into the muscle of Hael's arm, hoping to anchor him in place. 'Detective, I am the Enclave's Liaison. We are here to identify and claim the bodies.'

The detective looked her up and down, unimpressed with what he saw. 'I suggest you move. I won't have you contaminating my crime scene.'

Harper pressed her lips together. Like he cared about undertaking a proper investigation. She let out a breath, forcing a tight smile. 'Of course.'

She tugged Hael's arm, pulling him along with her to stand out of the way as more officer's came over to process the scene. Jacobs threw her a quick apologetic glance before following the Detective, arguing with him about control of the case. Hael's muscles shifted beneath her fingers as they tensed and twitched. He almost vibrated with the effort of keeping his emotions from showing.

Hael flinched as two officers pulled down the first body. They didn't worry about doing it carefully, tugging when flesh caught on the hooks. Harper swallowed down anger at the clear disregard for the victims, and she hadn't even known them. She needed to get Hael out of here. Glancing at him, she was surprised he'd shown this much restraint. He closed his eyes briefly, swallowing thickly.

'I've never been to the scenes before,' Hael said quietly so none of the humans in the room heard him.

His eyes drifted back to the sigils. Harper thought he was avoiding looking at the bodies, but it was more he couldn't take his eyes off the sigils, drawn to them the same way she'd been.

Harper turned to look at him. 'The sigils, you can feel them too?'

Hael looked at her, surprised. Before she could ask what that meant, several more police and coroner staff arrived, filling the warehouse with their chatter. Hael held out his hand towards her, tilting his head questioningly. Harper glanced back towards Jacobs, but she'd get more answers with Hael. She took hold of his hand.

Hael leaned in close to her. 'It's better if you take a deep breath.'

She did as he suggested, breathing deep. Flying with Hael was different when she expected it. The warmth of his body anchored her as the world seemed to shift around them. It reminded her of the old microfilm machines, a blur as you shifted through the images, slowing to check your place, before spinning on further as they took a couple of jumps to travel to Aeternus. They touched down just long enough for the air to be drawn out of Harper's lung, and to take in another breath before shifting again. They arrived at Aeternus, appearing in the private lounge.

'What happened?' Gage asked, barely waiting for their feet to touch the floor.

Gage spoke to Hael, but his brother didn't answer, heading

for the bar instead. Harper wasn't surprised, his hands shook as he let her go when they landed.

Harper looked around, unsure who Thorn and Valerie were, but they'd likely been family to everyone in this room. She never dealt with victim's families. Too messy. She was here now though, with no way to back out gracefully. Surprisingly, she didn't want to leave. She never met the two young Erinyes she'd just seen strung up like sick marionettes. But wanted nothing more than to stop the sick bastard that'd done that to them.

She took a deep breath. 'Jacobs got the call about half an hour ago. The vi...they hadn't been dead for very long when we arrived.'

'Is it like the other murders?' Gage asked.

Harper hesitated a second. 'Yes.'

Cole looked sharply at her. 'Yes, but...'

Harper returned Cole's gaze, he was clearly emotional, but steady and calm, unlike the brewing storm over where Hael tipped back another drink. He held a bottle of whisky in a death grip, it was a wonder he bothered with the glass.

'The killer took his time. There were a lot more sigils...more of them carved in their skin. It was more...controlled. Like he's getting closer to something.'

Cole glanced towards Hael before looking back at Gage. 'We need to let Ishta know.'

Gage's expression closed. 'You think I'm the best person to do that, or Hael?'

Hael let out a bitter laugh. The only sign he was still listening to them.

Ash stood up from where she'd been sitting quietly with Deacon. 'Deacon and I will go. She should hear it in person.'

Cole nodded. It surprised Harper he seemed to be the one making decisions. Deacon took hold of his sister's hand as he stood, giving it a squeeze. She appeared on the verge of tears. From her brief interactions with the woman, Harper expected Ash to be too self-involved to care enough about anyone else to cry over them. She felt a spike of shame at the assumption.

Deacon placed a hand on Cole's shoulder as he walked by. Deacon's gaze shifted to Hael. He hesitated, reluctant to leave, before leaning in closer to Cole. 'Try and keep him contained.' The words were quiet enough only Cole and Harper heard them.

Cole nodded. 'I'll keep an eye on him.'

Deacon expression turned sad in a way that had nothing to do with murdered family members. 'You always do.'

The room fell silent after the siblings left. Harper shifted her weight from one foot to another, dropping into a more defensive stance, suddenly uncomfortable. She stared down at her hands as her unease grew. All the hairs on her arms stood on end, like they were reacting to the static electricity in the air before a storm, while her skin warmed with a hot flush of standing too close to a fire.

Cole walked towards Hael, speaking to Gage over his shoulder. 'I suggest you offer Harper a cup of tea.'

Gage nodded, clearly not wanting to leave Cole and Hael alone. Harper considered arguing. Hael saw something at the crime scene, something he understood that she didn't, but an instinctual scratching at the back of her thoughts urged her to get out of the room as soon as possible.

Cole reached out to take the whisky bottle out of Hael's hand, but Hael pulled away. The control from the crime scene crumbled and fell away as Harper watched, a critical fault line that started as a tremor in his hand where in clenched the whisky and rippled out as Hael threw the bottle. It shattered against the wall. A surge of heat blasted into her. She swayed, dizzy and struck with the sensation of standing on the edge of a volcano looking down into lava gurgling up from deep within the earth. Harper took in a deep breath and the air burned her lungs. The emotions scrolling across Hael's face a silent picture of brutally raw fury and devastation. Gage grabbed hold of her hand, pulling her away as Cole reached out to Hael, talking too quietly for Harper to hear. She let Gage lead her away towards the kitchen, her steps loud and intrusive in the fragile intimacy of grief.

***

25

~ COLE ~

LONDON, 6TH NOVEMBER 1690

Cole chewed on a piece bread, still warm from the baker, as Hael joked with half a dozen street kids around them. A girl, maybe twelve, smiled shyly at him. Cole held out one of the warm buns. She grabbed it, splitting it in half and sharing it with a girl a few years younger. They looked enough alike to probably be sisters.

The streets were busy this afternoon, traders hocking their wares, the steady rhythm of the blacksmith, the back and forth of the city folk, few of whom paid any attention to the orphans, except to make sure their purses were safe from desperate fingers. Hael sat cross-legged in a sunny spot out of the way of the people on the street. He could probably be leading the Erinyes Council if he chose, instead he sat here, holding court with human street urchins. He already knew all their names. If they stayed much longer, no doubt he'd start teaching them to read and write. It's what he had done in Rome and Budapest.

For now, Hael seemed content regaling the children with stories. Cole only half listened. He took the Pleiades pendant out of his pocket. He hadn't shown it to Hael yet. Instead, he had spent the morning in the Enclave's archives looking for any possible meaning behind the Pleiades symbol but found none. Maybe someone just thought the star constellation made a nice decoration.

Hael started another tale. Cole recognised it as one of Deacon and Ash's favourites. He didn't need to listen, he practically knew it by heart. The twins liked to tell it to each other, voices deadly serious as they huddled in the dark trying to scare each other. He should have realised they'd heard it from Hael.

A millennium ago, or maybe two, there was a man, who wasn't really a man at all. He had green eyes, dark blond hair that burned like fire in the sun, and a smile he surely stole from the devil. He walked the earth in a time of screams that tore open the sky and rained down blood. Born of a love that doomed one race and gave rise to another, he wasn't the first of his kind, nor the last. He was just a man, who befriended the wrath that burns at the heart of the storm. Reaching out with curiosity, or maybe madness, reckless wonder or kindness, he touched pure fury with gentle fingers that never wavered with fear. The storm screamed, it roiled and raged, wild and untameable. The man didn't care, he didn't want to change the storm or pacify it, only to know it. He stood at its centre, with his stolen devil smile and sun touched hair, lightning struck all around, splitting the air with such force the ground shook in its aftermath, and he smiled.

The storm shifted, as if to accommodate his presence, this mad man who dared its wrath. The man looked up, caught in wonder, in awe, where any sane person would tremble and flee, and instead flew into the storm's heart. The dark clouds surged, towering, tumbling, consuming, until they took on a hint of green. From somewhere in the storm's depths, ice collided and careened earthward, and hail and wrath rained down, razing everything that dared stand in their path.

Some say, the man at the heart of the storm saved us from its fury, others that his madness only made it more unpredictable. The truth is, of course, far more complicated. The truth is both, and neither.

Cole startled as Wrathe chuckled, low and deep beside him. He hadn't even noticed him appear.

Wrathe watched Hael, amused. 'Sometimes, I think Hael forgets.'

'Forgets what?'

'The origin of the story of the heart of the storm.' Wrathe gave Cole a look like he was being particularly dense. 'A story about a storm, full of wrath and hail.'

Cole glanced across at Hael as he neared the end of the story. The children leaned in, all rapt attention for a story full of blood and terror. He laughed. It really was rather obvious.

'That story is about you and Hael.'

Wrathe smiled, a small shy expression that didn't dare show itself too much. 'Hael made it up. A long time ago.'

'Why?'

Wrathe shrugged. 'You remember that time in Madrid. You managed to get on the wrong side of that thug who had kids stealing for him.' Wrathe studied Cole like he was some unfathomable mystery. 'You stole all his kids. Tried to get them out of the city, but he caught you.'

Cole remembered. He remembered being dragged bleeding through the street to the markets. The thug owned the streets, no one would act against him, and he intended to make an example of Cole for trying. 'Yeah, I remember.'

'Hael scared that guy so much, I'm pretty sure he's still running.'

An understatement. Hael killed most of the man's gang while rescuing Cole, all the while telling the man a story about what happened to those who cross the Aesir. It had been a bit of a bloodbath honestly. 'So, he made the story up to scare someone?'

'It was more a cautionary tale. One the unfortunate soul failed to heed.'

Cole looked at Wrathe. The man could be utterly terrifying. 'Who taught them the error of their ways, you or him?'

Wrathe smiled. This time it was like watching sheets of ice shift against each other. 'Both of us.'

Wrathe reached across, gently pulling the pendant from Cole's hands. He studied it for a moment, thumb toying with the edges on the pendant, turning it so it caught the light. He looked up questioningly at Cole.

Cole looked down at the pendant. 'I took it from the man I followed into the sewers.'

Wrathe watched him, thoughtful. 'All stories start somewhere. Do you know the story of the Pleiades?'

The scrolls in the Enclave's library depicted several versions of the myth behind the constellation. 'Apparently there are several stories.'

'True, there's always more than one version of any story. But one story of the Pleiades is particularly interesting if this belonged to the man you followed. The seven sisters were the daughters of Atlas. He carried the heavens on his shoulders, and his fate so saddened the sisters, that they wanted to join him to keep him company. They were also being hunted, by Orion, so Zeus placed them in the heavens to protect them.'

Cole frowned. 'How does that relate to the Aesir?'

Wrathe held out the pendant. 'It doesn't really. Me on the other hand, is a different matter.'

'Don't tell me you're Orion.' It was weird enough that the two people closest to him were apparently the inspiration for a children's folktale.

'Not really. It's a loose retelling and myths have a funny way of contorting truths. They called Orion the earthborn, but his father was one of the gods.'

Cole thought for a moment. 'Orion is a stand in for the Erinyes.'

'Yes.' Wrathe handed the pendant back to Cole. 'And the Pleiades the children of a group known as the Order.'

'Hael mentioned them. He said you wiped them out.'

'We did. But it's hard to erase something entirely.' Wrathe narrowed his eyes. 'I know you want to ask.'

Cole studied the pendant. 'Hael said they took Erinyes, tortured them.' He looked up. 'They had you, didn't they?'

Wrathe turned to watch Hael. 'They had me for a very long time. The Erinyes Council skirmished with them for years. Hael thought they weren't doing enough to stop the threat the Order posed. He made a choice. Reminded me of one I'd made once, but that's another story.'

Cole pocketed the pendant as Wrathe hunched his shoulders, seeming to close in on himself. Cole got it, there were plenty of things he never spoke about either.

Wrathe stood. 'You should show that to Hael. If this is anything related to the Order, or someone following in their footstep, he needs to know.' He waited until Cole nodded, before he turned and disappeared.

***

26

~ GAGE ~

Gage absently pulled two cups out and started making tea. He lost count of how many sugars he put into one cup, distracted by the prickle of heat sliding across the back of his neck and down his arms like creeping fingers looking for a way in. Hael hadn't lost control like this in a long time. Gage flexed his fingers, taking a deep breath, holding it awhile, before letting it flow steadily back out. Cole had always been better at calming Hael than anyone else besides Wrathe. Which was ironic, given how often Wrathe or Cole were the reason Hael needed calming.

Hael's abilities were the kind most people dismissed as fanciful myth. Unfortunately, Hael also let his emotions guide him. Not always the best combination

Gage handed Harper a cup of tea, keeping the over sugared one for himself. He tried not to wince when he took a sip, putting the cup down on the table and pushing it away. He didn't really feel like tea anyway.

Harper flinched as another crash sounded from the lounge. She sipped her tea, looking across at Gage. 'Who were Thorn and Valerie?'

It was surprising it'd taken her this long to ask questions. 'They were my niece and nephew.'

'I'm sorry.'

Gage shrugged. 'I have a lot of nieces and nephews.'

Harper raised an eyebrow at him. 'Were you close to them?'

Gage sat back in his chair. He'd once flown to Italy to get gelato for Valerie's birthday because she mentioned a memory of eating it on the banks of the Tiber River with her brother as a small child. 'A little. They stayed here sometimes. They idolised Hael and were young enough that coming here was their way of rebelling against Ishta. She's their grandmother.'

Harper nodded, chewing her bottom lip, probably trying to get her head around the complicated Aesir family. 'I take it you don't get on with Ishta. Isn't she the head of your family?'

Gage laughed. Describing their family wasn't easy. 'It's complicated. She was our last representative on the Council, that might make her the head in other families. Ours doesn't really work that way.' That was an understatement. With so many powerful Erinyes in one family, it's a wonder they hadn't imploded, other families would have. 'She'll probably come to take her grandchildren's bodies home. If you talk to her, it'd be best not to mention Hael. Or me.'

'You think she'll come?'

Gage nodded. Ishta would never leave it to Hael now this

involved her direct family. She'd blame Hael if it was his fault or not.

Harper took another sip of tea. 'I don't do well dealing with grieving families.'

Gage looked across at Harper, he well imagined that. Harper seemed the sort of person who pretended emotions didn't exist, even when she obviously felt a great deal. It's why she fit in with his misfit family so easily. Cole rarely opened up to anyone, and even Deacon had barely protested over her presence.

He poked at the discarded cup of tea, watching as the liquid swirled. If Harper intended to get mixed up in their family, she needed at least some background to their issues. He didn't look up, tracing his finger through a drop of tea that sloshed out onto the table.

'My mother had an affair with Ishta's husband. It ended their marriage.' He looked up, shrugging. 'I've never had a great relationship with Ishta. Her history with Hael is more complicated. She blames him for the death of her oldest son, Shade.' Gage looked away again. He was as angry with Ishta over her treatment of Hael as her ostracization of his own mother. 'Shade was Deacon and Ash's father. They were only a year old when he died. Hael raised them. He avoided America for about two hundred years because Ishta didn't want him here.' That was putting it mildly. Ishta made damn sure Hael wasn't welcome in the Americas, believing he'd all but stolen her grandchildren from her on top of killing her son.

'Ishta is a powerful woman who garners a lot of respect. Don't underestimate her dislike for my brother and those who associate with him.'

Harper studied him, quietly assessing the information before finally nodding. 'Okay.' She paused, tilting her head in exaggerated confusion. 'Deacon and Ash are twins?'

Gage smiled. Deacon and Ash had been inseparable once. Hael liked to tease them for being little devil clones of each other when they were little. Gage always found it hard to imagine stoic suspicious Deacon and aloof Ash as two cheeky carefree kids who liked to laugh and get into mischief, but apparently it was true.

'They're different sides of the same coin once you get to know them.'

Harper shrugged. 'I'll take your word for it.'

She curled her fingers around the cup, sipping her tea as she took in the view out the glass wall. It was getting late, a few lights starting to come on across the Enclave. The silence was comfortable. It shouldn't be. He'd just lost a niece and nephew. There were things he should feel about that. He mostly felt numb. After losing Ara, nothing much mattered. It had been five years, maybe he was meant to move on, or whatever people did after they stopped grieving. He couldn't even talk about her. Ara deserved more than that.

He looked down, smoothing his fingers over the pattern on the warm cup of tea he'd abandoned. 'Ara...the first victim. She was my daughter.'

Harper nodded. 'I know. I'm sorry.' She shifted looking uncomfortable. 'I shouldn't have gone to her house.'

Gage shrugged. He'd been angry, but only briefly. 'Ara was always so happy, quick to laugh.' He rubbed his fingers back and forth across the cup. 'I'm not sure where she got that from. Certainly not me.'

'Is her mother...' Harper trailed off, like she wasn't sure what she wanted to ask.

'She was human. I thought we were in love. It didn't last.' Gage paused. The only good thing that had come of the relationship was his daughter in the end. 'She didn't want to raise an Erinyes child in the human city and refused to live in the Enclave. So, Ara lived with me.' He pushed the cup away. 'Maybe she would have been better off with her mother.'

Harper pulled out something from inside her jacket. She hesitated before handing it to Gage. It was a photo of Ara kissing Gage on the cheek. 'The pictures in her house...they all showed a girl who knew she was loved.'

He looked at Harper a moment before he took the photo. It was a nice sentiment. One he desperately hoped was true. He looked down at the photo, thumb brushing over Ara's face. He remembered the day it was taken, only a few months before she died. She'd been so young. He swallowed thickly, tucking the photo away in his own jacket as Cole walked in.

Hael followed Cole, which was a good sign, though his brother appeared about as calm as a hive of bees some curious kid kept poking. If they didn't find the killer soon, Gage doubted even Cole would be able to restrain Hael's self-destructive tendencies. The lot of them were particularly unstable peas in a pod. Harper would be better off walking out the door right now and not looking back. Gage traced the outline of the photo in his pocket and hoped she didn't. Harper was curious and unfazed by his family. They were an intense lot. People ran from less. But she didn't seem to be, not yet at least.

Cole sat next to Gage, picking up his abandoned tea and taking a mouthful. Gage raised an eyebrow.

Cole looked down at the cup. 'It's disgusting.'

'I know.'

Cole shrugged and continued drinking it.

Hael ignored them all. He faced the window, shoulders tense. Cole's phone pinged with an incoming text. He read it before pushing his phone across the table so Gage could see. It was from Deacon, and just said, maelstrom incoming. Deacon, always short and to the point. It'd be best if Harper wasn't here when Ishta arrived.

Gage leaned back in his chair. 'You should probably leave.'

Harper put her cup of tea down, shoulders hunching defensively as she looked between the Gage and Cole. 'Okay. There was a lead I wanted to follow up anyway.'

Gage didn't need to see Cole to know he rolled his eyes at the lack of tact.

'What Gage means is Ishta is on her way. If you don't want to get in the middle of awkward family drama, you might want to go.'

'Oh.' Harper's posture relaxed a little.

Gage shrugged. In almost two hundred years, neither Cole nor Hael's natural charm had rubbed off on him.

Hael shifted, drawing Gage's attention. His brother tilted his head slightly. 'Too late. They're here.'

Gage heard nothing. He assumed Hael sensed something from the building's wards. A few seconds later, Ishta stormed into the kitchen. She was a tall woman, regal, with an intelligent sparkle in her eyes. She might not be the head of the family, but she was a driving force within it. Gage wondered where she had been when the twins found her. Ishta wore an impeccably tailored business suit, her hair pinned down in a severe no prisoners sort of way. He could feel the turmoil her emotions were in as her gaze swept the room, lingering on Gage a moment, she ignored Cole completely, as usual. Gage wasn't the shy boy hiding behind his mother's legs anymore, but Ishta was still intimidating. She hesitated when she saw Harper.

Gage stood, hoping to forestall any heated words. 'Ishta, this is Caitlan Harper, Watcher Liaison. She acts as the contact between the Chicago Police and the Council.'

Harper stood, holding out her hand for a moment, before dropping it when she realised Ishta had no intention of taking it. 'I'm sorry for your loss.'

Ishta nodded. Swallowing as her eyes glistened. They may not have the best relationship with Ishta, but no one questioned how much she loved her family. She'd had ten children with Kazimir, half siblings to Gage and Hael, during a marriage that lasted almost a thousand years, and dozens of grandchildren and great-grandchildren. At last count she was matriarch to seven generations and a major branch of the Aesir family.

Ishta turned towards Hael. 'Do you have anything to say?'

Hael's shoulders slumped. His brother turned, looking at Ishta. 'I'm sorry.'

'Sorry? What good is sorry? How long have you known someone was targeting us? Did you do anything to warn anyone?'

Hael said nothing in his defence. He never did. Hael respected Ishta and refused to speak against her, despite the centuries she'd reviled him for Shade's death. Hael blamed himself for his brother's death as much as Ishta did, even though it hadn't been his fault. Hael had lived a long time and lost so many people, but he never dealt with grief very well.

Cole shifted behind him. 'We'll find who did this.'

Ishta didn't acknowledge him, angry gaze not wavering from Hael. 'And how many more will die before you do?'

'Ishta, that's enough,' a voice said firmly.

Gage flinched. He hadn't heard his father arrive. Kazimir walked into the room, standing between his ex-wife and eldest son.

Ishta glared at him, before looking away, tearful. 'Our grandchildren are dead.'

Kazimir reached out and held her. 'I know.'

Ishta pulled back after a moment, wiping away her tears. She turned to Harper. 'I assume the Watchers took possession of their bodies?'

Harper nodded. 'Of course.'

Kazimir smiled sadly at Ishta. 'Go, take Thorn and Valerie home.'

Ishta cast another accusing glance at Hael, before turning and walking out without another word.

Kazimir sighed. He was a tall man, though he didn't seem it at the moment, with his shoulders slumped and expression weary. Gage wasn't sure how many children and grandchildren he'd buried over the years. Kazimir looked up at Gage, tilting his head in Harper's direction questioningly.

Hael noticed the silent query. He turned back to look out the window. 'Harper can stay, if she wants.'

Gage was surprised. Either Hael had controlled his outburst of power, or he was comfortable enough with Harper not to care if she saw him this way. Harper looked around at them. Gage nodded at her, while Cole silently pushed the chair out for her to sit. She did so tentatively, like she didn't quite trust they wanted her here.

Kazimir rubbed a hand over his face, casting a worried glance towards Hael before turning to Gage. 'What do you know?'

'There have been several murders over the last few years. Most of the victims distantly related to the Aesir.'

'How do you know the murders are related. We're a big family prone to causing trouble.'

'The killer covered the crime scenes with Aionic sigils. It's almost ritualistic.'

'What sort of sigils?'

'Nonsense. They look random.'

Harper shifted at the words, like she didn't quite agree. But the flare of emotion from Hael was more telling. Despite his unpredictable and stormy personality, Hael excelled at keeping his true emotions hidden. He'd spent centuries operating as an information broker, a collector of secrets. He had a knack for broadcasting what he wanted people to see, rather than letting them see the truth. It was anger he had the most trouble keeping a lid on. The intense rush of emotion now, almost panic, was unusual to say the least. Hael reigned it in, but everyone in the room except Harper felt it.

Gage looked across at his brother, but he stared out the window, arms crossed tightly. Whatever it was, he didn't seem to want to discuss it now.

Harper spoke up, oblivious to whatever bothered Hael. 'I did have one lead to follow up.'

'You mentioned that earlier,' Cole said.

Harper sucked in her bottom lip, something Gage noticed her doing whenever she was thinking. 'Jacobs found the van used to dump Yuri's body. She said it's tied to the Descendants. Aren't they obsessed with the Aionic script?'

Hael turned to face them. 'The Descendants?'

Harper looked around at them all. 'Yeah. But aren't they just a bunch of humans obsessed with Aionic myths? Some sort of harmless cult.'

Kazimir shook his head. 'Not exactly.' He studied Hael. 'Didn't you have a run in with them once?'

Hael nodded. 'History likes repeating itself.'

Cole sipped at the disgustingly sweet tea. 'The Descendants have been around a long time.' He looked at Hael. 'Didn't think ritualistic murders were their style.'

'Whether the Descendants are connected or not, the killer is certainly targeting our family. I wasn't sure at first, after Ara, the connections weren't obvious until recently. But he's taken out two of Bodhi's and now Thorn and Val.'

Kazimir nodded. 'Do you know how they were taken?'

Hael sighed. 'I thought they'd gone home.'

Guilt rolled off Hael. Kazimir nodded, his attention fixed on his oldest son. Cole took the moment to offer Harper a chance to leave, holding out a hand to her. She took it and he pulled her to her feet, tucking her hand into the crook of his elbow and leading her out of the room.

Kazimir walked across to Hael, putting a hand on his shoulder. Hael flinched, like he wanted to pull away from the comfort. Kazimir pulled his son closer, whispering something in his ear. It was such a fatherly gesture, and completely foreign to Gage. He didn't resent the relationship Hael had with their father. It just wasn't something he understood. Hael was this ancient thing, so far beyond anything as mundane as a father, that it was odd to see the different shapes his relationship with Kazimir took, the way it flexed and flowed.

Gage watched them, waiting to escort Kazimir to the Watcher morgue to identify his grandchildren. In profile, it was easy to see the two men as father and son. The same fine, strong nose, same coloured eyes. But it was the presence the two men had that was more similar. Like beneath their skin they were made of something perpetual and unyielding. Even now it felt unbreakable, if a little dented. Gage looked away, acutely aware he wasn't made of the same stuff.

**

It was quiet as Gage walked through the halls of the Watcher's building with his father. Apparently, word travelled fast. Heads turned to stare at the Aesir Watcher, but everyone's eyes averted when caught looking. He wanted to scream at them. The last time everyone looked at him like this, was the day he walked through these same halls to identify the body of his daughter. He'd screamed that day, screamed until he was hoarse.

Gage clenched his jaw, trying to chase away the sensation of ghost fingers digging into his arms where Hael had forcefully pulled him away from Ara's body. He didn't remember much after that, it was a blank, until he remembered Cole holding the urn with her ashes out to him days, or maybe it had been weeks later. They stood on top of a mountain. Ara loved the mountains. She loved climbing them. Gage hated climbing. He would fly ahead, wait for her to catch up.

Gage hadn't been able to make himself reach out and take the urn from Cole. He'd stared at it. The first thing he remembered being aware of for days, the way the light caught on the simple silver. His knees ached as he fell to them, watching Cole empty out all that was left of her, watched as she flew away on the wind. It didn't matter how long he waited there on top of the mountain, knees sinking in wet earth. She'd never catch up with him again.

Gage took a breath, holding it deep in his lungs. Cole and Hael had waited with him for hours that day until he'd been able to stand. He clenched his fists, focusing on what was in front of him now. Ishta waited in the hallway. Harper had called ahead to speed the process along. The human police had been cooperative for once, delivering the bodies straight to the Enclave. Gage assumed Harper's Detective friend had something to do with it. Not that it mattered if they got the bodies back to the family faster. It wouldn't make the grief any easier.

It would get Ishta out of Chicago quicker though. Gage had been fond of Valarie and Thorn. He loved his brother more though, and Ishta being here would only push Hael towards an emotional edge it'd be better he didn't fall over.

Ishta refused to acknowledge his presence. She spoke quietly to Kazimir. At least it was Carellen who greeted them. He nodded briefly to Gage. As the registered family Watcher in Chicago, Gage needed to be the one to sign the release forms. Carellen offered no useless words of condolence. He smiled kindly at Ishta, briefly placing a hand on her shoulder and bowing his head. It was respectful in a way Gage expected from the older Watcher.

Kazimir and Ishta went in to identify the bodies. They'd be cremated here, and Ishta would take the ashes back to Los Angeles. Gage waited outside.

Carellen cleared his throat. 'I asked Harper not to get involved in the cases you assigned to her.'

Gage wasn't surprised. 'I'd have done the same.'

'She's too stubborn for her own good.'

Gage smiled. 'I know what that's like.'

'Your brother?'

Gage looked across at Carellen, sliding automatically into defensive mode. The man looked back at him openly though. 'Harper tell you that?'

Carellen shifted his weight. 'She might have mentioned something.'

'My brother isn't the only stubborn ass I have the misfortune of caring about.'

Carellen nodded. 'We all have people in our lives we care about, family, friends. Sometimes we do stupid things to keep them safe.'

Wasn't that the truth. 'Is that why you protected Harper, after her father died?'

Carellen eyed him, before smiling ruefully. 'Of course, you'd know about that.'

'She doesn't though, does she?'

Carellen paused before answering. 'No.'

Gage looked away and shrugged. 'Probably for the best.'

Carellen stepped closer to Gage. 'I don't care who Hael is, but others will.' He waited until Gage nodded. 'I received word this morning someone is offering a bounty for any Aesir. A very big bounty. I don't know who it is, but someone is coming for your family.'

Gage looked at Carellen. He was one of the few Watchers Gage respected. He trusted Carellen would only pass on information like this if he thought it accurate. Gage didn't say anything, just nodded as his father and Ishta returned.

'I'd say don't do anything stupid, but I hate wasting my breathe.' Carellen walked off, collecting Kazimir and Ishta and leading them away.

As Gage followed them, his father dropped back to walk with him. He looked weary, but like grief was something he was used to.

'Ishta will return home as soon as they process the paperwork.'

Gage nodded. Apparently not doing a good enough job of hiding his relief.

Kazimir smiled tiredly. 'I know. She'd only cause Hael more grief if she stayed.' He glanced across at Gage. 'How are you doing?'

Gage felt shitty the question surprised him. It wasn't that his father didn't love him. They just had a complicated history. 'I'm okay.'

Kazimir studied him for a moment, looking like he didn't believe him. 'I wasn't sure Hael did the right thing, letting you become the Watcher after...after Ara.'

Gage shrugged. 'Maybe he didn't.'

'I think he did. Sometimes, having something to focus on,

even if its rage, helps. I knew Hael and Cole would try to keep you from doing anything too reckless. And now, I think being a Watcher suits you.'

Gage laughed bitterly. He wasn't so sure about that. He hadn't exactly been making great decisions for a while now.

Kazimir sighed. 'I experienced the first death of a child over eighteen hundred years ago. It nearly destroyed me, and I still carry that pain with me. Don't be too hard on yourself for needing to grieve in your own way.'

Gage looked across at his father. This ancient man who he'd never really known. Hadn't let himself know, if he was being honest. He swallowed around the lump in his throat and nodded. He was quiet a moment. 'You should talk to Cole while you're here.'

Kazimir looked at him questioningly.

Gage hesitated, but Kazimir had always been fond of Cole. 'I don't think he's been doing too great.'

Kazimir nodded. 'I will. I still remember him as a teenager raging at the world.'

'I sometimes forget you knew him as a boy.' Gage looked down. 'These last few years...I think I messed up with him more than anyone.'

Kazimir smiled. 'I swear, Cole is one third Hael, one third Wrathe, and a third pure natural chaos. Somewhere in there he still fits a heart bigger than the Pacific.'

Gage couldn't help smiling. Chaos and heart, he'd never heard a more apt assessment of who Cole was. He looked down, debating whether to ask. 'Were you there?'

'When?'

Gage looked up at his father. 'When he became...our Cole.'

'Oh.' Kazimir walked in silence for a moment. 'No. I wasn't. And I never asked because I didn't want Hael to have to lie to me.'

'What do you mean?'

Kazimir stopped walking, letting Carellen and Ishta draw further ahead until they were alone before he answered. 'There are only two things Hael's ever truly chosen for himself. Loving Wrathe when he should have killed him. And raising Cole as his son. Everything else he's ever done has been for this family. Cole is over 370 years old. I'm not sure I even know the extent of his powers. However that happened, it's one of the few things Hael has ever felt he couldn't tell me.'

Kazimir paused looking down the empty corridor. He looked back at Gage, eyes serious. 'I have always trusted his judgement in the secrets he keeps. This is one you shouldn't try to uncover.'

Gage studied his father's expression. 'You know, don't you? He never told you, but somehow you know.'

Kazimir stilled, expression resolute. 'No...I have my suspicions, but I will never share them with anyone. Not even you son. I'm sorry.' Kazimir's expression softened. 'Hael made a choice a long time ago. I'll do anything I have to so Hael can keep that secret.'

Gage nodded, not sure Kazimir was still talking about the choice to blood Cole. 'Okay.'

Kazimir studied him a moment, satisfied by whatever he saw. 'Hael was right to make you our Watcher here in Chicago. And he was right two hundred years ago when he told me to let him take you and your mother back to Europe. I'm sorry I didn't listen to him. I was selfish and wanted to know you, my son. But trying to keep you close...I failed you and I failed your mother. I don't know if I can atone for that.'

Gage didn't know what to say as he stared at his father. He had held a grudge for a long time over his mother's unhappiness. He eventually formed a relationship with his father, though one built more on respect than love. Maybe it was time to let go of the past.

Gage looked down. He couldn't quite say I forgive you. But he could offer understanding. 'We all make mistakes.'

Kazimir smiled, a sad thing full of regrets. He reached out and squeezed Gage's shoulder, before turning and walking down the hall to find Ishta and Carellen. Gage took a deep breath and followed him.

***

27

~ COLE ~

LONDON, 9TH NOVEMBER 1690

Cole flattened his back against the rough bricks in the narrow alley. He sucked in a few deep breaths, before evening his breathing out, cocking his head slightly as he listened. He could hear the men following him. They weren't far behind. He looked along the alley, out the opening at the far end he saw the silhouette of the Enclave wall against the darkening evening sky.

He'd almost made it back.

Two figures stood on top of the wall. One crouching, head turning, looking. Looking for him. Cole could tell it was Wrathe, Hael standing by his side, waiting.

It wasn't far. He'd make it before those pursuing him could

corner him. But they wouldn't let the walls of the Enclave stop them. If he made it to safety, he would lead them straight to Hael and Wrathe.

Not an option.

Think damn it. He had to lose them. He had no other option. Lose them, get a message to Hael, then get out of the city and find somewhere safe to figure out their next move, because the men chasing him had an advantage. They knew Cole, knew his face and that he could lead them to the Aesir family.

Cole laughed. If he made it through this, Hael would kill him. He had gone back to look for his ring. It had been stupid. The men following him had found him poking around the sewers. He'd barley gotten out but hadn't been able to lose them.

Cole spared one last look toward Hael and Wrathe, and the safety of the Enclave. The two men would have no trouble killing those following Cole, but if they did, it'd draw attention. Whatever cult this was, they'd been chasing rumours about powerful members of the Aesir family. Cole wouldn't lead them to what they were looking for. He turned away from safety. Staying out of sight of the two men on the wall, he ran, back towards those chasing him.

This was not going to be fun.

Cole moved out of the alley, feet pounding along the cobblestones. He ran straight, making sure his pursuers saw him, before ducking left into an alley, angling away from the Enclave. There was loud cursing as he caught them off guard. He couldn't help grinning. He wouldn't be the dog they sent running to flush the grouse. Hael always said he got far too much pleasure doing the opposite of what was expected, in being unpredictable. Cole wasn't entirely sure Hael meant it as an insult or not. There was a fine line between genius tactician and obstinate stupidity.

Cole didn't waste time being discreet once he was out of Hael and Wrathe's sight. He ran, top speed, dodging the few people out on the streets, startling a horse and sending it skittering, its rider yelling at him. Cole didn't look back, putting as much distance as possible between him and the Enclave. Neither Hael nor Wrathe would wait long to come looking for him. He'd have to lose them as much as the men chasing him for this to work.

It was fully dark as Cole ducked into yet another alley. He slammed into the solid body of a man. One he had seen at least three times in the last hour. The man didn't hesitate, getting a solid punch to Cole's ribs. Cole twisted with the blow. Using his momentum to grab hold and pull the man to the pavement. Cole was nimbler, back on his feet quickly he aimed a kick to the man's head. He didn't wait to see if he got back up. Two more men and a woman came towards him. He moved, using the wall to push off and land a blow to the side of the nearest head. Twisting, he kicked out, hitting the next in the ribs. He landed and rolled, taking out the legs from the third. He kept moving, more intent on putting distance between himself and the attackers then putting them down. They wouldn't be the only ones, he needed to avoid rather than fight.

It worked for a while. Cole led them on a cat and mouse chase through the streets of London for an hour. He was well away from the Enclave now but wasn't making any headway.

There were too many of them. He lost a few, only to run into a couple more. Hael had been right to be worried about this cult. They were organised, and more than just a few fanatics obsessed with one of the older Erinyes families. They had purpose. Cole had no idea what it was, but they definitely had a purpose, and not one likely to be good for his family.

They finally cornered Cole in a random dead-end alley in Cheapside. Cole had gotten turned around, the memory of the twist and turns of the streets of his youth mismatching the rebuilt city. He spun and faced them, breathing hard. Taking down two more, he grinned even though he was dead on his feet and knew he was done. He hadn't made it easy on them at least. A hit connected, knocking Cole out.

***

Candlelight flickered. Cole blinked, vision swimming as he fought his way back to consciousness. He wished he hadn't bothered when he went to shift his hand, only to realise he couldn't. He was tied to a table. He couldn't move. Staring up at the dirty ceiling, he forced his breathing to slow even as panic clawed at his throat and ran riot under his skin, demanding he move. The panic feeding itself in a viscous loop when he couldn't.

Cole closed his eyes. Breathed out through his nose. His heartbeat settling as he listened, trying to map out the room by sound. He wasn't alone, and the person moving about him was clearly aware he'd woken but said nothing. The room was small, cool, damp. Probably underground. Once he had the panic firmly under control, Cole opened his eyes.

A man stopped what he was doing, coming to stand over Cole. He was stocky, had dark hair, eyes dead, expression completely disinterested, like Cole was barely worth his time. The man said nothing, just stared at Cole, waiting. Cole shifted his head. He saw rows of knives laid out on a table. Well, shit, this really wasn't going to be fun.

Cole let his head fall to the side and saw there was someone else in the room. Another man sat quietly in a chair in the corner. He was older, well dressed. A book lay open in his lap, he held a pen loosely in his fingers as he studied Cole.

Cole raised an eyebrow in question, unable to help himself. 'Well, should we get started?'

The man smiled, almost congenially. It was creepy. 'Okay, let's start with a name first?'

Cole looked back at the ceiling. 'Bob.'

The stocky man next to him picked up a knife and ran the blade along the soft skin of Cole's inner forearm. He was careful. The cut not deep enough to do any serious damage. More a warning than anything.

The man in the corner shifted in his seat. 'Are you human?'

Cole breathed out. 'No, I'm a marmoset.'

Another slice.

'Are you a member of the Aesir family?'

'Nope, orphan boy.'

Slice.

'Why were you following us?'

'I was lost.'

Slice.

'Why were you following us?'

Slice. Slice. Slice.

The man with the knife looked across to the man asking the questions. He set the knife down, picked up another one. This time he didn't slice, he peeled. Cole didn't bother trying to hold back the scream. Didn't fight it when it dissolved into manic laughter. He held no illusions. This would not end well.

The man in the corner spoke quietly, and the slicing stopped. The man cutting stepped away. Cole breathed in through his nose, out. He smelt his own blood, felt it dripping from his arm.

The man in the corner cleared his throat. 'Do you know who we are?'

Cole closed his eyes a moment, before letting his head fall to the side and looking at the man. 'Not really.'

The man watched him. 'Do you know who the Aesir are?'

Cole didn't answer.

'You're human. Or at least you were, before you let them taint you.'

Cole smiled at him. It wasn't a very nice smile, though it didn't seem to bother the man.

'I suspect you think you know who they are. The pretty story they tell. But do you actually know them?'

Cole refused to look away. He doubted anyone knew Hael or Wrathe's full story. But he knew enough. He'd spent twenty-four years with them. He had met a lot of the Aesir as well as Kazimir, the father of them all. Spent countless hours lying in the sun watching their children swim in the Mediterranean Sea, listening to the sounds of their innocent laughter, teasing them, carrying them home when they fell asleep exhausted. He knew the Aesir in ways this man never would and had no intention of sharing any of it.

'There are many stories about the Aesir. Carefully curated ones. It's the forgotten ones, the hidden ones that I'm interested in.' The man paused, tapping his pen against the book. 'You let them give you their blood. Do you even know what the Erinyes are?'

'They're not that different to us.'

'Oh, but they are. Do you know how the first Erinyes came to be? And I don't mean the fairy tale version.'

The fairy tale version told a story about the Aion who came to earth and brought a war with them, that they rained down blood on the humans which changed some forever. 'Which version do you mean then?'

The man leaned forward. 'The true one.'

Cole raised an eyebrow, curious despite himself. 'Who's truth?'

The man smiled. 'So, you're not completely stupid.'

Cole stared at him. 'There are as many truths in this world as there are people.'

'Perhaps. But maybe there is enough shared truth in some stories. The Erinyes didn't come into existence by accident, by bathing in the blood that rained down from battles raging in the skies. They had no choice at all. The Aion fought their endless war. One side wanted an advantage, so they perverted humanity, found a way to turn them into monsters, into a slave army to fight for them.'

The man paused, watching for any reaction from Cole. Cole tried not to give him anything. He turned his head, looking back up at the ceiling.

'When the Aion came, they were nearly the end of us all. Some called them gods. But they weren't. They were monsters, devils in beautiful disguises who slaughtered us by the thousands. They didn't care. I'm not sure they were even capable of caring. The things they turned those first helpless humans into cared just as little. The first cursed generation of Erinyes, monsters who lay with the beasts that created them and birthed even greater abominations. The Furiae. They're long gone of course, so I'm not surprised you don't know the story. We're just left with the Erinyes and their bastard offspring.'

Cole gritted his teeth, keeping his expression carefully blank, because he did know this story. He just had no idea how a human knew so much when history had mostly forgotten it. Cole heard it once from someone who'd actually been there. Furiae wasn't a name many knew. They were the offspring of an Erinyes and Aion. Few survived, but despite what this man thought, they weren't all gone.

'Do you think the Aion gave those first humans a choice?' The man continued. 'Did they ask if they wanted to fight in a war that had nothing to do with them. To die?'

Cole laughed. 'People who wage wars rarely offer much choice to those dying for them.'

The man leaned forward. 'You said you didn't know who we were. But we know who you are.'

'I doubt it.'

The man smiled. 'I would think, someone who was a child slave himself, forced to fight, would have issues with the creation of an entire race of slave warriors.'

Cole couldn't help reacting to the words, his heart rate picking up as it felt like his blood turned to a slurry of ice in his veins, slow, thick and suffocating. How the hell could he know that?

'Tell me, how old were you? Eight, nine?'

Cole swallowed thickly. 'No idea what you're talking about.'

The man hummed to himself, smiling knowingly. 'Yes, you do. How young do you think the humans the Aion took were? Did they take any children? Do you think they wanted to fight in a war they couldn't possibly understand?'

Cole shook his head, lips pressed tight together.

The man sighed. 'When the Aion first made themselves known to us, how could we do anything else but think them miracles?' He leaned forward, looking at Cole intently. 'They were not a miracle. They were a curse. They slaughtered their own kind in such numbers we still tell stories about blood raining down from the skies. What did they care about humanity? They turned our cities to ash. Have you seen the Shadows of Megara?'

Cole let out a breath that shook. He nodded. 'Once.'

'I was a young man when I saw the Shadows. Do you know the story?'

Cole licked his lips. 'The Aion destroyed part of the city. I don't remember when. People say the Aion burnt so hot as they fought, nothing but shadows of the people they killed were left behind.'

The man nodded. 'The first time I saw those shadows, all that was left of the humans who got in the Aion's way, I felt fear, deep in my bones. Then I felt relieved that the Aion no longer walked this earth. But we are still dealing with what they left behind. There is another story I wonder if you know. Have you ever been to Constantinople?'

Cole nodded. They stayed there once. They didn't stay long. Something about the city made Hael sad.

'They have their own story of destruction. The destruction caused by Erinyes. There was a revolt in Constantinople in the year 532. Erinyes destroyed half the city. The stories say it was a garrison of Erinyes. But the stories are wrong. It wasn't a garrison, it wasn't a hundred Erinyes, it wasn't even a dozen. It was two. Just two, and they destroyed half the city.'

Cole turned his head, studying the man. His words pushing against a memory of watching the sun set over Constantinople a few years ago, the way Hael had looked out to the north of the city. His shoulders tense, expression unusually melancholic. They had left the city the next morning.

'Can you imagine, the kind of power that could destroy cities, burn them to the ground, leave nothing but ashes and shadows on the wall?' The man looked at Cole, eyes hard and cold. 'That sort of power does not belong in this world.'

The man with the knives was back. He moved to Cole's chest, slicing, long even strokes.

The man in the corner sat back in his chair, opening his book once again. 'You will help me find the Aesir, and we will purge them from this world.'

Slice. Slice. Slice.

Cole let the pain find release in his screams. These people thought they knew him, but they didn't. He needed them to underestimate him. He needed to bide his time, wait for them to unbind him. They wouldn't do that until they believed they'd broken him. He just had to hold on long enough.

***

28

~ HARPER ~

Cole offered Harper a lift, but she took a taxi instead. The address Jacobs gave her wasn't far outside the Enclave. Harper tapped on Jacob's car window, before opening the door and getting in. Jacobs pointed down the street at the van used to dump Yuri's body. It was parked in a driveway of one of the abandoned buildings. It hadn't taken Jacobs long to find it.

Jacobs fidgeted with her coffee cup. 'I'm sorry about earlier.'

Harper scratched at an imaginary itch on her knee. 'It's fine.'

'It's not. It's bullshit.'

Harper leant her head back against the seat rest, looking out the windscreen at the unmoving van. It was what it was. The same bullshit she'd heard from countless cops and detectives, hell even some Watchers for years. Too few people gave a shit about a dead Erinyes, unless they were from a powerful family. If someone hadn't started targeting the Aesir family, would anyone care about people like Arty, and Yuri?

'Who was that man at the crime scene?' Jacobs asked.

Harper shrugged. 'I met him a few days ago. Those kids were his niece and nephew I think.'

'You think?'

Harper sighed. She couldn't complain about the world being full of arseholes, if she was one herself. She replayed the conversation with Gage. 'Uncle, definitely.'

'Shit. And you let him see them like that. Pretty cold Harper.'

'He can handle it.'

Maybe. She wasn't as convinced of that as she'd been earlier. Harper ran a hand over her forearm, chasing the memory of heat from Hael's emotional outburst. It had been visceral, so real and nothing like anything she'd felt before.

'He's an information broker of sorts. I'm hoping he can help find who's doing this.'

'Okay. It's your case. I'm just along for the ride at this point.'

Harper looked across at the Detective. 'You're officially off the case.'

Jacobs smiled ruefully. 'Yelling at the Captain apparently isn't an effective tactic for getting back on a case.'

'Feels good though, doesn't it?'

Jacobs grinned. 'Damn right.'

No one came near the van. It got darker as they waited, a light eventually turning on in the building. Someone was around.

Jacobs finished her coffee, setting the empty cup in the

centre console. 'You really don't know anything about these Decedents?'

'Not really.' Harper tapped her fingers on her thigh, remembering the comment from Kazimir. 'You were right, there might be something more to them though.'

'Your information broker know something?'

'Maybe.'

'I wasted my question on them the other day.'

Harper smiled. 'You really did.'

Jacobs rolled her head to look at Harper. 'Do over?'

There was nothing better to do while they waited. 'Why not.'

Jacob stared at her for a moment. 'I know this might be a touchy question. But why do the Erinyes put so much value on families?'

Harper raised an eyebrow. 'Aren't you always preaching the value of forging relationships?'

Jacobs rolled her eyes. 'You know what I mean. I get families. I sometimes want to kill my brother, yet I'd break the arms of anyone who messed with him. But I get the impression it's something more with the Erinyes.'

Harper stretched her legs. 'I don't know.' She looked out into the night. 'My kind were almost wiped out at the end of the Aionic wars. Looking out for our own increased our odds of surviving.'

Jacobs didn't say anything, just nodded.

'We live long lives, and those bonds become even stronger over time. The families grew so large they could ensure their own safety. They formed safe havens, the first Enclaves, and created the Council to formalise alliances between families.'

'So, the Council has always been controlled by the powerful families.'

Harper nodded. 'They created the Watchers to ensure internal family conflict didn't endanger the Enclaves and unaligned Watchers to protect the interests of anyone from families fragmented in human conflicts.'

'So not that different from us humans, except you live longer?'

'More or less.' Harper stared out into the dark. 'The unaligned Watchers do what they can, but the system makes it easy for those who don't have much family to fall through the cracks.'

'Like the victims in the cases you take?' Jacobs looked across at Harper. 'The ones even the unaligned Watcher don't want?'

'There's no justice without someone protecting those who have no one to watch their back.' Harper shrugged. 'That's something my father always said.'

Jacobs huffed a small laugh. 'I'm guessing you're a lot like him.'

Harper wasn't so sure about that. Her father had more trust and belief in people than she did. If she had emphatic abilities like the rest of her kind, would that have made a difference?

Harper chewed on her lip, remembering fragments of stories her father told her as a child. 'You know most Erinyes are empathic.'

Jacobs watched her. 'Yeah. I work with plenty of fools who think you're in their heads, making them do things they don't want to do.'

Harper laughed. 'Most Erinyes think I might as well be human, for how limited I am.'

'Gee, thanks.'

'Humans don't have a monopoly on arrogance. Erinyes can't control people or make them do something they don't want to. That's a myth created by fear.' Harper remembered the way Hael influenced her into telling the truth the day they met. 'A few can influence through suggestion. Inspiring you to want to tell the truth, or at least knowing when you're lying. We're empathic, not telepathic. I'm not sure I understand it myself, best I can explain it, is it's like trying to lie to a parent. You can still do it, but it's harder and they're more likely to see through the lie.'

Jacobs watched her, thoughtful. 'Makes sense I suppose.'

Harper thought of how Hael's reaction to the death of his niece and nephew tricked her mind into feeling volcanic heat that didn't exist. His emotion had overflowed and washed over everyone around him. She'd heard stories of powerful Erinyes who could freeze or burn with a touch. She'd always dismissed them. But now, she wondered what Hael was capable of if he controlled and focused that emotion. Or what would happen if he ever truly lost control. There was truth to some of the stories she'd once dismissed. What other myths might be true?

Harper shifted in her seat. 'My father told me stories about the Aion when I was a kid. How they drew strength from each other. Not figuratively, literally. An empathic connection to each other that amplified their powers. No one knows if the stories are true or not. But my father sometimes wondered if that's why we hold so tightly to our family bonds.'

Jacobs watched Harper. 'What do you think?'

'That even if it's true, none of the Aion are left, so what does it matter?' She spotted movement. 'Look.'

A man exited the building. He looked around, before getting into the van. Jacobs glanced across at her, Harper nodded. It was their only lead, they had to follow.

Jacobs kept well back. It was hard not to be spotted in such a deserted area. The man didn't seem to be in a hurry, twisting through the quiet streets. It took her a while to realise where he was heading.

'Shit. Pull back.'

Jacobs glanced across at her. 'What?'

Up ahead the vague outline of Enclave wall loomed in the night. 'He's heading into the Enclave.'

Jacobs slowed down. 'We can still follow him.'

'You have no jurisdiction in there. Neither do I.'

'Didn't you say you knew the Watcher for the family of the dead kids?'

Harper hesitated, unused to calling anyone for backup. She pulled her phone out. 'Follow him.'

Cole gave her his number before she left Aeternus earlier. He didn't answer, so she sent him a quick text. Hopefully he'd let Gage know. Even if they found anything, without a Watcher they couldn't officially do anything inside the Enclave walls. Hell, just bringing a human cop inside the walls would cause enough trouble with the Council.

The van entered the Enclave. They followed until it parked in an alley outside another abandoned warehouse. Jacobs parked on the street, and they watched the man get out and enter the warehouse. Harper checked her phone, but there was no response from Cole.

Jacobs looked across at her. 'What do you want to do?'

Harper chewed on her lip as she looked around. The area seemed abandoned. They weren't all that far from Hael's club, a few blocks maybe. The buildings here hadn't been converted into trendy lofts though, just left to crumble.

She sent another text to Cole with the address of the warehouse. 'Let's see what's inside.'

'Is that a good idea?'

'Probably not.'

Jacobs shook her head, smiling ruefully. 'And my boss kicked me off the case for failing to sign you into a crime scene.' She checked her gun before they got out of the car. She paused, lifting it up. 'Can I even use this in here?'

Harper shrugged. 'No. If that'll stop you from pulling it, you might want to stay in the car.'

Jacobs re-holstered her side arm, keeping it unclipped and ready to pull if she needed it. Harper wasn't permitted to carry a weapon outside the Enclave, she didn't let it stop her from carrying the two knives she always wore strapped to her back, easier to conceal beneath her jacket than a gun. They were more useful for close quarter combat, and she was better with them then a gun. Jacobs pulled out a couple of flashlights, tossing one to Harper.

They made their way down the alley. Harper took the lead. The area was poorly lit, so she moved slowly until they reached a dumpster that provided cover. She tilted her head, closing her eyes. The man they followed was an Erinyes. She sensed him like fingers creeping across the back of her neck, slick, sweet, trying to find a way beneath her skin. She breathed in and out, settling into the sensation to pinpoint his location. Usually, she avoided doing this, letting the impression trickle across her senses to feel out the shape of them. It made her sick, like she was losing herself, being pushed down and down beneath the earth, covered with dirt until she couldn't breathe, couldn't feel the edges of her own mind, only theirs.

Jacobs shifted behind her. Harper breathed out through her nose, opening her eyes. He was close. She saw a dim light coming through a doorway ahead.

'He's Erinyes. Stay behind me.'

Jacobs nodded.

Harper edged closer to the door. Jacobs reached out to touch her arm, and Harper stopped. She heard it too. Quiet voices. It sounded like two men. She only sensed one Erinyes. The other must be human.

Harper pressed herself against the wall, resisting the urge to look around the doorframe. She could just make out the words of one of the men. He spoke louder, the other's voice only a quiet murmur.

'She's getting too close.'

...

'This obsession of yours will get you killed.'

He sounded exasperated, like this was an argument they'd had before.

'You really going to keep arguing this when she's standing right outside?'

Harper drew in a sharp breath. She pulled a knife as she moved, letting her body flow around the door. One man turned towards her, the other only a shape in the darkness. She let the knife loose, watching it turn end over end toward the man facing her, who smiled and took flight. So much for the element of surprise. Jacobs was right behind her, following Harper's lead. She pulled her gun out but didn't fire. The man in the dark backed away, disappearing into the shadows.

With no idea where the Erinyes had gone, Harper followed the human. He moved deeper into the warehouse complex, clearly familiar with it as he moved fast. Jacobs pulled out a flashlight, lighting the way. Harper stayed in the lead, using the sounds of the man's footsteps as much as the light to guide her. They were gaining on him.

Harper turned a corner. Something moved in her periphery. Before she could turn to see what, a body slammed into hers. The attack knocked the breath from her. She pulled her other knife, slicing, but only catching air. The Erinyes disappeared again before she regained her balance. Jacobs got her attention, waving a hand to the left in the direction the human had gone.

Harper shook her head. 'No. Get out of here. I'll draw the Erinyes' attention.'

Jacobs paused, clearly wanting to continue, before yielding to Harpers judgement. The Detective turned back the way they'd come. Harper took a deep breath and pulled out her own flashlight. She continued following the human, hoping to keep the Erinyes' attention away from Jacobs until she could lose him.

The footsteps ahead of her stopped. Harper slowed. She saw a silhouette in front of her. The human wore a long coat, but she couldn't make out any other details. He stood in a doorway facing away from her. She wasn't sure why he stopped. He didn't turn around, but shifted his head a little to one side, not quite looking at her.

Alert for the Erinyes, Harper moved closer. 'Stop...'

The man lifted a finger to his lips. 'Shh.'

Harper hesitated. He dropped his hand and disappeared. She stared at the spot where he'd been standing in confusion. She'd been sure he was human. He'd felt human, there had been no trickle of sensation from him at all. Harper shook her head, trying to shake away the unease drifting in the utter nothingness left in the man's wake. If the attackers were both Erinyes, why hadn't they just flown as soon as they realised they'd been followed?

They hadn't taken flight though. They'd drawn Harper deeper into the warehouse complex. Shit, it was a trap, and she'd just walked right into it.

Harper turned, about to call out and warn Jacobs. She didn't even feel the hit. Just the sudden sensation of weightlessness as her legs crumpled beneath her. Gentle hands caught her, guiding her down to the floor.

Somewhere in the warehouse, she heard Jacobs.

'Harper? Harper, where are you?'

Harper tried to tell her to run, but it came out barely a whisper, before everything drifted away into blackness.

**

29

~ GAGE ~

Gage and Kazimir found Hael alone in the kitchen when they returned. Kazimir had convinced Ishta to return home. Gage wasn't sure she'd stay away. She was angry and needed someone to take it out on. He hoped making the arrangements for Valarie and Thorn would keep her busy and away from Chicago.

Kazimir grabbed three glasses from the cupboard and a bottle of whisky. He sat across from Hael, pouring three drinks. He pushed one wordlessly in Gage's direction, glancing up when he didn't sit. Gage shifted, full of energy that demanded release. At least the urge to scream himself hoarse had dissipated. Gage shoved the restlessness aside and sat next to his brother.

Kazimir took a mouthful of whisky. He swirled the liquid in the glass, watching it listlessly. 'I wish I could say it gets easier.'

Hael stared out the window, his drink untouched. 'If it got easier, we'd be the monsters they all think we are.'

The words rested heavy in Gage's gut. He had spent the last five years waiting for it to get easier, for the hollow spaces inside to fill with something other than anger. The loss of Ara was too great even now to feel more than a twinge at the death of the two young Aesir. His niece and nephew. Gods, Ara had adored children, and was particularly fond of Val and Throne. He'd almost forgotten that. Gage picked up the whisky and swallowed it down, barely tasting it. Was he becoming a monster? Someone who felt nothing. Had he really retreated that far into his grief. He reached a hand up, feeling the outline of the photo Harper had given him earlier in his jacket pocket. Ara had always delighted in making everyone around her laugh.

'Ara adored Thorn and Val when they were kids.' His voice was scratchy, but he continued. 'You remember that time they ran away, turned up on the doorstep here wet and freezing but so determined. Ara let them in. Made them hot chocolate. Promised them she wouldn't call their parents until morning so that they could stay long enough to see you, Hael.'

Hael smiled weakly. 'I remember.'

Kazimir smiled too. 'Ara rang me that night to let me know they were okay, but it was too late for them to come home.' He took a sip of whisky. 'Ara must have still been a teen herself at the time.'

She'd been maybe seventeen. They didn't see much of Thorn and Valerie until they were adults. Ishta kept her family away from Hael. How the two young children had found their way to Chicago was a mystery. He just remembered coming into the kitchen to see Ara making them giggle uncontrollably. Even Kazimir had barely seen many of his grandchildren with Ishta at the time. Kazimir had been trying for decades, centuries, to mend the rift, to no avail. He had a new family now. Gage had two young sisters he didn't know. They'd been born after Ara's death. He never even made the effort to meet them.

Kazimir looked across at Gage. 'I've lost too many children. Sometimes, it's hard not to lose yourself with them.'

The thread of emotion Kazimir pushed towards Gage was complicated but filled with understanding. Gage let himself drift in the comfort of it for a moment as Kazimir and Hael drank quietly. They'd slipped back from the father and son dynamic earlier to something different, to equals who had seen too much. Old soldiers in a war without end. In moments like these they felt unknowable. The father that kept his distance and the brother who kept Gage close enough to protect, but always that little bit separate, like Hael was something that belonged to the shadows and everyone else the light.

Hael had hardly spoken since their return. His brother had been off kilter since he came back from the scene of Valerie and Thorn's murder. He'd seen something he was refusing to talk about, and it had rattled him more than the deaths.

Gage's fingers itched, needing something to do. He thought about pulling his phone out to see where the hell Cole was, but before he could, Cole walked in, looking agitated.

'I missed a text from Harper. I think she's in trouble.'

***

Gage was grateful for the coat he'd grabbed hastily, the cold night air shifting around him as he and Hael landed. The address Harper had texted to Cole was for a warehouse. It wasn't far from Aeternus, but the area was deserted, decrepit and would probably be torn down soon. Hael gestured towards a car parked near the warehouse, and they moved closer. It was empty, but there were no other cars around, it had to be the detective's. It'd only been half an hour since Harper sent the message. Clearly, she hadn't waited for them.

Hael studied the building a moment before turning to Gage. 'Do you want to wait?'

Cole and Kazimir were following in the car. They should only be a few minutes behind. That might be a few minutes too late. 'No.'

Hael nodded and headed towards the entrance of the building. It was open. Gage took his phone out and used it as a flashlight. They searched quickly, going from room to room.

They found the Detective first.

Blood gleamed in the light from Gage's phone. Detective Jacobs sat slumped on the floor, back leaning against the wall. Her arms outstretched, steel rods driven through her wrists. Gage froze. Breathe catching. Throat tight. He saw a slit throat mocking him with its rigorous grin, beautiful dark hair turned red. The cheeky glint gone from her eyes, fingers hung limp instead of tapping to a beat only she could hear. His baby girl strung up like nothing more than meat, someone's macabre canvas, a plaything. It felt like his ribs were pushing inwards, clamping around his lungs. He dropped his phone.

Hael pushed past him, not hesitating as he fell to his

knees beside the Detective. His fingers went to her neck. 'She's alive.'

The Detective groaned as Hael tilted her head. Her eyes opened but they looked glazed in the dim light from his phone where it lay on the floor. She'd lost a lot of blood.

Gage tried to clear the fog in his head, forcing a deep breath into his lungs and his feet to move. He'd barely taken a step when he felt something bite his neck. Lifting his hand to swat at it, he found something sticking out of his neck. He pulled it out, and he stared down at it. A tranquilliser dart slipped through his numb fingers and fell to the floor.

What the hell?

Tranquillisers shouldn't work against an Erinyes. They metabolised most poisons too quickly. But he could feel it. His hands were cold and felt far away, his vision blacking out at the edges.

'Hael...'

He didn't get a chance to finish the warning, a dart striking Hael's chest. Hael looked down pulling it out and tossing it aside. He looked past Gage. There were three men in the hallway. One held a tranquilliser gun. The others had handguns. Hael shifted into flight, landing between them, he elbowed one in the head. Another dart was fired, this time into Hael's neck, a third into his upper arm. One of the other men fired, a bullet hitting Hael in the thigh.

Hael staggered a little. The three attackers took the opportunity to put space between themselves and Hael. One landed behind Gage and grabbed him in a choke hold. He needed have bothered. Gage's knees buckled, whatever was in those fucking darts was powerful. He blinked slowly, the world fading to black and slowly bleeding back in as he reopened his eyes groggily. He watched Hael fight one of the men, but his brother's movement were slower than usual. Another dart impacted Hael's upper back and he staggered. That was all Gage saw. His knees finally gave out, and he wasn't even aware of hitting the floor.

***

30

~ HARPER ~

Harper groaned, lifting her fingers to her temple. They came away wet and tacky. She stared at them, and it took longer than it should to realise it was too dark to see the blood. She frowned, trying to force her way through the haze. Someone had hit her. They came out of the dark. The warehouse...Jacobs.

Pain spiked above her left eye as she sat up too quickly. She fumbled around searching for the flashlight, eyes straining in the murky darkness for any danger. It was quiet. She was lying exactly where she'd fallen. Once again, whoever attacked her, hadn't been interested in finishing the job. Maybe they were interrupted? She couldn't even convince herself the attacker had been somehow foiled while she lay unconscious. The words she overheard when they entered the warehouse came back to her. One man accused the other of being obsessed.

Even if that obsession had kept her from serious harm twice now, it wasn't in any way a comforting thought.

There was a noise down the hallway, and she felt someone coming toward her. She tensed briefly, before recognising them just as the beam of a flashlight fell on her, the bright light making her wince.

Cole knelt next to her. 'Harper?'

She looked up as Kazimir appeared behind Cole. 'We were ambushed. Jacobs, did you find her?'

Cole shook his head, expression tight. 'No. We only just got here.'

She looked around, head protesting at the movement. 'Someone knocked me out. How long has it been?'

'Not long. Hael and Gage flew ahead. They should have been here.'

Gritting her teeth, Harper stood, Cole reaching out to steady her when she wavered. She tried to orientate herself once she had her balance. Jacobs had split off from her back down the hallway. 'This way.'

Harper backtracked, leading them toward the room where they first entered. She closed her eyes briefly, taking a steadying breath against a wave a nausea as the hallway swayed in front of her. Maybe she'd been hit in the head harder than she thought. She took another deep breath, holding it a second until everything settled back in place.

'Jacobs and I split up.' She pointed through a doorway. 'She went this way.'

It didn't take them long to find her.

Harper noticed the blood first. There was a lot of it. Bright red, drying to black. No sigils, but words this time.

Her breath hitched, edging toward panic as her eyes drifted down. Jacobs was propped up against the wall. Her arms were outstretched, held in place by steel rods driven through her wrists.

Harper, still woozy, half fell as she moved towards the Detective. Kazimir caught her, moving them to the side so Cole could enter the room. He knelt to check for a pulse. Harper held her breath.

'She's alive,' Cole said.

Harper's fingers twitched by her side as she stared at the white pallor of the Detective's face, in contrast to the dark red blood smeared over her pale skin. Kazimir let go of Harper and moved to help Cole. He grabbed hold of one of the steel rods, fingers searching around it, checking the Detectives wounds while Cole gently cradled the Detective trying to keep her still.

Kazimir looked across at Cole. 'We've got to get her down.'

'She'll bleed out.'

Looking at the Detective, Kazimir's brows drew tight. He shrugged. 'Maybe not.'

Jacobs had already lost so much blood. Harper shuffled forward, reaching out to brush the hair back from her face. Jacobs' cheek was clammy. 'We have to do something.'

Kazimir looked across at her, before his gaze shifted, caught by something. A phone lay on the floor. He reached over and picked it up, pressing his thumb down to bring up the lock screen. It was a photo of Ara.

'Gage's?' Cole asked.

Kazimir nodded, knuckles white where he gripped the phone tight.

Jacobs moaned, lifting her head slightly. 'They took him. Took both of them.'

The words were a barely audible rasp.

Cole reached out, gently tilting her head as she tried to move. 'Detective, what did you see?'

'They knew we were following them. Wanted to draw the others here.' She looked up at Cole, though she seemed to be having trouble focusing on him. 'The tall one didn't go down easy.'

'They were alive?'

She tried to speak again, but the words were mumbled. Her eyes closed as her head lay heavy in Cole's hands.

'Shh, it's okay,' he whispered. Though Jacobs couldn't hear him, unconscious once again.

Cole looked across at Kazimir 'Kaz, save her.'

Kazimir studied Cole a moment, before nodding his head. Harper stared dumbly for a moment before it registered what Cole was asking. Even if they could get her to a doctor, it would probably be too late. But Jacobs was human, they had another option.

'Will that work?' She asked hesitantly.

Harper knew academically about sharing of Erinyes blood with humans, but she had never seen it done.

Kazimir took out a small knife from a sheath she hadn't noticed before. He glanced up at her. 'When we pull her free, try to stop the bleeding as well as you can.'

Harper nodded, hoping he knew what he was doing.

He took a deep breath, before glancing at Cole and nodding. They grabbed hold of a rod each and pulled them free of her wrists. Harper felt sick at the sound of it, but Jacobs was free. Cole pulled the Detective toward himself, cradling her against his chest, while Harper grabbed hold of both her wrists to put pressure on the wounds as best she could. Kazimir sliced open his hand, cupping it so his blood collected in his palm. He tipped Jacobs' head back gently, holding his cupped hand to her lips.

Harper watched the blood trickle off Kazimir's hand, bright red.

After the first few drops Jacobs stirred. She drew in a loud breath, like her lungs had just figured out how they worked. Her eyes flickered behind her lids, rapid fire, before slowing. The blood oozing between Harper's fingers started to slowly ease. Gods let it be because Kazimir was healing her, and not because she was dying under Harper's hands. Kazimir continued to drip blood into her mouth for what seemed a small eternity, but was probably not even ten minutes, before he swayed a little, and sat back against the wall. Jacobs seemed to sink into Cole's arms as she let out a quiet sigh, the sound almost reverent. They watched her in silence as she took an easy breath, and another.

Kazimir appeared weary. 'It should be enough.'

Jacobs still looked to be on a first name basis with Death. But Harper would trust his judgement. She had no other choice. Erinyes didn't offer their blood randomly to strangers. They could have let the Detective die, and no one would have blamed them. Not even her. Harper swallowed her gratitude, unsure how to express it. Not when they had wasted precious minutes saving her while Hael and Gage were missing. Harper looked back up at the words on the wall, written in Jacobs' blood.

You'll never find them.

Cole shifted, staring out the door, fingers twitching where they held Jacobs, like holding her was the only thing keeping him from bolting out into the dark to look for the others. He had still asked Kazimir to save her though, knowing it would cost them time.

Kazimir stirred. 'You can let go.' He reached over and studied the wounds when Harper let go. 'It should be okay to move her now.'

The bleeding had stopped, and the jagged edges of the wound were showing the first signs of healing. Cole carefully slid out from behind Jacobs and picked her up. They followed as he carried her out to the car. Harper opened the back door, and he settled Jacobs on the seat.

Cole handed the car keys to Kazimir. 'Take her to Aeternus, I'll look around, see if I can find anything.'

Kazimir looked at Cole. 'Be careful.' It seemed like he wanted to say something more but changed his mind.

Cole simply nodded before he turned to Harper. 'You should go with them.'

Harper stepped back from the car, closing the door. She trusted Kazimir would keep Jacobs safe. 'No, I'll help.' Even though it would be futile. She was sure whoever had taken Gage and Hael would be long gone. She thought Cole knew it too. Harper looked around. 'The van's gone, the one we followed here.' She swallowed, a guilty ache wedge between her ribs. 'She said they knew we were following them.'

'Maybe. Maybe they just took advantage of the situation.' Cole glanced across at her. 'It's not your fault. We Aesir have been getting ourselves into trouble for centuries.'

She nodded, not really believing him. The Aesir undoubtedly had a talent for finding trouble, but this time felt like it was because of her impatience.

They searched the building room by room. Her shoulder brushed Cole's as they walked down a hallway. She felt a slight absence beside her that she would have missed it if she wasn't paying attention. It was almost like an empty space where Cole should be, an echo of him but nothing more. She'd never noticed it before and couldn't help but focus on it now. Humans felt like nothing, while Cole felt like an absence of nothing. She'd met Eshari before, and they felt the same as Erinyes only kind of faded, distant.

Her shoulders tensed. 'I can't feel you.'

'What?'

Harper tightened her fingers on the flashlight. 'My abilities are weak, non-existent really. The only thing I'm able to do is sense other Erinyes.'

Cole looked across at her, she couldn't see his expression in the dark but felt his scrutiny anyway.

'Sense them how?'

Harper shrugged. She could never explain it. 'Sensations. Like someone walking over your grave, or warmth like standing out in the sun, a soft wind on bare skin.' She felt him studying her and resisted the urge to fidget. 'It varies for each individual. How old they are, the strength of their abilities.'

Cole was silent as they searched through another room before moving further down the hallway. 'So, you sense more than just emotions?'

She thought he only asked to distract himself as they searched empty room after empty room. It didn't seem to be working, his movements tight with worry. 'I don't sense emotions. At all.' She didn't, not like most Erinyes who were empathic to varying levels. That'd actually be helpful, she'd probably be better at interacting with people if she had some sense of what they were feeling. 'It's different. One of the men that attacked us, the one that knocked me out.' She looked across at Cole. 'I couldn't feel him either.'

Cole paused, shifting his flashlight between them enough to see each other. 'You don't think...'

She shook her head. That probably should have been her first impulse. Before today, there'd been no one her senses failed to identify as Erinyes. She reached out to touch Cole's shoulder. She hadn't for a moment thought he'd been the one to attack her. 'No, I don't.'

Cole looked at her, brow creased, before he shook his head, looking away. 'You felt the other one though, right?'

Harper nodded. 'Yeah.'

'Would you recognise him again?'

'I would. The feeling, it's like hearing someone's voice, everyone's a little bit different.'

Cole nodded, moving again. They searched every room. The further they went the more tense Cole became. It soon became obvious no one else was in the warehouse complex. There was no sign anyone had been here in a long time. It looked like the two men she had followed had picked a random abandoned building to set an ambush. There was nothing to provide any indication what had happened to Gage and Hael or who had taken them. Wordlessly they expanded their search to the laneways, adjoining buildings. There was nothing. Gage and Hael were gone.

Harper hurried to keep up with him as Cole searched down another empty laneway. 'Cole.' He ignored her, turning another corner. She caught up to him, grabbing his arm. 'Cole, they're gone.'

He pulled away from her but stopped his frantic searching. He ran his hands through his hair. Harper didn't know what to say. There was nothing, no sign of the two men or a struggle, of anyone else in the warehouse.

'It doesn't make any sense. You said there were only two of them.'

He wasn't accusing her of lying, he sounded desperate. He looked at her, expression somewhere between fury and despair. She had no doubt that Hael and Gage were more than capable of holding their own in a fight, but Cole's anxiety made her gut clench with concern. She'd seen how Hael handled himself at the fight club against ten skilled opponents. He'd lost on purpose, but he'd easily taken most of them down first. Two men should have been no match for him and Gage. Yet they were gone, no, they'd been taken. Who the hell were they chasing?

Cole turned away from her, shoulders held stiffly as he breathed deeply. He moved suddenly, striking out at a dumpster with his fist. The sound reverberating in the quiet night made her flinch. His outburst subsided as quickly as it'd come. He closed his eyes, tilting his head back and taking a deep breath, holding it in a long moment. He let the air rush back out.

Harper walked closer once Cole had hold of himself again. This was beyond her usual involvement in cases. They were inside the Enclave. It was Cole's family, and she had little experience with feeling responsible for anyone else.

'What do we do?'

Cole looked at her, seeming suddenly much older. His expression schooled to something much calmer, though his eyes still held a determined wildness. 'We find them.' He nodded slightly, like he was trying to convince himself no other outcome was possible. 'We need to get back to Aeternus. Kazimir can help. We can reach out to some of our contacts. We'll find who has them.'

That sounded like a long shot at best, but she didn't say anything. They walked back to Jacobs' car. Harper got in the driver's seat, and Cole opened the passenger door, before pausing. He stepped away, pulled out his phone, and made a call. She turned away but couldn't help listening as the call went to voice message.

'Wrathe.' Cole's breath caught. 'It's Hael. He's...someone's taken him. I... just, can you call back? We need you.'

Harper started the car, swallowing guilt for overhearing something she shouldn't have. Cole ended the call and got in the car. She looked over briefly. He was staring at the phone still in his hand, expression painfully blank like he couldn't isolate just one thing to feel, so tumbled into nothingness instead.

***

31

~ COLE ~

LONDON, 10ᵀᴴ NOVEMBER 1690

Cole's skin was on fire. The pain from all the cuts merging into shifting patterns of torment each time he took a breath. He distracted himself by fantasising about how much he'd enjoy sticking something pointy in the eye of the man who'd spent the last few hours slicing away at him. Probably not as much as he'd enjoy killing the man with the oily charmed voice who did nothing but ask question after question in an irritatingly even tone.

Relieving that bastard from the weight of his head would be nothing short of blissful.

Cole kept his eyes closed as he carefully catalogued movement in the room. The man asking the questions had left a while ago. The man with the knives was currently cleaning them. He wanted to snarl insults and laugh in the man's face, but that wouldn't gain anything. He'd carefully let his glib answers to their questions devolve into screams and manic laughter the longer they cut at him. It hadn't been hard. Cole doubted anywhere on his arms and torso hadn't been sliced open. Blood dripped off him everywhere. He refused to give them any answers but let them think he'd given up.

If they were finished asking questions, maybe they'd move him. He hadn't been able to hear anyone else in the time he'd been here. They were underground. Maybe somewhere near the sewers where they'd first seen him, though it was impossible to tell. If there weren't too many, and he could get his hands free, maybe there was a chance. That's all he needed.

Cole discreetly flexed the muscles in his arms, trying to judge how much his injuries inhibited his movements. He healed much quicker now. It was a good thing his captors ended their questioning after a few hours. The first cuts were already starting to scab over. There'd probably been too much blood for them to notice.

Shit, if they'd noticed. He should never have let them capture him.

Cole swallowed painfully, replaying the stories his captor told as they cut him open. Stories about two Erinyes so powerful they had destroyed cities. Blood-soaked and dangerous, maybe the most pure-blooded Erinyes alive, a throwback to the days when the Aion still walked the earth. Cole knew who those stories were about, and at the heart of them was a truth. A truth that flowed through Cole's veins.

He'd heard others describe the slow process of blooding

a human. How the high it gave, and excess energy like you could run all day, wore off over several days. It took years of regular doses to maintain a permanent state of change because most Erinyes alive had been diluted after generations of coupling with humans. His own experience had been very different. The first time Cole drank Hael's blood it had been like inhaling a storm, lightning danced along his veins, white hot energy that never faded because Hael wasn't just another diluted Erinyes.

Cole already knew most of what the man had spoken of. How two thousand years ago, the first generation of Erinyes had been slaves. They hadn't been born, they'd been made, made to fight and die, and most of them did. They died for a war that wasn't theirs. They did something else too though. Something he doubted the man asking the question understood. The Aion felt the emotions of the Erinyes in a way they never could with humanity. They could feel the fear and pain as the Erinyes died, the same way they felt other Aion, and it changed everything. Some Aion recognised something of themselves in this new race they'd created, and through them, saw something in humans they never had before. A faction of Aion rebelled and befriended the Erinyes, lived amongst them, had families with them. They birthed the next generation who became known as the Furiae, half Aion and more powerful than the Erinyes. Few remembered the Furiae, because no one called them that anymore. Made or born, all descendants of those first generations called themselves Erinyes now.

Cole knew this, because Kazimir, Hael's father, liked to tell Cole stories. Stories about a very different world, about how Kazimir's own father didn't remember being human, but remembered the way it felt like the stars themselves burned through his veins the day he was made. The way the Aion who forced Godblood into his mouth barely spared a glance for him while he writhed in the dirt before moving to the woman next to him.

Kazimir's mother had been one of the Aion. Making Kazimir Furiae.

One cold night, Kazimir told Cole about the woman he'd once loved, the mother of his oldest child. Like so many stories the Aesir told him, Cole had never dared repeat it, not even in his own head. A story he had no right to know. A secret.

Kazimir was half Aion. His eldest son much more.

There was a shuffling sound to Cole's left as the man finally seemed satisfied his knives were clean. He moved back to Cole, reaching for the straps holding him down and undoing them. Cole waited, patient, for the right moment. The last strap came free, and Cole breathed deep, setting himself against the pain. He moved quickly, far more so than the man who had tortured him expected. He flexed his abs, arcing his body and flipping the man, twisting as he did so. The man was dead when he hit the floor, neck twisted grotesquely. Cole breathed deep from the exertion, his mutilated muscles screaming at him. He wavered on his feet a moment, clutching at the table. Gritting his teeth, he stubbornly held onto consciousness. He eyed the knives on the table. The safest thing would be to pick one up and slit his own throat. He could never betray the secrets he held if he was dead.

Cole reached out, fingers folding around the handle of the

nearest knife. He picked it up. He closed his eyes, dropping his head.

Not yet, not yet.

He kept hold of the knife as he pushed away from the table. He'd try to escape first. The knife would be a last resort.

Cole looked around the room. The book the man questioning him had been writing in lay amongst a bunch of scrolls on one of the tables. Cole grabbed it, flicking to the last pages, skimming it quickly. There were notes about the Erinyes. About their offspring with the Aion, the Furiae, being the purest blood that ever existed. Half the notes didn't make a lot of sense, written in shorthand. He skipped through until he saw notes about the Aesir. The man strongly suspected they were sired by one of the Furiae, and more powerful than many other families because of the purity of their blood. Cole ran his fingers over a note contemplating the possibilities of Furiae and Aion relations and froze.

If these fanatics were obsessed with the purity of Erinyes blood, they couldn't get any purer than Hael. Kazimir was half Aion, and the woman Kazimir loved, Hael's mother, had been an Aion. Furiae like Kazimir were rare after the wars and massacres of the last dozen centuries. But Hael, born of a Furiae and an Aion, was more Aion than Erinyes. If there'd ever been others like him, Cole doubted they were still alive.

Cole shoved the book in the band of his pants. He needed to tell Wrathe and Hael what he'd found. They needed to know the cult wasn't hunting the Aesir for some vendetta. There was another purpose here.

Cole peered out the door. The corridor outside was empty. He moved quickly. Apparently, he'd been right, this place was underground and sparsely manned. He only encountered one other guard on his way out, guarding the door to the street.

Cole moved as silently as he could, but the man heard him at the last moment, turning and blocking Cole's attack. He was strong, but Cole was desperate and very angry. He didn't bother blocking the guard's knife. What was one more cut at this point? Cole used the man's momentum to drive his own knife between ribs and into something vital. The guard let out a surprised gasp and slumped against Cole, breath gurgling. Cole pushed him aside and staggered past him.

It was dark and cold outside.

Cole looked around, not sure where he was. The street was deserted, half the buildings still under construction. He picked a direction and started walking, putting as much distance between himself and where he'd been held as he could. He looked down. His shirt hung in tatters. There was blood everywhere, a fresh streak coming from where the guard stabbed him. Cole didn't think it'd hit anything vital, but that might not make any difference. He'd lost too much blood and now that the adrenaline was wearing off, he'd would probably pass out soon. Frankly, he wasn't sure he'd wake up again if he did. Gritting his teeth, he concentrated on staying on his feet. If he figured out where he was, maybe he could find his way back to the Enclave.

He paused. He wasn't meant to go to the Enclave. It took a moment to remember why.

Hael and Wrathe. He had to keep the creepy cult from finding out who they were.

It didn't matter. Nothing looked familiar. He had no idea which direction the Enclave might be.

He started walking again. Maybe if he just kept moving a plan would come to him. It usually did. How often had he blundered into, then out of trouble and endured an angry lecture on stupidity and recklessness from Hael, while trying not to roll his eyes at the irony. Cole stumbled, crashing inelegantly into the brick wall of a building. He nearly blacked out at the jolt of pain. His knees buckled and he reached out, trying to brace himself, but only grazing his elbow on the bricks, barely slowing his fall. He landed in a heap, half slumped against the wall.

If he died in a random alley somewhere, Hael would be really angry. He would drink and destroy something. Maybe a lot of somethings.

Cole really hoped the twins would be too young to understand.

And Wrathe...

Wrathe let very few people know him. No one spoke about Wrathe's past. It was full of pain, that much was obvious. Cole didn't want to be one more thing that caused him pain.

He dug his fingers into the rough brick wall, trying to get to his feet. He barely even made it to his knees. Cole slumped his head, not wanting to give up, but his body just wouldn't cooperate. He sucked in a thready breath. Sometimes, when he'd been in trouble, serious trouble, the sort he didn't think he would get out of, Wrathe had somehow known. Maybe, maybe if he...

Cole closed his eyes. He thought about a little stone horse. One he thought long lost, and the way Wrathe held it gently while he watched over Cole. The way he tucked it away, the same way Wrathe tucked away how much he cared. Cole took a breath, deep down in his lungs, wrapped all his pain up and pushed it outwards, calling out Wrathe's name.

It left Cole hollow. When had he become such a sentimental fool? The pain faded away and he blacked out.

***

32

~ HARPER ~

Harper drove Cole back to Aeternus. The club was closed and Kazimir and the twins were downstairs instead of in the private lounge. Kazimir sat near Jacobs where she slept in a lounge booth while Deacon inspected her wounds. Ash was sitting on the bar, nervously chewing a nail. Harper waited until Deacon was finished before kneeling next to Jacobs, brushing a strand of hair back from the Detective's face. Her skin was cool to the touch, but her colour was looking better.

Deacon looked across at her. 'She's stable. I don't think there will be any permanent damage. It'll take her a few hours to wake up though.'

Harper nodded, not sure what to say as relief flooded her.

Cole looked down at the blood on his hands, and muttered something about needing to clean up, but Harper wasn't really listening. She gently brushed her thumb near the wound on Jacobs' wrist. It had scabbed over, the edges angry and red, but well on the way to healing. The rods probably damaged arteries, bone, tendon. She should be dead. Instead, she looked peaceful as she slept. Harper swallowed as she placed Jacobs' arm back to rest on her chest.

She never should have involved the Detective.

Kazimir reached out to Harper, laying a comforting hand on her shoulder. 'She's safe here. You're both welcome to stay as long as needed.'

At his touch her senses flared. She let herself focus on the sensation, needing a distraction as she tried to force her emotions under control. Kazimir felt like wind across a barren salt lake where life once teemed. It reminded her of the first time she met Hael and the single brief flash she'd felt from him before he'd somehow hidden it away again. Hael had been the oldest Erinyes she'd ever met by far. His father felt the same way, old, but with a kind of otherness as well.

She had dismissed so many of the stories her father told her about the Erinyes and what they had once been. Several things over the last few days made her think she shouldn't have. Her senses expanded out to touch Deacon and Ash who were like a sea breeze laden with salt. No otherness, they felt like any other Erinyes she'd known. Was it possible Kazimir wasn't just the oldest Erinyes she'd met, but the purest? That would explain the difference she sensed, and how Jacobs' injuries were healing when she should have died.

A door banged somewhere, jerking Harper's focus back. She could hear someone moving around in a backroom behind the bar, Cole she presumed. Kazimir looked in the direction of the noise, expression etched with worry.

Harper cleared her throat, pushing aside her guilt and worry. 'I want to help find Hael and Gage. If I can.'

It was Cole who answered her as he walked back into the room. 'Good. If you've got any ideas how, I'm listening.'

He'd changed out of his bloodied clothes and cleaned up a little, though flecks of Jacobs' blood remained on his arms.

Harper looked away, forcing herself to think. 'There were two men that we saw. Both Erinyes. The van they were driving belonged to someone Jacobs said was linked to the Descendants.' She chewed on her lip. There really wasn't much information she had to offer. Let alone any sort of plan. 'Other than the link to the Descendants, I'm not sure what else we have.'

Ash jumped off the bar. 'I almost forgot. Someone called in looking for Gage. He left a note.' She grabbed a piece of paper and handed it to Cole.

Cole glared down at the note as he read it, before scrunching the piece of paper up.

'What is it?' Kazimir asked.

Cole ran a hand through his hair. 'Gage went to see Tyriel, looking for information, seems he might have found something.' He turned to Ash. 'Don't suppose the bastard left a phone number?'

Ash shook her head. 'No, he didn't.'

Cole grabbed his keys from the bar. 'Guess I'm paying Tyriel a visit then.'

Deacon pushed his chair back. 'Like hell you are.'

Kazimir stood, looking between Deacon and Cole. 'Tyriel? Is that the owner of the fight club here in the Enclave?'

Deacon nodded.

Kazimir stepped closer to Cole, studying him intently. Even if Harper couldn't feel Kazimir's age and power, the man would be intimidating. Not in a violent way, but he possessed a gracious kind of nobility that made Harper want to stand a little straighter.

Cole held his gaze unflinchingly though. 'He might have information we need.'

Kazimir seemed to find something in Cole's expression, or probably picked up something empathically, that satisfied him. He reached out to grip Cole's shoulder. 'I've always trusted your judgement.' Kazimir dropped his hand. 'Go.'

Cole nodded, lips thin and tight. 'Can you and the twins reach out to our contacts, maybe we'll get lucky, and someone will have heard something.'

Harper watched as Cole picked up a holster with two guns and shrugged it on, before grabbing his coat. There wasn't much she could do here, but Tyriel had seemed willing to help her last time they spoke.

She stood. 'I'll go with Cole.'

Cole gave her a curt nod, like he didn't care one way or the other, and walked out.

'Wait.' Ash ducked behind the bar. She wet a clean bar cloth and tossed it to Harper. 'For your hands.'

Harper caught it staring down at her hands. She'd forgotten they were still covered in Jacobs' blood too. 'Thanks.' she mumbled.

'Be careful,' Deacon said, watching her wipe her hands. He paused, like he was unsure whether to say anything. 'Cole and Tyriel have history.'

He didn't elaborate, so Harper just nodded, tossed the cloth back to Ash, and followed Cole outside.

***

Tyriel's club was crowded, with a line waiting to enter. Cole led her away from the front entrance and pounded on a staff only door. A burly Erinyes opened it, glaring at them. Not giving him time to react Cole pushed past, twisting the man's arm behind his back and pushing him face first into the wall. He waited until Harper was inside before kicking the door shut.

Cole twisted the man's arm harder. 'I need to see Tyriel.' The man gritted his teeth but didn't answer.

Harper looked around. More security guards came towards them. Well, this had gone bad quicker than she'd expected.

Cole smiled in a frighteningly charming way, if you found cold killers charming. 'He's expecting me.'

A soft chuckle came from the hallway. 'Oh, Cole. You certainly don't disappoint.'

Cole didn't move, glare fixed on the man he held. Harper shifted to see Tyriel. He wasn't dressed for the fight club tonight. He wore an old pair of jeans and a t-shirt. The casual look suited him. He watched Cole, a small smile playing on his lips. She doubted Tyriel expected them, but he didn't look at all surprised. Tyriel's men shifted, looking uncertainly between the club owner and the intruders.

Tyriel realised his guards were waiting for clarification. 'Excuse Cole's manners, he's quite welcome here.' He waved a hand at his security in clear dismissal, and the tension in the room dropped.

Cole let go of the man he'd been holding who turned and glared at Cole, surreptitiously rubbing his wrist. Cole smiled smugly at him, almost daring him to react before moving to follow Tyriel. The club owner led them through the back rooms of the club to what looked to be living quarters. It was small, cosy rather than flashy like she expected.

Once they were alone, Tyriel waved a hand towards a lounge but appeared unsurprised when they remained standing. He leaned against a small cabinet with a decanter and several glasses but didn't pour himself a drink.

Tyriel studied Cole. 'I was expecting Gage?' Cole tensed and Tyriel noted the movement, eyes narrowing. He seemed concerned for the first time. 'Where's Gage?'

Cole shifted, clenching his fists by his side. 'Missing.'

'Missing, not dead?'

Cole nodded. 'Hael as well.'

A muscle in Tyriel's jaw twitched. He stepped closer to Cole. 'I know who ordered the hit on Gage.'

Harper looked between the two men, trying to catch up. 'The attack in the alley was meant for Gage?'

Cole glanced at her, mildly apologetically. 'We found the shooter.'

She squinted at him, confused. 'But Gage wasn't even there?'

Cole just shrugged. 'He wasn't a very competent hitman.'

Tyriel huffed a laugh, eyeing Cole. 'I hear young Henry's given up the hitman life. Pretty sure he's halfway to Argentina by now.'

Cole didn't seem the least bit interested in the where-abouts of the man who shot him. 'Who put out the hit?'

Tyriel looked at Harper for the first time, his gaze assess-ing. 'Someone your friend here knows quite well I believe.'

Harper's eyes widened. Who the hell did she know with the audacity to attack an Aesir Watcher? 'Who?'

'Viridian Astor.'

Harper stared at Tyriel. What the hell? 'He's just a kid.'

Tyriel shrugged. 'Weren't all killers once?'

Cole turned toward Harper. 'Who is he?'

'Someone I met on a case a few years ago. He's training to be a Watcher.'

Tyriel poured himself a drink, swallowing it down in one anxious gulp. 'I was looking into the kid. Didn't expect any-one to be stupid enough to make a second attempt on Gage so soon.'

Harper folded her arms, looking down. They probably wouldn't have if she hadn't been following them. She'd led Gage and Hael right to them.

Cole shifted on his feet, impatient. 'Did you find anything?'

'Kid seems clean. He's training with the Watcher's, works a couple part-time jobs. Apparently has a thing for under-ground fights. Explains why he was here. His family is inter-esting though.'

Harper looked back up. 'Viridian doesn't have any family.' It was one of the first things she'd known about him. He was an orphan.

'Yes and no. The Astor's owned a lot of businesses here in Chicago until they were almost wiped out about a hundred years ago. Viridian's parents died a few decades back, when he was still a kid. According to his sealed records, his brother adopted him, though I can't find any record of the brother at all.'

Harper chewed her lip. She'd known Viridian for five years. She'd always worried he'd turn up dead somewhere in a ditch. That was seeming a likely outcome with Cole looking ready to kill anyone who hurt his family.

'Where can we find Viridian?' Cole asked Harper.

'He trains at the Tower a few times a week. Works at a cafe.'

'Do you know where he lives?'

Harper shook her head. She had no idea.

Cole pulled out his phone and started tapping something in. She looked over his shoulder. He was using his backdoor into the Watcher database. He glanced up at her, like he expected her to say something about his hacking. She wasn't sure if she had a problem with it or not. Frankly, if she was capable of hacking in herself, she probably would have to find her father's file. Cole found Viridian's detail quickly. His address was listed as an apartment in one of the high rises in the Enclave.

Harper glanced out the window, thinking. There was no way he'd take Gage and Hael to his apartment. They couldn't be sure to even find Viridian there and didn't have time to stake it out and wait for him to return. Gage and Hael may not have that long. She thought about the scene of Valarie and Thorn's murder. They hadn't died quickly. He would need a place where no one would hear anything. Somewhere isolated, abandoned maybe.

She looked across at Tyriel. 'You said his family owned businesses?' He nodded, picked up a piece of paper and handed it to her. It listed several businesses the Astor family once owned. If Viridian was the last Astor, any assets may have passed to him. 'Run these, see if any buildings are still owned in the business names.'

Cole started searching. It didn't take long to find something. Three warehouses, all abandoned and still owned by a subsidiary of an Astor company. One of them, was the warehouse where she and Jacobs had been ambushed.

'As good a lead as we have,' Cole said, turning to leave.

Tyriel reached out to stop him. 'Hael saved my life that day. I want to help find him.'

Harper watched the two men, unsure what day he was referring to. Cole appeared to know what Tyriel meant though.

He pulled away from Tyriel's grip. 'Why the hell would I let you help?'

Tyriel shrugged. 'Because you'll probably need it. This kid can't be working on his own, not if he took Hael.'

Cole looked away, the muscles in his neck straining, like he would lash out at the slightest provocation. 'If you really wanted to help, you wouldn't still be running this place.'

Tyriel flinched and stepped back, like he was putting distance between himself and Cole's words. He nodded to himself. 'Okay.'

Cole glanced at Tyriel, brow creasing. His expression smoothed out quickly though, falling into an unsettling blankness. He walked out without saying another word.

**

They decided to split the two addresses, texting one to

Kazimir and the twins, and Cole and Harper heading to the other. Harper looked across at Cole as he parked down the street from the address. Kazimir and Deacon insisted on scouting the building only, to check for any activity. If Gage and Hael were being held at either location, they were supposed to call the others and wait. Harper doubted waiting would go well. Cole didn't seem to be in a patient mood.

They left the car and walked down the street. Cole led her to a fire escape on a building opposite the one Viridian's family owned. Cole moved silently, swift and sure in the shadows. Harper did her best to mimic his stealth, taking his hand when he offered it to help her off the ladder onto the roof which provided a good view across the street. Cole's fingers tightened where he still had hold of her. The building wasn't abandoned. The first and second floors were dark, but there were lights on the third storey.

Cole gently pulled her towards the edge of the roof, keeping low and out of sight. He knelt on one knee, eyes scanning the building. His hand was tense in hers, fingers twitching. They could see movement through the windows. If Viridian was involved, and she struggled to accept that, he wasn't working alone. Harper waited, keeping her breathing calm as she watched figures shift in and out of the light. She gently squeezed Cole's fingers to get his attention. He flinched, like he'd forgotten he still held her hand before he let go.

Cole pointed to his eye and then across at the building. He wanted to get a better look. She chewed her lip a second, but more information would be good before they went in. Harper nodded and followed him.

Moving further along the roof they could see into an alley

that ran down the side of the building. A van was parked in the alley. Harper pointed to it and Cole raised an eyebrow at her questioningly.

She leaned in closer. 'That's the same van we were following.'

If they needed any further confirmation that would be it. His eyes shone bright in the darkness. Harper saw him fighting the urge to rush in and get Gage and Hael out. After a moment, he closed his eyes, breathing out slowly and sinking down to sit with his back against the roof railing. He pulled out his phone and sent a text to the others.

Cole studied the building when he was done. 'There are at least five people inside.'

There was movement at a few windows, someone stopping to stare out before moving on. They were on the alert and keeping watch. She'd take his word on their numbers. He had more experience at this sort of thing.

Harper reached out and grabbed his arm as his fingers gripped the railing. 'Do I need to remind you that there are only the two of us? We are supposed to be waiting for the others.'

He turned to study her. 'How many can you sense over there?'

Harper let go of his arm, surprised at the question. She was so accustomed to suppressing her ability she hadn't thought to use it that way, especially not from this distance. Cole just tilted his head, waiting.

Harper wiped her hands on her thighs. She closed her eyes, concentrating. Cole's presence at her side drew her senses in like the pull of gravity. She took a breath forcing herself to push away from him, reaching out further across the street. She picked up indistinct flickers, sensing their movements first. It was hard to pick any of them apart. She pressed her lips together, angry at the inevitable surge of inadequacy. Breathing out slowly, she was aware of Cole shifting impatiently beside her. She tried again.

There.

She opened her eyes, gaze flicking across the building from window to window. She felt them. Six, no seven? As quick as it came, the sense of the Erinyes slipped away, but she'd felt them.

She turned to Cole. 'Seven, I think?'

'Could you sense Gage or Hael?'

Before she could answer, a scream came from across the street. Short, cut off, and full of pain. Cole reacted immediately. Harper reached out only to grab empty air as he launched himself off the edge of the building.

'Shit.'

Harper leant over the railing to see Cole land in the street below. He rolled, coming to his feet and running, losing no momentum. Harper ran to the fire escape, keeping her eyes on Cole. Her steps slowed as she watched him reach the building and jump, using a ledge to launch himself higher. He pulled himself up and into an open window on the second floor. Cursing, Harper ran.

She swung down the fire escape. Slipping on a step, she steadied herself, trying to keep some semblance of stealth. Once on street level she paused, unsure if she could climb through the same window as Cole, certainly not as quietly.

Harper moved out into the street, determined to try. Her

steps faltered as she felt an Erinyes a moment before he appeared. He grabbed her, pressing her into the shadows of the building. Instinctively she pushed back, shoving the man off her. She recognised him the moment she did, heartbeat still frantic.

'What the...'

Tyriel grabbed her again, pressing a hand gently over her mouth. He pulled her close as a man ran out of the building, jumping into the van and driving past them.

He let go of her once the van left. 'Where's Cole?'

Harper looked across at the building. 'He went in.'

Tyriel shook his head. 'Of course, he did.'

Before Harper could ask what the hell he was doing here, Tyriel ran across the street. He didn't try for stealth, kicking the front door in. Harper followed him. The sounds of fighting came from above. They moved through the darkened building, finding their way to a stairway. Harper barely saw the first attacker before Tyriel struck. He broke the man's arm in a single quick motion and kicked him down the stairs. Harper barely managed to dodge the tumbling body. The man groaned when he hit the bottom, still alive but no longer a threat. The second man went down easy, a series of punches from Tyriel, before Harper had even caught up. Tyriel wasn't so lucky with the next, taking a sharp hit to the jaw. Harper pulled one of her knives. She shifted around Tyriel, using him to block the man's attack, and sliding past to slash at their attacker's hamstring, aiming to disable him. The man cried out, stumbling. Tyriel knocked him out him with a vicious punch to his temple.

As they made their way to the third floor, they heard

a short scuffle and then silence. The quiet didn't last long, broken by sounds of a door being kicked in. They found Cole on the south side of the building. Four dead bodies lay strewn across the floor. Cole obviously hadn't been as concerned about casualties. Part of her wanted to react to the unnecessary killing, but the rest of her was too busy evaluating the room for any more threats.

'Cole?'

He didn't acknowledge them, moving on to kick down another door. Not finding anything he moved to the last room, pushing his way inside. It was empty as well.

Cole cried out in frustration, breathing heavily. 'They're not here.'

They weren't. Harper sensed no one else in the building. It didn't make sense. Cole looked across at her, clearly distraught. She had no idea what to say to him.

Tyriel, braver than her, took a step toward Cole. 'They could be at the other address?'

It was the wrong thing to say. Cole grabbed out his phone. They should have heard from Kazimir and the twins by now. Cole dialled, face falling further the longer it rang.

Tyriel turned to her questioningly. She wasn't sure how much to tell him. 'The others went to the warehouse on Harrington. We should have heard from them by now.'

Cole hung up and tried another call. Harper turned at a sound from outside.

'Cole.'

The others heard it now too. It sounded like several cars pulling up outside, the stomp of boots on the floors below.

Tyriel closed his eyes, cursing under his breath. 'They knew you'd find who ordered the hit on Gage.'

Harper looked between the two of them. 'What?'

Cole got it before she did. 'They knew we were coming.' He shook his head. 'No, they wanted us to come.' Cole backed away from the window, looking around calculatingly. They didn't have a lot of options for exits. He glanced at Tyriel. 'What the hell are you doing here anyway?'

'I followed you.' Tyriel answered, like it was obvious.

There were footsteps on the stairs.

Cole smiled. 'That was probably really stupid.'

Tyriel shrugged.

Harper shifted until she was shoulder to shoulder with Cole. She tilted her head facing the door to the stairway. 'They're human.'

'What?'

Harper looked up at Cole. 'I can't sense any Erinyes.'

Cole turned, looking at the window. She assumed he knew she couldn't fly. It would be in her Watcher records. Blooded humans couldn't either. If it was only humans entering the building, Tyriel would be fine, he could fly away any time he wanted.

Cole grabbed her hand. 'If they're human, we can probably outrun them. Unless they had gunmen already in place.'

Harper looked towards the door. 'I'll take that chance.'

Cole climbed out the window first, balancing on the ledge. He waited until she joined him, and they jumped at the same time. Harper landed awkwardly in the alleyway, stumbling, as Cole rolled nimbly. They scrambled to their feet. Tyriel appeared ahead of them. He looked around the corner into the street before pulling back and waving at them to wait. He disappeared a moment before reappearing next to Cole.

'There's too many of them in the street.' Tyriel held his hand out. 'Give me your keys. I can get the car and pick you up.'

Cole stared at him, like trusting Tyriel was the last thing he wanted to do. He dug into his pocket and pulled the keys out anyway. 'Pick us up at the end of the alley.'

Tyriel grabbed the keys and took flight.

Cole wasted no time second guessing. He led Harper down the alley. They ducked in and out of shadows, keeping out of sight. They were maybe a hundred meters down the alley when they heard footsteps behind them. Not bothering with stealth any longer, they both ran.

A gunshot sounded. It ricocheted off the wall near Harper's head. They ran faster. Tyres screeched ahead of them as Cole's car skidded to a stop. Tyriel reached over, throwing the passenger door open. Harper jumped in the front. Cole getting in the back. Tyriel didn't even wait for the doors to close before he gunned it down the alley. Another gunshot twanged loudly off the rear of the car, before they turned a corner and were out of range.

Tyriel drove wildly, tyres screeching around the corners.

Cole leaned forward, gripping the front seat tightly. 'Slow the fuck down. You crash my car and I'll kill you.'

Tyriel eased off the gas. 'Where are we going?'

Cole glared at Tyriel. 'I'm going to kill whoever took Hael. You're pulling over and getting out.'

Tyriel looked up at Cole in the rear-view mirror. 'You

don't care if I get killed, so why don't you just shut up and tell me where we're going?'

Cole glared at Tyriel but said nothing more.

Tyriel glanced across at Harper. 'I can let you out if you want?'

Harper looked back at Cole. This would be the perfect time to bail on all the madness. She'd already almost gotten Jacobs killed. This would usually be where she drew the line, keeping her nose out of anyone else's business. Actually, that time had come and gone days ago. Against her better judgement she was invested, beyond just solving her case. How the hell had that happened?

Harper shook her head. She wasn't going anywhere. 'I'm in.'

Cole, clearly too worried about his family, didn't argue. 'Go to the warehouse on Harrington. I've already called in all the backup we need. But I'm going in whether they're here in time or not.'

Harper looked back at Cole, wondering who he was expecting. And if both Tyriel and she were insane for sticking around long enough to find out.

***

33

~ GAGE ~

Gage groaned as he regained consciousness, arms a scream-ing mess of pins and needles. He clenched his jaw against the pain, shifting his weight. He looked blearily up at his hands tied above his head, flexing his fingers. His weight must have been hanging on them too long. The faint outline of a sigil was visible on the chains holding him. A simple but effec-tive one keeping him from breaking them or taking flight. Moving awkwardly, he got his feet under himself and stood shakily, relieving the pressure off his arms. How long had he been out?

Swallowing dryly, Gage looked around. Hael was chained the same way as Gage. He froze, this was not good. Hael wasn't looking at him. He was staring at a man sitting on a crate across from them. Hael's expression could freeze oceans, but the other man seemed unconcerned. Actually, he seemed a bit delighted. It was unsettling.

The man studied Hael, amused. 'Your friend seems to possess less fortitude than you.'

Hael said nothing. Gage didn't bother rising to the goad either, studying his brother instead. Hael seemed unaffected by whatever Gage still felt in his system. He tried to remember what happened. Whatever they'd been drugged with was damn effective. It had obviously taken Hael down too, though his superior healing must have burned through it quicker. What drug could do that?

Gage took in their surroundings now he was more aware. They were in an abandoned warehouse. Not the same one, or the others would have found them by now. The man smiled at Hael, the expression a combination of taunting and dismissive, before turning away to study Gage. Good, let him underestimate Hael. No one else was in the room with them, but Gage heard movement in another nearby, and voices too low to hear the conversation. The man wasn't working alone. Still, there was a good chance either this man killed his daughter, or he knew who did.

Gage's finger tightened into fists, jaw clenching. 'Who are you?'

'Me? I'm no one. Who you are is more interesting.'

'And who am I?'

The man smiled, but it didn't reach his eyes. 'You're an Aesir.'

Gage's eyes narrowed. 'That's not much of a secret.'

The man nodded. 'True. But you're no one too. There are a lot of you Aesir, easy to get lost amongst all those siblings and cousins I imagine.'

'If I'm just a no one, why put a hit out on me?'

'Oh, that wasn't me. That was someone less patient than I am. Internal politics, not really all that interesting either. What is interesting, is how you became the Watcher for your family here in America.'

Grinding his teeth, Gage barely resisted the urge to growl and lunge at this man. It'd do no good with his hands tied. He became a Watcher because this sick bastard or whoever he worked with killed his baby girl. 'You know why I became a Watcher.'

'I do. But I said how, not why.'

Gage glared at him, trying to figure out what the hell he meant. 'How? I filed the paperwork with the Council.'

The man laughed. 'What is it with you Aesir and smart mouths? I don't give a shit about Council bureaucracy. What I care about, is how a no one like you in a family full of more impressive people, convinces anyone to make you their Watcher, just so you can chase down your little vendetta?'

Gage kept his eyes on the man, careful not to glance towards Hael. He needn't have bothered.

The man smiled at him benignly. 'Gage, what's so interesting about you, isn't you at all.' He deliberately turned his gaze towards Hael.

Hael didn't react, content to let the man talk.

'You on the other hand, might be the most interesting person I've ever met.'

Hael shrugged casually, as if being chained in an abandoned warehouse wasn't a particularly concerning occurrence. 'I like to think I'm interesting. Generally, people go more with arrogant, reckless, or hedonist bastard. Which are simply different ways of saying interesting if you ask me.'

The man smiled, pointing at Hael. 'I think I'm going to like you.'

Two men and a woman walked into the room. The woman's gaze drifted past Hael and Gage like they weren't worth her time, to stare coldly at the man on the crate.

'Vellichor, you should have told me they were awake.'

Vellichor shrugged. The woman narrowed her eyes at him, before walking past him dismissively. Clearly, he wasn't in charge.

She looked Gage up and down. 'So, you're Gage Aesir.'

If she expected a response, Gage didn't bother giving her one.

She stared down her nose at him, like he was something usually found on the bottom of a shoe, before grabbing his chin, tilting his head. 'You're as pretty as all the rest of them I suppose.'

Gage pulled out of her grasp, refusing to look at her.

Vellichor kicked the heel of one foot against the crate, looking across the room with an oddly complicated expression. 'Maia's not fond of pretty boys.'

Maia ignored him. Hael didn't, though. His brother studied Vellichor shrewdly.

Gage looked at the woman. 'Who are you?'

Maia glared at him, before slapping him hard across the face. 'We will ask the questions.' She folded her hands primly in front of her, examining him. 'You're the Aesir Watcher. You lot usually take a lot more care in keeping things like that private.'

Gage said nothing. Neither did Hael. She was right. His family kept their business to themselves. They hadn't been on the Council most of Gage's lifetime. Almost no one outside the family knew the names of their Watchers. Gage knew the risks of replacing Deacon as their Watcher to officially investigate Ara's death. Hael had been unhappy with how public his name had become.

'From what I understand, family Watchers are respected members of their family. Intimate with all its inner workings and machinations.' Maia glanced towards Vellichor. 'Yes?'

Vellichor nodded in response.

'So, this...man, can tell me about the Aesir, where they are?' When Vellichor didn't answer, she turned her cold gaze fully on him. 'He will know, yes?'

Vellichor nodded, not looking at her. 'A Watcher should know, yes.'

'Should?'

Vellichor looked down. 'He only became their Watcher after Ara...his daughter, was killed.'

Maia turned back to Gage. 'Why does that matter?'

Gage wanted to rip the indifferent expression from her face.

'Only Watchers can access official records. They let him become their Watcher so he could find who killed her.'

Maia smiled, dark amusement dancing in her eyes, the sort of amusement psychopath kids got from pulling wings off flies. 'Then you and he should have a lot to talk about.'

The ground seemed to disappear beneath his feet. Gage jerked his gaze away from the smiling Maia to Vellichor, who stared at some point across the room, before his shoulders tensed and he slowly looked at Gage. Everything else seemed to fade out of existence until only Gage and Vellichor were left. Gage strained at the chains holding him. He threw his body in Vellichor's direction. His shoulders twisted, wrist bones grinding against metal. He didn't care. For five years he had hunted the bastard who killed his daughter. He finally had his answer, and he couldn't do anything about it. He wanted to rip the man to pieces. Gage's breath caught harshly in his throat.

The woman laughed. Gage tore his gaze away from Vellichor. He'd kill her too.

'You'll help us. One way or another. Either you answer our questions, or we sacrifice you next, and I'll keep killing my way through the rest of your family until I find it.'

Gage stared at her, her words finally registering. 'I don't know what the hell you're looking for. But I won't help you find a damn thing.'

Maia nodded to the two men who entered with her. They stepped towards Gage, each holding a baseball bat.

Gage had all but forgotten Hael until he cleared his throat. 'You know.' Hael ignored Maia and the men with bats, watching Vellichor instead. 'You had a good point before.'

Maia barely spared Hael a glance. 'What's he talking about?'

'Vellichor was just saying he didn't think Gage was particularly interesting. He was right.' Hael tilted his lips in a lazy, aw-shucks kind of smile. 'Me on the other hand. I'm much more interesting.'

Maia glared at Hael. 'Vellichor?'

Vellichor leaned forward, resting his elbows on his knees as he watched Hael. 'As I said. Gage became their Watcher suddenly. What I wanted to know is how.'

Maia turned to face Vellichor, shoulder's square and expression dour, like if Vellichor was wasting her time she'd be livid. 'How what?'

'How did Gage, a younger son, an all but outcast amongst most of the family in America if rumours are true, somehow become their Watcher, just like that.'

Maia's stance loosened, just a little. He'd piqued her curiosity. 'What are you thinking?'

Vellichor shrugged. 'He wouldn't, unless someone much more influential within the family let him. Someone close enough to him to care, someone who outranked Ishta?'

The fog of Gage's anger cleared a little. They knew both who Ishta was, and that she didn't favour Gage. He glanced across at Hael, but his brother's expression gave nothing away.

Vellichor tilted his head, still watching Hael. 'Most people are under the impression Hael is nothing more than an information broker. And while he is that, and an excellent one, he's even better at obscuring secrets than collecting them. Especially his own.'

Maia studied Hael more closely.

'What does anyone know about him, other than he drinks a lot and has a tendency towards rashness?' Vellichor continued. 'But I don't think he just associates with the Aesir. He is one. One I'm guessing, with enough say to dictate who becomes their Watcher.'

Hael smiled smugly. 'Told you I was the more interesting one.'

Vellichor leaned back. 'Maia, you've been searching for who has all the power within the Aesir family? Who leads them when we know it's not Ishta. I'd bet there's a good chance you're looking at him.'

Maia stared at Hael, like she could take him apart and find everything she wanted hidden amongst his insides.

Hael leaned forward, weight resting against the chains holding him. 'Nah, I don't lead our family. We're more an autonomous collective. You know. One for all and all for one.'

Maia flicked her hand. One of the men stepped forward. He swung his bat, slamming it into Hael's ribs. Gage gritted his teeth at the sound it made. The second swing hit so hard, Hael lost his footing, swinging from his arms as he grunted in pain. Gage snarled at them, fingers clenching uselessly, but they ignored him.

Maia stepped closer to Hael as he stopped swinging and regained his footing. 'There are a lot of interesting stories about the Aesir. I've been piecing them together for years, as my father did before me. My family has been searching for the head of the Aesir for generations. But you are a secretive lot.'

She nodded, and the man took another swing. Hael listed to the side, visibly struggling to breathe for a moment before coughing up blood.

'Your family is old. According to the records, very old. But it's not only your family who've been around a long time, but individual members too. Few people believe the stories, because they have no facts to back them up. Was it you who erased them?'

Hael grinned at her, teeth coated red. 'You're human.'

Gage looked at her, surprised. He should have known that. He'd been distracted and missed the obviously human swirl of emotion he sensed now.

Hael spat out another glob of blood. It landed at Maia's feet. 'You're human, a few generations are what, a hundred years? What do you know about history?'

Maia looked distastefully at the blood. 'You are an abomination.'

Hael's stare turned icy. 'Oh, you have no idea.' He glanced towards Vellichor. 'But it seems you work with our kind.'

'You have your uses.'

She sounded resentful about that.

Hael seemed to pick up the same thing. 'Him being here wasn't your idea, was it? You hate us, would kill us all given half the chance. Guess that means you're not the one in charge. So, who's pulling your strings?'

Maia glared up at Hael. 'You all think you're clever. Fortunately, I don't have to listen to you. I just need your blood.'

Hael stilled at those words.

Maia held out a hand and one of the men handed her a bat. 'If you're not the leader of the Aesir, it doesn't matter. It will be one more of you dead.' She tilted her head, studying Hael. 'Maybe Vellichor is right. Maybe you are more than you seem. It will be fun draining you and finding out. Take every last drop just in case and see if you're pure enough to open the gates.'

Gage didn't understand what she was talking about, but her words affected Hael. They stunned him into stillness.

'What gates?' Gage asked.

Maia's expression turned condescending, like Gage was a child waiting for a seat at the adult table. 'The gates to the heavens. The ones that were sealed to end the Endless War. Sealed with blood.'

Maia turned away, lifting the bat, she smashed it into Hael's left knee. It hit with a sickening crunch. Gage strained against his chains, helpless to do anything. Hael didn't even react, still staring at Maia, even as his leg struggled to hold his weight up after the hit. She readied to strike again.

Gage struggled against his bindings, futilely. 'What the fuck are you talking about?'

Maia turned her attention to him. 'You ignorant half breed. You don't even know your own history.'

She aimed at Gage this time. He tensed, but the hit still knocked the breath out of him. Hael leaned forward again, straining against the chains. His eyes seemed to darken, rage descending across his features like night falling. The muscles in his arms rippled as he pulled against the bindings.

'Leave my brother alone.' Hael's teeth were coated with blood. He looked almost feral. 'You talk about history. Like you know anything about it. They're just stories to you.'

Maia smiled, almost sweetly. 'Just stories? Stories start with a truth.' She poked Hael in the ribs with the end of the bat. 'So, you are an Aesir. Do you want to know the story that brought you here today? It's an old one, maybe you know it.'

'Two thousand years ago, at the end of the Aion wars, there was a group who called themselves the Order. They were old men, afraid of what they didn't know. But they found something interesting. On the day humans slaughtered the Aion, they found a man on the battlefield. He was unconscious, near death. Not unexpected given the circumstances. But the man's injuries weren't from battle. His body was covered with sigils. He'd carved them into his own skin.'

Gage tensed. He had thought Ara's death, the other

murders, had simply been the acts of a crazed psychopath who liked to play with his victims. He looked across at Hael. His brother had thought it might be something more. Hael returned from the scene of Valerie and Thorn's murder more shaken that Gage had seen him in decades, not since the day they found a barely recognisable Cole in Veracruz. Hael cared for the young Aesir siblings, but Gage should have realised it was something more. He remembered what Hael told him on the balcony a few days ago. About the secret he'd been protecting for two thousand years.

Maia smiled at Gage, noting his reaction. 'Yes, it was the sigils. You should have paid more attention to those. See, those old men knew they'd found something interesting. The man they found was an Erinyes. They took him, studied him. The only words he ever spoke were when they first found them. He said, it's done, I sealed the gates, they can't return.'

'The gates to heaven?'

Maia nodded. 'Exactly. Those fools had in their possession the man who ended the Endless war, and they didn't know what to do with him.'

Hael laughed, the sound like frost crunching underfoot. 'You've been killing people; over some fairy tale your daddy told you?'

Maia snarled, swinging the bat at Hael again. 'Fairy tale? You want to hear how the fairy tale ended? That Erinyes escaped. The Order underestimated him, and he got loose. He killed every last one of them. Burned them and half of Rome to the ground, destroying all their research. Well, most of it anyway. Enough survived for us to piece it together.

You think it's a fairy tale? I've seen the archaeological site in Rome, scorch marks still on the stone.'

'Okay, say it isn't a fairy tale. What do you want to use the sigils for anyway?'

'What else? To open the gates again.'

Gage stared at her in disbelief. 'So, you're insane? Why the hell would any human want the Aion to return?'

'Why, is none of your business.'

Gage sucked in a breath, every muscle in his body stretching taut. 'You killed my daughter.' His arms trembled, seeking release in violence but held in place by the chains. 'You killed how many people? You're targeting my family for some insane master plan, and you think it's none of my business.'

Maia gave him that same simpering smile. 'Well, when you put it that way.'

Gage glared at her, trying to think. 'So, you believe this story about what, some ritual to open the gates to the heavens? For whatever reason you're stupid enough to think opening them again is a good idea. What the hell does that have to do with my family?'

Hael's voice was quiet, he looked down, eyes distant. 'You know the story, but you don't know his name.'

Maia looked at Hael, clearly surprised. 'No, we never knew his name. History has forgotten him completely, human and Erinyes alike.'

'You don't know who he was, but you think he might still be alive.'

Maia shrugged. 'It's possible. Those early Erinyes were strong, especially those that were the bastard offspring of the Aion themselves.'

'Like my brother said. Why target the Aesir?'

'History has forgotten much about that time. There's a lot of speculation about the fall of the Order. One theory that persisted spoke of a rogue Aesir who was their undoing. Do you know the stories about your family? The famed Aesir, one of the oldest families, with the purest bloodlines left.'

Hael nodded to himself, like some puzzle piece had fallen into place. 'You're looking for a pure-blooded Erinyes. You think that's why your ritual isn't working.'

Maia studied him, genuinely curious. 'You're very perceptive. The Erinyes the Order held captive was powerful. He wiped out the Order single handed. Performed a ritual to close the gates no one else ever even heard of. Most people have forgotten the Furiae. They've forgotten how the Aion were tempted by their own creations and beget an even greater abomination. Half breed Aion.' Maia spat the words like they were a foul taste she couldn't get out of her mouth quick enough. 'You all call yourselves Erinyes now, diluted descendants of those first slave soldiers, but some of you are the offspring of those few half Aion, the Furiae.'

Hael shrugged. 'Born or made, you think there's that much difference?'

Maia lifted the bat, putting the tip of it under Hael's chin, forcing him to look at her. 'Oh, I know there is. You're so fond of stories and truth. Tell me, there are rumours the Aesir are sired by one of the Furiae. Is that true? Maybe it's even you?'

Hael looked over Maia's shoulder and smiled. 'Sorry to disappoint. But I've never fathered a single child. Him on the other hand...'

Gage followed Hael's gaze to see Kazimir behind one of

her men. His father snapped the man's neck without pause. A surge of relief flooded Gage. But it turned to granite dread as Maia turned to Vellichor.

'Shoot him,' she ordered.

Vellichor picked up a tranquilliser gun and fired a dart into Kazimir's neck. Five more of Maia's men ran into the room. Kazimir pulled the dart from his neck, looking down at it, as Vellichor fired another dart.

Hael strained against the chains holding him, frantic. 'Kaz, get out of here.'

His father looked up at Hael almost like he wasn't sure where he was. The drug in those darts was potent. Gage remembered the prick when he'd been hit and not much else after. It was fast acting. Kazimir was still on his feet at least, but his motions were sluggish. He turned to face the men approaching him, they all had batons. Kazimir would normally be more than a match for them. He wasn't a natural fighter like Cole and Hael, but strong and experienced. That didn't matter today though. Whatever Vellichor drugged him with, it turned his limbs to putty. Every move he made was easily blocked. Gage and Hael both cried out as Kazimir fell beneath a storm of baton strikes.

Maia's men grabbed hold of Kazimir, dragging him over in front of his sons, and shoving him roughly to his knees. Their father listed to one side, whether from his injuries or the drug was unclear.

Maia eyed Gage and Hael, noting their distress critically. She grabbed hold of Kazimir's hair, pulling his head back. 'So, who do we have here?'

Gage tensed, while Hael all but snarled at her.

Maia pulled a knife and held it to their father's neck. 'Tell me, or I kill him right now.'

Gage had no idea how to get out of this and glanced helplessly across at Hael. His brother always had a plan. A cold shiver danced across Gage's back at the expression on Hael's face. Hael's jaw clenched so tight Gage could hear his teeth grinding together. The threat of a drug capable of incapacitating them changed any of their usual tactics. He could practically see Hael sorting through ideas and discarding one after another.

Maia shifted the knife, drawing a bead of blood. 'Tell me who he is. Last chance.'

Gage bit his tongue. She was bluffing, right?

Kazimir coughed. 'Let them go.'

Maia looked down at him, tugging his head back harder.

Kazimir winced as the movement forced his back to bow, aggravating his injuries. 'You wanted to know a story about the Aesir?' He glanced up at Maia best he could. 'Yeah, I was listening. And you're right, our family are all descended from a Furiae. His father was Godblooded, and his mother an Aion. He was born over two thousand years ago, and you're holding a knife to him.'

Gage stared at his father. What the hell was he doing? Hael didn't react, trusting Kazimir knew what he was doing.

Maia lowered the knife. 'You're their father?'

Kazimir nodded. 'I was there during the Endless war, and I watched Aion fall from the sky. I'm half Aion, probably one of only a handful still alive today.'

Maia smiled triumphantly.

Gage stared at his father. 'What are you doing?'

Kazimir could barely move, his gaze fixed on Hael. 'I heard them talking. This is just a splinter cell. A field team for a larger organisation. They know too much.' One of the men kicked Kazimir to make him stop talking. He paused, coughing weakly. 'Gage, you remember what I told you earlier?'

Kazimir pushed a desperate rush of emotions towards Gage and for a moment he couldn't think what his father was referring to, but then it came to him. Kazimir had told him he would do anything to let Hael keep his secret, even if he didn't know what that secret was. Apparently, it was a pretty fucking big one if it had to do with how the Endless War ended and the gateway to the Aion home destroyed.

Hael's eyes pleaded with his father. 'You don't have to do this.'

Kazimir smiled. 'I know.'

Hael shifted, close to tears and unable to look away from his father. He seemed to come to a decision. He curled his fingers slowly around the chains holding him. 'My father was on that battlefield when the Order found the man with the sigils. Of course, he was nowhere near Rome the day the Order fell.'

The facade Hael usually put up crumbled and fell away as he tightened his fingers around the chain. Gage watched as Hael straightened, suddenly taking up far more space. The hairs on Gage's arms stood up as a flare of heat blasted outwards from Hael, gliding over skin like the sure creep of molten lava. Gage had rarely seen his brother like this. It was easy to forget how terrifying he really was.

Hael leaned forward, the corners of his mouth tilting upwards. 'But I was.'

Maia dropped her hand away from Kazimir, letting him slump back down. Kazimir stared up at his son. He tilted his head forward, a slight accepting nod Maia missed. Gage didn't understand the sad fond smile Kazimir gave Hael, or what the two of them were trying to do.

Hael's gaze settled back on their father. 'You thought the purest blood would be a half breed? You were wrong. I am Kaz's oldest child. I was with him the day the Aion fell. Do you know who my mother was? She was one of those Aion that fell, burning and screaming from the sky.'

Maia stared at Hael, almost reverently. 'That'd mean...'

'I'm more Aion than human.'

'You're what we've been looking for.'

Hael laughed, the sound almost manic. 'I'm really not. Even the purest Erinyes blood you could find won't work. Want to know why?'

'Why?'

Hael stopped laughing, leaning towards Maia conspiratorially. 'It's a secret.'

***

34

~ COLE ~

LONDON, 10TH NOVEMBER 1690

Everything was dark. Everything hurt. Cole flinched as someone gently shook him. He pulled away, the movement grating his tattered flesh. Dried blood and scabbing skin cracked. He opened his eyes. It was still murky. It took a moment to realise that was because it was night. A rough brick wall rubbed against his back. He was still in the alley.

He looked up. Hael?

Hael looked worried, or maybe scared. He reached out, cupping Cole's cheek, trying to get his attention. Cole listed to the side a little, unable to even hold his head up. He spotted Wrathe, standing guard over the two of them.

'Cole?'

Cole swallowed, trying to focus when he realised he hadn't actually replied yet. He coughed, vision nearly whiting out.

Wrathe looked around. 'We've got to go.'

Hael nodded, leaning in to lift Cole. Wrathe grabbed Hael's arm though.

'It'll be smoother with me.'

Cole smiled. Flying with Hael was like riding a hurricane sometimes. Wrathe a gentle summer breeze by comparison. It was funny, because in every other way, Wrathe was the hurricane. A dark and menacing storm, just like the story Hael made up.

Wrathe lifted him gently. Cole still had to bite his tongue to keep from crying out. He curled into Wrathe, barely aware of the way everything shifted as the alley blurred, the world drifting past in a swirl of colour like paint in water. They appeared somewhere more familiar and comforting. Cole had claimed this room in the family's Spanish Villa years ago. Wrathe settled him on the bed.

Cole looked around as Hael appeared a moment later. A spike of worry helping him find his voice. 'Where are Deac and Ash?'

Wrathe didn't answer, brow furrowed as he fussed with the pillows to prop Cole upright.

Hael knelt next to him, reaching out to squeeze his fingers where the skin was undamaged. 'Wrathe flew them out of London when we realised you were missing. They're downstairs with Bard.'

Cole nodded, incapable of doing anything else. 'Okay.' He just needed to tell Hael and Wrathe what he'd found, then maybe he could close his eyes again. 'The cult...'

His voice caught as he coughed. Wrathe glared at him, his expression a battlefield between anger and wild panic. Cole couldn't make himself look down at his arms and chest. But his injuries must look terrible to put that expression on Wrathe's face. He felt weak, lightheaded. Little flecks of light buzzed about, with an unsettling darkness around the edge of his vision. He flinched as Wrathe applied pressure to one of the injuries still bleeding. Cole thought it might have been the stab wound from the guard. He'd had his share of close calls before. Nothing like this, not since he'd been human. Cole looked up at Wrathe. Fear evident in the tenseness of his shoulders, the shallowness of his breaths.

Cole hated being the cause of that fear. 'I'm sorry.'

Wrathe glanced up at him. 'No, you're not, or wouldn't keep doing things like this.'

Cole couldn't help smiling. That was more like it.

Hael handed Wrathe another bandage. It probably wouldn't do any good, even with the healing abilities Hael's blood had given him.

Cole coughed again, wincing. 'The cult calls themselves the Children. They're obsessed with pure blood Erinyes. They knew stories, stories about the origin of the Furiae, about Constantinople, and the two Erinyes who destroyed half the city.' Cole swallowed, looking at Hael. 'They're not just after our family. They're after you, because you're more than you should be, because of your mother. They don't realise that yet, but if they find out...'

Hael looked away, swallowing thickly before looking back. 'You can tell us later.'

Cole grimaced. 'I'm not sure there will be a later, and you need to know.'

Wrathe glowered at the bandage he held to Cole's side, like he could cower the wound into submission. Cole shifted his arm, creeping his fingers closer to the book he'd tucked away in the band of his pants. They'd find it anyway, but he needed to make sure. Wrathe saw what he was reaching for and pulled the book out for him. He frowned at it and passed it to Hael.

'You need to read that.'

Hael took Cole's hand in his own again. 'Cole...'

'I didn't tell them anything, but they know a lot. They knew who I was, about my childhood. Don't let them find you.'

Wrathe pulled away the bandaged. Cole felt the wound bleeding, though sluggishly now.

'Hael, he's not healing.'

Hael looked like he wanted to break something, or maybe it was him that was breaking as he looked at Wrathe. 'Can you save him?'

Wrathe's brow knitted as he pressed the bandage back in place. 'I don't know. He's already a full Erinyes because of you. I have no idea what my blood will do.'

Cole glanced between the two men. 'What are you talking about?'

Wrathe looked up at him. He seemed fragile as his eyes searched Cole's. 'Do you trust me?'

Cole nodded. Answering on reflex he was so certain. 'Of course.'

Wrathe pulled a knife from his belt. He sliced open the

palm of his hand, grabbing a glass from the bedside table and catching the quickening drops of blood.

Cole didn't understand. 'Hael's blood stopped working on me a long time ago.'

Wrathe glanced down, taking a deep breath. He looked up and all his uncertainty slipped away. This was the man Cole imagined destroying cities.

'Cole, I'm not Erinyes.'

Cole stared blankly at Wrathe a moment, not sure what the words meant. He blamed the extreme blood loss for the slow uptake. His eyes widened. 'Oh.'

Hael stiffened, fingers twitching around Cole's. He seemed torn between wanting to make sure Cole never got into trouble again while keeping anything from ever harming Wrathe. Cole got it. Hael cared about nothing more than Wrathe, and if Wrathe really was a...

Cole swallowed, holding Hael's gaze when he finally looked up. 'Let me die.'

Wrathe flinched, and Cole wanted to snatch back the words. Hael looked like Cole just suggested they start eating babies.

Cole cleared his throat, needing to make them understand. 'I trust Wrathe with my life, I trust you with it. But I can't let you do this. They're looking for pure blood Erinyes. What do you think they'll do if they realise what Wrathe is?'

Now they both looked furious.

An argument bubbled up Cole's throat. A mess of reasons they should let him die to keep anyone from ever finding out about Wrathe. He didn't have time to voice a single word of it.

Wrathe's gaze was resolute. 'Cole, I'd stand on a rooftop and shout to the world what I am if it'd save you.'

Cole stared at him, wanting to argue but not sure how. He turned to Hael for help.

Hael shook his head. 'It's Wrathe's choice.'

Wrathe held out the glass filled with his blood. 'If the only reason you won't take this is because you want to protect me, you're as stupid and stubborn as Hael. Please...let me save you.'

Cole didn't have the energy or heart to refuse him. Not with the way Wrathe looked at him, like he was teetering on an edge waiting for Cole to push him over it.

Cole took the glass.

He remembered the stories Kazimir told about his father. About his memories of drinking the Godblood and turning into an Erinyes, the terror of it. Cole tipped the glass, swallowing the blood in a few quick gulps. Wrathe was nothing like those Aion that made Kazimir's father.

Cole emptied the glass. He looked up at Hael and Wrathe, at their matching anxious expressions. They'd shown a thousand times how much they cared for him. He might finally let himself believe it this time.

The blood slid down Cole's throat. Nothing happened for a second, then every muscle in his body tightened until they felt like they'd break. He screamed. Or tried to. But it wasn't possible when his lungs wouldn't work. His jaw clamped shut, and he was pretty sure he bit his tongue. Distantly, he was aware of two sets of hands trying to hold him down as his back arched off the bed.

It felt like his blood boiled. Pain exploded everywhere.

Cole closed his eyes. The world dropped away leaving him falling and falling into darkness. He could feel so much, too much. He felt the universe turn, the motion of galaxies drifting, spinning. Lifting his head, Cole watched in wonder as delicate filaments of a nebula reached across the eons to brush across his cheek with fingers made of dying stars. He tasted a thousand suns turn to dust.

Then, everything faded, leaving Cole bereft at the loss of perception. No matter how hard he tried to hold onto the stars, he fell back into his body and knew only darkness.

Wrathe and Hael were by his side when he woke, though he knew it was hours later. His body ached, but it was an itchy sort of ache. His wounds were all but healed, skin flushed pink and so sensitive the shifting air felt like fingers drawing random patterns across his torso. Cole opened his eyes, staring at the ceiling a moment as he slotted his thoughts back into the right order. He eventually looked to the side to see Wrathe sitting with his head slumped, elbows on his knees.

Cole wanted to reach out to him but wasn't sure how Wrathe would react. He might shatter with a wrong touch or word. 'No one else knows, do they? Only Hael.'

Wrathe looked up at the sound of his voice, smiling with tentative relief. 'No. No one.'

Cole nodded to himself. The last Aion on earth had died over fifteen hundred years ago. Or so everyone had believed.

'If I asked what your story was, would you tell me?'

Wrathe seemed weary, but certain. 'Yes.'

Hael shifted where he dozed on the floor with his back against Cole's bed, like even moving to the chair had been too far away.

Flexing his fingers, Cole could feel new strength in them, energy fizzing under his skin as it changed him. It was odd. He was a twice made Erinyes now. He wondered if that had ever happened before.

Cole was overcome with a surge of protectiveness for Wrathe, one that had been growing for years now. 'In that case, I'll never ask.'

***

35

~ Harper ~

Harper flattened her shoulders against the brick wall. Cole crouched beside her, looking out into the street while Tyriel remained in the shadows on the other side of the alley. There were maybe a dozen people outside the warehouse. All human, except the two people who were bound.

Deacon and Ash were on their knees, hands tied behind their backs. Blood streaked down Ash's temple. One of the men kicked Deacon. Ash glared at him like she'd rip his head off given half a chance if he hurt her brother again. Cole shifted and Harper reached down, putting a hand on his shoulder before he did something dumb. Cole dropped his head, breathing in through his nose, and letting the breath out through his mouth in a soft rush of air.

Harper knelt next to him. She squeezed his shoulder until he looked at her. She tapped her chest, and then pointed to the building. Cole watched as she repeated the gesture before nodding his head in understanding. She'd pinpointed the Erinyes at the last building, even if the humans waiting in backup had surprised them. She should have been able to tell Gage and Hael hadn't even been there. Hopefully, she could figure out they were in the right place this time before they rushed in. Cole settled back on his heels, slipping further into the shadows as he watched her, waiting.

It was odd to have someone trust her ability, after so long having everyone, even herself, focus and what she couldn't do.

Closing her eyes, she breathed out. She sensed Cole, and the oddly calm presence of Tyriel across the alley. She let the sensation wash over her, memorising it. Tyriel was the ghosting touch of sunshine in the dead of winter, caught somewhere between a sorrowful memory of the summer lost and a resolute promise of the slumbering spring. Expanding her senses, she recognised the hint of sea salt from Ash and Deacon. Five unfamiliar Erinyes waited inside the warehouse entrance and another dozen were scattered around the complex. There. On the top floor. The corner of her mouth twitched as a thrum of accomplishment buzzed somewhere in her chest. She could feel Kazimir, and the cool touch of Gage like a delicate frost that wouldn't survive the sunrise. There was a turbulent presence with them that had to be Hael. It was like trying to pick up detail of the horizon through shimmering heat haze, but she was sure it was him. Another unfamiliar Erinyes was nearby, probably in the room with them.

She opened her eyes. 'Gage, Hael and Kazimir are on the top floor with another Erinyes. There are five Erinyes inside the entrance, maybe another dozen in hiding.' Tyriel tilted his head, but Harper ignored his curiosity. 'No idea how many humans there might be.'

Cole shrugged, like that didn't matter. It probably didn't. Harper doubted anything would stop him from going in. His eyes flitted over the warehouse, looking for the best way in. There weren't many options. They'd scouted around the building when they arrived. The only accesses were the main and a rear entrance. Both being guarded. Obviously, they expected an attack.

Tyriel shifted in the shadows. 'We won't get in there quietly.'

Cole stood, flexing his shoulders. 'No, we won't.' He reached into his coat, pulling out his pistols. He handed one to Harper along with a spare clip. 'Stay here, cover our backs.'

He glanced at Tyriel but said nothing, resigned he'd follow no matter what Cole said, and rushed out into the light.

A dozen guns turned towards Cole. He moved fast, but surely he'd need the ability of flight to have any chance of dodging that many attackers. He didn't show the slightest hesitation though. Cole was going to get himself killed.

Harper reached for her knives but paused as Tyriel disappeared. He dropped back into sight a split second later, breaking the neck of the man who kicked Deacon before anyone reacted. Cole fired, taking out the one holding Ash, before shifting with a grace that seemed unnatural, dodging to the side. He'd moved so quickly he caught them by surprise, crossing the street before anyone got a good shot at him. He grabbed hold of Ash and, twisting in one fluid movement, pulled her into cover behind a parked car.

Tyriel slashed the ropes binding Deacon and the two of

them took flight. They landed next to Harper in the cover of the alley. Deacon crashed into the wall, barely managing to stay on his feet. Cole cut Ash loose, urging her to flee once she was free. She appeared in the alley as unsteady on her feet as Deacon, who reached out and put an arm around Ash's shoulder, pulling her close. They held each other upright. They appeared groggy, like they'd been drugged. Harper doubted either of them were capable of full flight at the moment. Any element of surprise was gone. Gunshots ricocheted off the vehicle Cole crouched behind as he returned fire.

Deacon and Ash were out of harm's way, but Gage and the others still inside might be in more danger now that their presence was known.

There was a sudden friction in the air, like incoming lightning, followed by a rush of sound as an Erinyes landed in front of Cole with an incredible amount of speed, a burst of displaced air accompanying his arrival. Harper raised her gun, but Deacon made a soft sound in his throat, shakily reaching out to push her weapon down.

'He's with us.'

Harper glanced at Deacon who smiled, though the expression was a little watery around the edges. She looked back at the new arrival. The man had long dark hair that obscured his face as he bent down to check on Cole, who grinned up at him. He must be the backup Cole called, Wrathe, she presumed.

The man let out an exasperated huff, and reached out to clap Cole on the shoulder, before disappearing. He appeared further down the street. Before he'd even fully landed, he struck out at one of the humans firing at Cole, twisting as he did so into a spin kick that connected with another man's head, snapping it backwards with sickening force. Before he finished the full turn, he was back in flight, a blur of movement Harper had trouble keeping track of. Cole rolled out from behind the car, firing in quick succession. He dropped one man, winged another. Rolling back into cover as shots shattered concrete around him, he looked down at his gun, before tossing it, out of ammo.

Harper hesitated, wanting to join the fight, but Cole asked her to cover them from her vantage point in the alley. As good as she was at close combat, she'd rarely put that into practice in an actual life or death situation. She fell back on the instincts her father had instilled. Soldiers followed orders in battle. Steadying her stance, she angled her body so she could duck back into cover easily but had a good line of sight. Aiming at one of the men closest to Cole, she fired. The bullet hit centre mass, and the man dropped.

She watched him fall with an odd detachment. She'd never killed anyone before. The man had been involved in the kidnapping of a Watcher, and had been about to shoot Cole in the back. Even so, she would probably have a lot to feel about it later, but for now, she took cover as their new ally appeared again.

Wrathe arrived with speed, face on to one of the attackers. He struck the man in the chest with his knee, the drive from his flight slamming the man backwards. He attacked the next man with a flurry of movement, blocking a hit he gripped the attacker's arm and flipped him onto the pavement. The man screamed as his arm wrenched backwards at an angle it clearly wasn't meant to achieve. The remaining humans turned their guns on Wrathe. Cole took advantage of the distraction, moving out of cover. He rolled, slamming into the legs of one man who went down hard. Using his momentum to come back to his feet, Cole grappled with another, a quick series of blocks and strikes before using a knife she hadn't seen him pull to slit the man's throat.

Tyriel had hesitated when Cole's backup arrived. He moved now though, appearing across the street, skilfully taking down one of the men at Cole's back. Harper sensed movement from inside the entrance to the warehouse. The Erinyes were coming. She aimed at the door as it opened, taking the first one out with a clean head shot. She fired rapidly as more landed in the street. She hit one in the shoulder, another in the arm, before she stopped firing as their ally moved into the fray. He grabbed one of the Erinyes attackers by his shirt and slammed a fist into his face, dropping him like a stone. The other Erinyes realised the mistake of coming outside and took flight. Harper sensed them falling back to a more defensible position upstairs, abandoning the last human who Tyriel quickly took down.

Cole turned to the man. 'Wrathe, you...'

Whatever Cole had been going to say died on his tongue as he and Wrathe both looked up suddenly, the colour draining from their faces. Wrathe disappeared. Cole didn't hesitate, taking off for the stairs. Harper felt it a moment later. A sudden blast of heat she knew in her bones was Hael. She wasn't empathic, didn't feel emotions like most Erinyes, but she could right now. Uncontrolled rage, sudden and fierce, the sort that left nothing but charred bones in its wake.

Harper swallowed thickly, the Erinyes had fallen back to

where Gage and Hael were being held. They had no idea how many more humans might be upstairs. She looked across at Tyriel. He shrugged, and they both followed Cole.

***

36

~ GAGE ~

Gage watched as Maia's hold on Kazimir loosened. His father sagged without her hold to keep him upright, still struggling with the effects of the drug Vellichor had shot him with. Maia stared at Hael, calculating, fanatically hopeful. Gage had no idea if Hael was telling the truth. Hael lied as easily as breathing, and Gage could only tell about half the time. It wasn't out of the realm of possibility he'd know something this group wanted. Knowing things was what his brother did.

Hael breathed heavy, every angle of his body screaming anger. 'If you want to know why your pathetic attempts at the ritual will never work, let my father and brother go.'

Maia tilted her head. 'Why should I believe you?'

'You want to know about the man the Order held prisoner?' Hael smiled, it was a twisted, ugly thing. 'I can tell you all about the room they held him in. I can tell you about the hooks that bit into his flesh. The way the Order stripped everything away until he could barely remember his own name. The countless drawings they made of him, of the way they cut into him and counted how long it took each slice to heal. I can tell you about the sound of the knife sliding into the left eye of the priest who'd tortured him for years, how damn good it felt.'

Maia made a whimpering sound in her throat. She stared at Hael with outright hunger now. 'The priest's left eye?'

'It was two thousand years ago, but I've never forgotten.'

Maia took a half step towards Hael. 'They found the priest the next day. We have the records of all the bodies, how they had found them, how they had died.'

Gage stared at his brother. If he was lying, how had he gotten such a small detail so right, it hooked Maia completely.

Hael looked mildly interested. 'Did they? I never knew. I left the city that night and didn't return for over a century.'

Kazimir groaned, looking up at his eldest son with a fierce pride even as he looked ready to pass out. 'Hael, are you sure...'

Hael nodded.

Gage's brain stuttered as it always did when thinking about how old his brother was, about all the things he'd done that no one ever talked about. Maia had been chasing myths of the man who ended the Endless War. But Gage was pretty sure it hadn't been his brother who closed the gates, who had been the Order's prisoner. What had Kazimir said earlier? That Hael had saved Wrathe when he should have killed him.

Maia lifted the bat again, settling it on her shoulder.

'Okay. Say I believe you. Why would I let your family go? Not when they are the perfect incentive to make you talk.'

She swung the bat.

Kazimir grunted, the hit to his side sending him off balance in his drugged state. He slumped, drawing in a ragged breath. Maia swung again.

Hael yelled. The sound rumbling from deep in his throat. 'Stop.'

Maia settled the bat back on her shoulder.

Hael took a deep breath, straining to contain his rage. 'If you ever want to undo the seals that closed the gate. You can't just use any Erinyes blood for the sigils, no matter how pure it is.' Hael clenched his jaw. 'You need the blood of the man who originally cast them. His fresh blood, taken while his heart still beats.'

Maia narrowed her eyes at Hael. 'And is that you?'

Hael's shoulders slumped. 'You've been looking for the Aesir who caused the downfall of the Order?' He looked up at Maia. 'That would be me.'

Gage looked at his brother, understanding what Hael was doing now, and why Kazimir seemed so resigned and sorrowful. If they managed to escape and couldn't kill Maia and whoever she was working with, Hael was using a half-truth to make sure it was him they would come after. And if they couldn't get free, Hael would make sure he died here. He would make Maia think she had killed the only man who could reopen the gates and hope that was enough to make her stop searching for the truth. It was a hell of a gamble, one likely to end with his brother's death.

Maia grinned at him. 'For all the hassle you and your

family have given me, I will kill this one.' She pointed the bat at Gage. 'I'll keep your father alive. For now.'

Was this how he died? Strung up by some zealot whose screws weren't just loose but missing completely. Gage looked across at his brother. Hael laughed. His body shook with it, eyes alight with dark amusement. Everyone in the room stared at him.

Hael grinned, trying to catch his breath. 'You know, as much as I hated those bastards from the Order. I learned one interesting thing because of them. See, they learned so much about Erinyes from studying us, dissecting and cutting. They were one of the few human groups who ever really grasped the use of Aionic script. So, aren't you curious how anyone escaped the Order when they knew so much about binding sigils?'

Hael shifted his weight. He flexed his hands, wrapping his fingers around the chains holding him. For the first time, Gage noticed the sigils smeared with Hael's blood were glowing. Before Gage could figure out why, the sigils flared and faded to nothing, like they'd never been there to begin with. It shouldn't be possible. Hael flexed his shoulders, pulling down on the chains, and snapping them easily.

The room was deadly silent as everyone stared at his brother in shock.

Hael rolled his shoulders to loosen them. As he did, the surrounding air shifted, shimmering like heat haze dancing on the horizon on a hot summer day. Cole had taken Gage to Hawaii once. They had gone to see one of the volcanoes. Stood and watched it bubble lava and gas, the billowing steam blanketing them where they stood on the rim. The heat had been aweing. That same kind of heat filled the room right now. Waves of it poured off Hael, but unlike the volcano, there was intent behind the fire burning in his brother. Hael smiled and it was terrifying, even Gage flinched.

Taking a step forward, Hael's gaze pinned Maia. 'You want to know the stories about us? Do you really? I could tell you all kinds of stories. I could tell you about what a city on fire sounds like. Or the sounds the old men from your Order made as they begged for their lives. But why should I tell you a damn thing? I've killed a lot of people to keep my secrets, what makes you think you will be any different?'

Hael reached out and grabbed hold of Maia by the neck. She swung the bat at him, but he didn't flinch as it bounced off his torso. Hael pulled it out of her grip, tossing it across the room. As he did, Gage noticed the sound of gun fire on the street below. Of course, Kazimir wouldn't have come alone.

Someone in the room opened fire, shots flying wild, but at least one hit Hael in the arm. He growled and tossed Maia at the man shooting, the two humans crashed into a jumbled heap. Hael turned toward Gage, but before he could release him, half a dozen Erinyes landed in the room. Hael shifted, placing himself between the attackers and Gage and Kazimir.

Hael stilled. 'Wrathe?'

Kazimir coughed, trying to stand, but only getting one knee under himself. 'Hael, you have to go.'

'I'm not leaving you.'

Kazimir shook his head. 'Go, I know what you're doing, and it'll only work if you get him far away from here.'

Hael didn't answer or leave.

The Erinyes who had arrived were clearly indecisive about

whether Hael or whoever was on the street below were the greater threat. Some of them faced the door, while others kept a wary eye on Hael, none of them seeming sure what to do with Maia incapacitated. Hael shifted his weight on his feet, trying to find the best position to defend them as he watched Vellichor who still hadn't moved. He was probably the biggest unknown. If he used the drug, this would be a short fight. Especially with Kazimir out of commission and Gage still chained. But Vellichor hadn't moved. He was staring at Maia where she lay unconscious but still breathing. His expression didn't show any concern, instead almost curious, like he was waiting to see what would happen.

Wrathe suddenly appeared next to Gage, landing so quietly he almost didn't notice. The tension in Hael's shoulders eased. Gage cringed as Wrathe ripped the chains holding him from the ceiling, the weight of them dragging Gage's arms to the floor with a painful tingling sensation as the blood rushed back to his hands.

Wrathe's arrival changed Hael's tactics from defence to offence. Everything happened so quickly. Hael moved, ripping the gun from one of the human's hands, throwing it at another man with such force his head snapped back from the impact. The shocked stillness dissipated and those left armed opened fire. Wrathe shifted in and out of flight with such incredible speed that even in the confines of the room it was hard to keep track of him. Gage had rarely seen the other man fight, though Cole had always praised his skills. Seeing them firsthand was almost indescribable. Hael's flying abilities were usually impressive, but they were nothing compared to what he saw now. Wrathe and Hael swirled around each other, appearing and disappearing as they dropped their Erinyes and human attackers alike rapidly.

Out of the corner of his eyes, Gage saw Vellichor finally act. Gage tried to move, calling out to get Wrathe's attention. Vellichor lifted the tranquilliser, waiting for the right moment before he fired. He'd aimed perfectly. Wrathe looked down at the dart buried in his chest, plucking it out. Tilting his head curiously, he flicked it away before looking up at Vellichor, who fired two more in quick succession. Wrathe moved forward like the darts hadn't affected him at all. The distraction was costly though.

One of the humans aimed at Wrathe while his back was turned. At such close range, a well-placed shot could be deadly. Kazimir, unsteady but on his feet, shifted, knocking the gun off target. His father was too weak though, and the attacker overpowered him. Grabbing Kazimir's arm, the man twisted it, forcing him to his knees. He aimed his gun point blank at the base of Kazimir's skull.

A single moment stretched, treacle slow. Gage watched as, impossibly fast to react, Wrathe shifted into flight, landing and killing the human, but not fast enough. It was too late. A fraction of a second too late. The man had already fired.

Kazimir was dead before he hit the floor. A single bullet, and a life spanning more than two thousand years was over, just like that.

Gage couldn't move, couldn't breathe.

His father was dead.

Across the room, Hael screamed. The sound reverberated, smashing into Gage with physical force. Every window in the warehouse shattered. Gage's legs buckled, shoulder glancing painfully off the wall before he steadied himself. It knocked everyone else to their knees. Even with his hands pressed tightly over his ears the sound pounded in Gage's head, before cutting off as suddenly as it had started. The silence in its wake was deafening.

Gage shook his head, trying to stop his ears from ringing as he looked around. Footsteps sounded on the stairs, and Cole burst into the room, Harper and Tyriel not far behind him. Cole stumbled to a stop when he saw Kazimir, the colour draining from his face.

Harper hesitated beside him, her grip on her pistol shifting. 'Shit.'

Her voice sounded loud, shattering the shocked stillness.

Hael stumbled, crossing to where their father lay. He fell to his knees like a puppet with its strings cut, gaze fixed on their father's body. He reached out, hands shaking as they hovered above Kazimir, like if he reached out and touched him it would all become real.

Gage shifted but didn't move any closer. His legs felt like they were stuck in thigh high drifts of snow, sluggish and the strength all but sapped from them. 'Hael?'

Hael didn't seem to hear him. His fingers hovered a moment longer, before Hael finally reached out, laying his hand gently on his father's unmoving chest. Hael's entire body shook. Gage barely had time to react before his brother cried out again. The sound primal, and unbearably raw. It shook Gage to his very bones. He pressed his hands to his ears, but it made no difference. The sound wasn't just vocal, it was pure power. A burning fury and visceral pain. Gage had never been close to his father, not like his brother. As waves of Hael's grief hit him it subsumed his own.

The air seemed to smoulder, almost to the point of conflagration and Gage swore he smelled ash. Wrathe moved quickly, twisting to grab hold of Hael and taking flight with him. The temperature dropped instantly. Wrathe couldn't have made it far as Gage felt a burst of white-hot energy slam into the outside of the building.

If Wrathe hadn't acted when he did, everyone in the room would probably be dead. Waves of energy battered against the building, slowly subsiding like aftershocks following an earthquake. Wrathe must have been in close range, Gage didn't know if he could survive a blast like that.

***

37

~ HAEL ~

23rd June 132BCE
Last day of the Endless War

Hael stumbled, almost falling. He caught himself at the last moment, using his sword to steady himself. He wasn't entirely sure where he was. They'd been fighting for a long time and the battle had drifted throughout the day. He was so exhausted his bones hurt. How was that even possible?

Hael straightened, looking up. The sky was dotted with drifting puffs of cloud. Clean and pristine white set against the blue. He wasn't sure he'd ever feel clean again. How could he? He was drenched in blood.

Around him, bodies piled on top of each other. So many. Mostly the humans they'd fought so hard to save. It had been years since his people first turned on their makers, the Aion, in a hopelessly one-sided fight. Too many of them had died at the whim of the Aion, expendable, forgotten. They fought now for their freedom, for a choice in how they lived and died. They had chosen to save the humans too, who were dying by the thousands in this war that wasn't theirs. It wasn't the Erinyes's fight either. They were pawns as much as the humans in the Aion's endless war.

No, it had to end. One side had to run out of people to kill sooner or later.

Hael moved, one foot in front of the other, though he wasn't sure which way he should be going. He stumbled along for a few steps, too tired to even try flying. Maybe today would be the day he died, and he could finally get some rest. Wouldn't that be nice.

He tripped over an outflung rotting arm. This time he did fall, landing hard on his knees. He barely registered the stab of pain amongst all the other aches. He dug his sword into the damp ground, using it to keep himself from giving in and laying down, here amongst all the corpses.

To the south, a flock of birds took flight. Startled by something, they scattered, black flecks in the sky. Hael watched them, wondering where the rest of his unit was, or anyone else he knew. He hadn't seen his father in a week, not since the surprise raid scattered their encampment.

Hael shifted his grip on the sword, flexing his fingers. He could feel something in the south, in the direction the birds had flown from. There was nothing to see. No movement. The battle had moved on and left Hael behind. He closed his eyes, trusting his instincts. There, a flicker of something. Some emotion that wasn't his.

Hael missed his twenty-third birthday last month. Completely forgot about it. But over the last few months, his powers had manifested. He was young, younger than most Erinyes when their abilities developed. He'd blamed it on exhaustion at first when he started to feel things from those he fought beside, from those he killed. He could feel their fear, their anger, grief, desperation. He'd thought it simply his own at first. But it wasn't. He'd reached out a few weeks ago to grab hold of an Aion attacking him and the man cried out in shock as his skin reddened like he'd been burned.

If he hadn't been so exhausted, it would have freaked him out. Instead, he'd barely had any time to think about the abilities growing faster than he could really handle. Instead, he unleashed them on their enemies. He'd figure out how he felt about that later. If he lived long enough.

Hael lifted his head, looking south. There was definitely someone there. They were alone. Desperate, but not scared. Whoever it was, they were drowning in the same bone-weary emptiness that had dogged Hael himself for a while now. The desperate desire for it all to end. But more than that, the will to make it end.

Hael opened his eyes, curious, but too tired to do more than idly track the ebb and flow of emotions as the Aion, and it was an Aion, Hael was sure of it, moved across the battlefield. He was a mile or so away. The Aion eventually stopped. Hael felt an echo of pain from him, pain that was growing. He looked up. The sky above the battlefield darkened. There were more Aion coming. A lot of them, converging on their lone brethren to the south.

Hael sharpened his focus, and it was like he was stood next to the solitary Aion. Waves of anger and grief that weren't his own tumbled over him, crashing down and pinning him to the ground. It was suffocating, pressing down and down until he couldn't breathe even as his lungs expanded, and expanded, crushing his heart.

Hael pulled himself upright, not sure why, but feeling compelled to do something. He'd barely made it to his feet when he felt the Aion scream. A massive wall of sound blasted outwards. A rush of air knocked Hael down again, tumbling him over and over. Hael screamed too, as unbearable pressure built inside his skull. Then, everything went silent. It was like the world drew in a breath and held it. In the stillness, Hael heard the Aion whisper.

'Forgive me. But this has to end.'

Hael closed his eyes, but even in his mind he saw the Aion. Saw him kneeling on the battlefield, shoulders slumped, torso bare and covered in sigils. A bloodied knife still gripped in the man's hand, before his fingers slackened, and he crumpled, falling to lay bloodied and alone on a battlefield filled with the dead and dying.

Hael opened his eyes. He wasn't sure how much later, but the sun had sunk low. He looked up and saw Aion. They tumbled from the sky. Hundreds, maybe thousands of them. Their wings burned as they fell, spiralling sparks flaring and dying.

Hael couldn't tear his eyes away from the sight, even as hands grabbed hold of him, shaking him roughly.

'Hael?'

Hael closed his eyes, seeing the afterglow of falling Aion behind his eyelids.

'Hael. Son?'

Hael opened his eyes and his father's worried face hovered above him.

'Father?'

Kazimir gripped his hand, closing his eyes in relief briefly, before turning to look up at the sky himself. 'They're dying. They're all dying.'

Hael squeezed his father's hand, not wanting to ask. 'Mother?'

Kazimir didn't look away from the sky. 'She fell. Just like them.'

Hael didn't react. He'd known before he asked. He'd wanted it all to end, and it was. Hael could feel it. Those Aion not dying in the sky above, were being slaughtered on the ground by humans. Hael turned his head to the south. Whatever that lone Aion had done, it had ended the war.

Tears welled in his eyes. There'd been so much death. For the first time, he let himself feel it. He felt the Aion screaming as they fell from the sky. He felt the spectre of so much pain and misery hanging above the corpses stretching out around him.

Kazimir pulled him up until he was sitting. He reached out, cupping a hand to Hael's cheek. 'It's over.'

Hael nodded, letting himself lean into the touch. It was over. Tomorrow, he would be glad of that. But now, he looked up as his father pulled him closer.

'How did you find me?'

'I heard you. You were screaming.'

Hael shook his head. 'That wasn't me. The Aion was screaming.'

Kazimir paused, hand tightening on Hael's shoulder. 'There was no one else. I've been searching for you since the raid on the encampment. You called out to me. You were screaming. I followed your call until I found you.'

Hael shook his head again. 'There was an Aion. He was alone, in pain. He was...I felt his sadness, his grief at what they'd done and what he was about to do.'

'Okay. It's okay.'

Hael let his head fall onto his father's shoulder, though he kept his eyes on the sky. For the first time in years, he let someone else hold him up. With his father, he'd bear witness as Aion fell from the sky. He felt each and every one of them flare and die out like embers in the night. It felt like part of him died with each one.

'I can hear them. I can feel all of them.'

Kazimir held him tighter. 'You can?'

Hael nodded, tears falling down his cheeks.

'It's okay. I'm here. I'm not going anywhere. Close your eyes son. It's okay.'

Hael felt like the boy he was as he closed his eyes, not the veteran soldier who'd been fighting for as long as he remembered. His father held him as he cried for the deaths of those who had been their enemy, for those who were more his brethren than the dead humans piled around him. Hael let himself fall apart in Kazimir's arms, knowing his father would hold all the pieces of him together.

***

38

~ GAGE ~

Gage stared numbly at his father's body. He couldn't be dead. It didn't seem real. Everything felt fuzzy around the edges, and just that little bit too far away. He took a step forward and the room felt like it swayed. Gage closed his eyes, swallowed dryly. When he opened his eyes, Kazimir was still dead, body slumped on the floor where he'd fallen.

Like a rag doll, tossed aside.

Gage stared at the body. He wanted to scream, he wanted to reach for that anger that kept him going after Ara, but there was nothing there. Just a great sucking void. It hurt to breath. He wanted to close his eyes, look away, but he couldn't move, breathe, think.

'Dad...' Gage barely recognised his own voice.

Cole shifted, letting out a shuddering breath. Gage slowly turned his head to look up at the older man. Cole clenched his fists and turned towards Vellichor, who was the only attacker still on his feet. The Erinyes took one look at the expression in Cole's eyes and fled. It was a smart choice. Every plane of Cole's body screamed fury, tightly coiled and ready to spring. He didn't give chase though. Tyriel hesitated a second before taking off, presumably going after Vellichor, though really Gage had no idea what the club owner was doing here. Cole rolled his shoulders and turned on the two humans left alive where they groaned on the floor.

Gage had no idea if he meant to kill them or not.

Harper intervened before he could if that was his intent. She quickly found something to bind Maia and one of her men. One of the Erinyes on the floor groaned, apparently not dead, only unconscious. Gage looked down at his wrists, still held in the warded manacles. Harper noticed, and frisked the two humans she had bound, finding a set of keys on Maia. She quickly unlocked the chains from Gage and snapped the cuffs onto the unconscious Erinyes. With the attackers no further threat, she looked around, seeming unsure what to do next.

It was Cole who acted. As it so often was.

Kneeling beside Kazimir, Cole shifted his father's arms so they crossed over his chest respectfully. He placed a hand gently over Kazimir's. Cole bowed his head and whispered words too quiet for Gage to hear. A private goodbye meant only for Kazimir.

His father had always been so fond of Cole.

Cole took a deep breath, steadying himself, and Gage could feel him pushing aside his grief, shoving it deep down inside so he could move.

Cole looked over at Gage. 'Deacon and Ash are across the street. They were drugged but otherwise seem fine.'

Gage nodded, thoughts feeling heavy and slow, like they'd been swimming too long against the current. 'They drugged us too. I'd like to know what with.'

Cole turned to look at the prisoners. 'Which one of these should I be getting answers from?'

Gage pointed at Maia, who glared at him. 'That one. Her name's Maia.'

Cole knelt in front of her, smiling charmingly. 'Hello Maia. My friend here would like to know what you drugged him with. Be a sweetheart and tell him, won't you.'

Maia spat at him. 'I know who you are. The filthy tainted human, begging for scraps from the Aesir like a stray dog.'

'Well, aren't you charming.' He reached out and patted her cheek. 'Be careful. Stray dogs have nasty bites.'

Gage glared at the woman. 'They're part of the Descendants. Following the work of some long dead human cult to open the gates of heaven.'

Cole looked up at Gage. 'The Order?'

'Yeah. How'd you know?'

Maia laughed, looking up at Gage. 'Even the filthy dog knows more than the Aesir Watcher.'

Cole's expression hardened. 'What else did she tell you?'

'They've been following stories about an Aesir rumoured to have ended the Order a couple thousand years ago. They thought he'd know about some ritual used to end the Endless War by closing the gates to the Aion world. They want to reopen them.'

Cole looked back at Maia. 'What the hell for?'

She laughed. 'Why does anyone do anything?'

Cole reached out and grabbed her by the throat. He stared

at her in that unnerving way he sometimes did, like he was seeing right down to her soul. 'Tell me.'

Maia smiled, and it was frighteningly manic. 'We will open the way for the gods. The pure, and undefiled. We will ascend and claim our place amongst them.'

Cole let her go, looking distant like he was seeing things not in this room. Gage startled as Hael landed beside Cole. His brother was pale, expression drained of any emotion as he reached down and squeezed Cole's shoulder, seeming to bring him back to himself. Cole looked up at Hael, expression grim.

Hael's voice had no inflection. 'They're fanatics who'll get us and the whole damn world killed.'

Harper moved forward. 'We need to turn them over to the Watchers and the Council to question.'

Gage looked across at his brother, knowing that was never going to happen.

Hael looked over his shoulder at her. 'No.'

Harper moved to stand between Hael and Maia. She lifted the gun she held. It was one of Cole's. Loaded, ready to fire. She didn't raise it all the way but held it ready. 'What are you going to do?'

'What I need to. This ends here. Now.'

'You can't...'

'You think you can stop me?'

Hael moved before she could answer. He ripped Cole's gun from her hand, aiming it at Maia's head and firing. Cole shifted, grabbing hold of Harper before she could react. She struggled against his grip, but he held fast.

'You can't do this.' Harper's words were quiet, like she knew the futility of arguing.

Hael didn't stop. He fired a single bullet into the head of each of the remaining captives. Then, he methodically put a bullet in the head of those they'd assumed were dead, to make certain they were.

Maybe Gage should be surprised at his brother's actions, feel some sort of horror at the ease of it. But he didn't. Hael had a lot of blood on his hands. He followed his own code, and never cared much if it was legal, or even met the moral standards of others. If killing was the surest way to protect his family, Hael would do it.

Hael came to a stop in front of Harper and looked down at her. 'Trust me. You don't want anyone to know it's even possible to reopen those gates. Let alone how.'

Harper stared at Hael in shock but said nothing. He turned away from her and handed the gun back to Cole. Hael walked to their father's body. He paused a moment, a trickle of emotion falling across his expression, before being consumed by the blankness that settled over him. Gage hesitantly reached out empathically, and felt nothing at all from his brother, the void even more jarring after the outpouring of emotion earlier. Hael reached down, picking up Kazimir and carrying him down the stairs without another word.

Gage stared after Hael. He took a breath, and it felt like his feet finally unstuck from the floor. He followed, drawn after his brother and the body of his father.

***

39

~ HARPER ~

Harper stared down at the bodies Hael left in his wake. A pool of blood spread around the woman, Maia, where she had fallen. Her hands were still bound. There had to be a dozen bodies in the room, plus those on the street outside. Hael hadn't even hesitated, like it was the easiest thing in the world. She watched the pool of blood widen and tried to sustain her outrage at the immorality of killing unarmed and bound prisoners. But as the shock of it settled, she felt oddly empty.

She stared at Maia, and thought of Yuri and his brother, of the two young Aesir strung up like marionettes.

They had died slow.

Harper looked down. A fleck of dried blood was still on the toe of her left boot from when she had stepped close to examine the bodies of Valerie and Thorn Aesir. She wasn't sure if it was right or not, but she was glad Maia was dead. Even if she may have taken valuable information to her grave.

Harper looked around, unsure what to do now everything was over. Though Maia hadn't been working alone. Was it really over?

The room was quiet, though Harper's ears still rang. She'd never before seen or felt anything like Hael's grief. The hair on her arms still stood on end from the blast of energy he'd let loose. Even now, despite the fact he was downstairs somewhere, she could feel odd eddies of warm air shifting about in haphazard patterns. Just how powerful was he? She looked around at the bodies again, suspecting he was capable of much more destruction than this. But could she really hold these deaths against him? These people had been targeting his family, they had killed people Hael cared about. He had just watched his father die. She wiped at her cheek, surprised when her fingers came away wet. She'd never been able to feel the emotions of others, but the waves of emotion coming off Hael had been overwhelming and intensely clear. Enough for her to shed tears for a man she didn't know.

Killing Maia and the others hadn't been justice. But had it been wrong?

Before she really thought it through, Harper knelt and unbound Maia's hands. Then did the same for the other two bodies. She had tried to stop Hael from killing them yet found herself oddly unwilling to let others who hadn't been here judge him for his actions.

She turned to follow the others downstairs. Wrathe, the strange Erinyes was standing behind her. He'd been so quiet she hadn't heard him land. Moving silently, smoothly, like water flowing from one place to another, he shifted to stand beside her. He smiled shyly at her. It was the first chance she'd had to get a good look at him. He was startlingly beautiful, but it was a broken sort of beauty. Distant, fragile, like a flake of snow drifting in the air. A prism of ice lonely in a dark night sky.

'Harper, I presume?'

His voice was deep and gentle, not what she expected from someone as deadly as he seemed.

'You're who Cole called. Wrathe?'

He looked down. 'I should have come sooner.'

Cole had only left the voice message two hours ago. It seemed he'd come as soon as he'd received it. He studied her a moment. She felt an odd sense of vertigo, a little like staring up at the night sky and suddenly realising just how big the universe really was.

He looked around at the bodies. 'I know what people think about him. What Hael wants them to think about him. He might be reckless, and he definitely drinks too much. But killing isn't easy for him. He feels too much, it's always been his biggest fault.'

Harper could easily believe that.

Wrathe glanced across at her, enigmatic, and held a hand out to her. She looked at it dumbly a moment, before recognising the gesture as the same one Hael used to ask if she wanted to fly with him. Whoever this man was, she'd bet money he'd spent considerable time around Hael. It was easier to focus on the familiar gesture, then the fact this was the second man in as many days to display an ability she'd thought impossible.

The others were waiting downstairs. There was no need for him to offer her a lift just to save a few flights of stairs. It was a show of trust she realised. Though she had no idea what she had done to earn it.

Harper reached out and took hold of his hand. He smiled at her again, a tiny thing that was barely there. He pulled her closer and they took flight. She sucked in a breath, expecting the same unsettling mad plunge through space as with Hael. Before she'd even fully drawn in the breath though, he set her gently down on the street outside. Wrathe let go of her, stepping back. Harper instinctively reached out to compensate for the sudden shift in location, trying to orientate herself. She accidentally did so with both her hand and her senses. Wrathe didn't seem to notice, he crossed the street without another word to her, unaware of her shocked indrawn breath.

Harper's senses roared at her. It took everything she had not to fall to her knees. She stared across the street as Wrathe stood next to Cole. Wrathe hovered close like he wanted to reach out and offer comfort but wasn't sure how to do it. Cole swayed a little to brush shoulders with him.

Harper let out the breath that had caught in her lungs. Wrathe was old, beyond old. It felt like witnessing mountains rise and fall to dust as she looked at him. The age she sensed from Hael and Kazimir had been immense, but this was humbling. So much raw energy streamed off Wrathe it washed over her like a wave. She struggled to pull her senses back from him. It felt like she was trapped between shifting sheets of ice, being dragged beneath a glacier as it ground down mountains. Her eyes widened. It was impossible. No Erinyes could have the amount of power she felt flowing from

Wrathe. The burst of energy from Hael earlier had been more than she ever thought possible. This was so much more. There was only one possibility, but it was impossible.

Harper sucked in a thready breath as she tried to reign in her senses, only dimly aware of Hael placing Kazimir's body on the backseat of Cole's car. Gage's expression crumbled as he stepped back from the car, the shadows bending around him. Harper blinked, and he was gone. Deacon helped his sister into the front seat, before getting in the driver's side himself. They drove away, leaving Cole, who watched as Hael walked down the street a way, as if drawn after the car carrying his father's body.

It all happened in a haze as Harper's senses kept being pulled back to Wrathe, the immensity of him pulling her in like gravity.

Cole's shoulders slumped as he looked across at her, smiling sadly in a way she thought was meant to be reassuring. 'Call this in to the Watchers. We'll be at Aeternus if you need us.'

Harper just stared at him, barely comprehending the words. They were letting her go. Distantly, part of her was surprised Hael hadn't put a bullet in her brain too, after what she had witnessed.

Cole took a deep breath, fortifying himself, before following Hael. They spoke quietly when he caught up. Hael stopped walking, every line of his body weary. He stood still a moment, looking up at the sky. His hands were shaking. Wrathe joined them, reaching out and taking Hael's hand. Hael leant into the touch briefly, before closing his eyes. He let out a soft breath and took flight. Wrathe sighed, then pulled Cole close and flew away with him.

Harper stood alone in the street full of human and Erinyes bodies.

She took a deep breath and let it out slowly, trying to wrap her mind around what she had just felt from Wrathe. She had no idea who he was, but what he was? It was impossible, but there was nothing else that would explain what she had felt from him. He was too powerful, too old. There was only one thing he could be, an Aion, one of the supposedly long dead gods.

Someone grabbed her from behind, yanking her body into theirs roughly. A hand clasped over her mouth, stifling her surprised cry. They twisted her around until she looked up at him. It was Hael, but the charming man she'd been getting to know was nowhere to be seen.

Hael's ice-cold eyes stared at her. 'I know you can feel it.' His voice, full of menace, was almost unrecognisable.

She stared up at him, too shocked by his sudden appearance to react to the threat in his voice. 'You know what he...'

He tightened his grip. 'If you ever utter a single word, you even say it aloud in an empty room...I will break your neck and not think twice about it.'

Harper stared at him, her spine turned to ice, shards that shifted and oozed ice water into her veins. She'd never been more certain of anything than the promise of death in Hael's eyes.

He shook her slightly. 'Do you understand me?'

Harper was barely able to nod her head, every muscle screaming at her to run.

Hael studied her for a moment, before his expression softened. He removed his hand from her mouth, still holding her close, he cupped it around her cheek instead. He looked infinitely sad. A man who'd seen and lost too much.

'I won't let anything happen to him. I can't.' His words were barely a whisper, a quiet promise.

Harper stared up at him, every ounce of her common sense screaming at her that this man would kill her without thought. It'd be the surest way to ensure her silence. But he hadn't. He was dangerous, but all she could see was someone who cared too much, who'd just lost his father, and felt that loss so deeply it swarmed out of him and overwhelmed everyone in that room. Wrathe's words came back to her. He feels too much, it's his weakness.

Hael was terrified, she realised, of her, and what she felt from Wrathe, what she knew. That knowledge was dangerous.

If there was even a possibility Wrathe was an Aion, how many people would want him dead? Humans and Erinyes alike. How many would want him captured. Harper had read stories about what happened to the last Aion on earth two millennia ago. The slaughter, the experiments. Had anything really changed since then? If anyone knew what Wrathe was, he would never be safe.

She nodded again, this time steadier. 'Not a word. Never.'

Hael studied her a moment, expression conflicted. He gently pushed the hair out of her face, tucking it behind her ear. Then he was gone, leaving her stumbling in the empty street. She sucked in a shaky breath trying to calm the frantic beat of her heart. The Aesir were gone, and with them, the last Aion. It was impossible but true nonetheless.

Harper barely felt her fingers as she pulled out her phone, fumbling as she dialled the Watchers. She had no idea how she was going to explain the street full of bodies or anything that had happened tonight. Would they even believe her?

She'd wanted to find a killer, to help this family she inexplicably found herself caring about. But she'd stumbled into something much bigger.

Something that was probably going to get her killed.

***

40

~ VELLICHOR ~

Vellichor landed painfully on his knees. He looked up into the wide eyes of his baby brother. The Mother pressed a knife to Viridian's throat, the blade drawing droplets of blood. He clenched his fingers, resisting the urge to rip the knife from her hands. He couldn't. His brother wouldn't get out alive.

Gritting his teeth, Vellichor looked down subserviently. 'Maia found something, Mother.'

He'd never believed in the Mother's fanatic ravings. But Maia had. The gates became her obsession.

'I know why the sigils haven't been working.' He swallowed thickly. 'You need the blood of the one who originally cast them.'

The Mother loosened her hold on his brother, the knife dropping away from his throat. 'What do you know?'

He knew a lot. How much he could keep hidden while ensuring his brother's safety wasn't one of them. He closed his eyes. Think damn it. Hael had been desperate to hide something. The man seemingly spilled much in his fury, but he was clever. He'd given up his own secret, the secret of his heritage to protect another, bigger truth. Vellichor was certain of it. He was also sure he didn't want the Mother to open the gates and let the Aion pour through to smoother the earth once again. Hael was protecting something, or more likely, someone. Sacrifice, that, Vellichor understood.

Vellichor looked back up at the Mother. He'd give her the same truth Hael had, to hide another. 'The man who destroyed the Order is Hael Aesir. He is who you need.'

The Mother smiled as she pushed Viridian away. Vellichor scrambled to his feet, catching his brother. He really hoped Hael was good at running, because the Aesir had just painted a massive target on his back. The Children would come for Hael, and they wouldn't stop until they had what they wanted.

***

About the Author

K. D. Edley is an Australian author who recently found a story she wrote when she was six. It involved a prince and princess who lived in a castle that collapsed, and they were never seen again. Apparently she has always preferred stories a little bit on the darker side. She also enjoys drinking tea, reading and daydreaming.

Harper and the Aesir's story will continue in book two of *Songs of Shadow & Sorrow*.

Between Fury & Silence
Long buried truths, love and loyalty. How easily their undoing comes about. The Aesir family struggles to maintain its secrets, even as they are falling apart. Seeking unlikely allies as they are forced to make the hard choices, knowing there will always be sacrifice in the end. But is it a sacrifice they can live with?

Subscribe to K. D. Edley's newsletter for all the news and release dates.

www.kd-edley.com